RATS

VIVIEN LEANNE SAUNDERS

Cover design and Illustrations by Vivien Leanne Saunders
Source images all public domain from Unsplash
Edited by Vivien Leanne Saunders and George Glass

This book is a work of fiction. Names, characters, places, and incidents either are products of the author's imagination or are used fictitiously. Any resemblance to actual persons, living or dead, events, or locales is entirely coincidental.

Vivien Leanne Saunders
Visit my website at
https://sivvusleanne.wixsite.com/authorvls

Printed by KDP Direct
First Printing: 2019
This Edition: 2020
ISBN: 9781661203849

For Ellis
Good Luck

PREFACE

The ballot was held on the first day of autumn. The men and women of the tribes could not spell their own names, but they counted off the days of the year with ferocious attention. Every year, without fail, scores of ragged scavengers poured into the neutral zone to gape at the flawless creatures on the stage.

As soon as the smoking lights began to flicker the bids started to flow. The creatures grew eyes and freckles when the blaze subsided, and their beautiful clothes betrayed loose threads and ragged hemlines. They were old, these creatures, or else bent from hard work and calloused from the sun. Their eyes held – what? Jealousy, perhaps, or fear. Some of the youngest looked nervous, but it was a rare creature who could hide their excitement at being on stage. They had watched the ballot all of their lives, and now that it was their turn they could barely contain their pride.

The scavengers watched them, and bid, and when the bidding grew too fierce they began to fight. It was a rare ballot when nobody died; the officials would wade in eventually with their short staves and shorter tempers, but even they knew better than to argue with the clansmen on such a day. Men and women fell, and their bodies were trampled by the seething crowd.

One by one, the creatures were won and escorted off the stage. The officials gripped their wrists as they walked. Some fought, dragging uselessly at the armoured hands until their skin shone white with bruises. Some had to be helped away, their faces waxen and horrified. Out of the tens of men and women who had walked so confidently on to the stage, only a handful looked pleased to be leaving it.

The scavengers watched them, and shoved at each other. There was no anger in their violence now; another death would be meaningless. The people who had won their bids stepped forward, and the others drifted away.

The ballot was held in the spring. The children were born when the first snows fell.

PART 1: BALLOT

CHAPTER 1

Elizabeth's daughter was born with eleven toes.

For the first two days of the squalling infant's life, the mother smothered every plaintive cry with her hard, calloused hand and huddled in the corner of her bed away from the light. Every time the hatch opened she flinched and shrank back, but it was only the strangers of her clan. Those men and women climbed into their metal bunks too exhausted or indifferent to even ask the young woman if she thought the child would live. Most didn't. That cruel indifference protected the mother for the first few days, but still she trembled at the sure knowledge that her sanctuary would crumble.

Now, there was no husband to demand his rights, to drag the blanket away and inspect the flecked, mole-ridden flesh of his progeny. Soon he would return. The strangers did not care about someone else's brat. They scowled and blocked their ears with scraps of fabric when the child cried, and returned to their scavenging when the sun had grown less fierce. But her husband would look at the child's body before he even cared to name her.

Elizabeth cowered in the stinking mess of sweat and pain which the baby had dragged out of her womb along with its twisted foot. The extra toe was long, more like a finger than part of a foot, and it had a crumbling brown callous along its tip like a rusted claw. No matter how hard she rubbed at that nail, it never came clean. The baby screamed in her arms, but she kept rubbing until the toe was red-raw.

Her husband would return soon. Elizabeth knew that he was not dead. The strangers would have spared a few words to tell her that, but they did not bother to tell the pallid woman what else he was doing. She was told less about her husband's life than she had been about the humiliation of childbirth. She only knew that she was afraid, and that the baby was crying, and that the cries hurt her ears far more than the other harsh sounds which haunted her life.

She could not explain her failure. She would not be able to apologise. When she was a child she could speak, but at some point the words abandoned her and now the thought of forming the stranger's guttural language made her feel dizzy. The baby sobbed so loudly she found it hard to believe that it was a part of her, but it was. That fact, above all others, had scared her to the core. It had taken her long minutes to summon the will to raise her knife and split apart the cord which bound them together.

How had she felt, then? She felt tears on her cheeks, but perhaps they were from the pain and fear of such long hours alone. The strangers had not returned until the bleeding had stopped. The child was sleeping. Her tiny chest rose and fell, but a soft whining noise crept from her nose with every exhale. A small flaw, but an obvious one. Even without peeking beneath the blanket, the officials would know that the child was spoiled.

The knife lay next to her for those two endless days, and on the third day Elizabeth knew she had no choice. She waited until the strangers left, and listened her daughter whining out her dreams into the stale air. Biting her lip, the woman reached down until her fingers found the knife. Just her fingers; nothing to do with her. She couldn't even see the blade. She couldn't even feel its sharpness, just the dull pressure of twine. It was really nothing, nothing at all, to press it down towards the earthen floor.

The people who told this story said that her husband arrived just in time, and that the child was saved. Others delighted in brutal details. They said that the mother sliced through the toe with the same cold detachment with which she had severed the umbilical cord. By the time her husband returned home, the scar on the child's foot was nearly healed. She might have gotten away with it, those people said, but...

Well, it didn't matter which story was true.

Elizabeth was caught, and her child was taken to the ballot and never seen again. That was the usual fate for the children who were born wrong, and Elizabeth should have known better than to try to hide her daughter's deformity. Only one child in six was born right. She knew that as well as any other woman. Her crime, like so many other young women's, was born from her loneliness and her fear. Perhaps she thought that the flaw was so small that it wouldn't really matter. A toe, a whining throat – she had seen far worse.

If she could speak she would have pleaded with the officials, as they tore the child from her arms. She might have shown them the child's healthy pallor and clear, bright eyes. She could have let them watch the way it latched onto her breast and drank with the strength of any growing, healthy animal. As other infants were carried away with emaciated limbs and sickly pallor, she could have pointed at their blind ravaged faces and asked how the officials could possibly think her own child was flawed.

But she did not. Her husband had chosen to reveal her crime, and she could no more deny it than she could hide the love in her eyes when she clung to the baby.

After her child was taken away, Elizabeth fell back under the eyes of the strangers, and she was scorned. They said that her missing voice was a flaw, and that she had brought the weakness down upon her own child. They could not accuse her in public since she had spoken well enough as a child, but once the rumour began it was almost impossible for the young woman to redeem herself. Her score fell, and before long her husband sent her back to the ballot.

She was chosen by a lesser man, with fewer strangers in his home, and she carried her quickened belly into his bed along with her silent loathing.

The child who was born six months later had ten perfect toes, and even as an adult he did not snore. Elizabeth was punished for entering the ballot while carrying another man's child. By then, Lawrence's father had been killed... but the law still had to be obeyed.

She was a lowly twenty eight by the time that her daughter was born, always silent, always afraid. The child found out about her mother's life by eavesdropping on the old women at the ballot. She stopped listening when she realised that the wretched creature they were laughing about was her own mother. The story of Elizabeth had fallen from rumour into fable, and finally had become a joke. Where, they asked, had she hidden the toe?

Elizabeth screamed when her son ran away. It was the only time her daughter ever heard her voice.

CHAPTER 2

Tiria was three before her parents bothered to name her. The infant's tongue could only create nonsense sounds. She would point at the rusted piles of scrap which littered her father's home and practice speaking to them, watching her mother carefully to see when she would smile. Elizabeth smiled so rarely that one day the child climbed onto her lap and pointed at her face, stubbornly determined to know what she could do to make it better. She felt moisture, and pulled her chubby hand back to see water which was clean and clear instead of yellow and murky.

"Is?" The child asked, fascinated by how it shone. Her brother looked over distractedly.

"Tear." He said, and came over to kiss his mother's cheek. She caught his hand for a moment, and then shooed him away back to where he was sorting through the cans. The infant looked at her hand, where the shining water had already dried.

"Tir-ia?" The girl burbled. Her mother smiled then, and the child was so pleased with herself that she clapped her hands together and sang the word out over and over again. She must have crowed the word at least twenty times that evening, delighted by the smile which crossed her mother's solemn face and the teasing laughter of her brother. By the end of the week she was known as Tiria, and by the time she was old enough to deserve a name the nonsense word had stuck.

Elizabeth beckoned her to the fireplace one day and knelt down to draw a symbol. It was a closed eye with a trickle of water running down from it. It was Tiria's name, she knew - her mother's silent way of speaking to her, and only her. Whenever the woman scratched the name into the ashes Tiria would curl up in her lap and watch her mother closely, chewing on her chubby fingers and learning the odd signs which her mother only made with her children, and no-one else. When her husband came home Elizabeth always pursed her soft lips and blew the ash away. No wonder, then, that he never called Tiria by name. To him she was girl, and to her mother she was a line, a smudge, a whirling cloud of ashes. Over time the eye became less curved, the water more direct, until the name was nothing more than a horizontal line with a long stem falling from its centre.

T. Her brother whispered it to her. T for Tiria.

M for Mama, a soft pair of lips bowing into an endless frown. The raised fist and striding leg of F became their father, and B for brother, but he was always L to Tiria. L for Lawrence, sitting strong and straight with his head held high. There were other letters, too, and other men and women whose shapes were mimicked in twisting lines. Hobbling C, pregnant R, the twisting deviousness of the letter S – all of these people danced in front of Tiria's eyes, until her father came home and they disappeared into the swirling dust.

Until she was six, old enough to go to her first ballot, Tiria knew more letters than she had met people. She did not believe that the world could hold many more people than her own small family. They were always cold, or sick, or hungry, so she could not imagine sharing their miserly rations of food with another person.

When Tiria saw the crowds at the ballot she was amazed.

"Stop gaping, girl." Her father growled, and shoved her back into the arms of her mother. Elizabeth held her closely for a moment, and then closed her fingers around one of the child's braids and gripped it tightly. Whenever Tiria dawdled, staring at someone who was uglier or taller or thinner than anyone she had ever seen before, her mother would give her hair a sharp tug.

Other women shouted at their children. Of all the wonders the Tiria saw on that day, that one stunned her the most. They raised their voices - high, but rich, more like Lawrence's than her own - and they spoke in clear, sharp words which fell easily from their lips. The child looked back at her mother in amazement. She had honestly believed that all grown women were mute.

She told her brother as much that evening, and he laughed at her frank surprise. "That explains why you talk so much now, Ti. You're scared that one day you'll outgrow your own tongue!"

The girl stuck it out at him. He grinned and ruffled her dark hair. He was older, and wiser, and he never let her forget it. He had spent the day swaggering around with the other boys, but now that we were huddled down in the corner of the overcrowded room he was simply her brother again, silly but sensible enough to be trusted with a little girl while his parents drank liquor with the other adults. He slouched back against the wall and pulled the girl back into his arms, tugging the blanket up over both of them.

"Why do you think she doesn't talk?" Tiria asked sleepily. Lawrence didn't have an answer straight away, but a gentle frown made his forehead pucker.

"I think she's sad." He scratched his nose awkwardly. "She doesn't talk; she doesn't smile either. I reckon if we could make her do one she might remember how to do the other."

"Will you shut up?" One of the other children hissed, prodding at them with his boot. Lawrence's eyebrows flew up, and his eyes glinted with childish mischief. He reached down and, instead of pushing the foot back, whipped the shoe off it and threw it over the sleeping children and through the doorway. The other boy let out a cry and stood up, hopping on his one shoe to fetch the other before someone stole it.

"Stretch out," Lawrence said quickly, and pushed the girl into the spot the boy had left. She smiled sweetly and wriggled into the space. She was already snoring by the time the boy returned. If there was a scuffle Tiria didn't hear it, but the next morning she was well rested, and her brother had a shining black bruise on one cheek and a smug smile below it.

The adults barely acknowledged their families once they were safely in the theatre, and so the hallways were rife with packs of screaming children. The officials would occasionally wade into the fray to take a child for questioning or examination, but even they were cowed by the near-feral way that even the youngest children fought and played.

Tiria was only just six, and small for her age. She spent most of her time on her brother's shoulders jeering down at the other girls who begged for a ride. Lawrence enjoyed being her protector, but he quickly grew bored. Eventually he dumped his sister onto the ground and wandered off to drink liquor and smoke dog-end cigarettes with the other older children. Tiria spat after him and cursed, and the pack swallowed her up. She learned how to fight, and how to speak to other children. She quickly worked out that they did not all think and speak like her brother, and that the tricks she used on him would not work on the sharp-minded scavenger brats.

Since she was so small and weak, the little girl quickly learned how to use her wiles to win food, or to befriend allies in the endless scuffles. Other children were not so lucky – the slow witted and cowardly ones often went hungry for the whole ballot, unless one of the others relented and shared their hard-won food. The officials did not care since a child could not die from a few day's hunger. The children all knew that if they were truly desperate they could find their parents. Doing that would have made them the laughing stock of the pack, and so many children preferred to watch their waistbands sag than admit that they were hungry.

Tiria was proud that she never asked for help. After the first day she didn't even ask Lawrence for a share of his bread, even though he freely offered it to her. She had bitten a girl's ear to steal away a baked horse-chestnut, and the malty taste still lingered deliciously on her tongue. Lawrence grinned as his sister exaggerated her daring battle, and then shoved a mouthful of bread between her lips to shut her up.

"Did the ear taste good?" He asked. Tiria pulled a face, chewing hard, and punched his arm. He pretended that he hadn't felt a thing until she threw herself at him. She had never actually fought with her brother before, but Tiria quickly learned that he could pin her in a second. Over the next few days she begged him to teach her how to fight properly. He made a huge fuss about being seen hitting a little girl, but finally agreed to teach her in secret. They stayed up late every night, and used the empty corridors to practice until Lawrence admitted that he had nothing left to show her.

While they practiced blocking each other's blows, they made plans about how to help their mother find her voice. Finally, they decided that the best thing to do was to search the wastes for something that could be utterly her own. Elizabeth had nothing that didn't belong to her husband. While he brought home useless treats and alcohol for himself, she never scavenged anything more luxurious than a ball of yarn. A present, the children decided, would make her very happy.

Tiria only had a vague idea about what lay outside of the shelter. She knew that everything good came from outside. If they were cold, then the wastes gave them fuel. If they were hungry, they only had to go outside and food would fall from the sky. It stood to reason that *happiness*, like any other good thing, could be found out there too. Lawrence was older if not wiser, and so his ideas were more cynical: there was nothing good inside the shelter, and so if he was going to make his mother happy, he would have to look beyond it. They both muddied each other's childish thoughts as they coaxed each other through the theatre doors, and as the sun started to rise they giggled and hugged each other.

What had they expected to see? They had only been outside with the adults before, and they were always being hurried along. Now that they were alone the world felt far too solid. The red light slowly rose above the ruins, and the black peaks of the buildings were silhouetted against the morning mist like jagged teeth. The birds were raucous, and their shrieks seemed to come from everywhere at once. There were deeper noises in their chattering calls which made the children imagine worse creatures growling from the shadows. Their nerve almost failed them, but they were both too stubborn to be the first one to turn around. They held hands, and stepped forwards. The road crumbled beneath their feet. A slight wind blew, and the dust was so fine it whipped into their eyes like shards of glass. Tiria muffled a cry with her hands, and Lawrence spat dust onto the ground.

It felt like they walked for miles, but fear made them misjudge distances. They imagined that the wealth of the wastes would be lying a few streets away from the theatre, and that they could sneak out and snatch something before anyone noticed they were gone. It was an idiotic idea, as Lawrence burst out after an hour: "Every scavenger for fifty miles came through here. They've picked it clean!"

Tiria had already fallen into a sullen silence. She was cold, and her feet were sore from walking on the glassy shards of stone. She pouted out her lip and kept walking, making stubborn little thuds as she headed deeper into the ruined city. There were more complete buildings here than there were near their home, and she refused to believe that there wasn't something in one of the hundreds of brick cubes. There must have been thousands of dust-eaters living here. Surely one of them had been clever enough to leave their treasure hidden somewhere that only a little girl would think to check? She puzzled over fireplaces and kicked at skirting boards, but all she found were mice and insects.

They made their way through the empty shells of so many buildings that Tiria lost count, and Lawrence had turned from irritable into taciturn. Neither of them wanted to be the first one to turn around, and so they were almost two miles from the theatre when they heard the voices.

One of them was crying.

"Come on," Tiria whispered, reaching for her brother's hand. "Let's go home."

He shushed her and shook her off. Hurt, frightened, the little girl watched her brother clamber clumsily over a mound of stone. There were branches of barbed wire sprouting out from the bricks like macabre plants, but the boy bit back the urge to cry out when one wrapped around his hand. He pulled his palm free from the twisting metal and kept moving. After a moment he felt the ground sliding away behind him, and looked to see his little sister stubbornly following him. Lawrence knew better than to send her away – she would raise a fuss, and they would be discovered. Instead, he helped her up to the top of the stack and held her still as they peered over to the other side.

The people on the other side weren't even trying to hide. They didn't need to; the two adults were armed, not only with knives but with short, fat sticks which Lawrence told his sister were called *guns.* One of the adults was an official – a muscular man shrouded in the same blank mask as all of the other officials. It was so peculiar to see one outside of the ballot that the sight of him would have been remarkable alone. He was speaking to a scavenger woman, who was dressed from head to foot in leather which faded perfectly into the shades of the dust. If she had been standing still she would have been invisible, but she was moving. Her hands were animated, and her mouth was an angry blur. The crying was coming from the two children who were trying to pull themselves free from a short rope which was wrapped around their wrists. The adults didn't seem to hear them, but while they were arguing they kept gesturing to the squalling pair.

"Look." Lawrence murmured, and pointed at the older child. It was a boy, about nine years old. His head had been shaved, and a swollen bruise of flesh blossomed from the shorn roots. Below the bruise, a strange lump of bone curled up like a ram's horn. Tiria gasped at the sight of a living mutation. The boy must have hidden the deformity under his hair – or, at least, his parents had. She knew that people were executed for hiding mutations. As she looked at the boy, she slowly realized that he must be completely alone in the world. His parents would both be locked up in the theatre, waiting to be hauled onto the stage and thrown into the grasping claws of the scavengers. The boy would never see them again. In that moment, the loneliness seemed far worse to Tiria than anything else.

The horn seemed to be bothering the woman, too. She kept pointing at it until finally the official snatched up her hat, pressed it hard onto the boy's head, and growled a few words. The woman folded her arms, and then a grudging laugh rang over the children's sobs. She nodded, shook her head at the younger boy, and then pulled a purse out of her pocket. The money she counted out would have fed a whole family for a year. The official held out his hand, and when she placed the coins into his hand he folded the fingers up and over like a piece of cardboard.

Then he reached down, drew his knife, and calmly slit the younger boy's throat.

Tiria screamed. She couldn't help it; the sound was out before she even knew she was frightened. Lawrence turned to hush her, and they slipped a little over the edge of the mound. They scrabbled frantically up, desperate to get to the other side, and heard a loud noise booming out behind them. Lawrence looked back, choked out something incomprehensible, and shoved his sister over the pile.

"What happened?" Tiria gasped, dragging her brother down the other side and starting to run. Lawrence kept looking back, tripping giddily over the sliding scree as they ran.

"She tried to shoot us!" He panted, and started pulling the girl along when she slowed down. His face was as white as milk. "The gun exploded in her hand! She... she..." He stopped and was sick, the vomit exploding from him without warning. Tiria cried out in disgust and dragged herself away. When he reached for her she pulled a face, not wanting to touch his filthy hands, until he swore at her and hauled her over his shoulder. She screamed and beat at his back as he started to run again.

Lawrence pulled her hair sharply to make her behave. He could not spare the breath to scold her. He had no idea if the official would be following them. The woman had been smiling, calmly cocksure as she aimed the gun at Tiria, and then half of her body had exploded into liquid and lumps of flesh. The boy bit back another wave of nausea as he remembered, and forced himself to keep running. The official had seen them. He knew they were children – and who would believe a child over an official? Would the man return to the ballot and look for the faces of two brats who had seen him selling mutations to the slavers? Would he be able to recognize them?

For the next two days, Lawrence followed his sister like a shadow. She had forgotten most of her fear after a few hours, and he didn't tell her that they were still in danger. For all that she knew, it was perfectly normal for officials to sell scavengers like chattel. The boy knew better. He followed the girl, and whenever an official passed by he would pull her into the shadows, or goad her into chasing him in the opposite direction. He stole extra blankets to pile over her when she slept, and fought some of the older girls to win a ribbon here, or a belt buckle there. By the time they left the ballot Tiria looked utterly unlike the frightened waif from the ruins, and her heart was overflowing with gratitude for all of the pretty presents her brother had given her.

Lawrence gave a pretty scarf and some ribbons to his mother. She shrugged, and handed them to her daughter. Gifts meant nothing to her, after all. The boy thought back to what he had seen in the ruins, and found his mother's silence creeping into his own body. It felt cool, not cold, as if it was refreshing his body and making him clean. If Tiria had been silent in the ruins then they would not have been seen. He had been silent afterwards, and it had kept them safe. Silence was not unhappiness, it was just a way to survive. He resolved to capture the feeling, and over the next few months he found that he could retreat into his own silence without feeling like he had lost anything.

Elizabeth's silence was just as deliberate. Lawrence never found out what she was protecting herself from.

CHAPTER 3

Within a year, Tiria's brother had been scarred
and sunburned into a creature she barely knew. The
soft, boyish mischief had fled soon after the ballot.
He had grown solemn and silent. However much
Tiria peered at him, she could not see him as the
child she loved. Now, he was another adult, and so
she felt like she was not allowed to understand him.
The separation was agonizing. She had known his
whole mind! They had whispered together every
night, planning how to make their mother smile,
but after they had ventured into the ruins he didn't
seem to care anymore. She had been so young that
the terrifying memory soon faded, but as the years
passed the lingering disquiet never fell from
Lawrence's eyes.

When their father decided that Lawrence should
earn his keep, he presented the boy with a pair of
solid leather boots. Elizabeth gave him a sturdy
rucksack, and a worried smile. Lawrence held his
sister tightly and made her giggle with his
ridiculous excitement, promising to tell her

everything he saw in the ruins when he returned. She forced herself to stay awake that night, her eyes burning and stinging, but when the hatch opened her mother shushed her stream of questions. Lawrence dumped his bag onto the floor and crawled into his bedroll without a word. Elizabeth, watching him, kissed the top of the girl's head and tucked her into her own blankets. Lying down beside her son, she wrapped her arms around him and nestled her head against his back. Tiria watched her brother, taller than his mother even at fourteen, fighting not to cry.

In the morning Elizabeth was shaken awake by her husband. She looked around at the man balefully, and for the first time Tiria could remember, she refused to obey him. Stroking her son's hair, she pointed at a bruise and stared accusingly at the boy's father.

"It's his own fault." The man spat, and walked away.

"He hit me." Lawrence whispered to his mother later that day, and she shook her head angrily. The wastes were dangerous enough, she knew, without her husband's petty spite making things worse. Tiria brought boiled water to wash the dirt away from the bruise, but when she tried to hug her brother he shook her off. Hurt, she retreated to her corner and hid her tears.

That was how things stayed for years. As time passed, her brother's skin toughened and his tears turned into a stoic silence. Sometimes he would come home and sleep alone, but he still cuddled up to his sister on the worst days, and she wrapped her arms around him with tearful, stubborn love. He smelled of metal and dust, and his voice became deep and rough. He smiled so rarely that she wondered if, one day, he might stop speaking altogether.

"Don't worry about me." He ruffled her hair, as he had done when he was a child, and smiled at her squeak of annoyance. "It'll be the ballot soon, Ti. I can volunteer when I'm seventeen. I only have to put up with father until then."

Tiria smiled and nodded her head, but her heart chilled at his words. He was going to leave her. Was their father really that bad? She watched as the weeks passed, and both of the men grew increasingly taciturn. The only time Lawrence seemed to smile was when he talked about the ballot. The months crawled by as they gathered supplies for the winter, and oddments and luxuries to sell at the market. Finally, they counted their hundred and fiftieth day, and pushed the hatch open to start the long journey across the wastes together. As the metal hatch boomed shut behind the siblings, their father turned around and fixed Lawrence in his glassy stare.

"You won't enter the ballot today. I'd have to give my consent, and I won't. You haven't learned enough to be an adult, and you still owe me for all I've taught you."

It was as if the boy had been burned with a flame. He stood bolt upright and even his words seemed to tremble. "But... but..."

"I won't have you shirking your debts just to lay with some bitch high." The man drawled crudely. When Lawrence paled, the man smiled sickly and turned on his heel. Catching Elizabeth's hand, he squeezed her fingers until she caught her breath in pain. Lawrence darted forwards and pried them loose, then glared at the man.

"You're disgusting." He spat, his hands trembling against Elizabeth's skin. The older man shrugged, and grinned lazily. Lawrence was visibly shaking when he looked up at his mother. She smiled wanly and touched his cheek with her bruised hand. The boy took a deep breath and turned away. "Next year I'll be eighteen. You'll have no choice."

The old man grinned more widely, said nothing, and began to walk. Lawrence followed with Elizabeth's hand nestled in his elbow, walking with her like a child while Tiria sulked along behind them. That year, none of them entered the ballot.

The new year was even worse than the months before. When Lawrence brought food home he shared it amongst the whole family, but when his father found supplies he refused to give any to his son. "If you're hungry, you should find more food." He would say. Both Elizabeth and Tiria tried to share their food with Lawrence, but he stubbornly refused to accept any. As the months dragged by, he grew thinner and more serious.

"Father is using you as a slave." Tiria whispered one night, after her brother came home with fresh bruises and a growling stomach. The boy didn't answer, but he pressed his face into the pillow. The girl persisted, "He sells the things you find and eats all your food. He beats you if you don't find enough, but he never brings back half of what you do."

The boy shivered, but he still did not answer. His sister knew what he was thinking. He only had to hold out until the ballot. But that was many months away, and who knew what might happen before then?

Sixty days before the ballot, their father found a supply of liquor in the basement of one of the ancient hotels. He buried most of it, licking his lips at the fortune the find would bring him at market, but he brought a barrel of it home. The ugly, stained container took up so much space that he shoved Lawrence's bed roll against the damp clay wall to make room.

"What is that?" The boy demanded when he came home and saw it. "We can't eat it or wear it. Why waste a whole day on it?"

The man scoffed and shook his head. "What I do on my own hunts is none of your business." He announced, and then took his son's portion of food from Elizabeth as she mutely held it out. Lawrence muttered an oath and snatched the plate away.

"I found this, and traded for it, and I spent my time on it." He growled. "It's mine. You drink your wine."

"Elizabeth." The older man said, and held out his hand. The woman silently took the plate back, and handed it over. Her head was downcast, and she breathed shallowly, but her eyes sought out her son's and were filled with a desperate apology. Taking a large mouthful of the food, the old man belched and then held his son's gaze. "If you can't bring home enough food for me, then take your sister with you. She can help you carry that chip on your shoulder."

"Ti's too young." The boy said too quickly, and his father latched on to the fear in that sentence. He stepped a little closer, still chewing, and caught the little girl's shoulder in a vice-like grip. She moued in pain, and Elizabeth made an involuntary movement towards her before the man stopped her. His glare never moved.

"If you want to keep her safe, you'd better keep your mouth shut."

"Don't you dare threaten her." The boy hissed.

"Don't whine at me. She's not even your real sister, dead man's get."

Lawrence froze, and looked at Elizabeth. The woman looked away and stared at her feet, but then her mouth set in an odd smile and she nodded. Tiria watched colours shift in Lawrence's skin. The idea didn't bother her at all, so she could not understand the peculiar pain on her brother's face. This was how she saw it: He was not her father's child. He was still her mother's son. He would be her brother until the sun burned out. Nothing her father could spew would change that. She crept forward and took Lawrence's hand, not because he was going to disown her, but because she wanted him to draw a breath.

"I'm glad." Lawrence spoke to the old man as if he hadn't noticed his sister at all. "You don't deserve me."

The older man made an involuntary sound, halfway between scorn and laughter. "What part of your twisted mind do you think I want?"

"The part that brings you food." The boy's eyes sharpened, and he gestured around the meagre shelter. "The part you forbade from entering the ballot. If I tell the officials you're not my real father they'll punish you for stopping me. You didn't have the right."

"I sheltered you for eighteen years." The man growled. "No-one else would take you in after what your father did."

Lawrence shrugged. "He can't have been any worse than you. Even if he was, at least he had the courtesy to die."

Gathering up his weapons and clothes, the boy made a bundle and shoved it into his bag. Elizabeth watched him for a moment, and then started packing up food. She did not try to argue, nor write in the ashes to try to explain. It was obvious that Lawrence didn't care. In the heat of the argument, the only thing that mattered to him was getting away from the man who had delighted in torturing him for long, pointless months. Tiria darted forward and clutched her brother's hand.

"Don't go." She whispered.

"No, Ti." He spoke quietly, the last words he would say to her. "If I stay he'll use you and mama against me. If I leave, he has no reason to do that."

She didn't understand, but her father did. He tried to shout something, but for the first time Lawrence had outwitted him. The boy silenced him with a glare, and then threw the hatch open without another word.

The old man yelled after him, "Rat me out and I'll tell the council what you've done! I'll tell them every disgusting thought in your head!"

Lawrence never answered him. Tiria didn't see which way he walked, or whether he wept. Her mother watched him, her chest heaving, and then she sobbed out a great cry and fell to her knees. She folded her little girl in her arms and wailed. In that embrace, in that heart rending sound, the child knew that her brother was never coming back.

CHAPTER 4

Out of the hundreds of times that Tiria had crawled out of the hatch into the wastes, she could never remember coming home without a new kind of pain. The sun had not quite been strong enough to burn her eyes, but she felt her skin beginning to crawl and knew that it would sting that night. She was relieved that the night was turning cool. Not for the first time, Tiria was grateful that her father was too lazy to scavenge every day, as he had when he was younger. She wondered how Lawrence had managed to do this for so many years, with the bastard breathing down his neck. It was difficult enough without constantly worrying whether the sour old man would snap.

Over the years she had searched every shelter and every solid building for miles around, even the ones that had been picked clean, for the slightest clue that her brother had been there. Some part of her knew that he was too clever to leave a trace, and that more people than just her father wanted to find him. He had broken the law, and he would have to hide for the rest of his life for it. But still, she felt instinctively that if he wanted her to find him, he would have found a way to reach her. She was closer to him than anyone else in the world, and she could not believe that he would simply disappear.

She had returned home empty handed so many times that even her father had gone hungry, and for the first few months she pretended that it was because she was a bad scavenger. After that, she could not hide behind the excuse. Her months of searching had given her a sharp eye and a heightened perceptiveness which even her father could not scoff at. She could see a shelter or a bolt hole from far away, and could tell at a glance if anyone was nearby.

When she had to fight she was quick enough, but she was glad that for the most part, she didn't have to. Unlike her father, she never stumbled across the outer tribes by accident, and she tried not to disturb other scavengers. The clans were fiercely territorial, and she knew that a young girl was more likely to be robbed than her burly father.

That night, the sun burning her arms, Tiria wondered how many years she had been doing this for. There was no-one left at home to count for her. The days stretched into a vague endlessness. How old was she? Had she changed in the same way that her brother had?

When she looked down and scratched at the tickling sunburn her limbs looked strange to her, outlined in a dim blue aura which made the wrists look dark and thin. Her fingers looked like claws, the arms too short, and although it was the coolest time of the day a fine sweat made her palms itch. She sped up, sure-footed over the chalky ground until she found the solid rocks which she had been born beneath. Taking one last, shallow breath of the fresh air, she dragged the metal hatch open and crawled inside.

Her father was already asleep. Tiria heard her own sigh of relief and clapped her hand over her mouth, hating the bitter taste of sweat and the close air as much as the treacherous sound. The old man groaned in his sleep, but did not move. She crept past him silently. As soon as she was in her corner of the room, hidden behind the empty wine barrel, she eased a book out of her bag and slid it under the mattress. When she had found the dusty tome she had seized it without thinking. Perhaps it was that which had made her mind spin as she walked home. The book was dangerous, and forbidden, and by taking it she felt closer to her outcast brother than she had for months.

Her father woke her up a few hours later by holding the torch up to her eyes. She squinted up at a face that was lined with age and, today, disgust.

He sounded resigned. "You're filthy, Ti."

"Yes, father." She mumbled, and realised that her sheets were stained with grime. Groaning, she dragged herself upright and winced as some of the fabric stuck to her back. Even her brother had not dared to come home so filthy, when her mother was around to glare at him. A thrill of guilt ran through the girl. "I'll clean it, I promise."

"Make breakfast first." He said shortly, and took Tiria's scavenging bag away with him. As he sat cross-legged on the floor and tipped it up onto the low table, the girl crawled to the fire pit and started blowing the embers into a flame. The smoke filled the room, and her father made a great show of coughing before he bothered to move a few feet to open the hatch to the outside.

"Something might get in." Tiria said, mimicking the warning he had scolded her with so many times. He sniffed and sat back down at the table.

"Let's hope you found a weapon, then." He rifled through her finds for a moment, and then laughed. Most of what Tiria had found last night had come from an old clothing shop. The roof had groaned loudly when she finished digging through the wall.

She was scared that it would fall and crush her, so she had stuffed as many plastic packets as she could find into the bag without looking at what they held.

Her father chuckled as pair after pair of ladies' socks, in wonderfully lurid colours, emerged from the rucksack.

Tiria breathed out, relieved to see his yellow-toothed grin and not his furious scowl. She quickly explained what had happened. He nodded and peered at one of the packets more closely. Breaking the plastic seal, he drew out a piece of card and left the useless flimsy material in the bag.

"We can make more money if we sell these separately," He looked at the pictures approvingly. His daughter blinked at him. He was holding a cardboard image of a woman wearing a pair of stockings. Her legs were long and sickeningly pale, and she was smiling down at her feet as though the socks were the only thing she had ever wanted. She had perfectly combed hair, and paint on her face, and jewels hanging from her ears, but she was smiling at a pair of socks. It was the stupidest picture Tiria had ever seen in her life, and she told her father so.

"I don't know who would buy that!" She shook her head and pointed at the socks with the mixing spoon, flicking a bead of porridge across the room. "At least people can wear those silly things."

"Things to eat and things to wear." He chanted mockingly, and shook his head. He threw over a packet of yellow stockings. The girl caught it and looked at him blankly. He shook his head. "When we go to the ballot, you take that picture to another woman and you ask her why anyone would buy it."

"Couldn't you just tell me?" Tiria sounded irritated because she knew she wouldn't see another woman for weeks, or even months. She wasn't allowed to talk to the traders, and she had lost count of the days until the next ballot. A slight flush spread across her father's cheeks at her tone.

"Ask a woman, Tiria." His voice was icy, and although he looked away the girl shivered. He started disembowelling the packets so fiercely that she knew the discussion was over. Biting her tongue, she turned back to the porridge. The dust from the open hatch had littered the surface. She stirred it in and watched the mixture turn from yellowish grey to brown.

The next day was her father's turn to scavenge. The tiny shelter wasn't worth raiding, but many of the outer clans got burned half into madness by midday, and everyone had heard the stories about what the sun-struck savages had done. The man opened the hatch cautiously and looked outside with a piece of reflective metal before he raised his head.

After what had happened to Lawrence, Tiria still shuddered at the thought of her father exploring the wastes. She had nightmares about the day that he had found a scrap of material from Lawrence's shirt and returned home. He sauntered around brandishing it with a sick grin on his proud face as her mother wept.

Tiria kept her fingers clenched around her knife until her father left. She stayed frozen into place until his footsteps faded. Then she darted forwards and bolted the hatch. As always she enjoyed a moment's delight at the action, imagining leaving him locked outside to rot. This time, though, she raced back to her bed. Holding her breath, she reached under the mattress and slid the book out.

It was the first time she had looked at it properly, and it was... terrifying.

She could think of no other words for it. She recognised some of the letters and clung to them like old friends, but she couldn't even read the first word. Then the book fell open and there was a picture.

A woman was standing on the top of a great tower. Tiria could tell how high up she was, because the trees beneath her were so small that they might as well have been daubs of moss on the muddy ground. Even though the world was etched in black and white, she could tell that the sun was rising and painting the world a sickly yellow. Or perhaps her mind leapt to that colour because of the flames licking at the walls beneath the woman's feet. They reached up to her as if they could snatch her down, but the woman barely seemed to notice her danger. Instead, she was looking up at a bright soaring bird, reaching her soft hands up as if she knew she could fly after it.

The girl stared at her for so long that her eyes ached. Who was this woman? What was her picture doing in a book? Tiria had heard that books were dangerous, but the woman looked so breathtakingly happy that her heart leapt in her chest. What was happening to her?

The hatch creaked, and Tiria gasped aloud. She shoved the book back under the bed, crumbling the spine between her fingertips in her haste, and caught her breath just in time to see the old man dropping through the hatch. He scowled at his daughter's flushed face and guilty expression, and then smiled slowly. Tiria's face grew even redder as she worked out what he was thinking.

"I was... I wasn't..." She choked back her words, realising that she shouldn't have spoken at all. The more excuses she made, the more her father probably believed his own sordid imaginings. He chuckled and ruffled the girl's hair as he moved past, laughing louder when she flinched away.

"Did you find anything?" I asked. He slumped down at the table and linked his hands behind his head.

"Don't be a scold, miss." He drawled idly. "My old dig has been picked clean."

"Then, did you look for another one?" Tiria imagined him sauntering up to an empty ruin, poking around it a few times, and then ambling home. It was probably close to the truth. He turned his grey eyes onto her, and they were small and shrunken in the reddened sockets.

"You can do that, if you're so desperate to go digging in the dirt." He snapped. "I guess you'd rather not, though. Not when you can get so hot and bothered back here."

The girl felt her cheeks grow red and turned her face away so he couldn't see her shame. It would have been less humiliating if it were true. "You'll be ready for the ballot soon enough." The man said, and Tiria shuddered at the laughter in his voice.

Perhaps it was embarrassment that made her do it, but the next morning Tiria decided to take the book back to where she had found it. The vast hallway had been left alone by most of the scavengers, who knew that food and clothing came from small homes and from abandoned markets, not from the marble and stone palaces of the old people. This place was full of wooden shelves, covered in dust and scraps of decaying paper. Tiria had been searching the small atriums at the back of the hall, wondering if someone could hide in one of the storage cupboards, when she had come across a flight of stairs. Tripping down it, she had found a second room filled with metal and glass cabinets, held together with gears which snapped when she tried to turn the handles. One of them creaked open, and when she peered into the slit of space she caught sight of the bright red cardboard of the book. It had been so easy to reach in and snatch it. Now that she was going to replace the book, getting back into the basement seemed wrought with danger.

She held her breath as she turned the winch, and cursed when the ancient metal snapped off in her hand.

"I thought someone was sneaking around." A voice said.

Tiria flinched back from the cabinet and held her torch up like a weapon. The woman laughed, and the sound amazed Tiria so much that she lowered the beam. It sounded so utterly different to any laughter she had heard before. Even her brother's laughter had been soft, smothered between his large, calloused hands. This woman didn't cover her mouth or bite back the sound, and the bright trickle of her voice rang through the room so sweetly that it echoed back from the glass.

"Who are you?" Tiria asked. Her voice was a dry croak. Monstrous.

The stranger took a step closer, smiling as she asked, "You live in a hole, don't you?"

The girl gaped at her and lowered the torch completely. Seeing Tiria's expression in the darkness, the stranger made that astounding sound again and her pale hands fluttered in an odd gesture. "My mother told me that you rat people all live in holes in the ground. She says you only come out to scavenge for food. I never thought I'd see one of you for real." She took another step closer and her eyes were wide. "You don't look like a rat."

"I'm not a rat." Tiria told her indignantly. "I..."

"Oh, I don't mean a real rat." She prattled on, so brazenly loud that Tiria cringed back from the echoes. Her words never seemed to end. "I've seen rats. I'm not stupid! We just call you rat people because of the way you..." her eyes widened even further, and the scavenger wondered if she was really an owl, grotesquely bulging irises and all. "Oh, I'm sorry. Did I offend you?"

"You called me a rat." Tiria's voice was icy as she turned away. "A rat person is still a kind of rat. It's like if I said you're not just stupid, you're... really stupid."

She sighed as if she was disappointed. "Moronic?"

Tiria didn't know the word, so she shrugged. The awkward silence healed some of the insult, but she raised the torch again and made herself look severe. "What are you doing here? In this hole?"

"It's not a hole. It's far more than that." The stranger sounded aloof and fluttered her birdlike hand towards where the books were hidden. "I always... wait, what are you doing here, Rat?"

"It's a hole." Tiria said, and felt her lips curve into a grudging smile. "So I'm scavenging in it."

"There's nothing here." The stranger replied too quickly. "Go away."

"When I'm ready." Tiria ambled away breezily and made a great show of rifling through the few cabinets that had been left open. The books there had crumbled into dust, but she dug into the soft fabric with slow, deliberate fingers. The owl followed her anxiously, fluttering around making odd shooing motions with her pale hands. Every time she did it Tiria slowed down, ponderously running her fingertips along every inch of every drawer.

"Safety pins." She said, at one, and "Coins." At another.

The owl groaned loudly and stomped away, and even her footsteps were louder than any other person Tiria had ever heard. As soon as she had disappeared into the gloom the girl made a beeline for the bookshelf, reaching for the book in her satchel so she could put it back. She could not resist peering in to the shelf one last time, hungry to see the rows of neat covers which had coaxed her to steal the book before. To her horror, the glass case was empty. She stood frozen, with the book dangling from numb fingertips.

The owl returned, but before she could draw breath Tiria rounded on her. "You stole them!" she cried, not bothering to lower her voice. "You... you...!"

"The books?" The girl drawled, and Tiria realised that she had known all along why she was there. Her hands were planted on her hips, and the scavenger saw that one of them was close to a knife sheath on her belt. Now it was her voice which was hard, but Tiria knew that the girl's was no act. She narrowed her eyes dangerously. "I noticed one was missing.

You're going to give it back like a good little rat, aren't you?"

Tiria had planned to put it onto the shelf, but now she bristled and shoved the book back into the depths of her satchel. "I'm not a rat."

"And I'm not playing around." The owl said, stepping closer with a menacing expression. "I know you have my book."

Tiria's mouth fell open, and without realising it she leant closer to the stranger. "Have you... have you seen it?"

"Read it?" She had a puzzled line between her eyes. "Yes."

"What is it about?" The girl pressed, excited beyond all sense. "Please, can you tell me why the lady is on the tower? Can she fly? Does the book teach you how to fly?"

"Fly?" The owl gaped at Tiria as idiotically as she had gaped at her. She nearly dropped her knife as she burst into great guffaws of laughter. "Of course not! It's just a story."

"A story?" Tiria echoed, and ran her fingers along the book. Flakes broke off the spine and buried themselves in the creases of her hands. She felt oddly disappointed, although she knew she shouldn't have been surprised. Even a seventeen year old rat knows better than to think she can fly.

The owl must have seen the regret in her eyes, because she smiled gently and sheathed her blade.

"It's a story about two women and a man." She said softly. "One of the women tells us the story, and the other woman keeps all of its secrets."

"What does the man do?"

The owl made a disparaging huff. "He makes silly remarks and lies to everyone, and in the end he burns for it."

Tiria took the book out of her bag and opened it to the extraordinary picture of the woman in the tower. The owl pointed her pale finger towards the base of the building, where a dark silhouette was crying out to the woman, trapped in eternal silence.

"That's him." The girl said, rather coldly. "I don't like him."

"I would have never guessed." Tiria returned, and the owl burst out laughing again. This time the scavenger joined in, amazed at the way that their voices mingled together. She was so used to being quiet that creating such an uproar made her feel giddy.

"Can you tell me more of the story?" She asked when they both had our breath back.

The owl frowned. "Didn't you read it?"

Tiria interrupted the stranger before she had a chance to mock her, although the joke fell flat. "Rats can't read."

"Oh." She chewed her lip, and then held her hands out. Tiria gave her the book willingly this time, and the owl ran her palm gently along the leather cover. "It's very old." She said hesitantly. "We only take a few out of the cabinets at a time, otherwise they start to decay."

"I didn't know that." Tiria felt an odd pang of guilt. Covering it with an awkward smile, she described the strange thrill which had made her take the book in the first place. The owl's cautious smile grew more genuine. It was as if someone had lit a flame behind her eyes. She turned from a strange, feathery creature into a girl a few years older than her companion. She leaned her chin on her hands when she was curious and smiled broadly when she was happy.

"I'm Farren." She said, and the smile danced across her face like the crescent moon. "I'm sure your name isn't Rat."

"I've been thinking of you as Owl." Tiria admitted, and explained why. When Farren finished laughing, the other girl introduced herself.

Farren – Owl, she was always Owl to Tiria - asked Tiria many other questions. The girl didn't answer all of them. Owl was as fascinated by the rat as Tiria was by the book. She was curious about Tiria's home, her life, the weapons she carried and even the colour of her hair. By the time she had run out of questions, the other girl's tongue was tired from answering her. Tiria yawned and suddenly realised that they had been talking for hours. If the sun had set she would be trapped here until dawn. She knew that her father wouldn't worry, but she knew far too well that the dark wasn't the only dangerous thing waiting outside.

"I have to go." Tiria said it so abruptly that she interrupted Owl mid-sentence. The girl caught her breath (she breathed in less than most people, probably so she could fit in more words) and looked up at the roof.

"It's still light." She said softly, wistfully. "Isn't there time for one more question?"

Tiria wondered why she felt so guilty for leaving her here.

"I'll come back," Tiria said. "I'll come back... not this week, it's the ballot."

"What's that?" Owl asked quietly. Tiria blinked, wondering if she had heard her right, and then laughed nervously. It was the kind of joke her brother used to make, but coming from a stranger it seemed almost disgusting. They were so close to the ballot that she could see the bid's faces in her dreams; it was horrible to joke about them when their own sleep must be full of nightmares.

"I'll come here the week after that. If you're here, I... I hope..." She cleared her throat and shrugged. The wasteland swallowed so many people that hardly anyone bothered making friends. Apart from her own family, Tiria had spoken to fewer than ten people in her entire life. Owl gave her the same rueful look, and waved her fluttering fingers at her in farewell. It was only after Tiria had crawled out of the ruins that she felt the yawning emptiness in her bag. She had left the book behind.

CHAPTER 5

The ballot was held twice a year. It was different from the trading markets, although everyone took the chance to bring their goods to the ancient halls where their clan met. For three days the theatres, or shopping centres, or schools, were such a hive of activity that cobwebs crumbled down from the ceiling and the floorboards were pounded into dust. But the ballot was not a market in the strict sense of the word; even if a family had no goods to trade they were still expected to attend. Every single person in the clan poured into the ruins of the city, and for two days they slept together on the floor like the rats they were.

For those two days every person was examined by the officials. When Tiria was a child she ran away screaming at their flat, empty faces. Even after she realised that they were wearing masks, she still shuddered when one of them walked by. After she found the stockings she recognised the sheer fabric, but even knowing that they were dragging old stockings over their heads didn't make the twisting bulges of their noses and mouths any less grotesque. The faceless officials prodded and poked every part of her, made notes about how tall or sick or wrinkled each person had become, and then sent them back into the pack.

Another group, again with covered faces, would ask the clans to report on their own lives and those of their families. The strange symbols which they scrawled onto misshapen paper pads had always fascinated Tiria, who always gazed in delight at the letters that she recognised. Did her words really become such ugly, cramped little symbols? When she was younger she prattled on with delight, knowing that every word she said would blossom into those eternal words. It made her feel powerful, in her own small way. She didn't realise how much harm she was doing.

All of this was done so that each person might be given a score. They would get points for their health and their character. It kept people honest in the furies of the wastes – or, at least, it was supposed to. If a man had been caught muddying a clean water source, his score would plummet. If he spent the next three months giving aid to his neighbours and leading them to rich supplies of food, then he could work his way back up quite quickly. It was a strange, clinical system, but it worked. If the council kept punishing someone for something done in desperation years before, then sooner or later that person would turn to worse crimes to support himself. With the score, he could become accepted again after just a few years – and he could take part in the ballot.

Tiria's number was sixty, because she was still beneath anyone's notice. Children died so easily in the wastes. They were protected by their families, and weren't expected to put themselves in even more danger by helping the clans until they were strong enough to support themselves. When she reached her next birthday and entered the ballot, Tiria would begin to have her own crimes recorded in those cramped letters.

The girl dreaded that year. She was scared of her own strong will, but she was more terrified of the ballot. The higher numbers were allowed to bid for any lower partner they desired. Lawrence had told her not to be scared, that the rule was there so that they could help the lows to rise. He had been hoping for something like that to happen to him, so that he could leave his father's home and do more with his life than simply slave away in the ruins. But Tiria could not share his dream. As much as she hated her father, she had found a quiet peace in the freedom that scavenging gave her. The lows had no freedom.

The only way to leave their new homes was to rise above them, or to disgrace themselves.

Some people never got to make their own choices. Elizabeth bore the brunt of her husband's complaints for years until her husband was disgusted by her and cast her out. Tiria started searching for her mother the second she crawled through the narrow gap into the theatre.

The room was already milling with people, and the girl had to cover her nose against the rancid stink of so much unwashed skin. After a few hours she knew that she would barely notice it, but for the first few minutes it was eye-watering. The atrium was a fevered nightmare of bodies pressing against each other and then breaking apart. She couldn't help remembering what Owl had said about rats.

She searched every face in the crowd with her sharp eyes, but there was one corner that her gaze refused to settle upon. Idling in the corner were a pack of the lowest men and women, their bodies draped in thin fabric and their faces painted in bright colours. Those lows were the old, the sick, the wicked or the ugly. Every single one of them was starving, living off any scraps they could scavenge from unclaimed areas and sleeping out in the open, or wherever they could find shelter. Their faces were dried out with sunburn and their limbs were emaciated from hunger and thirst.

The ballot was the only time when they could mingle with anyone who might help them. Whenever a high walked past their fingers would reach out, clutching at clothes and wrists and even hair in their desperation to be noticed. Most of the highs walked past without glancing around, but some of them stopped and spoke to the lows in hushed voices. Even as a child Tiria knew what was happening; her brother had tried to shield her eyes from the sight, but she had been curious enough to look. Everyone pretended not to see the writhing, sweating limbs wrapped around each other in dark corners of the rotting building. As often as not, the lows would be cast aside and forgotten the moment their prey had finished with them. They would straighten their clothes, wipe their eyes, and return to the pack. What else could they do?

Tiria finally steeled herself and looked for her mother amongst them. The short, thin woman was not there. The girl breathed out sharply, barely aware that she had been holding her breath. It was a comfort to know that her mother wasn't as desperate as that. At least she wasn't fated to freeze in the wasteland, like those poor frantic souls. If she wasn't here, then it meant only two things. Either she was sick, or her new high had taken her to a different ballot. Tiria prayed it was the second, although her throat closed up as she realised how desperate she had been to see her mother.

Before Tiria could search another room, her father's hand caught her wrist. He knew who she was looking for. His face betrayed nothing, but his fingers sank into her skin and squeezed. By the time he let go, his daughter's arm was bruised purple. She shook her hand out, meeting his eyes expressionlessly, and then turned away.

The rats scurried into the main hall when the officials shouted for them to attend. Holes had been poked into the ceiling to make the huge auditorium bright, and the sun shone down in thin slices onto the seething crowd. Tiria pushed her way through to the second floor, clutching at the balcony and scanning the people milling around below her. The rats behind her jostled, and she sank her fingers into the wooden posts to stop herself from being pushed over the edge.

The criminals were brought out first. They were dealt with in a brisk, dismissive way. The ones who had stolen goods or beaten their families were lashed and branded before they were shoved back into the jeering crowd. Men and women who had spread dissent were publically humiliated. The rats threw rotting food and garbage at them, taunting them to respond, while the traitors bit dumbly at their gags and glowered back. They were finally sentenced to slavery on the farms, and herded off the stage. There were a great many of them; the winter had been hard, and the officials had halved the ration allowances. Finally a chain of guards set up a perimeter along the stage, and the officials brought on the condemned. Murderers and rapists struggled to escape from their bonds until the soldiers lowered their pistols to their heads. The rats fell silent. The shots echoed through the auditorium.

There was a girl who was going savage. She was brought onto stage last. Her eyes were frightened, and the soft ballot dress she was wearing billowed around her ankles. Her skin was sunburned and her limbs were strong and graceful, but one sleeve had been torn away to betray the black, rotting abscess which had sealed her fate. The crowd was still silent, but this time they swayed a little as families reached for one another's hands. Tiria sank her fingers into the balcony and forgot to look for her mother. The mutating girl was only a little older than she was. She must have been stupid, to come to a ballot when she was so obviously contaminated. The girl's sweet eyes were a little clouded, and Tiria told herself that madness was already making her simple. The alternative was too awful to think about.

The soldiers gripped the girl's her shoulders and turned her so that the crowd could see more of the marks. The sores looked like spots of ink. The crowd murmured, and the front few rows took a step back as a doctor came onto the stage. The doctor's masked face caught the darkness and made him appear demonic as he opened a metal box and drew out a glass syringe. The rats held their breath. The man tapped the bubbles from the vial, and slipped the needle into the girl's arm.

She shut her eyes, and her body twitched a little. The poison took a few moments to work, but everyone in the crowd knew what it was doing. The yellow liquor would not hurt a healthy person, but anyone who had begun to mutate would have their corruption sped up by it. The doctor had given the girl enough to transform months of decay into a few minutes.

The girl made an odd noise, and the crowd's whispering grew louder. It wasn't an execution, it was a warning. People were supposed to report their mutations the moment they appeared. The girl had tried to conceal hers. She could have fallen asleep, dosed by the doctor's drugs, until her heart eased if she had told the truth – but she had put her family in danger to protect her own skin. There was no mercy, because if she had gotten away with it she would have shown even less to her kin. One savage could slaughter an entire family in minutes. The sores would have grown worse, stinking and carrying disease, and then her mind would have started to crumble. Long before her limbs grew soft and brittle, she would have used her teeth and nails to tear at any person who came near her.

The crowd could see the sickness now. They watched the girl's skin boil and burst. Oily pus trickled down her bare legs with the urine which her frightened body could not hold in. Her soft eyes had grown milky, and her feeble struggles slowly changed into snarling lunges at the soldiers. She screamed, and her voice was rough. Her face was almost gone now; the white eyes blazed from skin so pock-marked that many in the crowd had to look away. The sound of retching filled the theatre as the stink washed through the crowd. The girl, now fully savage, laughed and gurgled as blood filled her mouth.

The doctor drew out a gun, and shot the girl once through the temple. She thrashed before she died. There was little difference between the death rictus and the feral fury which had come before. She fell to the floorboards, and the crowd was completely silent as she was hauled offstage.

Tiria took a deep breath when she got back into the foyer, and rested her head in her hands. She had seen it happen before, sometimes to two or three people at a time. It never got any easier. She wondered what it must feel like to know the person on stage, and to watch them changing from someone you loved to a creature that you hated. A lurch of icy fear ran through her stomach. What would she have done, if the doctor had dragged Elizabeth or Lawrence onto the stage?

She began her search anew, but with less hope. She found her father instead, and stood awkwardly beside the man. He looked impatient, but it wasn't his usual taciturn ire. There was something else in his eyes: a triumphant, impatient look which the girl had never seen before. He drew her a little closer and pushed her long black hair behind her ears, smoothing down the tangled locks. It was only then that Tiria noticed that another man was standing beside him, looking speculatively down at her. She shivered and stared at the floor, wrapping her arms around herself.

"How old is she?" The man asked, leaning so close that the girl could smell the liquor on his breath. The old man cut in before she could speak or move away.

"Tiria is eighteen." He lied, and then caught sight of the open disbelief on both of their faces. Before Tiria could tell the younger man the truth, her father scowled and muttered, "She's seventeen. But her birthday is next week."

"Then she's a child." The man sounded disappointed. The old rat smiled, and Tiria felt her nails biting into her palms. She wanted to smash his yellow teeth in.

"Is a week a long time to wait?"

"You can't bid for me!" Tiria burst out, feeling sick to her stomach as she realised what was going on. "I'm not in the ballot."

"They won't begrudge you a week if you can be useful, Tiria." The strange man said, and despite all of the nightmare Tiria's head spun at the fact that he managed to sound earnest. It was almost as if he was giving her helpful advice rather than throwing away her last month of freedom. "By the next ballot you'll have wasted months. They won't like that. It's seen as selfish. It's far better for you to volunteer."

"She wouldn't want to be selfish." Her father said pointedly. "Eating my supplies, taking up room..." He waved a hand. "Especially since I'm taking in a new low this month."

The other man smiled widely and shook the old man's wrinkled hand, congratulating him on his generosity. The man who had given her life smiled smugly at Tiria and gave her a meaningful, warning look. She scowled and bit her lip. She had already worked out what he was thinking. He wanted to start again, with a new woman and a new family. Now that Lawrence was gone, she was the only thing reminding him of his old, depraved life. The sooner he got rid of her, the sooner he could pretend that his children didn't even exist.

"Father," She tried pleading with him, and felt tears sliding down her cheeks, "Please..."

"I've already put you into the ballot." He said shortly. "You'd better start smiling if you don't want to be chosen by an old man."

He was not a clever man, but after a few hours Tiria realised that her father's cunning had outfoxed her. A volunteer had to have their parent's consent. The man had simply told the officials that he was there to vouch for her. Once her name was on the ballot list, it couldn't be taken back, and if she argued then it would make her look like she had lost her nerve. It was better to go through with it than to be branded as a coward.

Tiria was so wretched as she moved through the crowds that she didn't think to look for her mother's face. She couldn't remember what her mother's high had looked like. Elizabeth's husband had done the same thing to her as he did to his daughter, waiting until she had arrived at the ballot before announcing his plan. Elizabeth had slapped him in the middle of the crowd, losing some of the scant few points she still had by flaunting her bad manners in public. It was deeply satisfying for her to finally strike her husband, but daughter was nervous to be seen with her after that.

"Don't you care about your score?" Tiria had asked, gulping back her fear. Elizabeth had smiled and kissed her forehead, and she walked away with her new high as freely as a bird.

Tiria milled around the market in a daze, trying to think of a way to take her name off the ballot. When her name was called to be examined she begged the officials to intercede, but they had heard the same story so many times they were deaf to it. They looked at her body and her father's consent, and said that *biologically* and *legally* (words she didn't know) there was no reason for them to intercede.

The woman was already opening the door when she said this. Tiria fell to her knees in front of her, clutching at the soft grey fabric of her dress.

"Please," she croaked, and then choked back her pride and begged again. "I don't want to do this."

She looked down, and Tiria thought the woman was surprised. How could she tell that through the mask? Perhaps in her fear she was only imagining it, but she could hear that the woman's voice was tired. "It's not about what you want."

"But, my father..."

"Your father knows what is best for you. It's better to enter the ballot early." The woman sighed when she caught sight of the girl's horrified expression and rifled through her notes. A glimmer of hope rose in Tiria's chest when the doctor kicked the door closed and sat down on the ancient row of folding seats which served as an examination bench. She wished she could read over the woman's shoulder, but the dark marks made as much sense to her as the cracks in the tarmac roads outside.

The official whispered under her breath as she read, and it took her a long time to finish. When she closed the folder there was more sympathy in her voice, but it was ringed with a vein of iron. "I see your father has chosen a new low. He's doing his duty. Can't you follow his example?"

Tiria laughed at that, a strange choking noise which echoed in the grey room. The official's voice turned sour, and all of her sympathy faded.

"The ballot isn't about what you want. The council understands that you're too young to know the right thing to do. By the time you've made up your mind, it might be too late. Our world is too cruel to us for you to waste time worrying. Every month which passes is another person growing sick, or getting killed, or going mad. Every person who we lose is a part of our world which is gone forever."

Tiria struggled to understand the peculiar words. Later on, she found out that all of the officials had learned the same speech off by heart. It had made sense years ago, when the world was so bleak that most children were born dead and most adults had the sickness. But there were hundreds of healthy people gathered in the theatre that day, and just as many in other cities across the wastes. A hundred people could have mutated or died without threatening everyone's survival. Tiria knew that instinctively, and so she hoped that she could refuse the ballot without anyone caring.

She was wrong. They were used to people refusing. They had heard it all before.

The official gave her a piece of honeycomb to calm her down. Tiria devoured the rare treat in a few thoughtless bites. By the time the second officials called her name, her head was swimming and she could barely see.

Tiria thought: *They're used to people refusing. They knew what to do.*

The ballot officials saw the vague shadows in her eyes, and when she mumbled her fears to them they didn't bother answering. She clumsily handed them the stockings her father had given her, hoping the bribe would make them help. Instead, they added five points onto her score and said it was her civil duty to contribute to the cause.

"Don't worry." One of them said, his voice kind behind his empty mask. "You'll be chosen quickly with such a high score!"

Tiria spat at him, losing her five points, and clawed at his hands when he half carried, half dragged her into the theatre hall. Before he left he spitefully fined her five more. That was how Elizabeth's daughter entered the ballot as the only new bid with a low's measly score.

All the others were dressed in smart clothes, with their hair washed and braided. Some of the women were wearing long, flowing skirts which they had brought to the city in their bags and changed in to. Tiria was so used to seeing everything stained with dust that the brightly coloured fabric was stunning. When they moved it flowed around their ankles. The men were just as smart, wearing shirts with flat collars and shoes which shone. They looked at the girl, reeling dizzily in her dust-stained travelling clothes, and hid their smiles.

Tiria had a dress at home. Elizabeth had helped her to make it.

Tears rolled down the girl's cheeks, but she saw the dress as clearly before her eyes as the swarming faces of the highs. Against their jeering and fighting, she imagined the dress. Every panel of it was a different colour. The shining fabric had been scrounged from hundreds of nights digging through the ruins of old clothing stores. It had a long, flowing skirt. It had buttoned cuffs on the sleeves.

Tiria looked down at her heavy boots. There was a dark, wet stain on the wooden floor. She didn't look up again. She heard one of the other girls laugh. It echoed strangely in her ears.

The auditorium was filled with so many people the dusty velvet seats had completely disappeared. Behind the bids, a great swathe of canvas swayed backwards and forwards across the stage and sent eddies of dust into the air. Tiria sneezed. The other bids sneered. A low doesn't even have the self-control to hold her breath!

Tiria had watched countless ballots from the auditorium, but from the stage it was a completely different, terrifying experience. She had not imagined standing there, feeling hundreds of eyes on her. She couldn't see. She tried to tell from a shouting voice whether the man was old, or young, or kind. When she finally heard a friendly voice, she knew that he was going to be passed over for a crow-like ancient croak with one point more to its name. She felt sweat pouring down her neck and goose bumps itching on her arms, and wondered if the people in the crowd could smell her fear.

Then she was afraid to breathe in case they disliked the shape of her mouth or the flare of her nostrils. Her ears felt blocked as if she had been dragged under water, but she heard her score being shouted out across the room like a brand searing into her flesh. There were jeers, and laughter. They made jokes about how she must be mischievous or a chatterbox, and the other bids turned their mocking, frozen grins onto her so that the crowd would turn against her even more.

In the end, Tiria had no idea who won her. She could hear them arguing over her, because even a low could be young, and strong, and comely. As to what kind of person chose her, she could not say. Standing on the stage, Tiria listened to an unearthly voice singing in her ears until the hot, choking air in the room swallowed her whole. She fell to the dusty floorboards in a heap, and the last thing she heard was the sound of laughter.

CHAPTER 6

Tiria woke up in the doctor's rooms with her head aching fiercely. She had seen people faint during the ballot before, and when she looked around her she saw beds full of other people who were still unconscious, or holding their heads in their hands. The water the officials had left them tasted like metal and dust, but it cleared Tiria's pounding head and calmed her sickened stomach. Now that she had actually been won the officials ignored her. Their task was over.

She made her way back to the darkness of the atrium and leaned against the wall, drinking in the thick, cool shadows. It was night, and the thin strips of moonlight which had broken through the cracks in the walls were smothered by smoke from the torches. A faint sound of snoring came from the theatre. Tiria's aching head buzzed with the low roar of hundreds of sleepers twisted together. Her bag fell to the floor from her numb fingers. The girl felt desperately tired, but she knew that if she joined the sleeping pack her mind would be too full to sleep. She couldn't bear to open the door and wonder which of the sleeping men was going to take her away in the morning. For a long time she just stood in the dark smoky hallway and felt tears rolling down her cheeks.

"Are you alright?" Someone asked. The girl opened her eyes and looked into a blurry haze.

"I'm fine." She said, and because it was the ballot she recited the pledge for good measure. "I embrace the rebirth of mankind."

"I'm glad to hear it, but that's not what I asked. I saw you fall down." The voice said, and there was a glimmer of laughter in it. Tiria blinked away the dim haze of tears and glared up. The man was holding a bright, battery powered lantern, which made her swollen eyes sting, but the silhouette behind the light seemed harmless enough.

"I waited up to make sure you weren't hurt." He told her. Then, to her numb horror, he raised a hand to her face and caught her chin so he could look into her eyes. "I thought so. They drugged you, didn't they?"

Tiria shook herself free and shoved him away, scowling when the man barely moved. "I'm still armed, even if there are two of you."

He spread his empty hands in a gesture of surrender. He took a further step back and shook his head apologetically before he spoke. "I'm sorry, perhaps you wanted to be left alone."

The girl scoffed but didn't answer. The stranger stood there in silence for so long that the emptiness stretched between them. After a while Tiria spoke just to make some noise: "I shouldn't have been in the ballot."

Those words hadn't saved her before, but she needed to mumble them one last time. It sounded like a record scratching out the same line of a dead man's song, but Tiria still needed to find someone who would listen. "I'm not a coward. I don't normally faint. I just wasn't... ready."

The man was silent for a moment, and then he lowered the lantern a little. His weather-worn face was thin and solemn, but he was smiling ruefully. "I don't think anyone could ever be ready for something like that."

The girl shook her head emphatically, and then let out a great sigh and sagged back against the wall. For a moment the man looked unsure of himself, and then he put the light onto the floor and leaned against the wall beside her. Tiria watched him out of the corner of her eye. For all she knew, he was an informant. He scratched his wrist awkwardly, and she caught sight of a beaded bracelet before he shook the sleeve back down and cleared his throat.

"It's a worse trial than the one they give to criminals, you know. At least they don't have to face down all of those people."

She had never seen a criminal trial. "They don't?"

"They only have to face the council." The man shrugged. "Not the mob. Lots of people asked for you."

"They wasted their time." The girl spat, with some energy. "I didn't want to be chosen."

"No-one ever does." He looked sad for a moment, as if he were remembering his own ballot. It must have only been a few years ago; he looked as if he were twenty five or so. Not a young man, but not old enough for the sun to have carved him out of sandstone, either.

His silent empathy was touching. For most of the year the only people Tiria spoke to were her family, or the odd scavengers who she met in the wilderness. Her father wasn't in the habit of putting his emotions on display, and the scavengers only trusted their own clans, not the strangers they met in the wastes. Sooner or later the empty buildings were picked clean, and a rat could lose far more than pride in the territory disputes.

The ballot was supposed to help with that, but nobody could remember when it had ever truly worked. No-one wanted to risk getting close to their bids, and not many people left their old families to make treaties. After all, if they had left their family they had either been sent to the ballot, or cast out into the wilderness. People who left of their own accord were rare, and people who could survive on their own even rarer.

Tiria thought about that whenever she missed her brother. She wondered what he would have done, if he had been with her when their father tried to sell her. She wondered what his own ballot would have been like.

She shivered and turned away from that line of thought. The man standing next to her was neither an outcast nor an informant. Neither of them would be stupid enough to show vulnerable emotions around another scavenger, even a miserable scrap of a girl. If Tiria hadn't been so desperately miserable she would have been disgusted at herself.

"Do you work in the council?" She tried to change the subject, remembering what the man had said about criminals. Her voice sounded sluggish and dour, but at least the tears had stopped. The man looked sidelong at her, and then the edge of his mouth lifted in the same rueful smile which he had worn when he began to speak. His voice took on the odd lilt of a storyteller.

"Once, I saw a woman who had stolen her sister's baby. They both insisted the child was their own. The officials couldn't work out who the real mother was, so they suggested that both of the women care for the child. First, they told them, one of you needs to change the child's nappy. One of the woman gave a disgusted cry and gave the child to the other. The judges laughed and said to the disgusted woman: "That proves you are not the mother!" The woman replied, "I am – I just remember what I fed my baby last night! She's welcome to change him!""

Tiria smiled shakily and shook her head. "That didn't happen."

"I swear it!" He made himself look far too innocent and then grinned at her expression. "Don't you believe me?"

"Of course not! I don't know you." She said, and just like that her tears were back. She shook her head, feeling suddenly angry at his foolishness. "All I know is that... that you wouldn't be making jokes if you felt like I do. Save your silly stories for the poor woman who chooses you."

"Alright," He sounded a little taken aback, but then the odd note of laughter was back in his voice. "I'll do that."

They fell into silence again. Tiria's mind was reeling. He had said so many people had asked for her. If they had been arguing over her, and all of them had numbers higher than her own, then the person who had won must have been very high. That must have annoyed her low father! For the first time the girl felt a small spark of happiness at how things had turned out, although it was nothing compared to the black mood which eclipsed every other part of her heart.

"Did you..." She started, and then tried to think of a tactful way to ask. "The person who chose me... was their number..."

"I thought you said they were wasting their time?" The man said flatly. He didn't seem to be able to stop making smart comments. Maybe something was wrong with him. Tiria bit back a frustrated sigh and shoved at his arm petulantly.

"Don't be an ass. I want to know." She thought about it, and then added, "So I can find out who they are and tell them they wasted their time *personally.*"

"A very fine plan." He said seriously, barely raising an eyebrow but somehow still making it seem as if he was laughing at the joke. He studied the girl for a moment, as if trying to guess her reaction, and his voice grew serious. "You were chosen by a ninety-two."

"A what?" Her jaw dropped, and then she broke into a kind of wretched laughter. "You're teasing me. What was it really?"

"Ninety two." The man said, and then looked her dead in the eyes. "My name is Seth."

CHAPTER 7

Seth asked Tiria if she wanted to go home and pick up her things. She shuddered at the thought of facing her father. Before she could refuse Seth caught her arm and lowered his voice.

"We can go early." His whisper tickled her ear, and she fought the urge to pull away. She was so distracted that she didn't hear what he'd said until he repeated it. "We can go tonight; your father won't leave until tomorrow."

"We can't leave." The girl used her scorn as an excuse to break free. "Someone will notice."

"Who?" He made a show of looking around the dark atrium. "We've both finished our work here. They made sure we haven't turned into savages and they've put you through hell. There's no reason for us to stay, unless you wanted to watch the rest of the ballot."

Despite herself, the girl whitened at the thought of going back into that room. Even the idea of watching the nightmare happen to other people made her feel ill. Seth frowned at her and picked up her bag.

"Come on." He said shortly. "You're not staying here."

She followed him numbly. It was almost obedience, but even though she wouldn't dare to disobey, Tiria would have laughed at the idea that Seth owned her. He had asked for her, and won because his score was so impossibly high no-one else who wanted her could bid. Instead of money or rank, he had bartered something far more valuable. He had volunteered to take a stranger into his home, share his supplies and shelter, and teach her the skills that she would need to rise to his rank. In return, she would help him make children.

The bids were supposed to be grateful. A high could easily choose someone of their own rank and leave the lows at the bottom of the heap. Lows were given fewer rations, smaller homes and scavenging rights in far more dangerous areas. Tiria grew up in a hole in the ground; her parents' scores never rose above fifty or so. Her brother had been desperate to enter the ballot, telling her that the higher you became, the more choices you got. There were farms in the east, and people who got to travel between cities carrying messages. You could even train to become an official, if you wanted to. But everyone started as a bid.

Tiria's situation was unusual. Normally a new adult would be taken in by someone of a similar age who was just a few points above them. This gave young men and women the chance to start their adult lives as equals and make their own choices at the next ballot. Because of her low score, none of these people had wanted anything to do with Tiria. Men on their second ballot would not dare to risk their few hard earned points on a girl who hadn't even lasted an hour without a penalty. Most of her bids had come from old men and work-worn sixties who saw her as a drudge worker rather than as a human being. Then, Seth had bid for her.

Tiria didn't know how to think about her new partner. His high score meant that he probably lead a life she could only dream about. But if Seth didn't grow tired of her, the only way she would ever be free would be to reach a higher score than him. Higher than ninety two! She had never even met an eighty. She had thought they were all doctors or officials. Officials never put themselves into the ballot.

Seth wasn't either of those things. She didn't know a single thing about him, much less how a man as young as he was could possibly have gotten such a high score. But she knew that if she lived for a thousand years, she would never be able to match it.

They walked in silence for most of the night. Seth followed the girl's directions without comment, and she took the chance to watch him. He was tall, but it was a solid height unlike the starved lankiness of her father. He walked with the same ponderous gait all of the scavengers used, lifting each foot carefully away from loose stones and tree roots and planting it deliberately into the dust. His hands were thin – she remembered their strength from the way he had caught her arm in the theatre, but while they were walking he moved branches aside with a curious grace. Other than that, he was shockingly unremarkable. His clothes were the same dusty colour that everyone wore, repaired so often that there was no colour left. His weapons looked sharp and well used.

Tiria wondered if he was handsome. She had no idea how she would decide. Lawrence used to tease her about her first ballot, describing scores of milk-faced swains with desperate hearts. His own perfect partner was light haired with the kind of curves that even drab clothes couldn't hide. When the girl pointed out how unlikely it was that a woman like that would want a frog-faced creature like him, he started sulking.

"You're not so precious, either." He retorted, tugging at her braids. "Do you think they're going to fight over your grumpy face?"

If faces were the best clue, then Seth was definitely not handsome. He had the same kind of wide eyes as the Owl, but nothing else about him was remarkable. His nose was sharp and his lips were thin, and he had a bruise above one eye which made him squint. He looked cross-eyed until it faded, by which time Tiria was so used to his lopsided expression that she laughed at his normal expression, thinking he was pulling faces.

She couldn't see his face when the sun set. The moon was barely a sliver in the sky, and they kept walking by the light of a flickering oil lamp. The girl pretended she could tease out the mysteries of him from his silhouette until she grew bored, and then she caught up to him.

"Why did you choose me?" she asked bluntly. He looked down absently, almost as if he had forgotten she was there.

"Don't you know better than to talk so loudly at night?"

"You're talking too." Tiria knew she was being brazen but she didn't care. Being attacked would have ended her surreal day perfectly. Seth shrugged and kept walking. After a few minutes the girl couldn't hold back any longer: "You have to tell me."

"You told me yourself, you were too young to be in the ballot." He said, evading the question again. "So until you are an adult, I don't *have* to do anything. I certainly don't have to answer annoying questions from a child."

The sharp words made Tiria shrink back. It was the first time he had been anything but patient, and she imagined a shade of her father in that cruelty. How angry had Seth been, when he found out that he had been tricked by the old man? Nobody wanted to take on another person's child. They were weak, untrained, and barely acknowledged by the council.

The book burned like a brand in Tiria's mind. As a child, she might have been forgiven the natural ignorance which made her peek inside. As an adult, she had committed one of the worst crimes imaginable.

She swallowed back that thought and looked up at Seth. She don't know why she had thought he could read her mind. Her guilty thoughts seemed to be tumbling so wildly about her ears that she was sure he would be able to hear them. And yet he walked calmly, watching the dark ruins rising around them with the patient eyes of an experienced scavenger. The buildings had been picked clean, many of them by Tiria herself, but the savages wouldn't know that. Even in the darkest hours of the night the fragile torch could have brought hundreds of them crawling through the dust, dragging their emaciated hands through the sharp shards of stone and glass until the air stank of copper and pus.

Seth's hand was nowhere near his weapons. He watched but he was unafraid. Tiria wondered if that meant he was stupid, or brave. She decided that she wouldn't like to be chosen by a brave man. The stupid ones and the cowards tended to live longer. Her father's magnificent laziness had taught her that.

The Owl had been right, Tiria thought with sudden bitterness. They were more like rats than any other creature. They would hide away like animals in their nests until one of the diseases drove them out, and then they had no idea how to care for each other. Elizabeth had been clever, and when Lawrence and Tiria fell sick she had spent long sleepless weeks fighting against the pox. That plague was the worst anyone could remember. Other people dragged their wretched bodies out into the fresh air to get away from the stink of their own flesh, and they withered away into the sun. When his family was too ill to hunt for food, Lawrence captured the birds that come to peck at the strangers' bones. The meat was tough, but rich; he threw away the claws and burned the feathers before anyone could use them. Nobody would dare to sleep on a pillow haunted by the screams of the dead.

The memory made Tiria shiver and stumble, and Seth looked around. She mentally cursed her clumsy feet. She could climb through crumbling buildings without dislodging a single stone, but while that man was near her she couldn't even breathe without feeling awkward and loud. He smiled a little, and the girl blushed and looked away.

She wasn't so naïve that she didn't know why the ballot had to be held, nor had she blocked her ears at past ballots, when her brother and the other older children told their stories in the whispering hours of the night. Tiria knew that if one of the old, sun-maddened men had won her, the last few hours might have been far worse for her. A man like her father could have easily won her, and her life would have been just as wretched as it had been before. Still, at least she would have known her place. She found it hard to imagine anything more humiliating than trailing pathetically after a stranger in the middle of the night, begging him for a single word of explanation. Her embarrassment made her clumsy, and her whirling mind made her careless. She honestly believed that in those first few hours her new husband thought that she was an idiot.

They stopped after several miles to rest. Seth sat beside her on a low brick wall, and shrugged when she pushed herself further away. Tiria had barely noticed his casual closeness when he had leaned beside her in the theatre, but once she knew who he was, she felt his body heat searing her flesh.

She told herself he must hate her for being a sly low, who had lied about her age to attract a ninety two. It was easy to imagine that he was disappointed. It was easier than trying to guess what he was really thinking.

"I'm sorry they tricked you. I didn't mean to lie to you." she said. "I wouldn't blame you if you refused to take me."

He looked offended. "You didn't lie. Your father shoved you into the ballot without your consent, and every single person in that building went along with it." He spat in disgust, and shook his head at the thought. "Would you have rather I left you there? I wouldn't even do that to a dog."

"So you chose me because you felt sorry for me?" The girl's voice rose as she asked. He made a frustrated sound and shook his head.

"No."

"Then why?"

"You'll find out when it matters." He said curtly, and stood up so quickly the girl flinched. Before she could draw a breath he had stalked off again. Tiria gaped after him for so long that the pool of light had nearly disappeared before she could convince her frozen feet to move.

They reached Tiria's shelter just as the sun was starting to colour the horizon. It was impossible to think that they had walked all through the night, and even more dizzying that not a single thing had come out of the shadows to face them. Tiria opened the hatch and they climbed in clumsily, pulling the corrugated iron sheet down behind them. It was only after the girl heard the familiar sound of the bolt sliding into place that the full shock of the past few days hit her.

"You live here?" Seth was saying, looking around with obvious amazement. Tiria nodded, and then shook her head, and then threw herself down onto her bed and burst into tears. Seth stood awkwardly for a moment, hunched over under the low roof, and then turned away and busied himself going through the store cupboards. He found dried food, stale water, tins and foil-sealed coffee, and made a great deal of noise clattering the pans around until the girl had finished sobbing her eyes out. When she raised her head he handed her a hot drink, a cold bowl of canned peas, and a handkerchief.

"We'll sleep here." He told her, watching her eat. Tiria nearly choked, and he pulled a face at her wary expression. "Don't be an idiot, Tiria. I'm not going to touch you."

"How would I know that?" She demanded, feeling mortified by the blush rising up her cheeks. It was the only answer that still made sense! "Why else would you want me?"

"I don't want to assault you." He told her icily. "What kind of monster do you think I am?"

"I don't know! Why don't you tell me?"

He shook his head, frowning, and that was the end of that. Whatever his reasons were for choosing her, Tiria decided that she wasn't going to humiliate herself by begging for an answer. The idiot probably didn't even know the answer himself. She bitterly told herself that she was probably just a whim for him. Well, good. He would get bored of her quickly, and then he would send her away. She would be free to choose her own partner at the next ballot.

If she was good, of course. Tiria made up her mind to be the most perfect little scavenger in the entire county. It would serve him right!

The girl slept uneasily, dreaming of roaring shadows in the darkness, and woke up when the sun was a lurid pink outside the small gap in the hatch. Seth was still sleeping, curled up on the ground with one arm thrown over his face, the other resting beside his knife. For a second Tiria thought he had been waiting for her father to return, ready to cut the man's throat for his cruelty and lack of unburned kitchenware. She smiled a little at the fantasy, but it didn't even play out in her mind before she guessed the truth. They had made too much noise the night before, and Seth had been wary of something following them.

Home. She looked around and remembered that today she would be leaving it forever. It was only a small hole in the ground, but she could see the shadows of her mother and brother in every corner, working and playing and laughing. The lurking fiend of her father was there too, raging at Elizabeth or stroking her soft black hair with his calloused fingers. Tiria looked around the home she had grown up in and her eyes filled with tears at the thought of leaving. When she thought of her father the sorrow turned into anger. He shouldn't have cast her out.

She remembered his triumphant smile and her hands curled into fists.

She swept through her father's home like a whirlwind, tipping every drawer and chest out onto the floor. She took everything which she and Lawrence had scavenged or repaired over the years. As she piled everything up she realised how little was left behind. What had their father done for himself? He looked for things which he could trade, not supplies to keep his family fed and warm. Tiria thought about his smug smile whenever he took goods to market, and the vague excuses he made when his trading only brought home a few tins of food. He said that he was bad at bartering; she had believed him. She had never asked herself how a lazy, sour man had risen high enough to bid for a new wife.

She had helped him to gather bribes. Tiria kicked angrily at the ground and tore her blanket from her bed, twisting the crocheted fabric between her hands. She should report him. But who would listen? If they punished him the bribes would stop.

The girl woke Seth up with a prod of her toe and edged backwards as his hand closed around his knife. "It's me." she said, and he blinked in sleepy confusion at the anger in her voice. "Wake up. We're leaving."

She left a single can of food in the store, hefting the others onto her back. The old man would probably eat it himself, and then his new wife would know exactly what kind of person had chosen her. Tiria strung the second bag - her mother's - across her shoulders. Then she turned her attention to the dirt floor, digging furrows into it with the heel of her boot. Up until this point Seth had been silent, but when he saw the girl reaching for a bottle of cleaning fluid he stopped her. Tiria struggled - she could already see the room going up in flames.

"Don't."

She whirled around, hating the note of command in his voice as much as the ghost of her father, and her voice came out in a sharp hiss. "You have six days before you can order me around. Until then I belong to myself."

His eyes narrowed. "No, Tiria. You have six days to prove you can be my equal. Until then I won't let you act like a child. This is madness."

"He deserves it!" she retorted. "You don't know..."

"I don't want to know." He interrupted with a harshness which shocked her into silence. His eyes were too fierce for the girl to meet. His fingers dug into her arm, stopping her from pouring out the noxious mixture of chemicals and alcohol, and he kept speaking angrily. "You can't destroy the only shelter for miles around."

"So what? He can dig another hole." she replied savagely. "He doesn't deserve this one."

"And what about the other people – the ones who get lost or need help?"

"Father always turned them away." Tiria told him in a cold, bitter voice. Seth's hand fell from her shoulder as if she had burned him, and for a second he was at a loss for words. Then he cleared his throat, and when he spoke again it was in the cool, distant voice of a ninety two.

"It's your choice." He said, and climbed out into the night. From his footsteps she knew that he was already walking away.

Tiria poured the fluid into the furrows and watched it seep into the soil. She picked up the matches. She climbed out of the hole. And then she stopped.

The acrid fumes stung her throat. The girl thought burning her home. She would be executed or locked away while her father carried on his new life, in some new home, with his smug smile on his face.

Tiria tucked the matches into her pocket and stood up. Her father would know how close she had come. It was enough.

CHAPTER 8

Seth hadn't been as guarded as usual in his anger. His words stuck in Tiria's mind as she ran after him. You *have six days to prove that you're my equal.*

What had he meant by that? He had chosen her, not the other way around. She didn't have to prove a single thing.

Her plan to behave herself had already failed. She supposed she needed to start again.

For his part, Seth was quite indifferent to her. After she had raided the shelter he seemed to give up trying to be friendly, and although he asked some questions he was unimpressed with most of the answers. They had no reason to speak to each other, and since making too much noise was dangerous they had the perfect excuse to dwell in their own thoughts.

Tiria's awkwardness left her in a slow way that she didn't notice at first. One morning she woke up and realised that the stranger who was sleeping beside her was nothing to her. Just as surely she knew that she was nothing to him; when he woke up first he always seemed to find something to do so that he could move away from the blankets as quickly as possible. He never tried to touch her.

He was odd in ways Tiria could not quite explain, even to herself. There was a way he spoke which made her think that he was mocking her, using words which were too long and drawing out his sentences into complicated strings. She mimicked them sometimes, but she could never quite get them right. He never laughed at her for trying, but she saw the light in his eyes blaze, and knew that he was amused. It was not the only way that he looked at her; she often noticed him watching her in the same way that she would look at a building. She would be working out its weaknesses and watching to see if it would collapse; he seemed to be curious if she would do the same thing.

Strangely, Tiria still didn't believe that he was regretting his choice. She didn't dare to ask him, He had openly mocked her for calling him her husband. He was so disparaging about the whole sorry mess that the girl didn't understand why he had even bid for her in the first place. Perhaps his sense of duty was stronger than his disgust – or, at least, it had been during the ballot.

Tiria had tried being obedient, and he had barely noticed. After a few days her temper flared, and she decided she would show him how bad a choice she was. She thought about piercing holes into their water bottles or losing some supplies, but she was not stupid or angry enough to do it. Instead, she dragged her feet and complained, demanded they stop and rest five times more often than they actually needed, and developed a strange fever which only a few days' sleep in the same place could heal.

Seth humoured her on the last one, but he clearly did not believe her. After a few hours it was embarrassing for her to keep up the pretence. She lowered her hand from her forehead and pressed her face into the blankets, willing the soft darkness to swallow her up so that she didn't have to see the blank stubbornness in his level gaze.

"What do you want?" He asked, so softly that the girl barely heard him. Tiria looked around and saw that he had moved closer, not to be intimate but so that he could speak without being overheard. It was that practicality that riled her, and she raised herself on her elbows to meet his eyes.

"Tell me why you chose me. What you want from me."

He sat back on his heels and shook his head. "I can't tell you what I want. You'll understand when we reach the city."

"What's that?"

"It's a shelter buried a week's walk from here. Maybe more, if you keep play-acting. I know you're better than this."

Tiria reddened, feeling scolded. He ignored her embarrassment and waved a hand idly back in the direction they had come from, his voice coolly listing facts so that she could take no pride in his observations, merely feel terribly small knowing that he had been watching her even more intently than she had feared.

"You're a competent scavenger, or you wouldn't be alive. Your hand falls to your knife at the smallest noise, and your eyes see everything before mine do. You're sure-footed and even quiet, when you want to be. So I want to know what's upset you, so that we can move on without the charade."

Abandoning the pretence of being sick, she sat up and looped her arms around her knees, pressing him for more answers now that he was actually saying something. "You still didn't say why you chose me."

He shrugged. "I don't know."

"Oh."

"Oh." He mimicked with a sudden grin. "That's it? After all that pestering, you're happy with that answer?"

She nodded. "The ballot's like that, isn't it? My father only chose my mother because she was low enough that he could bid for her."

"But I'm high enough to choose whoever I wanted." He prompted. Tiria smiled at him, almost mischievously.

"You wanted to get out of there the second you found me." She held up her hand, miming running with her fingers. "Arguing over a high takes time and patience, and I don't think you have much of either. So you could have chosen anybody, but you chose me because I was the first idiot up there."

He regarded her archly for a moment, then smiled and looked away. The soft expression made his lean face look much more gentle, and Tiria wondered how old he really was. It was his stubborn arrogance which made him seem older than her, she thought, not his looks. If he stopped looking like the whole world was annoying him then he might even have looked almost attractive.

Now that she knew they were going to the city - whatever it was - and that there was no ill will between them over the ballot, Tiria started enjoying their cool companionship. Seth demanded nothing of her, and she had walked further from her home than she had ever dreamed of. The buildings she had grown up around were far behind them. First there had been other buildings like them: straight roads of square, squat houses, and huge buildings with crumbling letters fused to their faces.

Then there were smaller buildings made of stone that was as black as night or as white as a frightened eye, whose broken window frames made surprised arches as they looked into the dust. The scores of buildings always made Tiria's head spin. She couldn't imagine how many people there must have been in the world, to have needed so many buildings. It also made her shiver to think of how many of them had died so quickly that their carefully stored food had never been touched. Tins and dried packets had lain uneaten for so many years, waiting for a scavenger to find them.

Lawrence had told her that once he had broken into a basement and found a whole family, their brittle skeletons preserved in the airless space. The building had collapsed on top of their bunker and suffocated them, he said, or maybe they had taken the easy way out. They had been clinging together, and it was impossible to tell whether it was in love or in fear. His footsteps disturbed the air, and when he walked towards them they crumbled into dust.

"What's the easy way out?" Tiria had asked, who was helping her mother to soak and weave thin strips of wood into a basket. Lawrence had paused, gauging her age, and then glanced at Elizabeth before he crouched down.

"We can't begin to imagine what it was like for the first people. So many of them were killed in just a few days, and we're still digging up the bones. But there are still stories, and... it would have been impossible for them to be strong. There was nothing to fight against and nothing to protect. All they could do was wait, and hurt, and wonder if they were dying slowly or fast. Lots of them found drugs, or sharp blades, and made sure that they left this life on their own terms."

She was too young to feel empathy, but she was old enough to understand. After that, when she was walking to the ballot or exploring the ruins, she felt as if the first people were watching her. These were their homes and buildings, and she was stealing from them. After a few weeks she shook off the guilt and stopped looking over her shoulder for the dead. They were long gone, and if she wasn't haunted by the people who were executed at the ballot or murdered by the savages, then she shouldn't be troubled by the long-dead.

The new buildings she and Seth walked past made her remember her childish fear, but she looked at their boarded up windows with sharp interest. They were too far from the official's reaches to be in anyone's territory, which meant that these buildings might still hold treasures – a few packets of rice, perhaps, or even some canned fruit.

Seth saw her interest and made them push on. He knew better than she did that un-assigned territories were thick with crawling nests. If they were lucky, it would be the mutie dogs and not the savages who caught their scent. Still, after days of walking he was growing bored with the endless tedium. When they made their way through the next village he held up his hand for her to stop.

"This is someone's territory." Tiria whispered, recognising the way he was scanning the buildings for entrances. She had seen the scraps of tattered fabric knotted in rotting window frames and around branches, although she was too far from home to recognise the markings on them. Seth's eyes narrowed, and he was about to ignore her when she grabbed at his hand, stopping him from drawing his knife. Gritting his teeth, the man shoved the blade back into its sheath and lowered his voice.

"These creatures steal from the dead while they're still bleeding out. They tried to add me to their number the last time I was here. I owe them."

"I don't believe that." She hissed back. It was true – he hadn't spoken in anger, but with a kind of baited glee. Biting off his retort, the man straightened up and studied one of the larger buildings.

"You don't have to come with me." He said, "I understand if you're afraid."

She almost ran after him, drawing her own knife without thinking. "I'm not afraid of...!"

He grinned at her and kept walking. Tiria realised she had been fooled just as the shadow of the building spilled over them. It felt like cool water, while the shivering excitement froze and warmed her at the same time. She was used to running away; if she found an inhabited building she never ventured inside. Other rats attacked each other, but she had always steered clear of that kind of scavenging.

Seth pointed in one direction, and then whispered to her that she should find a quiet way to sneak into the building, and try not to be seen while he flanked the people inside. If there was anything worth taking, he whispered, she just had to keep hidden for long enough to sneak it back outside. She nodded at the peaceful sounding plan, but was dubious. Seth's face was alight with a grim kind of contentment, which made her uneasy. He didn't look like he simply wanted to tiptoe away with a few packets of dried food.

The man slipped into the shadows like a ghost and was suddenly gone, his dust-stained clothes camouflaging him perfectly against the dingy stone wall. Tiria almost shouted after him when she realised how stupid she was being, and slipped along the wall in the opposite direction. After a few nooks she found a ground-floor window which had been kicked in, and slipped down into the building.

It had been a school, she realised as she looked around. She recognised the white board which was stuck to one wall, and the walls held remnants of brightly coloured paint even if most of it had flaked down onto the floor. There was no sign that a clan lived here, despite the territory flags outside - she couldn't make out footsteps on the floors, and the rooms had hardly been picked clean. She crept from door to door searching every corner, but there were no bed rolls or cooking fires. The school was not empty, though. She knew the stale stench of still air, and in this place the air breathed. She guessed that there was a squatter here, or maybe two - outcasts, not rats, using the territory flags to keep scavengers away. She listened for footsteps, but all she could hear was her own breath. The doors were mostly barricaded shut, and the windows were blackened by the ancient fires.

She gave up Seth's flanking plan and acted as she normally would, finding the stairs and searching the building floor by floor. She started in the attic, opening ancient boxes which crumbled under her fingertips, and then she made her way down through labs of broken glass, tiled rooms filled with metal hooks and cabinets, and finally back to the ground floor, leaving Seth to search the basement. Her pack was filled with things she could use – undamaged metal jars, pencils and satchels from the lockers, and more – and she stopped at the base of the stairs to rearrange the heavy load, knowing that the smallest clink could give her away.

Too late. The man was on her before she even heard him breathe, and suddenly her arms were trapped and he was dragging her back and up towards the wall. She screamed, and stamped on his feet, but his thick boots protected him and he slammed her hard against the wall to wind her. His breath stank as he kicked open a door and dragged the girl through. She cursed broadly and struggled until she felt an odd heat against her temple. Her breathing hitched as she realised it was pain, not heat. It was the kind of sharp pain which could not be argued with. The man had his blade pressed so hard against her skin that it felt bruised, but she knew that the warmth must be blood, and that he only had to twitch to shove his blade straight into her skull.

Perhaps she was too breathless to cry for help, or maybe pride kept her silent, but the man soon grew impatient and bellowed across the ruins, "Don't you see I have your woman?"

He knew we were here. Tiria thought frantically, looking for a way to break free. *He knows there's two of us.* She managed to look at the man out of the corner of her eye, and saw that a livid bruise was spreading across his eye. She hadn't done that. He must have been in the basement. He had escaped from Seth only to stumble across the other intruder.

Seth sauntered out into the hallway, for all the world as if he were back at the ballot instead of covered in his own bruises. His eyes were angry, but he didn't look at the man. All of his fury was directed at the girl. "Why the hell did you let him catch you?"

"Let him?" She gasped, and clawed at the man's hand. He growled and the blade slipped, cutting away long strands of hair before it came back to rest against her temple. She laughed hysterically. "It was your idea to scavenge in someone else's land!"

"I found this." Seth said, and lifted something up. Even in her fear the girl could see that it was beautiful: a tiny, transparent woman, her arms lifted in a birdlike arch as she rose above a mirrored disk. It was a beautiful, useless toy.

"You're telling me off for getting captured when you came charging in here for... for that?" She shrieked. The man looked up.

"I didn't charge, I walked. I had a plan which you ignored. The man next to you found an intruder on his land, and has every right to shove that ice pick into your brain."

"Are you two done?" The captor growled, losing patience again. Tiria shoved her elbow back into his stomach but missed, earning herself another haircut.

"Do you want me to help you?" Seth asked. There was no sarcasm there, just a genuine question which he waited for her to answer. She stared incredulously at him.

"If it's not too much trouble!"

The captor, by this point, was almost stunned by the argument. All of his fury had trickled away, and in its place was the dawning realisation that the diffident man standing in front of him was armed, scarred from countless fights, and looking at him with a half grin that made him want to hide. "Look." He said, "If you want the girl you can have her, just give the bauble back and I'll let her go."

"This?" Seth raised his eyebrow and lifted the dancer. "Where did you get it?"

"Seth!" Tiria hissed. The man narrowed his eyes at her.

"Don't interrupt, Ti. It's rude."

"I'm not interrupting, you moron! He has a knife to my head!"

"Well then, just be grateful he feels like talking and not stabbing." The man said archly, and then turned his cold eyes back onto the captor. "I apologise. You were telling me why you want this toy back."

"The officials are coming. They want to see it." The man interrupted Tiria's swearing quickly, his voice thick with relief now that it seemed like the threat was passing. "They say … they say that it can't be from the ruins, because it wouldn't have survived in the heat storm. They say it must mean that there's somewhere nearby that the bombs didn't touch."

Seth laughed mockingly. "The bombs fell everywhere. The officials don't believe in fairy tales."

"They're coming here to look." The captor replied in a surly monotone. "They say there must be a vault."

The other man tilted his head to one side, grinning wolfishly. "You are full of nonsense, aren't you? The officials will be furious with you for telling them such stories. I might stay and watch." He met the man's eyes with a smug smile, and then dropped the bauble on the floor. A long, dark crack pierced through the dancer's body, and then Seth rested his boot on her face and slowly, deliberately, pressed down. They all heard the thin crack rattling into the dusty air. When he raised his foot, there was nothing left but a few shining shards.

"What have you done?" The man breathed, and then his face turned red with fury. "What have you done?"

"Seth!" Tiria cried out, just as horrified, and then she choked and struggled as the man's arm locked around her throat. Instead of dragging herself against the stranglehold, she leaned back into his body and then span, using the small space to plant her knee firmly between his legs. He howled and his hands constricted around her, tearing into her clothes and her hair even as his knife clattered to the floor. In the heat and the chaos she felt that they were falling, tangled around each other, and suddenly he was on top of her and his weight was crushing the air from her lungs as his hand searched grimly for her throat. Then there was freedom - air - as the body pressing down on her suddenly reared back. She gasped in breath after breath as she clawed at his fingers, feeling her hair being torn loose as he was hurled away.

Now the captor fought with pure fury, blinded by his rage so he could only see the man who had smiled as he shattered his one chance at riches. Seth waited for him to stand up, Tiria saw in a dizzy haze. Blood ran from her forehead and dripped into her eyes, but she saw the men grappling like children at play, their arms locked and shaking with the effort of shoving each other away. She gasped and pushed herself upright as Seth lost his footing and fell hard against the tiles where she had been lying seconds before.

She laughed giddily. "Do you want help?"

To her amazement, he grinned back and pulled himself onto his knees. Waiting for the other man to run towards him, he braced himself against the floor and lifted his shoulder just as the captor tried to slam into him. Instead of landing the blow, the man stumbled and crashed into the wall. Now, Seth didn't wait. He stepped forward and quickly drew the man up, looping his arm around and pressing the captor's hand into the small of his back. The other man cursed and reached for his knife, reeling around with wild roundhouses as he realised the blade was gone. The second one of hits strikes connected with flesh, Seth yanked his hands upwards. There was a sickening crack, and the captor howled in pain. Seth let go and backed away, his hands moving cautiously to his side. The punch the captor had managed to land had made its own horrifying sound, and Tiria's own ribs ached in sympathy.

There was a triumphant yell, and they both looked up just in time to see the captor running forwards with his recovered knife gripped in his good hand. The other hung limply at his side as he swung, not caring who he hit, his eyes manic and dizzy with pain. He stumbled and Tiria shoved him away, but her arms were still rubbery from lack of air and she only managed to move him a few inches. The knife skimmed across her cheek, and she cried out in pain.

"That's enough." Seth growled, and locked his hands around the man's broken wrist to drag him away. The captor screamed, screamed so loudly that the dust seemed to rattle, and then he fell silent. Tiria forced her streaming eyes to open, and then shut them again. The hilt of the knife was sticking out of the man's chest, and his mouth gaped in a graceless O, sucking air in and out as blood trickled slowly from the edges of the mortal wound. Seth was frozen, his hand still gripping the knife. When the dying man clutched at him he lowered his head down so he could hear his gasping words.

"You didn't have to... kill me."

"The officials would have killed you, too." He murmured as he looked around. The struggle had disturbed the dust, which flew around in swirling eddies, and the glass shards had completely disappeared. Nobody would know they had ever existed.

"You're from the vault." The dying man croaked, his eyes bulging. Seth grinned and leaned closer.

"Of course I am." He whispered so low that Tiria couldn't hear. The man choked and then forced his eyes open again, the whites milky with insane laughter.

"They're coming. They'll hunt you down like a dog."

"Better hunters than them have tried." Seth nudged the hilt of the knife idly, and then tore it free. The man shuddered and lay still, his lingering pain suddenly over. Tiria struggled painfully closer and crouched down, barely giving the dead man a glance.

"What did he say?" She asked. Seth shook his head and rifled through the man's pockets, pulling out a scrap of paper and screwing it up into a ball.

"Stupid sod probably couldn't even read." He muttered, and threw the note away. "Come on, girl. We're done here."

Their first miles were painful and slow, but once they found a rhythm they walked with more purpose than they had before. Tiria was glad to be putting distance in between themselves and any scavengers who might be returning to their haunt. Seth knew that there was nobody to run from, but he easily matched her pace. After several hours they stopped beside a slow trickle of brackish water, and washed the blood from their hands. It was too dangerous to drink, but Tiria risked rinsing her mouth with it to clear away the taste of blood. When she spat it out her mouth tasted of mould and metal, and she gagged.

Seth unzipped his pack and handed Tiria something. She gaped at the faded blue wrapper – chocolate! The officials made it with scavenged powdered chocolate and with honey from the farms, and gave it away as a reward. Most people preferred to sell it on than to actually eat it, although as time passed every bar betrayed a series of tiny nibbles around the edge. It was such an extravagance that

Tiria had never even held a whole block in her hands.

"I... can't..." She stumbled, handing it back. He frowned and closed her fingers back around the priceless morsel.

"It's a fair trade. Food for information." He said conversationally, "He wouldn't have told me half as much if he hadn't thought he was in control."

She blinked, looked down at the chocolate, and then watched it fall into the mud as her fingers turned numb.

"You knew I'd get caught." The revelation was astounding, as was the utter disdain in his eye when he looked across at her. The man's stubborn expression faded, leaving a half smile in its place.

"No, but it was useful."

"Useful! I might have been killed!"

"I assumed you wouldn't."

"You assumed?" She spat on the ground and pointed back at the building. "What was that thing you were looking for? You never said a word to me!"

"You would have been a terrible hostage if I had." He picked the chocolate up from the mud and shook the brown drops of water away from it. This time when he held it out she snatched it, broke it in half, and threw the two pieces in the river. He laughed and shouldered his pack. "I wasn't looking for anything, girl. Chasing rumours is far more interesting than treasure hunting."

"You liked killing that man, didn't you?" She asked, stopping him in his tracks. He paused and looked at her with a challenge in his eyes.

"You've killed as many men as I have."

She looked down at her footprints in the mud. "That doesn't mean... I don't know if I like it."

"I don't know either." He shrugged and caught her chin with one hand, turning her face to look at the cuts. Something changed in his voice. "He hurt you. I enjoyed returning the insult."

She shivered a little. "It doesn't hurt so much."

"That's not the point." He turned her face the other way and then stopped, running his finger lightly along a bruise. "You've been telling me for days that I own you. I don't like it when people break my toys."

She pulled away, eyes burning with tears of anger. "I'm not...!"

"You're not?" He grinned and tilted his head to one side. "When did you change your mind? Before or after I saved your life?"

"You used me as bait!" She growled, and remembered him crushing the glass dancer under his boot. He had worn the same grin there, the same challenging smirk that had made her captor snap and run, screaming, into his blade. She pulled herself back from the same brink, knowing that he could see the battle in her eyes.

"It's against the rules." She spat, when she could finally draw breath. He straightened up, his grin vanishing.

"Ah yes, the rules. I might have guessed. Can you run away from me now, little rat?"

She bristled. "You know I can't."

"I can't help wondering what I could get away with, before you got desperate enough to break your rules." He said in a thoughtful, cold voice that chilled her blood. Raising her chin again, he looked straight into her eyes and smiled a little. "Tell me, Tiria, how are you going to punish me for risking your obedient little life?"

She blushed, confused, and stumbled over the words that suddenly seemed so feeble. "I... I'll report you at the ballot."

"I look forward to it." He sneered, and strode away.

That night they sheltered in a small room at the back of one of the looming stone buildings. By barricading the narrow entrance and piling stone between their room and the massive main building, they made quite a secure bunker and rested there, managing to avoid even looking at each other despite the cramped space.

Seth finally unpacked a first aid kit from his bag. Calling Tiria over, he wet a piece of lint with alcohol to clean the dust from the wounds on her face.

"Fixing your toy, are you?" She asked, refusing to come closer. He sighed.

"I'm tired of bickering, girl. If you want your face to rot off that's fine by me."

She yawned, rolled her eyes, and submitted to being swabbed until her cheek burned and stung. By the time he was finished she was half asleep, lulled into the soft silence by the heavy weight of the day. They had laid out their bedroll before her cheek started to itch, and by the time they lay down it licked at her flesh like a candle flame. She fidgeted and scratched it so many times that finally Seth held her hands still and growled some sleep-drugged nonsense as he fell back asleep. It was torture, but she was too proud to pull her hands away. The slow tickling pain trickled from her cheek down to her spine, until she was aflame with the insect-bites that demanded to be scratched.

Seth's hands relaxed, and he turned over in his sleep. Tiria's hands fell free, but she grit her teeth and refused to surrender. Instead, she crept away from their bedroll and silently dug in to the stone barricade, a stone at a time. She squeezed through the gap she had made, and found herself in a room so vast that she couldn't see the roof. It was broken in places, and she could feel the dew of rain on her face, but the darkness was so rich she could taste it. She did not dare use a torch in case something saw the light, but when the rain eased the moon shone through the open windows and she gasped.

The room shimmered with colour, red and violet and gold all tumbled together and bathed in the blue moonlight. Every step she took was on a different shade, and when she looked at her thick boots the colour clung to them. She tried to pick some of the red up and gasped, sucking at her finger as blood seeped from the wound. It was a shard of glass. How could glass be so beautiful? The only glass she had ever seen was yellow and dusty, protected from the wasting by thick walls or heavy furniture.

Something else shone at the head of the room. She moved carefully through the shards and picked it up, frowning. It was a cup, shaped like a flower with a long stem and delicate leaves at its base. She sniffed at it curiously, but it only smelled like metal and dirt. When she tapped her nail against it the metal made a dull ringing sound, and then a flake of it fell away. Beneath the shining surface was a different metal, ugly and grey. She bit her lip, thinking of the book she had damaged in another life, and took the cup back into the atrium.

"What did you find?" Seth asked, when she lay down next to him. The girl flinched, and then sighed and handed him the cup. Of course he had woken up. The man turned the shining flower over in his long fingers, frowning intently, and then handed it back to her. "Very pretty."

"I should leave it here." She murmured, tracing one of the petals with her fingertip. "It can't be eaten or worn."

"What does that mean?" The man asked, yawning. Tiria gaped at him.

"It's the scavenging code. How can you not know that?"

"I'm not a scavenger." He interrupted her next question before she could ask it. "For the love of God, Ti, don't ask me what I am again. Even you must get tired of pestering me at this time of night."

She made a mocking grunt and put the cup down. "If you can't eat something or wear it, then you have to ask yourself - would I die to possess it? I don't think many people would die for a shiny cup which would fall to pieces the minute they tried to pour water into it."

Seth fell silent, and then his voice was thoughtful. "Where I come from, people trade weeks' worth of rations for things like that cup. We think that beautiful things are worth protecting."

Tiria laughed and shut her eyes. "Your city must be full of pretty, starving fools."

The man was silent again, but this time he wasn't thinking of an answer. He rolled onto his back, away from her, and as she fell asleep his eyes stayed open, staring at the hole in the ceiling as the rain began to fall.

CHAPTER 9

Seth found himself watching the girl more closely. He was naturally suspicious, and life had taught him that the most dangerous people were the ones on the wrong side of your shelter door. He couldn't puzzle out the oddities of the Tiria's mind, the way her eyes flickered constantly away into the ruins as if she were searching for something. Her confused obedience had kept her safe for many days, but Seth knew that she was too clever to surrender to it. When she turned on him, would she fight him, or run?

His hand hovered over his knife, as it never did when he prowled through the savages' lands. They were close to the sanctuary now, very close, but the girl's patience was stretched into a brittle thread. He waited for it to snap.

She had already turned against him, and that was his fault. He had been curious – a flaw his father had detested – and his boredom had made him careless. They were close to home now, and perhaps the false safety of that made him complacent. He couldn't resist the temptation to goad her, but every time she answered he hated her a little more. There was a bovine quality to her resentment which disgusted him.

No matter; it was too late to change his mind.

The girl woke up, and her sleepy eyes fixed on the golden communion cup she had found the night before. Seth saw a softness in her eyes which made him uncomfortable; he trusted her sharpness, and the merciless coldness in her heart. He respected that. He didn't like to think of her as gentle.

He remembered seeing the girl on the stage at the ballot, swaying and pale from the drugs which the officials had fed her. Her eyes had been dilated and clouded, barely open, and then she had raised her head and stared wildly out into the auditorium. Even in the smothering grasp of opiates her eyes were fierce, moving over the cloud blindly but still searching, hunting, desperate to find something beyond her grasp. Others stared out, but their eyes held fear or pleading. Seth scoffed at them, but he could not laugh at Tiria. He knew her mind even then, recognised the near-physical urgency to *know*. What could a scavenger brat possibly be searching for, so passionately?

He wondered if the same light shone from his own eyes. He hoped not; he had practiced hiding his thoughts with such grim diligence that now he had to concentrate to make himself smile. Every expression, every affectation, was an act. He was an accomplished liar, and he was proud of it.

Was Tiria a liar? If she was, she was terrible at it. He saw through her thoughts so easily that he grew frustrated with her, the thinness of her mind and the pettiness of her questions. He had been amused when she had left her father's home undamaged, but he could easily put that down to her grudging obedience. She believed in her indoctrination, even as she loathed it. Another weakness, and an insuperable one. If she was so easily swayed, it would be a mercy to kill her now and carry on alone.

Seth thought this, and rolled onto his side, and felt the heat of her body against him. He thought: she doesn't trust me any more than I trust her, but I sleep armed. He had thought that she was more practical than that, but then he remembered her diatribe and almost groaned aloud. She slept unarmed because it was a part of her contract. He knew that in the wastes, the only person you could trust was yourself. She knew, just as erroneously, that they were responsible for one another. If something attacked them at night, then as far as she was concerned they both had a weapon. He was simply... looking after it.

He couldn't kill an unarmed woman. She wasn't a danger to him. Not yet. The realisation that she actually trusted him was astounding to Seth.

Tiria, studying the cup with sleepy eyes, was thinking about her brother. He liked beautiful things, and when he scavenged he always used to bring home little things for his mother and sister. There were buttons, pieces of metal with embossed scrolls on them, scraps of old tile and other things that even their father wouldn't bother to sell. Elizabeth lined the children's corner of the room with the oddities, pushing them into the soft clay of the wall until they stuck. Tiria fell asleep every night tracing her finger around ancient blue birds, the curves of spiral etchings, and stems of broken flowers.

After Elizabeth had been sent away, her daughter ripped the ornaments out of the wall and dumped them into the wastes. It hurt her so much to be reminded of her brother that even the memory of her mother's love couldn't eclipse the pain. She had searched for Lawrence knowing full well that she wouldn't find him. He would be far away, where the council members wouldn't know his face. It was the only way he had any hope of surviving.

When the familiar buildings of her territory had faded into the distance, a small bead of hope had warmed in Tiria's stomach. Perhaps, if she walked far enough, she would still be able to find Lawrence. He could have followed the same ancient road. He might have even reached the city, following rumour or luck to its sheltering gates. She stared at the golden cup, and wondered if Lawrence had sheltered here, too.

It was this softness that Seth saw in her eyes, and the same softness which disappeared the moment she realised the man was awake. He watched her eyes shift from peace into fear, an odd glimmering secret, before her habitual wariness returned. It was like watching someone slip on a mask.

"Is it time to go?"

Seth shook his head a little. It was safe here, and it would not take a full day to reach the city. When he told her how close they were the girl's face lit up with an unusual emotion – excitement. She tried to hide it, but it was too vibrant for her to disguise.

"What are you looking for?" Seth asked her, tactless because he wasn't thinking clearly. The girl's eyes opened wide, and he pressed her. "Do you think it's in the city?"

"I've never been there." She said, guarded and dismissive. "What would I be looking for?"

He had no idea, and so he made himself smile and shrug. To his surprise she smiled back – a mocking smile, but full of relief, as well. Whatever she was hiding must have meant a lot to her, he thought. For some reason it made him feel a little jealous.

"Are you allowed to keep secrets from me?" He teased her. She raised her eyebrows at him.

"Allowed? I thought you didn't believe in our contract."

"I don't, but I suspect you're still diligently obeying your side of it. I'm curious to know what that actually means."

"If you don't know what my duties are, then how do you know I'm obeying them? For all you know I'm supposed to cook you breakfast every morning."

"I've tasted your cooking, and if that is a clause in our agreement then I'd rather we continue to omit it."

"What?" She pulled a face at him, half annoyed. "Did you just insult me?"

"No, just your cooking." He grinned when she shoved at him and wondered at it. Teasing the girl genuinely amused him. Growing more serious, he asked her again about the contract. She bit her lip as she thought.

"Well, the contract's not so much words as... just accepting it. I'm meant to learn from you. Not what you teach but more... who you are. If you're a good person then it makes sense that there should be more people like you."

He laughed. "I'm not a good person, Ti."

"You're a high, which is the same thing." She rolled onto her side, and her voice was quite serious. "My father traded stolen goods and bribed officials to raise his score. His wife could copy him, rise in the same way, and earn her freedom. Father's not a good person, but he is a clever trader and he gives his wealth to the right people. The officials would value that more than if he... if he spoke politely to everyone."

"And would his wife think that was an ethical way to act?" When Tiria looked confused, Seth rephrased his question. "Would she want to learn how to steal and bribe?"

"Why not, if it helps her rise?" Tiria shrugged. "Perhaps then she could find someone who could teach her how to farm, or to fish. After that, she might learn how to weave or how to treat sickness."

"But that's all luck." He persisted. "And in return, these men and women agree to... to enslave themselves?"

"Everyone starts out that way. It's fair. If you don't like your high you only have to spend a year with them, as long as you're higher than them by the end of it. It makes people want to improve themselves. Once you're free, you can choose whatever life you like."

"As long as it's not a life above your grade - otherwise, you have to go back into the ballot and hope that the person who picks you shares your ambition, right?"

"Some people meet each other before the ballot, arrange the bids... or bribe people not to bid for them." Tiria looked uncomfortable. "It's not really allowed, but since it's hard to prove the officials ignore it. My father told people that if they paid him for me, he would stop anyone else from bidding. I hope after you won they all took him aside for a painful talk about that trick."

"But still, the whole system... the fact that you willingly walk into the home of a complete stranger just because they bid for you..."

Tiria interrupted in a slow, patient voice. "How can you learn anything without sharing someone's life?"

"You could just... just talk to each other!"

"Talk to who? And when?" She laughed and shook her head. "Are there so many people where you come from that you can just run into each other in the ruins? My clan covers the whole valley - hundreds of miles - and the sickness buries as many of us as the ballot sells. You and I haven't seen a single friendly face, and we've been travelling for days. And even if there were that many people, what good can talking do? I could teach you how to search the ruins better, Seth. I could try talking, say 'look more closely', but that's not how you learn. It takes months of watching and asking questions and practicing. Those are months that we need to spend gathering supplies so we don't starve when the pox comes, or freeze when the black winters come. It can even take years to learn anything worthwhile. And if you're spending years with someone..." she shrugged, and looked a little awkward. "It makes sense." She finished lamely. "And if you can only make mutations then you can bid for someone else and try again. Some people just can't..."

"Stop." He held up a hand, "I don't need you to explain that part of it to me, if it's all the same."

She blushed but looked scornful. "You don't?"

He scowled at her. Tiria blushed, suddenly feeling foolish. She didn't know a single person who could count their siblings on two hands... nor, for that matter, many people who were lucky enough to have even one full-blood sibling. The mutated babies were taken away as soon as they were brought to the ballot, and although the officials in charge of inspecting the new infants tactfully stayed in a room

129

away from the chaos, you could hear the women wailing and pleading even through the walls.

Elizabeth had tried to trick them, Tiria knew, but she had been discovered at once. The officials could smell the fear on her, so different from the cool pride of the women whose children were pink and whole and healthy. Tiria often dreamed about her little baby sister being taken away. Her name would have been tied around her soft, pudgy leg on a paper strip, and she would have been stripped of every garment Elizabeth had lovingly made. The masked, robed women who took the children away never said a word.

The women wept. But how could you plead with someone with no voice? The officials rarely spoke, and the ones they called midwifes were as silent as the dead.

Tiria, like every other child, had been examined by those faceless crones. She was one of the few who were lucky enough to come back out.

"Do you have any children?" She asked Seth, wondering how she still knew nothing about him. He cleared his throat awkwardly and scratched his nose.

"Two stills and a mutation."

"I'm sorry." Her voice was soft. "My father only ever had stills. He got drunk every time. After that he acted like it hadn't happened, but it must have hurt."

"He had you."

"Ah, but he didn't like me." She smiled and shook her head. "I didn't like him either, so I didn't mind. And my mother hated him."

Seth steepled his fingers in front of his nose and frowned thoughtfully. "Then why did she let him near her?"

"Don't joke about it." Tiria knocked his fingers down and sat up. "The sun's rising."

He reached up and grabbed her wrist, his eyes oddly intense. "I'm not joking. I've never forced myself on a woman who didn't want me, and I would refuse any woman who tried to do the same to me. I don't understand why you seem to accept that your mother - and even you - are so blind to how... how foul..."

"I'm glad you were lucky enough to like your high. My mother just wasn't lucky." She returned stiffly. He flinched.

"Stop saying that. Can't you even hear yourself? Are you seriously telling me that life is what you'd want?"

She gave him a withering look and pulled her hand free. Seth fought back a wave of genuine anger. He couldn't break through to her, and she didn't understand how dangerous her apathy was. Without thinking about it, he yanked her arm back down and pushed her down against the blankets. He tore open the top buttons of her shirt, straddled her hips and pulled the fabric away. She lay still, watching him silently, her hands curling into fists at her sides but otherwise staying completely still, not trying to push him away. She breathed a little rapidly - frightened, he knew, not excited - but her eyes were steady and guarded as she looked at him. He moved his hand down her body, and stopped when she finally flinched and looked up at the ceiling.

"Look at me." He said. She did, and he cursed in disgust. "What the hell is wrong with you?"

She spoke flatly. "You're my husband."

"Saying that word doesn't give me the right to touch you." He said icily, and pulled away from her. He felt unclean. She didn't try to sit up, and her blank, passive fear made him hate himself even more. "God, you would have let me do that the first night I met you, wouldn't you?"

"Of course." She looked confused, and he bit down the urge to shout at her, to explain to this scrap of a girl how horrific the whole arrangement was. She saw a little of it in his face, and for the first time her own expression hardened.

"I agreed to this. You accepted me."

"You didn't agree to anything." He said in a harsh snap, taking pleasure in the way she flinched. "Your father sold you."

"That doesn't mean I had no choice. I could have run away days ago and reported you." She lied, just as fiercely. "If the council found out that you don't even know the rules, then what do you think they'd do to you? Even Lawrence..." She stopped and bit her tongue so sharply it bled.

The slip of the tongue saved her life. Seth's face had darkened in anger when she'd threatened him, and his hand had moved to his knife. When she stumbled over her brother's name he stopped, challenging her to finish her threat before he drew the blade. The girl looked more frightened for saying another man's name than she had when he had thrown her onto the bed, but when she saw the knife she her skin went white. She could read death in his eyes. She took a shallow breath and deliberately turned her back on him, buttoning up her shirt with shaking fingers.

"My brother is an outcast." She told the ground in front of her. "He disappeared. If they find him, they're going to kill him. If I report you... they'll wonder if I'm the same as he is."

He grasped her chin with one hand, forcing her to meet his eyes. He felt a lingering wave of disgust at the feeling of her heart racing under his fingertips, and the mulish way she still forced herself not to pull away. He let go of her with a curse. "Tiria. Would you betray you had nothing to lose?"

"I don't know." The girl shook her head slowly, and moved her hands through the air as if she was shaping the answer in front of her. "I know you're not who you say you are, but that doesn't mean you're a bad person. I have as good a chance with you as I would with anyone else."

It was an insulting answer, but it was enough to make the man back down. Tiria's hands had closed into fists, he realised. When she uncurled them there were red marks on her palms where her nails had bitten into the skin.

She needed to force herself to be still. She wanted to fight back, Seth realised. He watched her with an expression which was half frustration, half grudging respect. She reddened under his gaze and looked back with such hostility that he almost admired her, until she realised what she was doing and forced herself to look down, meek and obedient. The man sat back on his heels and spoke without thinking.

"I could have done anything to you. *Anything.* Not just... Tiria, please look at me. Try to understand what they've done to you. Does finding your brother mean more to you than your own safety?"

"We both have to get something out of this arrangement." The girl growled, and then stood up and shook out her torn clothes. She didn't look at him at all as she left the room, but her voice was harsh. "I'm going to keep looking."

Seth followed her outside a few minutes later, his hands raw where he had scrubbed them with soap and sand. He wondered if he would ever feel clean again. He pretended not to notice the red marks around the girl's eyes. Even while he was assaulting her he had hoped that in her blank obedience, there was something in her that would scream and fight back. He desperately wanted to know there was something else, a trapped voice inside her which he could force into sound. Now that he knew some of her thoughts, he was sickened by his selfishness, his delight in forcing her to break. He pushed down his aching need to understand her mind, and instead looked at her as the girl he was supposed to protect.

He had hurt her. Not her body, but something else inside her that was too brittle for her to defend. Seth knew it was too late to apologise; he had only been trying to make her understand, and she had been too stubborn or frightened to truly listen. All he had proven was how easy it was for him to overpower her. Whatever fragile trust their indifference had given them had been shattered in a few thoughtless moments and angry words.

"I'm sorry." The man still tried to say, as they started to walk. Tiria looked around, and her voice was scathing.

"No, you're not. You won your argument, didn't you?" She paused, and folded her arms around her as she glared at him. "You're such an idiot. We're only stuck with each other for a few months. Whatever I do afterwards - wherever I want to go, or whoever I want to find - is none of your business. I'm not scared of you, and I don't care about you stupid opinions." She leaned closer and her voice was deadly serious. "I own you just as much as you own me. Pry into my life again and I'll cut your tongue out."

He set his jaw and forced himself to shrug. He walked away from her in silence, and if he still felt wretched he swallowed the feeling back. His hand drifted back to his knife, and he watched the girl as she began to cross the wastes.

CHAPTER 10

The route which Seth had taken them on had twisted and turned, but mostly headed through lands either patrolled by a branch of the council, or else picked clean by the scavengers. There was nowhere for the savages to scrounge food, and so the travellers could walk the trails in relative, watchful, safety. Their packs grew lighter as the days passed, and they rationed out their water in careful sips, but they both knew that it was far better than being attacked.

Their good luck didn't last forever; on the last day they were both tired and caught up in their own thoughts, too angry or bitter to meet each other's eyes or pay attention to the dangers the other person might put them in.

The savages were on them before they noticed. The ground erupted, and hands clawed at them from under the shards of rubble, and both of the scavengers leapt backwards with cries of horror as scores of desiccated bodies seethed out of the shadows.

"There!" Tiria gasped. She pointed somewhere behind Seth's back and took off, her boots kicking up dust as she ran. She was unusually quick - her backpack didn't seem to weigh her down at all. But then, of course it didn't: she was used to running with it full of tins, or fuel canisters. There was no way she would have survived if she had let it slow her down.

Seth had no idea what she was planning, and he hesitated for too long for it to make a difference. There was no way that he could outrun the savages by then, and he was too proud to make the attempt. Instead, he stood his ground and sized up the creatures. His hand moved slowly to the small of his back.

Tiria climbed the side of the crumbling building, the hot sun-baked bricks burning her bare hands. She forced down the pain and kept going, making her way all the way to the top before she looked behind her. They were close behind her, as she had known they would be, but the baking stone had confused them enough to slow them down. They slithered up and down buildings as if gravity didn't apply to them, but they preferred the shadows to the sun. In the burning light you could almost smell the meat falling from their rotting bones.

While she caught her breath and waited for them to make a move, Tiria looked down at where they had been ambushed. She shook her head in self-disgust: the buildings formed a perfect circle, and they had traipsed right into the middle of it. She couldn't believe that they had been so stupid. The savages would have been hiding in the dark shadows, flattened out under the rocks and bricks. They hadn't even needed to run, they just waited.

Seth was standing in the middle of the circle, and he was surrounded by the creatures. He stood quite still, as if frozen by fear. Tiria scrabbled for a loose brick and pried it free of the building, feeling her nails break and bleed as she ripped it free.

"Hey!" She shouted, and hurled the brick . "Up here!"

The brick hit one of them - a lucky blow, but it made more of them look around than just her shouting would have done. They peeled off from the group, leaving a gap. Tiria watched, holding her breath, expecting Seth to see the gap and break free of the circle. He turned his head a little, and then he looked away. He still hadn't moved.

"What's wrong with you?" She shrieked. "Run!"

He didn't react, but his hand twitched at his back. His head moved slowly from savage to savage, and now they were so close that she wondered how he wasn't retching from the stink of them. Then he pulled a weapon out from the back of his jeans and pointed it at one of them - not the closest, but the one who moved the fastest. Aiming carefully, he pulled the trigger and watched the creature's skull explode into a mess of blood and pus. Turning on his heel, he aimed for a second creature and did the same thing. Tiria watched in amazement. She had never seen such flawless aim - who had time or ammunition to learn? Seth had been watching the savages, not frozen but choosing his targets, identifying the most dangerous ones - and now he moved with careful, deadly precision. His unhurried steps made the girl's skin crawl.

She had been wrong. He wasn't a coward. He acted confidently because he simply had no reason to be afraid.

The sound of falling bricks brought her back to herself, and she looked down the side of the building to where her own hunters had finally started climbing up. Grinning, she reached up for her next handhold and swung herself up onto the overhanging lip of another building. Rooting in her bag, she drew out a bottle of powder and, very carefully, poured it around the overhang. Then she jumped up to the next level - a statue of an ancient, faceless animal - and lost her grip. Gasping, she landed on all fours back on the dust, and pulled herself away from a scrabbling hand. They were almost on top of her now, their hands covered in the black powder. She caught her breath and ran towards the statue again, launching herself into and landing so hard that she was winded. Fighting for breath, she tore open her bag and pulled out the book of matches. Striking one, she lit the entire packet and waited for it to flare. Every second felt like an age, and she could taste the filth of them in the air, and then the box exploded into flames and she threw it down into the powder.

The explosion blew her back, and she scrabbled desperately at the smooth stone as the building shuddered and groaned. Great chunks of stone shattered in the square far below her, and Tiria caught her breath as she watched them. The savages shrieked as they lost their grip, and hurtled down the jagged peaks of seething rubble in a series of sickening cracks and screams. They writhed when they reached the ground, and Tiria hoped they were dead. She wasn't scared of them any more - she couldn't bear to hear their sobbing cries. Clambering back down the ruins, she drew her knife and slit the throats of the broken creatures who were still shuddering.

"Tiria!" Seth shouted, and she looked up just in time to see a savage charging towards her. She leapt back with a strangled cry, lost her footing in the rubble and fell hard onto her back. Winded, she tried to crawl away, her eyes full of the anger in the savage's eyes and the black, filthy claws he was raising towards her. She kicked out with both feet, gasping when her back screamed in pain, and scrabbled in the dirt for her blade. She couldn't find it, but her frantic fingers found a brick and she raised it, ready to throw. She knew she only had one chance. The creature staggered to its feet and slithered back towards her, dragging its twisted feet. A long thread of saliva hung down from its bared, yellow teeth. Tiria waited until it was close – closer – too close, with the reek of its rotting breath and maggot-ridden flesh stinging the back of her throat – and then she drew her hand back and smashed the brick over the savages' head. It connected with a sickening crunch and she reeled back, retching, as thick viscous blood flowed into the creature's eyes. It glared at her, and she held it back with both hands, trembling in terror, until she realised that it was dead. Shoving it off her, she dragged herself to her feet and looked around for her knife.

"Ti." A voice brought her out of her daze, and she had spun around with a snarl before she remembered that the savages couldn't speak. Seth caught her wrists and held her still, his own breath panting with effort. "It's okay, Ti." He said. "They're gone. They ran away."

Tiria looked around in frank disbelief. Alongside the ten or so which she had killed in the explosion and the falling rocks, she counted fifteen bodies strewn in the dirt. Each one of them had a smooth, burned hole etched into its forehead, right between the eyes. The last few were contorted as if they died fighting, and when she looked at Seth Tiria saw why. The man was just as bruised and bloodied as she was, and his knife was drawn and stained. A deep gouge had been sliced into his arm, and the fabric below it hung in sodden tatters.

"Are you hurt?" She asked, rather stupidly. He shook his head and looked up at the destroyed building, his dark eyes studying it with the same sharp interest he always wore. Now that the danger was passed, he looked at blackened explosion site, and then back at Tiria, as if the whole fight was another problem he had to solve.

"Come on." He said. "Let's go."

CHAPTER 11

They dragged themselves through the crumbling arches of the city long after the sun had set. Tiria had fashioned a rough tourniquet to stop the bleeding in Seth's arm, but he was still pale from blood loss by the time they reached the decaying buildings. The girl shook him out of his daze and pointed up at the carved stone.

"Where do we go?" She asked. "There's nowhere to hide."

He didn't answer, but his energy seemed to come back. He made his way through the columns and then, as if following some invisible map, turned sharply to the left and strode along the city wall. It was just as damaged as the rest of the buildings. Tiria was about to suggest they crawl into one of the old houses where they could at least barricade themselves in when a low, booming noise made her jump. She stared at Seth, who was impatiently kicking the heel of his boot into the ground. It looked like the same ancient tarmac as the stretch of road they had walked along for days, but it sounded like hollow metal. A hatch, Tiria realised, making her exhausted mind see it through a scavenger's eyes It was so neatly camouflaged that even she couldn't see the edges, but it lifted up and a hand waved them down.

She followed Seth, expecting to find herself in the same kind of hollow hole that her father had lived in. As soon as she dropped down into the darkness a wash of warm air struck her, and her hand met a smooth surface when she reached out for the wall. She waited until she heard the stranger close the hatch and then closed her eyes, waiting for the inevitable flair of light. Her eyelids shone red, then purple, and she opened her eyes to see a room that was still so bright her eyes burned.

"Who the hell are you?" Someone demanded. She squinted around at a silhouette, raised her hand to her eyes to block the light, and then gasped when Seth took her arm.

"You're safe now." She heard him say, and there was something so gentle in his voice that she thought she'd imagined it. The man moved closer, touched her cheek lightly, and then looked around at the stranger. "Give her a moment to get used to the light. She's never seen fluorescent strips before."

The stranger made a scoffing sound and there was an odd click, which Tiria would later find out was a pistol's safety being snapped on. All the sentries wore them on their hips. "Are you hurt, sir?"

"Not really. They've started setting up ambushes." Seth said in his indifferent way. Tiria blinked her eyes open and saw that he had bled through the strips of fabric she had looped around his arm. In the blinding light the stain looked far too bright, more like lipstick than blood.

"Is there a doctor here?" She asked softly, and looked around until she found the guard. He looked surprised, and she explained, "He's been stabbed."

"He's used to it, miss." The man shrugged, and smiled viciously at Seth. "No lights... no doctors... where did you find this one? Anyone might think that the great Seth has found himself a little pet rat."

Seth ignored the man. "Are we too late to get in tonight?"

"What do you think?" The man picked at his teeth for a moment, and then shrugged a shoulder at a wide inner doorway. "We're all cosy and locked out until morning. There's blankets and benches in decon, you know the drill. Just don't let that creature touch anything until you've hosed her off."

Tiria opened her mouth to retort but Seth caught her hand and tugged her away. She followed him grudgingly into the next room. It was just as glaring and smooth as the last one, but it had square cubicles lining the walls with metal contraptions hanging over them. Checking that the guard hadn't followed them, Seth leaned closer to the girl. She flushed and tried to pull back.

"Don't be an idiot. He'll be listening." Seth said so quietly that the man could not have overheard. Tiria blushed at her foolishness and leaned in so the man could whisper into her ear.

"Don't let them turn you away. Remember that. If they think you're a spy or a scavenger then they'll shoot you so you can't tell another soul how to find this place."

"They've already worked out I'm a rat." She said sulkily, looking over to see that the guard was watching them. Seth nodded, and smiled a little.

"That's fine."

"Then what else am I supposed to say?"

"Nothing." He looked a little embarrassed and then stroked her hair back from her eyes. She jumped, and bit her lip when the guard cleared his throat. Seth didn't look up at the man, but his hand fell to her shoulder. "Ti, just make sure you tell them the truth. That stupid contract should be enough to convince them. I'm your husband, right? If I'm going to get you into the city, they need to believe that. Convince them that I'm besotted with you. That I brought you home because I couldn't bear to leave you to die in the wastes."

She tried not to laugh. "You're joking."

"I'm deadly serious." He looked it, too, with his eyes fixed on her so intently that this time even the guard could not distract him. Tiria bit down a hysterical giggle and almost shook her head, and then she nodded. She was burning with curiosity about this place already, and she couldn't begin to imagine what might be beyond the next set of doors.

"Alright." She said. The man smiled, and it was a smile which lit up his whole face. For a moment Tiria was captivated for it. He only looked genuinely happy when some part of his plan was falling in to place. She hadn't seen him look so self-assured since he had met her at the ballot.

Seth opened one of the lockers which lined the wall and pulled out two towels. As he handed her one, he pointed to a second locker and told her that when she was clean she would find clothes in there. When Tiria reached to open the door he stopped her.

"You have to be clean, first." He said, and Tiria heard the guard laughing mockingly at her. She reddened and stomped into one of the cubicles, expecting to find a bucket of water and a bar of soap. Instead there was only the metal contraption, and a pump holding an oily gel. She stared at the contraption in absolute bafflement until there was a hissing sound, and the pipe in Seth's cubicle started raining down a torrent of water. Gasping in delight, she fiddled with the buttons on her own contraption until a flood of stinging warm water sprayed over her whole body. She laughed and spun around in it, not caring that her clothes were drenched, or that they were dripping grey mud onto the shining tiles. In the end Seth pounded impatiently on the metal divide between them, and she made a rude noise before she stopped dancing and stripped off the sodden rags.

Water. It smelled nothing like the stale, metallic pools which littered the waste lands. Even the rain was hard and acrid, and when she had grazes on her hands they dried out and cracked wherever the water touched. Water was yellow or grey, and she had to filter out the dirt before she could drink it. This water was so clear that Tiria could see straight through it to the tiles, and it was so sweet that she could taste it in the air around her.

Her hair was hopelessly tangled. She felt sure it would fall out before she had it properly clean. Long strands of it came loose and coiled around her feet before she shook them off, and they slipped down the drain. The gel smelled like a bar of soap, but it felt more slippery and was easier to rub into the long strands. After a few rinses her hair felt unsettlingly soft, and she pulled the knots apart expecting the gossamer threads to simply snap. By the time she was satisfied her skin was puckering as if she had spent the day in the rain.

She wrapped the towel around herself and went to fetch the clean clothes. When she opened the cabinet she understood Seth's warning - the fabric was soft and pale. A single dirty fingerprint would have been painfully obvious against the light yellow cotton. Looking back at her own clothes, Tiria felt herself blushing. They had moulded themselves into a brown pile, and she could barely tell the dirt from the cloth.

Had she been so filthy? She had washed whenever she could, but that wasn't often enough. After her mother had left, there hadn't been much point. Her father didn't notice, and she was often too busy or tired to want to fetch extra buckets of water. When she had been young her mother would fetch endless water, and Tiria remembered being cradled in the woman's lap sneezing at the harsh smell of soap, with the gritty water coursing through her hair over and over again. Afterwards she would smell metallic and clean, not like a little girl at all, but like a new creature Elizabeth had moulded from love and water.

Tiria slipped the soft clothes on and sniffed at them curiously. They smelled sweet, but she didn't know the scent. She smelled the same, she realised. Her hair plastered itself to her neck and she ran her fingers through it irritably. Now that it wasn't tangled, it felt inches longer and a hundred times lighter – but the loose strands tickled terribly. She searched inside the locker, and found a soft hat which she stuffed her hair into until it was a bulky, sodden mass.

"Don't wear that, it's a soldier's hat." Seth said from behind her, and she jumped as he snatched the hat from her head. She planted her hands on her hips and scowled, feeling her hair tumbling back down her back in an infuriating, soggy mess.

"If you love me, you'll love the things I wear and be happy about it."

He didn't answer, scratching his cheek thoughtfully as he looked her up and down. For some reason, Tiria was suddenly burningly aware that her feet were bare. She couldn't remember ever having bare feet around another living person.

"It didn't suit you." He said. "You look lovely without it."

She reddened and looked at her feet. The guard probably saw it as some nonsense girlish shyness, but in truth she was mortified. She knew that Seth was lying, and so she heard the unspoken mockery behind every word and recognised the mischievous glint in his eyes.

"If you think I'm lovely, shouldn't you kiss me?" She goaded him back. "Or will you give my hat back after all?"

"I don't want to make a scene in front of the sentry." Seth replied easily. Tiria shook her head, her weariness coming back as her body revelled in the warm room and soft clothes. She noticed that while she had been in the cubicle, the man had taken the time to find a clean bandage. He had wrapped it around his arm, but the ends were untidy and the knot was already coming undone in the steamy air.

"Here." She said shortly, and untied the knot. Tearing the ends of the bandage, she made a series of smaller knots and tucked them behind each other. When it was secure she checked the rest of the dressing for overlapping edges, and smoothed it out. Seth watched in silence, and flexed his arm experimentally when she was done.

"Where did you learn to do that?" He asked. The girl shrugged and yawned. Glancing at her, the man's eyes softened and he held out a hand. "Come on, let's make a nest."

She rolled her eyes at the stupid word, but followed him to the far end of the room. It was drier, and a little cooler. A strong door was bolted shut in front of them, where Seth said the officials would meet them in the morning.

"Officials?" Tiria asked, feeling numb. "Is this a ballot?"

He shook his head, hiding a yawn, and fetched a bundle of fabric from the lockers. He had brought mostly blankets, with all of the remaining towels which he used to make a rough mattress on the tiled floor. She got the distinct impression this wasn't the first time he had slept here. It was only when he finished and looked at her that she balked. For the first time since they had found the city, Seth's self-assurance seemed to fade. He cleared his throat and glanced towards the sentry, but for the first time since they had arrived he didn't put on an act.

"Ti, you know I'm sorry for what happened this morning. I was... trying to prove a point."

"That I'm an idiot to sleep with a stranger from the ballot." She finished for him, and then crossed her arms stubbornly. "Can you see the irony, here?"

"This is only sleep." He said quietly. "We were arguing about something else."

She bit her lip and looked down at her bare feet. "If you do anything like that to me again, I'll hurt you." She murmured, and there was a vein of iron in her voice which promised that it was the absolute truth. Seth nodded, and wondered why he suddenly felt relieved. It was respect, he realised. He hadn't truly believed that she could turn away from her training.

"Don't hurt me. Kill me. I would expect nothing less." He held out a hand and she shrugged and took it, wriggling into the blankets. They were just as soft as the clothes, and she sighed in pleasure as she lay down. Every part of her body seemed to ache, and even the irritating web of wet hair on her neck couldn't make her uncomfortable.

"I don't know if I could kill you." She replied drowsily.

"Why? Are you that fond of me, little wife?"

"No, idiot." She rolled onto her side to shove at him, remembered his hurt arm just in time, and settled for poking him in the chest. "You carry more weapons than I do. I've never seen anyone fight like you."

"It's mutual. Let's stay friends. I suspect you'd cripple me with your gunpowder before I slit your throat." He yawned again. "And then who would bandage me up?"

CHAPTER 12

The door opened quietly, and so the officials were gathered in the room before Tiria was fully awake. She mentally cursed at the lapse, knowing that if she hadn't been so tired she would have been alert enough to hear the bolts clicking back, at least. Seth was wide-eyed, which annoyed her. He might have woken her up! When she stirred he rested his hand on her shoulder.

"Seth." A woman was saying. "We were beginning to give you up for lost."

"You say that every time I leave." The man said in a soft, respectful tone. "I always come back."

"You've been away for months. We were looking for a replacement! What is - that?" The woman interrupted herself mid tirade. Tiria refused to answer to *that*. She shook her dark hair over her eyes and wished she could stand up to stare the woman down, but Seth was keeping her sitting quite still.

"I'm Tiria, miss." She muttered.

"This is my wife." Seth spoke so stridently that she flinched. As one, the officials in front of them took a sharp breath, and Tiria couldn't resist peeking up through her hair at them. Their faces were transfixed in disgust - some looking at her, but just as many staring at Seth. It was as if he had admitted to lying with a dog, she realised, and the thought made her redden.

"Seth," She turned to him shyly, making her voice as soft as she could and thinking of the gentle way her mother moved. "I thought I was still dreaming. I can't believe we've finally made it here! It's just like you said." She thought of her brother, forcing his broken heart into her mind until her eyes filled with tears. She let the officials see them before she buried her head against Seth's shoulder, sobbing out, "I can't believe we're finally safe!"

He stroked her hair and she felt him move as he looked up at the officials. "We were attacked on the way here. I couldn't risk leaving Ti alone up there when... well, you can see that she's in shock."

"I thought you were lying to me!" She wailed, taking some pleasure in thudding her palm a few times into his chest before she relented and sniffled into his shirt. "I never thought this place was real! I'm sor-ry!"

"Ssh." He held her closely, waiting for her to calm down while he answered more of the official's fierce questions. When the girl was quiet he helped her to her feet. Tiria wiped her eyes and refused to meet the officials' hostile, curious gazes. Finally, one of the officials cleared his throat and glanced at the others. They nodded slightly.

"If Seth vouches for her, then we might as well let her in." When one of the others moved to interrupt him, the man's voice grew more pointed. "Who knows what he might have told her?"

"She knows how to find this place, which is bad enough." The interrupting man shot an accusing glance at Seth, who affected a rueful smile.

"I do tend to talk in my sleep, sir."

Tiria ducked down her head to hide a giddy laugh and reached for Seth's hand. He held it clumsily, as if he wasn't sure what to do with all the fingers, but his skin was warm and calloused. To her surprise, Tiria could feel his heart racing under her fingers. Surely he wasn't nervous? He was talking to these people as if they were beneath him, or at least irritating equals. He had seemed so sure that they would gain entry into the city that she hadn't thought to doubt him, but now she felt the thrill of fear running through his body and it made her stomach tighten. Moving a little closer to the man, she held his hand more tightly and peeked up at the officials through her eyelashes.

They looked normal enough - too clean and soft to her eyes, but not particularly forbidding unless she looked at their eyes. Those, she saw, were as blank and cold as the strips of light which glared from the ceiling. They didn't look happy as they argued with each other, but they weren't calling the sentry over. After a long argument they fell into silence, and one of them nodded. That was enough, it seemed - the men and women all trailed back through the doorway, and it seemed that the newcomers were allowed to follow them.

When Tiria moved to the entrance one of the women blocked her way with one meaty arm. The girl hissed through her teeth and stopped, looking at Seth to see how she should react. The man was frowning, as perplexed as she was.

"You're not letting this thing in to the city until it's been cleaned." The woman said, ignoring Tiria to speak to Seth. The man was about to answer when Tiria cut in.

"I had a wash already."

"She needs to be decontaminated. Quarantined. Who knows what filth you've caught from this creature?"

Tiria bristled, but Seth shrugged and scratched his nose, unabashed by the snide implication. "Screen her by all means, Agni. Just give her back before the day's over. I need to report to the council, anyway."

"And you?"

"What about me?" He asked, and there was something so flat in his voice that Tiria was sure the woman would start screaming at him. Something odd happened, instead. Agni balked and her hand closed around Tiria's shoulder, and through the fabric the girl could feel the warm moisture on the woman's sweating palm.

She's afraid of him!

Agni dragged her away without another word, branching away from the main corridor at the first fork and turning again so many times that Tiria could not have found her way back to the entrance in a hundred years. There was a strange pressure in her ears, and she felt as if the corridor was sloping downwards at every step. There were flights of stairs as well, always going down, but the lights stayed so bright that Tiria had no sense of being underground. There were even windows - artificial rectangles which spilled bright light into the corridors to make it feel like the surface. The whole thing sped by in a dizzying blur.

Agni was breathing heavily as they walked - the girl guessed that walking was the most exercise she ever got, and the woman was determined to plough forwards at top speed. Trailing after her like a stray dog, Tiria only got brief sights of the rooms they were sailing past. A small, dark space with a square of light on one wall. A large area with green plants - more vibrant than she had ever seen - covering every inch of space. A room which buzzed as if it were full of flies, with the most amazing sweet smell coming from it. Tiria tried to stop there, but the woman growled a curse and dragged her on.

"Here." She said abruptly, and stopped in front of a white door that looked just like all the others. Tiria ran her fingers along the symbols on its nameplate but Agni slapped her hand away. "Don't touch!"

The girl glared at her, lowered her hand, and then deliberately leaned forward and ran her tongue along the sign in one slow lick. The woman flushed brick red and her chin quivered in fury, but before she could explode the door opened. Barely able to form words, the bull of a woman shoved Tiria through the doorway. A woman in a white coat looked up in surprise.

Agni began to speak, and once she began the words flew through the air like bird shit. The rat had to be screened. She was too thin, too gaunt, her legs were too thick and her skin was too scarred. She was filthy, bug-ridden and diseased. Tiria listened in silence, vowing to lick every object the woman owned before the end of the week. Finally, Agni ran out of air and slammed the door behind her.

"You've upset Agni." The woman in the room said. "Well done."

Tiria didn't answer, but she rubbed her stinging hand and looked around the room. Like many of the others it was white, with the same strips of light in the ceiling. A low bed was pushed against one wall, and most of the furniture looked like it was made from metal. A compartment like the one in the entrance room stood in another corner, and Tiria pointed at it dourly.

"She said I'm not clean enough. I already used one of those."

"I can see that." The woman said, and Tiria heard the laughter in her voice. Looking up, she saw that the woman was also plump, but it made her look more like a ripe fruit than a rampaging bull. Her soft smile wavered a little when she met Tiria's eyes, and she took a step back. "Are you really from the wastes?"

"I'm a rat." She mixed the insult with pride, enjoying the shred of fear on the woman's face. After the way Agni had spoken to her, and the way she had acted with Seth, she wanted to hold her head up high. The woman was silent for a moment, and then when she spoke again the warmth in her voice was completely gone.

"You'll need to be screened for disease and contaminants. Also..." She took out a wand-like machine and waved it over Tiria's skin, frowning when it made a clicking sound. "You will need to take another shower."

She handed her some soap which smelled pungent, completely unlike the soft, oily stuff from the other room. By the time the girl had rinsed it off her skin was burning. Her clothes had vanished, and she wrapped herself in the towel as she looked around.

"I burned them." The woman said, gesturing to a chute in the wall. "Just in case."

"What on earth do you people think is wrong with me?" Tiria demanded. The woman's eyebrows shot up, and she gestured for the girl to sit down. Before she answered, she brought over a tray of needles and told the girl to hold out her arm.

"These are inoculations." She explained, and pressed the first one into the girl's arm before she even had time to look at the needle. The girl jumped and was swatted for her trouble. "Sit still! Don't you have doctors in the wastes?"

"Oh, doctors!" Tiria looked suddenly suspicious. "I haven't mutated."

"Yes, we look for mutations. Do the doctors in the wastes do anything else? They must help you when you're sick."

"Sick?" The girl shook her head. "No, they only look for mutations. If they have time then they look at us for bites or injuries. I got looked at a week ago and I'm fine." She gritted her teeth as another needle stabbed at her. "What's that for?"

"Measles." The woman muttered, and put the last needle down on the tray. "Lie down on the bed."

"I swear that Agni woman told you to jab me as payback."

"What did you do?" The woman shone a bright light into each of the girl's eyes, and then briskly opened her mouth and shone the torch down her throat. When she was done she repeated the question.

"I licked a sign." The girl looked up at the woman's snort, and then added more slowly, "I'm Seth's wife."

The woman snorted derisively, and then her eyes opened wide. "Wait, you're serious?"

Tiria looked away. "I don't think Agni likes it; she didn't laugh like you did. She told him he should be decontaminated, too, but she was too scared of him to drag him down here."

The doctor stopped examining the girl and spoke very carefully. "If I were you, I wouldn't tell anyone that Agni is scared of Seth."

"She is."

"Many people are." The woman was silent for a long time. When she finished poking and prodding the girl, and gestured for her to sit up. "Agni has her own reasons for appearing strong. By controlling Seth's wife the second she came into the city, she will make people think she has some influence over him. Which may have been the case, apart from the fact that you're not really his wife."

Tiria blinked. "Yes, I am."

"You're a virgin." The woman said simply, and turned away to a cabinet. By the time she had found some clean clothes the girl's blush had nearly gone. The doctor spoke quite flatly. "Seth plays games with people. Agni is a sly busybody, but she's not as clever as Seth. He takes advantage of that. If he's got you acting out some role then you'd better make sure you don't mess it up. One or the other of them will make you regret it."

"I'm not acting." Tiria pulled on the clothes and spoke mulishly. "He really is my husband. He hates the Wastes laws, but he still won the ballot for me. It doesn't matter why he did it, or whether he wanted to breed, and I don't care what games he plays. That's not the point."

"The wastes don't have laws." The doctor interrupted her, sounding tired. "Whatever barbaric code you follow doesn't apply here. We don't *breed* or fight each other for bread or kill our old folk in the winter. Seth follows our laws, not yours."

"Then why does he go into the wastes at all?"

The doctor pretended she hadn't heard her. "I won't tell anybody the truth. I don't want to be involved. In return, you won't tell Seth that it was me who examined you."

"Why not?"

"Your 'husband' doesn't like anyone to hold secrets over his head."

Tiria agreed wearily, and then shook the woman's outstretched hand. She wondered if she should offer the woman a bribe, but nearly everything she owned was still in her rucksack in the entrance. For all she knew, they had burned that, too. As soon as they had made their deal, the doctor treated her as brusquely as if they had never spoken at all.

An hour later, Tiria felt as if every inch of her skin had been prodded, jabbed and scraped. She might have been protected from the pox, but she felt as if she had suffered through all of its welts and rashes in one go. Her hair had nearly dried, but her arms ached too much from the inoculations to tie it up. The doctor took pity on her and braided it back into two long tails, which hung down over her shoulders. Tiria wondered how her hair had grown so much in the past two days, and then realised that the snarls had been making it twist around itself. When it was clean and combed it fell almost to her waist.

"Dangerous." She muttered, feeling the braids tangle against her arms. "I should cut it off."

The woman frowned and sat down next to her. "When you're clean and sitting quietly you could almost pass for normal." She tugged at one of the braids, and Tiria suddenly remembered her mother doing the same thing the first time she had taken her to the ballot. It was a sudden, blinding memory which made her eyes sting with tears, and then it was gone.

She turned away from the soft, pale woman and saw herself reflected in a mirror - hard and dark, her eyes red and swollen, her hair so long it made her look smaller, almost childlike. A changeling wrapped in their clothes. As she sat in their sanctuary Tiria felt as if her body and the world she had understood was crumbling to dust around her. Every word the doctor spoke struck her like a blow.

All she wanted was her family. If they were here she would know for sure that she belonged. She had clung to Seth in the entry and tried to convince herself that once they were through the door he would stay with her. The pretence would continue, and that he would finally explain why he had brought her here. But he had let her be taken away, and he hadn't looked back. The doctor was right; he was playing some kind of game. Tiria wondered how small and insignificant she was, if he saw her as a faceless stone on a checkers board he could move where he pleased.

Her reflection blinked back at her, the eyes hating her for every broken word she hadn't dared to hurl at him. She reeled away from the mirror and was sick, suddenly and violently sick.

The doctor's hand patted her on the back. "It takes a while to get used to filtered air."

The air... the lights... was nothing real here?

Tiria curled up in the chair, and wished for the rough grit of dust beneath her feet.

CHAPTER 13

"I won't do it."

Seth folded his arms and spoke through gritted teeth. "Tiria..."

"No! If you're leaving, then I'm coming with you." She growled, and looked around the room that they were sitting in. It was large, at least the size of the atrium in the theatre, and filled with tables and benches that felt cold to the touch. They had taken trays of food from a counter at one end of the room and sat far away enough from the serving woman that she wouldn't be able to overhear, but there were other people in the room who were obviously listening in. Tiria cynically wondered if Seth had chosen this place on purpose, so that she wouldn't make a scene.

"You need to stay in the city." He said impatiently. "It's safe here."

"Do you think I care about being safe?"

"No, but I care about you being safe." He returned just as stubbornly. Tiria snorted incredulously, and he sighed. "Ti, I took a risk getting you in here. They think I did that to rescue you from the wastes. I need them to believe that. If the first thing you do is start clawing at the walls and following me back out there then the whole thing falls apart."

"What thing?" She pressed. The man gave her a blank look, and she bristled. "Oh, I see. You need me to play your stupid game, but the terrifying Seth..."

"Don't call me that." He interrupted her. She glared.

"Why not? You called me Ti. Only my brother calls me Ti."

"You didn't object before."

"That was before I found out you were a pompous, lying ass." She bit into a roll with a vengeance. "You gave me six days to prove I'm your equal, right? Well, you had six days to order me around. Now, I get to ask questions."

"Fair enough, but for all you know every single one of my answers will be a lie."

She scoffed. "Try me."

He opened his hands in a questioning gesture, and she sat back watching him carefully. "Why did you bring me here?"

"To keep you safe, little wife."

"Why do you want to do that?"

"Because I love you."

She flinched at the false warmth in his voice, the way he made *love* sound like *hate,* and glowered when he looked amused. Raising her chin, she tried again. "Why does Agni hate you so much?"

"She wants me for herself. The moment she saw you, she knew she could never compete with your radiant beauty and your sweet nature."

Tiria laughed grudgingly at that nonsense and unfolded her arms. "You're not so much of a prize, Seth."

"Ouch, my poor wounded heart." He clutched at it, and grinned when she laughed again. "Staying here isn't so bad, is it? I'll be back soon."

"What am I supposed to do?"

"Everyone gets set a work detail. Unfortunately you have fallen into the hands of the caretaking branch. None of the others wanted you. I suspect that Agni wants to keep a close eye on you."

"Agni?" She echoed dumbly. "You want me to work for her?"

He shrugged, but there was an odd light in his eye that made her think he was pleased about the arrangement. Tiria found herself growing angry again. Was this another part of his game? The doctor had said that Seth hated Agni; why would he agree to put his new wife into her clutches?

"Some people are saying that she has influence over you." Tiria muttered. "That's why you let her take me away."

"Who told you that?"

"I overheard it." She raised an eyebrow at him. "Is it true?"

"You watch Agni while I'm gone, and when I'm back you can tell me that yourself." His eyes sharpened. "This is the last time I'll let you lie to me. Next time you 'overhear' some gossip, make sure you remember who said it."

She raised an eyebrow, supremely unimpressed. "Sure. They had a pale face, big owl eyes and a chubby body like every other person here."

"You'll get used to them." He shook his head at her description, but didn't argue with it. Now that Tiria had seen where Seth had come from, she could see the marks of it in his hair and his eyes - the darkness of his skin was sunburn, she realised, and not the natural rich shade that the scavengers possessed. He moved like a rat: careful and quick. Amongst all the soft city people, she and her husband stood out like a sore thumb.

"What work detail are you from?" She asked. He stood up.

"I'm not. Come on, I'll take you to Agni."

It was another trip down long, endless tunnels until Tiria felt sure that they would simply step out onto the opposite side of the earth. The pressure in her ears grew almost unbearable and then they popped, and she could hear properly again. She supposed, like the air and the lights, that the weight of rock above her head was just something else that she was supposed to get used to.

The caretaking wing was smarter than most of the others, with shining floors and gleaming white walls which Tiria diligently left finger prints on every time Seth wasn't looking. Finally Seth stopped at a door, and the girl wondered how on earth the people in this place knew where they were going. Apart from the incomprehensible writing on the doors, every apartment looked identical. It was only after you went through the doors that you could see the differences. A plain, grey door could lead into a broom cupboard or a vast hall of empty seats.

Seth brushed down the creases in his shirt and nonchalantly said, "Right, you're here. I'll see you later."

Tiria almost laughed, and then realisation hit. "Wait - you're going *now*?"

"I'm not going to spent my hard-earned free time with that old bat." He said archly, and then lowered his fierce eyes to the girl. "People are already going to think they can talk to me in the canteen."

Tiria wondered how he must have acted before she had arrived. If it was so extraordinary for him to even eat with a friend, then he must have been close to a recluse. It was pathetic, really. A grown man hiding from people! He didn't even work for his clan! And he was acting as if she was the one being unreasonable?

"I'll be back in a few weeks." He told her, quite diffidently. Tiria reddened, then went pale with anger.

"Weeks!"

"Oh, come on. It took me a month to bring you home, and I own you. You can hardly expect me to come back in a few hours when your friends in the wastes..."

She barely heard the last part as her blood boiled. "You don't own me!"

"No?" He leaned closer. "Then why didn't you run away?"

"You would have followed me. Killed me." She returned flatly. The man looked at her appraisingly, and then nodded slowly.

"If I thought you capable of betrayal, I would have done. But I don't think you have it in you to rebel. As long as you stay loyal to me, you'll be safe."

She grit her teeth at his insulting words. "Do you have any idea how much it costs me to follow you around? I'm not a dog trailing after you for scraps, I'm your wife. You act like obeying you is easy for me. I'm not afraid of you, or in love with you, or any other thing that makes me mindless. I'm loyal because, at the moment, you haven't shown me you're worth betraying. That's all."

"Tiria, I've threatened you, insulted you, lied to you and damn near assaulted you. What else do I need to do to make you turn against me?"

She was silent, and he sighed. Under his weary gesture was a vein of anger, the same frustrated fire which had flared at her in the church.

"I wish you would disobey me, Tiria. You argue with everything I suggest, but you always end up obeying me. I have more power over you than any living being has a right to. Do you know the worst part? You tied that rope around your own pretty throat. You somehow convinced yourself that your slavery is some kind of freedom, because you have no idea what freedom could be."

She stood silently against this tirade, her nails biting into the palms of her hands. He was trying to make her angry, she told herself. He wanted her to stay here, and not want to follow him. She told herself that, but she couldn't force herself to believe it.

"Your people are locked away from the sunlight." She said icily. "I'd never let you stop me from seeing the stars. I've had more freedom than these worms could ever dream of."

"They know that." He shook his head. "They're no better off than you, but at least they never lie to themselves about being buried alive."

Tiria glanced up at the roof and shivered. "Please don't leave me here."

"Just walk out, if you want to go."

"That sentry will kill me."

"Doubtless, but at least you can die following your precious master into the sunlight."

She let out a strangled shriek and flew at him, trying to claw at him as he caught her wrists and held her back. He was smiling, she saw - the real grin which said that he was genuinely enjoying what he was doing. She swore and kicked at him. "You don't own me! Stop saying that!"

"No?" He brought his arms down around her and held her still, his hands digging in to her arms. She cursed and tried to writhe her way free, but he held her tighter until she stopped. Panting, she glared up at him and saw that he was still smiling, watching her as if her fighting was a game that he wanted her to win.

She was suddenly too aware of how close she was to him, of the strength of his arms around her and the scent of his skin. Heart racing, she stopped trying to hurt him and simply tried to push herself away, wishing she could catch her breath and make her writhing, confused thoughts settle. She hesitated, her palm resting on his chest, when she felt that his heart was racing as fast as her own.

"Maybe I shouldn't go." He murmured, his hands still holding her closely. Tiria froze, and gasped as he pulled her even closer, and finally managed to drag one hand free. Reeling in the sudden freedom, she spun around and slapped him hard across the face.

He grinned, let her go, and opened his hands in a gesture of surrender. "Well done." He said with an ironic inflection, and then he sauntered off.

"Don't bother coming back!" She yelled after him, and then gasped when she realised there was someone standing behind her. She didn't have to hear the woman speak to know that the heavy breathing and stale odour came from Agni.

"What the hell are you looking at?" Tiria growled. The woman scowled and pointed one finger toward the door, which the girl kicked open and stomped through. Staring speculatively down the corridor, Agni scratched her head and then followed the savage girl through the door. She was cursing under her breath and pacing around the room, ignoring all of the other people in the room who were staring and backing away.

"What is Seth thinking, bringing this thing home?" One of them whispered to another. Tiria glared at them, but once they started mocking her they didn't stop.

"Do you remember when he found that mangy old dog?" A different man replied, laughing in a creaking huff. "I used to swat at it with a broom, horrible thing."

"At least it used to hunt." Another sniffed. "Does this one eat rats?"

They laughed, and then Agni yanked at one of Tiria's braids so hard that tears sprang to her eyes. "We should cut this off." She muttered. "It's probably crawling with lice."

The girl dragged herself away and spat in the woman's face. "Maybe I should cut your nose off, witch!"

The other women fell about cawing with laughter while the crone pressed her gnarled hand to her cheek and glared at Tiria. When the laughter faded into a nervous silence, the girl looked into her black eyes and saw something close to pure hatred in their milky depths. For the first time since she had come to the city, she wished that she knew how to talk to these people.

Before either of them could say another word, one of the younger women pulled her to her feet and marched her away.

"You mustn't upset Agni." She hissed once they were out of earshot. "She tells all the other women what to do."

"They all made up their minds long before I spat on her." Tiria said sullenly. The woman tutted between her teeth and her grip on the girl's wrist grew tighter.

"She assigns work details. You're lucky she already wrote yours out." She pulled a folder out of a cabinet and then whistled through her teeth. "Or not. You're right, she already hates you."

Tiria grabbed one of the buckets that littered the room and dully saw that it was filled with cleaning rags and bottles of fluid. Seth had brought her to a buried city to make her clean things. She remembered pouring chemicals onto the floor of her father's home and wondered what would happen if she did the same thing here. It probably wouldn't even catch alight in their processed air. The girl handed her the folder, and Tiria blinked at it wearily.

"I can't read."

The girl gave her a withering look and shoved the folder into the bucket. "I hope you've got a good memory, then. I'll show you where to go today, and tomorrow you're on your own. I won't risk a beating for a rat."

PART 2: SANCTUARY

CHAPTER 1

After the first few weeks Tiria's curiosity about the city faded. It wasn't that the shining floors and gleaming furniture were any less remarkable, but she was so captivated by loneliness that the wonder of it was lost on her. The women who gave her orders had not warmed to her in any way, and there seemed little point in trying to impress them.

The city followed a pattern of days and nights, with the lights growing darker throughout the evening and then cutting out entirely when everyone was supposed to sleep. That much was the same as the wastes, but when the 'sun' rose the citizens obeyed incomprehensible shapes on the faces of metal mechanical disks, which littered every room. Tiria was too stubborn to ask what the devices were, but she learned to move to another task when she heard other people moving between rooms.

She was just as baffled by the way the people looked. There were hundreds of them, far more than Tiria had ever imagined in one place, but they all had the same soft look which made her wonder if they were a single tribe. There was black hair and yellow hair, dark and light skin, but the plump limbs and lazy eyes were on all of them. It was ridiculously easy to sneak up on them, and Tiria made a game of edging closer and closer to a different group at each meal. She listened to their gossip without interest - it was always about people she didn't know, small scandals which she didn't care about.

The more she listened, the more she wondered if these people were truly stupid. They seemed to weep over the pettiest things - a damaged trinket, a torn shirt, a bad haircut - as if all they cared about was how they looked and what they owned. Seth had told her, in the church, that these people would pay dearly for beautiful things. As she looked at them, Tiria began to understand why. There was nothing else in their boring lives for them to care about. They had their work, and their gossip, and then they ate and slept and started the whole thing over again. The only thing they really struggled for was leverage - a bit of gossip here, an embarrassing secret there...

Tiria began making lists in her mind of what would happen to these people in the wastes. Most of them made it through a week before the dogs got them. She grew bored with the game, and with the gossip, and soon her own life became as tedious as their own. Work, fighting with Agni, being slapped and scolded by the other workers, and then sleep. She had nothing else to do, nobody to talk to, and no idea how long her purgatory would last.

Any day, Seth was going to reappear and take her away. Tiria told herself that after every cruel word spat at her, but as the days crept by the certainty crumbled. No-one else seemed to think Seth was coming back for her. Apart from the short hours they had spent together, no-one even seemed to remember that there was any link between them at all. People spoke about Seth in hushed, serious voices, but they did not look at Tiria or mention her name. She tried to ask questions, but most of them laughed at her until her stomach churned and she hurled herself at them in furious outrage.

When they unlocked her room they did not say a single word, only marched her towards a new set of rooms and told her to clean them. It was as if they were resigned to her fighting, and they expected her to act like an animal. It was probably close to the truth, Tiria knew. Even when she tried to bite back her quick anger, they still called her a rat.

Usually the rooms she cleaned were living quarters, which she scrubbed while the residents were out doing their own daily chores. It seemed odd that they would push their own work onto another person – Tiria imagined a whole string of people all queuing to carry out the next person's chores. She counted herself firmly at the end of that string, scrubbing floors on her hands and knees and retreating back to her own filthy rooms too tired to clean another inch. Sometimes, though, the rooms were different. Once she was sent to a room so far underground that her ears rang in the silence, where endless lines of square, deep cabinets were labelled with hundreds of names. She peered at the letters as she wiped the dusty plastic, but they were written in an ornate, scrolling way which made the ones she knew difficult to work out.

Another day she was sent deep into the sanctuary with a jar of beeswax, and told to polish the pews. The door opened to a vast room, which swallowed her footsteps into a heavy, soft silence as she crept inside. The walls were not made of stone, but glass. Instead of the murky yellow shards she was used to, every pane was stained a bright colour. Lights blazed behind each pane, which made colours spill onto the floor in a shimmering rainbow. She cautiously tiptoed around a yellow patch and reeled dizzily. The floor looked like it might twist and swallow her up. However beautiful it looked, the colours were a riot of swelling, shrinking rises. She had no idea what a pew was, but made an effort to polish the wooden benches which ran along the walls, since they were farther away from the light than any of the other furniture.

The last room which she was sent to was the most extraordinary, but when she first stepped in it looked quite plain. Like her own room, the walls were bare plastered concrete and the floor was made of solid stone tiles. The cabinets which filled the corners were grey and didn't even have labels to peer at. But in the middle of the floor was the table, and it was the things on the table which made her freeze and catch her breath.

Animals. Not the twisted, rabid fiends of the wasteland, but small, soft creatures which moved slowly and squeaked at her. Their fur was white and black and orange rather than dingy brown, and they cleaned themselves with tiny pink tongues until the fur shone. Tiria moved slowly from one of the plastic boxes to another, her cleaning rag falling from her hand. She recognised some of them - the larger crates held animals not unlike the feral cats, but these ones were smaller and made mewing noises when she pressed her nose to the plastic. Then there were mice, and animals that looked like rats - but they had large, bushy tails, or short stubs which waddled between their haunches, and their noses were blunt rather than pointed. She could not imagine catching them in a trap, or killing them for their meat. It seemed sacrilegious to even wonder what they tasted like... although her mouth watered when she saw how chubby some of the cats were, and how they would walk willingly into her hands.

Another tank caught her eye, and she stood up straight to stare at it in wonder. A small creature was... there was no other word for it... waving at her. A small arm was lifted, and a hand was moving back and forth so deliberately that she waved back. The animal turned its head, fixed her in one beady eye, and then waved again. It paused, and waited, and Tiria realised she was holding her breath. Raising her hand, she moved her hand in an arc - and as soon as she moved, the animal copied her.

She stepped closer, and knew her eyes were bulging almost as large as the animal's. It was some kind of lizard, she knew that, but she had never seen anything like it in her life. Most lizards were thin and bony, designed to slip under stones and hide. This one was so large she wondered if it was a mammal carrying its young, or at least filled to the brim with food. As soon as she thought that, it occurred to her that the lizard wasn't actually that fat. Its body was scrawny and small, but it was built in such a peculiar way that it seemed out of proportion. Its stomach bulged out from under its four gangly arms, and a great sack of chin rippled down from its stubborn mouth all the way to the paunch. The lizard studied Tiria as fiercely as she did it; unlike Tiria, the lizard was obviously deeply uninspired by the vision before him.

"Hello," Tiria said. The lizard tipped its head to one side and goggled at her, and then raised its chin and sauntered away. It left deep footprints in the sand as it walked, as if it was deliberately stamping its feet.

"What are you doing?" A voice snapped out. The girl jumped and looked around for her cleaning rag. Diving to pick it up, she waved it like a flag until the scientist sighed and tapped his foot. "Okay, fine, but be quick about it. Don't upset the animals!"

"What is that, please?" She asked meekly, deciding to be polite for the first time in her life as she pointed at the tank. The man glanced at the retreating lizard and scowled.

"Bearded dragon. That one hatched last season and came out of the egg sulking. Don't touch it if you don't want your fingers clawed off."

Tiria looked nervously at the lizard's paws. There were indeed claws, and they looked long and sharp. The lizard gave her a smug look.

She cleaned the room as slowly as she dared, watching the scientist as he moved from tank to tank. Sometimes he touched the animals, or gave them water. Sometimes he checked a chart which was stuck to the side of each case, and frowned at the creatures inside. After nearly an hour of this he picked up one of the plastic boxes, filled it with the stumpy-tailed mouse creatures, and headed into another room without a word.

As soon as he had left, Tiria sped towards the bearded dragon tank. She looked down at the lizard, and chewed her lip. The animal looked up at her with a surly, arrogant expression that made her smile. The little creature looked like he was reading the inside of her own mind.

"Shall we be friends?" She asked. The lizard closed its eyes and yawned. Tiria looked up at the door once, and had closed her hand around the lizard before she even thought about the sense of it. The man would know it was her. He would report her.

Her fingers closed around the fat little belly, and she smiled in wonder at how soft the lizard's scales were. On his back they were sharper, tiny spikes in a criss-cross pattern, but she felt like he was easing himself gently into the curve of her hand. She raised him to her eyes, and he licked at the air lazily.

By the time the scientist came back, they had gone.

CHAPTER 2

The lights had dimmed to amber before anyone came looking for Tiria. She was curled up in her bed, fussing nervously with a bit of yarn, when the door slammed open. She sat up and glared at the intruders, who returned her anger tenfold.

"Where is it?" Agni demanded, already pulling clothes down from the shelves to search. Tiria made herself look baffled, and folded her arms.

"Where is what, ma'am?"

"Don't be cute." The woman snarled, and spun around to snap at the other two intruders, "If you want to find the stupid thing, then at least start looking!"

The older man shot Tiria a quick, resentful look as he started opening drawers, but the younger one looked amused. He beckoned the girl forward and smiled. Her heart sank as she recognised the scientist from the lab.

"You took my dragon." He murmured, making sure the others weren't listening. "I realised he was gone when my finger stopped aching - he hadn't bitten me all day! I thought he must be sick!"

She hid a smile and made herself look serious. "Does he get sick often?"

"No, no, he's very healthy. He's quite easy to look after, really. I just have to make sure he stays warm and eats lots of bugs." The man raised an eyebrow at her, "And lettuce. He likes lettuce."

"Lettuce." Tiria folded her arms again. "Your rabbits will be happy he's gone, then. There'll be more food for them."

"There's more than enough food for them. Someone could steal a bag full every day and no-one would be any the wiser."

She sighed and hid a grateful smile. "You idiots are terrible at rationing."

He grinned at her and then cleared his throat. "Agni, are you sure the girl has the lizard? I don't see it anywhere."

"She's probably hidden it." Agni scowled, "Or eaten it."

"I don't eat lizards. There's no meat on them." Tiria raised her chin proudly. "I didn't steal anything. Why would I want a lizard, anyway?"

Under her shirt, George sank his claws into her collarbone. The girl winced and covered the expression with a faked coughing fit. Agni looked at her suspiciously, but even the indomitable hag could see that there was nothing in the room. The few things Tiria owned were scattered on the floor, broken and stepped on, by the time they stopped searching. The old crone eventually gave up, but instead of stopping her search she turned around and gripped the girl's wrist.

"Where did you put it, you little witch?"

"Hey!" The scientist stepped between them and yanked Tiria's hand free, pushing her a little behind him. "We don't even know that the girl took the damn animal in the first place!"

"She was the only other person in the lab today, and I'm certain we had four infant pogonas when I left this morning, Walker!" The older scientist had to stand on his toes to look the younger one in the eye. Walker obligingly hunched over a little. He met his superior's eyes for a moment, and then looked around at Tiria. She couldn't read the expression in his eyes, but she knew that her own must be pleading with him, because when he turned back he shuffled his feet nervously.

"Sir, I didn't tell you this but... when I was changing their water this morning I may have... I was distracted, and..."

The other scientist stared blankly at him for a moment, and then groaned loudly. "Don't tell me."

He covered his face with his hand and sighed. "I thought the ferrets were bad enough."

"Oh, it's just one lizard." Walker's voice was over-bright. "He'll probably eat a few spiders and then come sulking back when he gets bored. I'll keep looking for him, sir."

The older man's eyes fixed on him with beady irritation. "Then why did you torment us with this... circus?" He gestured to the floor around them, at the chaos, and only belatedly at the girl hiding behind his assistant. Walker's ears turned red.

"I said I... I got distracted."

The scientist glanced back at Tiria, and his mouth quirked in a smile. He tried to hide it, but he suddenly looked far more friendly than frightening. She met his eyes briefly and smiled back, and his mouth split open into a grin. "Have you been distracting my lab assistant, girl?"

"I don't think he needs my help." She muttered, trying to work out if she was still in trouble or not. The man laughed and reached up to pat Walker's shoulder, and then he turned to leave, still chuckling. Agni took a creaking breath and then smiled. Unlike the old man's, her smile was utterly false.

"This still doesn't settle the issue of where you hid the animal, Tiria."

"Maybe it's in your room." She returned wearily. The woman rolled her eyes and would have moved closer, but her eyes flicked up to Walker's and her smile managed to stay in place. Tiria had the strangest feeling of safety, as if this gangly scientist was holding a shield up for her. It was a peculiar feeling, feeling protected without resenting the person doing it. Agni sighed dramatically and opened her hands.

"Well, when I find it... you'll know." She turned on her heel to leave the room, and then turned back trilling pleasantly, "And Seth will hear about how distracting you're being while he's away, dear."

Tiria blanched, and took a step backwards without thinking. Agni laughed cruelly and shut the door. Her snide words seemed even worse now that they were shut in a small room together.

"Seth?" Walker asked. Tiria shook her head and opened the door, making sure that the woman had gone.

"He's my husband." She explained. "He won me in the ballot last spring."

Walker's eyes widened. "You're the rat!"

Tiria scowled and slammed the door wide open. Seeing her anger, the scientist raised his hands and babbled, "No, no, I didn't mean that in a bad way, just that... I thought you were a maid, that's all, and... look, can you please stop glaring at me?"

She tried, but had to settle for glaring at the door instead. "I knew you didn't know what I was, or else you wouldn't have helped me. I guess you'll want your dragon back now."

"No." He said it so quickly that the girl flinched, and she heard him take a deep breath. "Look, can we start over? My name is Walker."

"I know that."

"You're meant to tell me your name, back."

"I know that, too. My brother taught me how to be polite." Tiria snapped, and then realised how stupid she must sound. Forcing herself to calm down, she raised her eyes. "I'm Tiria. Please don't call me a rat again. Even Seth doesn't do that."

"I don't know Seth." Walker spoke carefully, as if he was tip-toeing past a creaking building. "I wouldn't assume anything about him."

"Whatever that means, I'm sure you know more about him than I do." She shrugged and fiddled with the door handle. "Everyone seems scared of him, but whenever I ask why you'd think he was a king or something. People seem insulted that I even talk about him, even though he was the one who brought me here. I didn't have any choice."

"Doesn't he care about you?" Walker blurted out, and then blushed at her horrified expression. "I'm sorry! It's just... does he know how badly that woman treats you?"

"I don't think he cares." She shrugged. "He'd say, it's better than being out in the wastes."

"Is it?"

Tiria burst out laughing, shock running through her whole body. No-one had even thought about asking her that, after all the weeks she had been here. Walker looked like he wanted to ask another question, and then stopped and smiled ruefully. Instead of saying a single word, he tapped his chest with one hand and then pointed at her. Tiria winked and unbuttoned her jacket. There, clinging to her shirt, was a very snug, very comfortable dragon. Feeling the cool air on his back, he wriggled a little and sank his claws deeper into the seams.

"Lettuce and bugs, right?" Tiria asked. Walker smiled and nodded.

"We call him George."

The lizard's eye flicked around, and he stuck his tongue out towards his old master. Walker stuck his out back, and then planted his hands in his pockets.

"Let me know if you have any problems with him," He said, and then laughed. "It looks like you'll be better with him than we were, anyway!"

"Thank you." The girl whispered, and then buttoned her jacket back up. "I needed a friend."

"You're welcome to as many as you can steal." Walker teased, and then held out his hand. "And I'd be honoured if you'd count myself among them."

"Do you eat bugs, too?"

"If that's what it takes," He said seriously, "Then sign me up."

CHAPTER 3

Tiria fussed over the lizard so much that he became utterly spoiled. At first she was worried because he was too sluggish, content to snuggle into the increasingly frayed breast pocket of her shirt and nap while she carried out her chores. Every night she would set him down on her bed and try to coerce him to play, tapping his nose with her finger and trying to get him to chase pieces of yarn, but the little animal refused to budge. The only way she could get him to move at all was when she planted him in the far corner of the room, where he would waddle towards her, glaring malevolently, until he could climb back up her leg into her lap.

"He likes the warmth." Walker told her, when she finally cracked and asked for help. George yawned widely as the man added, "Besides, bearded dragons are naturally lazy."

"Does he care about me at all?" Tiria had told herself the dragon came to her because he liked her; it hurt a little to think that he was just coming to her for warmth. Walker glanced at her, and then tugged her braid with a smile.

"Are you joking? He's never even tried to bite you! I think he must really love you."

She snorted at the word and ran her finger gently down George's beard. The scales there were a deep yellow shade, almost orange, and his eyes closed in contentment. That night she kept him in her lap, stroking him thoughtfully. The next morning, instead of giving him food, she put a piece of lettuce in the corner of the room. He stomped over to it, turned his nose up at it, and made a great show of sulking away under the bed. There was a scuffle, and Tiria gasped at the sound of scrabbling feet. She dragged the bed to one side in a squeal of metal, and stared under it at the carnage.

Several dead cockroaches were lying on the floor, many of them bitten into pieces. George was slowly crunching his way through another one, raising his head with an arrogant pride which clearly told her that lettuce was for lesser lizards. Tiria bit her lip at the sight and waited for him to finish before she cleaned up the rest of the bugs. She found out they were coming from a hole in the floor, and blocked it up with a piece of rag. George gave her a filthy look as she pushed the bed back into place, and that night he slept as far away from her as he could. The next morning, she pushed the bed back against the wall and unplugged the hole. As scores of beetles poured out, the bearded dragon launched himself over the slick floorboards in utter delight. His tail stuck straight up, and he scurried from bug to bug with a grace that belied his fat belly.

"I found a way to make him exercise." Tiria told Walker, and explained what had happened. He winced when she described finding the infestation in her room, but grinned at the solution.

"You keep him inside your jacket, don't you?" He asked. Tiria nodded, and the man scratched his nose thoughtfully. "If you ever need to hide him, I'll look after him for you. Nobody pays any attention to me."

"I do." She pointed out, faking a grimace. "You never leave your rabbits unguarded for long enough for me to make a nice stew."

"You don't count." He stuck out his tongue and held out his hand. Tiria shook it strongly, grinning at the formal gesture. When they had done, she picked up George and waved until he raised his paw to wave back. Walker took the tiny paw and shook it, and then yelped when the lizard snapped at his fingers.

"He's just playing." Tiria said, and started laughing. "Why are you scared of him?"

The man shook his stinging hand and shrugged. "I never underestimate a lady's loyal knight."

The girl blinked at him, and after a moment Walker explained that he was talking about a kind of story which children read. She shook her head and asked him where he thought children could find books out in the wastes. Frowning, the scientist excused himself, and came back a few minutes later with a thin book.

"If you haven't read much, it's a good story to start with." He said, a little awkwardly. She didn't dare to touch the book, remembering what Owl had said about their fragile pages. Walker held it out impatiently and finally she pointed at the cover.

"That letter is a T, and that one is an L." She tilted her head to one side. "I don't know many of the others."

"It says Fairy Tales."

Tiria's lips moved silently as she sounded out the word, and then she frowned and looked up. "Walker, have you ever heard of a person called Owl? No, I mean... Farren? She likes books."

The man shook his head, asking a question with his eyes. Tiria told him about the strange girl she had met in the wastes. "She didn't know anything about the rats, or even the ballot. When Seth brought me here I figured she must be one of you."

"I don't know the name." Walker looked intrigued. "But I've heard that there are other sanctuaries in other parts of the country. Maybe she came from one of them?"

Tiria thought this over, and it made her want to laugh. After generations of starvation and sickness, it was despicable to find out that so many people had been hiding behind the thick walls of their cities. It would be even worse if this was not the only one, as if the rats were just the people who had been left behind. Yes, laughing would be best, because otherwise she would start screaming and tearing at the walls.

She dragged her mind back to the book and forced herself to focus. "Walker, have you ever seen a story with a picture in it of a lady and a bird?"

He raised an eyebrow, and she continued lamely, "The woman is standing at the top of a tower, and she's about to jump off and fly, and the tower is all on fire around her and a man is trying to pull her back down. Owl told me it's a story about a man who has two women in love with him, and that he's not a very nice person, and the woman thinks she can fly but she can't."

Walker put the fairy tale book down. "Do you mean Jane Eyre?"

"How would I know?"

He rolled his eyes. "I've read it, but the copy here doesn't have any pictures. It's not the best book to start with, if you want to learn how to read."

She folded her arms and fixed him in her sternest gaze. Usually he would tease her for this, but when she had asked him about books something had lit up behind his eyes. Without another word he left again, and this time the book he returned with was large, with a hard black cover, and the pages were dense with words.

"Sit down." He said, and pulled out one of the laboratory stools. "If you're determined to read this, then we have a lot of work to do."

CHAPTER 4

Seth's eyes opened as the footsteps echoed through the building, but no other part of him moved. Even while he slept, he had been quite still. His clothes were covered in so much dirt that he almost disappeared into the wall, and he breathed so shallowly that he appeared not to move. Even if someone had seen him, they might have thought he was dead – the man held stillness in the same way a wailing infant shrieked out sound – obstinately, and bluntly, but very effectively.

The footsteps were in the floor below him, and Seth held his breath as he listened. There was more than one person – three or even four, he guessed, counting the different voices as the men spoke to each other. Their voices were rough and the words were almost garbled in their thick accents. Not clans people, then, but if they could speak then their minds were nowhere near as degraded as the savages'. Traders, maybe. Seth moved slowly and pressed his ear to the floorboards. Minutes crawled past, and finally he heard the soft sound he had been searching for. A humourless smile crossed his face, and then he was still again.

He heard the woman's footsteps climbing the stairs, and the men following her. Her footfalls were as unsteady as theirs were loud. Seth listened, and didn't move. He heard the doors opening, the men laughing. He heard the woman crying. He listened, and when the men had finished he leaned back against the wall and closed his eyes.

The hours trickled by. When the sun had set, the men began to snore. He counted their nasal tones – two downstairs, and one with the woman. The woman, Seth knew, was not asleep. He stood up, walked down the corridor, and when he pushed her door open he pressed a finger to his lips.

She almost screamed. Almost, but then she bit her lip and looked away. He didn't look at her shame or nakedness, but watched the way her eyes flicked nervously to the other side of the bed. The man smelled of liquor and sex, and when Seth slit his throat the hot blood loosed filth from his clothes until the bed was soaked in such a putrid fluid that the woman turned her face away and gagged.

Seth cleaned his knife on the end of the mattress and then looked down at the woman. There was something dead in her eyes. He cut one of the ropes which tied her to the bed frame. It was enough for her to roll away from the dead man and cover herself, but when she looked at him with pleading eyes he shook his head. The other ropes would stay tied.

"Why did you do it?" He asked softly. The woman refused to meet his eyes. Her voice came out in a broken croak.

"There are more of them downstairs."

"Answer my question."

"They'll come if I scream."

"I don't think they would. They're not exactly falling over each other to defend you, are they?"

A tear spilled from the corner of her eye, and she shook her head numbly. Seth crouched down beside her and helped her to pull on her dress. The soft pastel fabric was completely unrecognisable, and she winced when she folded her bruised arms into the sleeves. Her skin was burned and hardened by the sun, her city plumpness erased in just a few weeks.

"Tell me." He ordered, and then added in a quieter voice. "I'll listen to you. Don't you want your family to know what became of you?"

"I had a baby." She said finally. Seth shrugged, about to ask her another question, and then she looked at him and repeated in a stronger voice. "It was a mutation. A beautiful, strong little mutation with his father's blue eyes."

He caught on quickly, and scratched his nose as he thought. "How did you get it out of the city?"

She laughed, a torn and wild sound. "I thought I was degrading myself. It was really nothing. Nothing!"

"Who with?"

"He... I didn't ask his name."

That was a lie, but Seth let it pass. He could find out the truth from the guards themselves, once he was back in the vault. They would tell him, and he would pretend to write down their names, and then things would return to normal. People who were determined to escape could cause more trouble than they were worth, and so when they slipped away the guards had a habit of letting them go. The same men who helped this woman escape had immediately reported her to the council. Still, it was worrying that they had demanded sexual favours from her. Usually they simply asked for bribes, which the committee then reclaimed for the traitors' families. It seemed that the guards were trying to get something extra out of the melting pot.

He could hear the soft noises of the other men turning over in their sleep.

"What happened to the baby?"

She gestured around her helplessly, to the ruins and the filthy bed and the man whose blood was clotting into the blankets. "What do you think?"

"I'm sorry." The man said, and the woman flinched and met his eyes. The honest sympathy in his face made her eyes well up, and she started sobbing into her hands. Seth stood up, letting her have some privacy while he checked outside.

The men had fallen back asleep, disgustingly accustomed to the sound of the woman crying herself to sleep. She had been with them a few weeks, Seth worked out, if not months. She had run away soon after he had left the city to search the ballots, and it had taken him several days to find her trail. The dancing trinket he had destroyed in the ruins had belonged to her, and the city council had sent him to recover the rest. They could not risk the clans finding any more evidence of the vault. What would happen if the officials found a women in the wastes who could lead them right to the front door?

People had run away before. They had different reasons, and they all regretted their choice within a few hours of leaving, but their treason was always treated the same way. Seth, and his family before him, hunted their own kind with every scrap of ruthlessness the council called justice.

Still, he felt sorry for this woman. He pushed down the feeling, mentally cursing himself. So what if she had left to try to save her child? Was the infant's life more important than the hundreds of innocent citizens she had left behind? Was her ambition any nobler than those people who wanted to escape from their menial lives, or look into the depths of the sky before they died?

He had followed people who wanted to bring home riches, and people who trudged through the dust with the shadows of history pushing them onwards. He had thought that they were the worst. Some people read the histories and were broken by the truth. They walked into the arms of the forgotten dead with their eyes lost and their hearts leaden with disgust. Seth had thought that he was immune to it. He told himself that the poisonous knowledge which sickened the citizen's minds couldn't touch him. When the vault grew too close, he returned to the surface. When the surface tried to destroy him, he welcomed its assault with candid brutality. That was the world their ancestors had left them, and the people who tried to blind themselves to it were simply not able to survive.

He returned to the room and watched the woman, who had stopped crying and was staring at her skin. Her hands were bloodied but soft, having never needed to grow the hard callouses which clanswomen wore. Her skin was blue-white where her clothes had shaded her, and burned everywhere else. Her stomach was loose under her thin dress. Her hair was bleached by the sun, and her feet were red and raw. Seth hadn't asked what she had been, under the surface. He hadn't even asked her name, he had simply taken his orders and followed her. Now, looking at her, knowing nothing of what she had been, he saw all of the things which she could never be. She had none of the hard, strong flesh which the wastes demanded. Her body and her mind were too fragile to bend against the dust storms, and so she could do nothing except yield.

Perhaps that was why she had lived for so long. Most of the citizens died in just a few days, but she had survived. But then, he had seen the death in her eyes. She knew she was never going home, and she had accepted that. He wondered if it was part of the numb thrall that her child's death had cast upon her.

He dragged himself quickly away from that thought, and sat down beside the woman. Her eyes flicked to his knife, but she didn't flinch or move away. Yielding, again. The only way she could have survived. Her tenacity was oddly touching.

"I can't let you go home." Seth told her. His voice wasn't made to sound comforting, but he at least managed to speak softly. "You've already put everyone in danger."

She nodded, not looking up from her hands. He pressed her. "Do you know what that means? Do you understand why I'm here?"

"If you're going to kill anyone, why don't you kill them?" She asked, just as quietly. "It wouldn't take more than a few minutes. Then I could run."

"Where would you run to?" When she fell silent, Seth sighed and shook his head. "You know where the city is. We can't risk you telling anyone that."

"Cut my tongue out." She retorted, and then smiled wanly. "It's not like these savages can read."

Her sudden sharpness took the man aback, and despite himself he smiled. It was so much like something Tiria would say.

"I'll kill them." He said. "You deserve that much, at least. Do you want to watch?"

She shook her head, looking nauseous as she gestured to the corpse. Seth nodded and left her again. If he left his spare knife beside the bed, it was clearly by accident. If the woman happened to see it, to cut her ropes and slip away, then it wasn't his fault. He could always find her again. He knew she wouldn't get far, but she had enough courage left in her to try.

The sleeping men barely cried out. Seth knew how to be quick, how to share his silence with sharpened steel. He was almost grateful to them for their animal stupidity. They never knew what a rare creature they had caught, or how she could have changed their outcast lives. They had only seen weakness, had smelled it on her delicate skin. The next group would do just the same, and likely the ones after them. There was no reprieve; the woman did not understand the wastes enough to find shelter.

She had been desperate enough before to trade for food, giving away her dancing trinket, but the kindly man had betrayed her by morning. Her trail was easy enough to follow after that; her captor had marched her from camp to camp before he sold her. As he sat at the outcasts' campfires Seth asked the right questions.

The man had been a slave-taker - the same man who had captured Tiria, just a few weeks ago. How easily would she have fallen into this life? The thought made Seth uneasy, but he scolded himself for it. Sometimes he taunted the girl, calling her a slave when her doglike loyalty grated on his nerves, but he couldn't see himself as a slave-taker. They were low, disgusting outcasts. He shook away the sharp guilt and returned to following the woman.

Even if the woman had found the clans folk she would have been treated badly. Their territories were far enough from the city to make it unlikely, but there was always a chance. The rats were clever enough to see some of what she was, and they would trade her to the officials as quickly as they could for their precious points. After that, it would all be over. This woman's life, and the hundreds of people she had left behind, would be worth less than dust.

Seth told himself all of this, and sharpened his knife, and climbed the stairs. He moved slowly. His feet felt heavy, as they always did at this moment, but he kept moving.

When he returned to the room, the sharp smell of blood was almost overpowering. The floor was sticky with it. The woman lay on the bed, and the knife had fallen onto the floor beside her. One wrist dangled from the mattress, and he could see the deep slices she had cut into her own flesh.

Courage, then. She had more of it than he had thought. Seth walked over to her and closed her eyes. He didn't flinch away from her waxen skin. He had done this too many times to be squeamish.

But this time, looking at her, he felt as if he should do more.

He pushed the man's body off the bed and lay the woman out in the centre, folding a tattered blanket over her body. He crossed her arms over her chest and covered the wounds with the fabric. Finally, he smoothed her short hair into neatness and stepped away.

"I'm sorry." He said, and left her there for the rats to claim.

CHAPTER 5

There were many things about the city which made no sense to Tiria. When she had been alone she ignored them, pushing aside her burning curiosity and stubbornly keeping her eyes down and her hands busy. If she thought that no-one could see her then she would look around, as she had in the chapel, but the soft people were still far too curious about her to allow her to spend much time alone. Even when she returned to her own room she was watched, as if she could commit some horrific crime in the space of a few sterile corridors.

She looked forward to the time when she could bolt the door behind her and truly be alone, knowing that the only person she had to answer to was herself. It occurred to her that even that was no longer true; she was far from her father's control, but Seth had demanded a different kind of loyalty from her. She had no idea what he actually wanted, and she didn't know him well enough to try to guess, so for a few weeks she decided to behave herself. Much as it had in the wastes, her resolve didn't so much waver as get thrown to the wayside. Stealing George had only been the beginning. After that, with Walker's encouragement, she began to look beyond her boring, menial chores.

Walker started teaching her the names of his animals, making her write them down in her slow, looping letters. *Hamster, pig, squirrel.* He unlocked a cage of odd mewling creatures and took one out, saying, "This is an easy one. *Cat.*"

"We call them Feral Cats." Tiria said, sounding the word out in her mind. She chucked one of the kittens under its chin and smiled when it purred. "I thought they looked similar. These ones are sweeter, though."

"Well, feral means wild. Something that hunts and lives by its wits out in the wilderness." He cut his eyes up at her. "Some people say that's what you are."

"Feral?" She echoed, looking up. "I guess that makes sense. I like it more than rat."

"But it also means... dangerous. Vicious. Savage." He tried to be tactful. Tiria laughed hollowly.

"I'm not a savage. You should pray none of them ever make it down here."

"I do." He spoke softly, putting the cat back in its cage. "We all do."

She frowned and put the pencil down. Kicking her feet against the side of the chair, she chewed on her lip and finally lowered her hand to her belt. Drawing her knife, she spun it slowly in her hand and then held it out to Walker, handle first. He balked and stared at her, then took it as if it were made of glass.

"If they do make it down here, wishing them away won't help." She said quietly. "There's no point being afraid of them. If you really want the nightmares to stop, then learn how to use a knife. It's better to be feral than to be dead... and the savages will kill you slowly."

He paled and dropped the knife down onto the table. "They won't come in here."

She grinned wickedly and took her knife back, dragging the point along the table. It made a nail-biting sound. "Let's hope you're right. Let's hope they don't break down the door or crawl through the vents."

Walker looked up nervously, his eyes fixing on the grate in the ceiling. "They couldn't fit through there."

Tiria leaned forward. "You'd smell them first, you know. Their skin rots off their bones, and sometimes you know they're coming just by the reek. Sometimes I dream that they crawl past my room, and the stink comes through the grate. You never forget the smell. And they laugh. They don't sound happy, but you can hear the air croaking out of their throats when they dig their nails into your skin. If they catch you, they kill slowly. They like to hear you scream." Her voice had lowered to a vicious hiss, and then she shrugged, sat upright, and spoke normally again. "So... I hope you're right."

He held his hand out, and she placed the knife into his palm. This time his hand closed around it strongly, and he met her eyes with fierce determination. "What do I do?"

When she wasn't reading, or training with Walker, Tiria liked to explore. She practiced moving silently through the corridors, disappearing into the shadows in the same way Seth had done. He made it look so easy, but for the first few weeks all Tiria managed to do was earn scathing remarks when the citizens saw her flattening herself against their walls.

The city was vast, far larger than even the ruins above it. The seemingly endless corridors and living quarters of the upper levels gave way to the more functional rooms everyone disappeared into when the lights blazed yellow - laboratories like Walker's, or offices, or strange store rooms where people collected linen and home wares to take back to their rooms. Nobody seemed to trade anything, but Tiria saw some people leaving with far more than others. She remembered their faces, and saw the haughty way they raised their chins.

They were officials, Walker said. Tiria thought about the officials in the wastes and wondered if they were the same. These city men and women mingled with the normal people. Nobody in the wastes even knew and official's name, they simply appeared for the ballot and left when it was done. Walker asked her if they were closer to the highs that she had told him about, but again the girl shook her head. The highs worked hard to earn and keep their score; they walked as if they had earned that right, not that other people owed them their respect. If a high had sauntered like the soft city folk he would have been laughed at. Who knew what fate might befall a high in a year, or even a month? It was best to be humble.

The city folk talked about something called status – the closest Tiria could find to any of them making sense. Some people had a higher status than others. To her, that made perfect sense. But the status didn't seemed to be earned, and that confused her. The people who took more goods from the store rooms were not smarter or stronger than the others, it was just that their families had always taken a larger share of supplies, and so they had inherited that right.

"But why doesn't anyone refuse?" She asked Walker, pressing him for an answer which she was sure was just beyond her grasp. The man looked uncomfortable, and the more he tried to explain to her about social structure, the more confused she got. Finally, he gritted his teeth and said, "Where do you think Seth got all his fine things from?"

"Seth?" She asked, and laughed shortly. "What fine things?"

"In his rooms. Do you think we all live like that?"

"I've never been there." Tiria answered absently, and then realised that she had made a misstep. She hastily corrected herself: "There wasn't enough time for him to show me before he left. I live closer to Agni because it's... it's just easier."

The man shrugged and refused to meet her eyes. His voice was a little cool. "It's cruel to criticise people when you're looking down on them, Tiria."

"Down?" She echoed, thinking of her tiny, cold room and the way Agni's women tripped her in the corridors. Her blood heated a little when she worked out what he was implying. "I'm not Seth, you know. Even if he looks down on you silly people, I don't get to. He left me at the bottom on purpose."

"You think you're at the bottom?" Walker looked at her in some amazement, and then laughed. Shaking his head, he checked the clock and stood up. "Come on, you have half an hour before your lunch break finishes. I need to collect some samples." When she hesitated, he sighed and added more pointedly, "I want to show you something."

He took her down to the fourth level, which she had never been allowed to see. He had to key a code into the elevator, which hummed as it dropped through layers of bedrock away from the shining world above. The rest of the city was built into caves, Walker explained. They had been shored up and blocked when the bunker was built, and as the centuries passed the citizens had carved deeper into the stone for more room. The lift seemed ridiculously clean when the doors opened and they stepped out. The steel corridors had disappeared, and in their place were soft, porous sheets of some material which exuded an odd, sticky fluid. Tiria winced when she touched it. She wiped her fingers onto her shirt, choking back the urge to gag at the sharp, acrid smell. The air was damp with condensation, and she felt as if the sticky mess was trickling down her throat and oozing into her lungs.

Walker looked around when she stopped. His voice was mild. "You can go back upstairs if it's too much."

She scowled and pushed him onwards. They trailed through a series of long, low rooms which connected to one another with thick iron doors. As they walked through each room the weeping walls became thicker with moss, lichen and fungi, as the lights moved from nocturnal hues to cool, weak light and, finally, the blazing warmth and heat of an autumn sun. Tiria stopped under this last great bulb, barely daring to breathe.

The floors – the walls – even the ceiling – were covered in plants which were more green and vibrant than anything she had ever even imagined. Every succulent leaf and flower was dewed with moisture, and the air was rich and sickly with the perfume of blossom. The reek of the sticky sap ran through the perfume like a sputum of mould, making the delicate scents turn bitter and pungent.

"What is this place?" She asked, peering around with a mixture of fascination and disgust. Walker was chewing on his fingernail nervously, but when he saw her expression he quickly stopped. His footsteps were childishly loud as he lead her through the next doorway, and when Tiria saw the vast cavern she understood.

The ground was golden, and green – every inch of it caressed by stems of grass and herbs, ones that she recognised and ones which were completely unknown. Even the plants she knew were monstrous, huge and brightly coloured compared to their shrunken counterparts on the surface. The thick air held a soft, artificial breeze. Under the sun lamps, insects and butterflies skimmed through the air, pollinating and feeding the birds, who soared even higher. There were other animals, too, but they were kept in cages along the far walls. She recognised some of them from the books she had been reading. Pigs, sheep, goats and dogs. There were other rooms, Walker said, but none of the others were as vast as this.

It took her a long time to notice that there were people in the fields. They carried tools on their backs, and walked with careful steps, but when she looked more closely Tiria realised that they couldn't stand up straight. Walker scratched his nose nervously when she pointed it out to him.

"Some of the caves are very small." He muttered. "You have to crawl through the tunnels to get between them. And... and the air down here is good for the plants, but even the animals get..." He stumbled to a halt and then shook his head. "It's a choice between the chemicals or the radiation, and people have to eat. It was a problem in the first generations, until someone closer to the surface had the bright idea of sending people down here to punish them."

"They're criminals?" Tiria asked. Walker wiped his sleeve across his forehead.

"They were. Criminals have children, just like everyone else."

"Children work down here?" She was appalled, and strained her eyes to see. There were more of the people everywhere she looked. Some of them could barely walk. Others were harvesting a large patch of land, pulling swollen potatoes out of the soil. The chemicals made the vegetables enormous, and the gardeners' arms strained with effort as they lifted each one into their baskets. Their eyes were puffy and swollen, constantly weeping out the sticky moisture in the humid air, and the sound of their coughing drowned out the bird song.

"It must be nice to live on the surface and think there's nothing lower than you." Walker said, and Tiria looked at him sharply. His words held such a peculiar mixture of accusation and wistfulness that she didn't know what he meant. She felt her face growing warm at the insult, though, and bit her tongue. She had never felt ashamed before.

"Seth didn't tell me about any of this." She whispered, and then thought back to the few short hours that they had actually spent together in the city. Her shame turned against him. "He didn't tell me about anything."

Walker cleared his throat. "I don't know Seth."

"Oh, don't you dare prattle that nonsense at me." She planted her hands on her hips. "If you're afraid to talk about him then it already means you know far more about him than I do! The way everyone around here whispers in corners makes my ears ring."

He lowered his voice. "You're not the only one who listens at corners, Ti."

"Are you telling me that Seth...?"

"No, not him." Walker looked up at the ceiling nervously, and then relaxed a little. Tiria looked up, and then shrugged. Whatever city device he was looking for would have been a mystery to her, anyway. They turned to leave, walking quickly back through the caves and sighing with relief when they got into the cooler air of the elevator.

"Do you think I would tell Seth about you?" She asked, changing the subject with a shaky grin. The man looked uncomfortable, and she laughed. "Oh come on, Walker! He wouldn't believe me if I told him the sky was blue!"

Rather than laughing, Walker frowned and shushed her. She bit her lip and quietened, remembering too late that Seth's apparent affection for her was the only thing protecting her from the hostile citizens.

The man said, very carefully. "Seth's family trained down here. They taught each other how to track every animal and recognise every leaf. Your husband spent his childhood with a notebook in his hand and a knife strapped to his belt. They disappeared down here for weeks, and while they were down here you can bet we all avoided this level. It's dangerous enough down here. Sometimes the vents get blocked, and when the animals down here breathe in too much of that liquid air they go... bad.."

Tiria shrugged. It seemed like a normal enough childhood to her, however disgusted Walker looked by it. He tried not to look appalled at her indifference, but couldn't hide a shiver as he carried on. "Once some of the gardeners went bad, too."

"They went savage?" Tiria couldn't imagine the savages slithering along these moist floors. Walker shook his head, and then nodded, and then breathed out in a huff.

"We all heard the gunfire. Everyone who came down here came back out. We waited by the lift and counted them. Ten security officers, two scavengers, and a ten year old child walked past us covered in blood. Nobody said a word. By the next day the mess was all gone, and we all acted as if nothing had happened."

"But?"

"But?"

"There must be something he did, or something he said - if it's just his job, then why is everyone scared of him?"

"His job isn't to clean out the vents, Ti." Walker looked at her dumbfounded, and then he shook his head in wonder. "God, you really don't know. I thought at least you..."

She scowled and folded her arms, glaring at the man until he gave up. Taking a deep breath, he explained, very carefully, what her husband did outside of the vault.

Tiria listened, said nothing, and when he was done she walked back to her room alone. She locked her door when Agni came looking for her. She barely heard the bells ring for dinner. When the lights dimmed she sat there, alone, and stared into the darkness.

CHAPTER 6

It was purely by chance that Tiria found out that Seth was returning. Agni called her in to give her the week's schedule, as she always did, but there was something peculiar about the way the woman looked at her that made Tiria suspicious. The woman asked far more questions than usual, prying into nearly every facet of the girl's life until Tiria grew impatient and pressed her lips firmly together, refusing to say another word. While Agni amused herself by mocking the girl's 'idiot tongue', she let her eyes wander over the room.

She had learned to read enough now to make out basic words, and when she looked down at the notes on the old hag's desk she saw a word she knew - Seth's name. As much as she squinted she couldn't make out the rest of the note upside down, and she didn't want the old woman to know that she had learned to read. For the rest of the day she loitered around the office whenever she had a free moment, until finally she could dart in and snatch up the note. It was short, thank god, but her heart pounded in her chest as she painstakingly sounded out each word.

Council meeting tonight at 6: Seth's report on Jane Mallard.

She bit her lip, and then gasped when the door started opening. Slipping the note back into its place, she fled into the supply cupboard and clattered around the tins, dropping half of them onto the floor. One of the other maids stood in the doorway and pressed her hands to her hips.

"I was looking for the furniture wax." Tiria gasped, scrabbling around to pick up the tins. The girl scoffed, threw a stray tin hard at the girl, and left. Tiria bit back a yelp when the tin struck her arm, but she didn't follow the maid. Her mind was racing. If Seth was back, she had to see him. She had to ask him about what Walker had told her. She had to... to...

She wanted to hurt him. She dropped a can from numb fingers and caught her breath. The thought was so intense it stung her eyes. She wanted him to feel how lonely and pathetic he had made her, by leaving her here. He had no heart, no feelings. Words would only be laughed at. She wanted to wrap her hands around his throat and squeeze, and laugh at all his secrets that he would never hide again.

No. She didn't want that. Tiria rubbed her aching head with her hand and winced at how cold her fingers had become. The note had made a wave of confusion rise in her, and as soon as one emotion flared up another eclipsed it. She was glad he was back. She could talk to him. She could be excited, now he would take her outside. Or perhaps he would tell her his plan, now that she knew the rest of it.

She smiled and nodded to herself. Yes. She would listen to his plan, and then strangle him.

Tiria finished her work diligently and crept up to the upper level, where the council members shared their opulent corridors with the wealthy citizens. Seth's room was there, she knew, although she had never been sent inside it. She had cleaned other houses, but no-one ever went into his. She would have knocked, but then she tried the door handle and found that it was unlocked.

She hoped to find Seth alone. She knew that the things she wanted to say would seem childish if anyone else could hear them. If she said them to him – only him – then they might sound angry and not petulant. As she thought this her stomach churned, remembering how he had cast her aside when they had first come here. The last thing she wanted was for him to be so angry that he would leave her here forever.

Her resolve grew stronger. Scared or not, she was sick of being treated as if she did not matter. Even if Seth refused to help her, he could at least explain why he had brought her here in the first place. He owed her that much.

Like the rest of the corridor Seth's room was dark and warm, with rough wooden panels caressing every wall. There were panes of glass between the timbers which drank in the soft light and made it shine. Every lantern cast pools of colour onto a different shelf or cabinet. Unbelievably, a banked fire was spilling soft orange light onto the carpeted floor.

Later, Tiria found out that the apartments the wealthiest members of the city lived in were designed to mimic the luxurious homes their ancestors had left behind: their walls held glass panels which mimicked the rise and fall of the sun, and even glittered with ice or rain drops when programmed to act out winter or spring. The doors were made of the same sterile metal as the rest of the complex, but clad in thin sheets of wood or stone. The fire was an illusion, a metal plate with false flames and real heat.

On one of the shelves there were scores of tiny glass jars, each one tinted a different colour or blackened by decay. On another there were dolls with white china faces, their eyes askew but lustrous in their deathlike masks. When the girl stepped forward she caught sight of a third shelf and nearly gasped aloud: it was full of books. They weren't crumbling like the rare artefacts from the wastes, or the much-thumbed replicas which Walker had leant her. They were beautiful, wrapped in soft colourful covers embossed with writhing creatures, empty-eyed faces, endless maps and scrolling words. Tiria held her breath and stepped forward, stopping herself from touching the books but unable to resist reaching out to one of the beautiful crystal bottles.

"Tiria." Seth said from behind her. The girl's head snapped around, her hand frozen an inch away from the shining glass.

"What is this?"

"It's called *don't touch*." He snapped, and then yawned. By the time he had finished Tiria had perfected her glare, and he smiled wearily at the obviously-rehearsed expression. "What are you doing here, Ti?"

"I was looking for you."

"Well, I don't think you'd find me in there." He picked up the bottle and held it up to the light with a wan expression. "Even the genies would find that a bit cramped."

Tiria blinked in confusion. It was hard to cling to her carefully nurtured anger when he spoke so strangely. "What on earth is a genie?"

"A man who lives in a bottle." He replied as if it were an obvious answer, and put the bottle carefully back into its place. Tiria remembered that the maids had said Seth liked to collect things. He gave the bottle a little twist so that its label faced the same way as the others, and then looked up. "How did you find out I was back?"

She didn't answer, but ran her thumb along the bookshelf. The dust was gritty under her nail. She knew that a few months ago she never would have noticed it, but now the privacy of his sanctuary struck her. None of the caretakers or cleaners were ever allowed in here to clean it. She wiped the dust onto her shirt. "I won't stay long. I'm not supposed to know anything important, so I don't know you're back. And you're not supposed to know how I've been treated. I figure that by tomorrow everyone will know you're here, and Agni will be bragging to you about the three meals a day she's been feeding me. I wanted to see you before... before all the lying starts again."

Seth sat down on the back of one of the chairs. He looked tired, a little thinner, but otherwise unharmed from his time in the wastes. His hair was still damp from the decon showers, but he was wearing the smart, impractical clothes which citizens wore when they were summoned by the council. Tiria felt sure that every council member was having their own hushed conversation at the same time as this illicit meeting.

Seth looked at her levelly and then sighed. His face took on the stoic, emotionless hardness which she remembered with loathing. Until he spoke, she had forgotten how much his flat voice made her skin crawl.

"I heard you've been unhappy."

She gaped at him and folded her arms. "You heard that, did you? So sweet of you to care."

"I didn't say I cared. It was hard to ignore. Everyone is talking about you."

"I know." The girl managed, "But they..."

"They what, Ti? I thought you would like it here. It has to be better than scratching a living out of that hole you used to live in."

"Everyone knows that lie about my home. They treat me like an animal. They say I deserve it."

He fell silent and his jaw set with anger. He had heard more than just her side of the story already, then. It was exactly what Tiria had been afraid of, and already she was regretting her sharp words. She took a step back and flinched when he caught her arm, stopping her. His voice was cold.

"You promised me that you would try to fit in. Now I've found out that when you first came here you screamed and hit anyone who came near you."

"They hit me back."

He growled a curse and let go of her arm. "They're scared of you, you little idiot."

Tiria gaped at him, and then a hysterical laugh bubbled from her chest so loudly that it hurt. She clutched her stomach in pain but could not stop laughing as tears ran down her cheeks. It was such a stupid thing for him to say, and it was a foul excuse for the way his friends had treated her. As she thought that her tears turned bitter and her whole body was wreaked with sobs.

She felt his hand on her arm again, and shoved him away so violently that his dog sat up and growled. Seth had left the animal in the gardening level while he was away, but now that he was home the ancient mongrel protected him with ferocious loyalty. Seth turned away from the girl to calm the animal down, crouching down with one hand buried in its soft fur and his hard eyes fixed upwards.

"At least that thing has teeth." Tiria choked, pointing at the mongrel. "They hate it, but they like it more than me. They say it gave me fleas. Are they scared of fleas, Seth?"

"No." He spoke quietly, forcing the girl to breathe more evenly so she could hear him. "They've seen fleas before."

"Well, they beat me because they said I brought them in." Heedless of her own embarrassment, the girl rolled up her shirt and showed him her newest bruises. It took her only a few words to explain how she had gotten them, and tens of others before. Seth's eyes moved to the blue and purple weals, and for a moment the girl shivered stubbornly under his critical eye. Then disgust flooded over her and she shoved the fabric back down.

"You did this." She hissed. "You brought me here. Don't you dare say it's my fault."

He scratched his nose awkwardly and beckoned her to follow him to the fire and, rather impatiently, told her to sit down. Tiria thought about staying standing, arms folded obstinately as she glared down at him, but the soft cushions on the chair were irresistible. Seth stared at the fire for a long time, and his voice was hard.

"I'm trying to make you understand." He said, not looking around. "They're not scared of what you're doing. They're scared of you. They've never seen anything like you."

Tiria scoffed and kicked at the chair leg. For the first time since he had grabbed her wrist, Seth seemed to grow angry and he looked up with fierce eyes. "Why do you think I brought you here, for god's sake?"

"You wouldn't tell me." The girl reminded him. He drew a deep breath, and then thought better of whatever he was about to shout and looked back into the flames. The silence stretched on for so long that Tiria couldn't help but fill it. "You wouldn't tell me *anything.*"

"And you know now, do you?"

"Yes." – softly – "I do."

He looked sharply at her and Tiria found herself shrinking away, not from the man but from all of the stories and rumours which he had become to her. It seemed like months since she had seen him, not weeks, and the last time they had been together she had almost trusted him. Now...

"I thought about running away." She looked up at him, saw his eyes growing harder, and shivered at even that small proof. "You told me I could run, if I dared – but you didn't tell me how far I would get before you found me. They say you find everyone, in the end."

"You would be more of a challenge." He admitted, still not softening as he studied her. "You might even make it out of the ruins."

"No, I don't suppose the people here make it very far." She returned, and every word she spoke was an accusation. "They're too soft, too... too weak. Do you feel good about hunting them down? Do you like being in the vault and walking past them, knowing how much they're afraid of you?"

He snorted, almost laughing at her. "What do you think?"

"You don't do anything to change it though, do you?"

"Why would I?" He looked archly at her. "Better they be afraid of me than go into the wastes. Do you think your soft, frightened little friends have any idea what it's like out there? It's easy to tell yourself you're not afraid, when you don't know what's waiting for you in the dark. It's harder to talk yourself into running away if you have to see the person who will hunt you down, if you can look into his eyes and see that he wouldn't hesitate – that might make you change your mind. Their fear keeps them here, and their fear keeps them safe."

She looked away, and swallowed a few times before managing to say, "It's like you're talking about children."

"Children have more sense." Seth scowled and finally looked away from her, his voice growing angry again. Something made him curt with her, as if he had betrayed some real emotion in his blasé' explanation. "I don't kill innocents, Tiria. The wastes do that for me. I've been doing this since I was a child, and I have only drawn my blade a handful of times in all those years. The stories they tell are far more comforting than the truth. I follow them, yes. I hunt them down to bring back their belongings for their families, and to destroy anything which could betray the city to your clans."

"You kill the runaways." Tiria whispered. "Everyone knows that. The only way to stop them from telling the clans officials where this place is, is to..."

He looked coldly at her, daring her to finish her sentence, and when she couldn't he shrugged and moved away. Opening his pack, he began pulling out the filthy clothes and supplies he had taken away with him. "Did you come here to tell me you've been gossiping, Tiria? I'm tired."

"No, I..." She started, and then shook herself out of the darkness into the more familiar anger. She was too confused to remember everything, and the few words she produced "I wanted to ask you why you left me here. You should have taken me with you."

"Murdering my scared little runaways is more fun than dusting furniture, is that it?" He mocked her savagely. Tiria bristled and rounded on him.

"You should know you're not allowed to give me to other people. I'm not a slave. If anyone deserves to be beaten it's you. The ballot was created to strengthen bonds between the tribes and to create children. Nothing else, Seth."

"Don't quote that nonsense at me. You can't tell me you'd still rather have children with a complete stranger than work for Agni?" He looked incredulously at Tiria when she nodded and, with a great sigh, he rested his head in his hands. "That nonsense diatribe has made you an idiot. I had no idea they were still using it to brainwash children."

"I'm not a child."

"Of course not." He smiled sarcastically. "You're old enough to breed. That's old enough for your father to sell you."

Tiria remembered the pathetic lows from the ballot and whitened. Surely he wasn't comparing her to them? Was that how he saw her? She was so appalled that she stood up, her hands clenching into fists. He had been sharp with her before, but never deliberately cruel. As she stepped towards him something made her stop. There was a pain in his eyes which he had tried to hide, and she couldn't help wondering if his cruelty was some twisted way of hiding it.

"There'd better be something really wrong with you." She growled, not backing down. "I told you I'd cut your tongue out, and I meant it."

He grimaced and held up a hand. "Tiria, please just... I'm sorry, okay? I spoke badly. I would rather talk to you tomorrow. I really am tired."

"Tired." She echoed, and he looked hostile when she folded her arms. "Seth, I won't go."

"You know what my job is, Ti. Can't your ferocious mind work out why I'm in no mood to talk to you right now?"

"Jane Mallard?" She asked, and watched him flinch. He hauled himself up out of the chair and opened a sideboard cupboard, pouring himself a glass of some liquor and drinking from it before he answered, with a sick smile.

"Jane Mallard." He drank again, and then shook his head. "That was her name, was it?"

Tiria tensed when he moved again, but she heard the chiming of glass and realised that he was pouring out another drink. He held a small glass out, but Tiria cringed back from the sharp smell.

"Drink it. We'll both feel better." He said, and pressed the glass into her hand. Watching her sniff suspiciously at it, he sat back in his chair and made a meaningless gesture with his free hand. "I apologise, Ti. I shouldn't have spoken about your father. I promised myself that when I saw you again I would move past all of our arguments. I'd appreciate it if... if you could do the same. We need to start again."

Tiria sipped the liquid cautiously and forced herself to calm down. It took her a long time to make her eyes stop burning, and every vicious curse word she knew screamed in her mind whenever she dared look up. She couldn't find the words to argue any more – she was too tired of all his secrets. As much as she hated Seth, he was the only person who actually told her anything. Walker only told her what he knew, and it was shockingly little. People in the city seemed to exist on nothing but rumour and gossip. They knew nothing about life in the wastes.

"If we're going to start again, then... tell me: how did you enter my ballot?" Tiria asked in the end, thinking back over her scores of questions. "You're not one of us."

He grinned and raised his glass in a mocking toast before he sipped the wine. "I'm whoever I need to be. It's not so hard to convince a few illiterate officials."

"But... ninety two?" She raised an eyebrow at him, and was secretly amused when he reddened.

"I needed to be sure I'd win."

"You would have won me at seventy. No-one higher would be stupid enough to want me. You made yourself look like an idiot."

"Because of your number?" He leaned forward, his eyes suddenly sharp with interest. "Doesn't anyone ever take a risk?"

The girl scoffed and looked away. Only stupid people matched themselves with the lows. The only times she had ever seen it, the low had been exceptionally lovely, and the high had been so old that their scores would not have enough time to fall. Many people prayed that their children would be lucky enough not to be born beautiful. It was dangerous to be singled out.

"Did you feel sorry for me?" Tiria interrupted Seth's next question with her own, flat words. He blinked and looked as if he was going to pull his indifferent mask back on, but then something thawed in his eyes and he shrugged.

"I needed a rat. I couldn't kidnap one of you, not with the way you all fight, and I couldn't coax one away without risking the whole wasteland finding out about this place. The ballot seemed like the safest bet, although it was a risk. I spent months drifting between the shelters, stealing the documents I needed and letting my face be seen until I reached your theatre. I wasn't going to risk it that night, but I saw a man in the crowd who was selling banned goods to anyone near him – pictures, jewellery, and … and his daughter. After he sent you to the ballot he went from man to man whispering in their ears about you. I reasoned that if he was that desperate to get rid of you, you'd be more interesting than most of those brainwashed idiots. That's why I bid for you."

Tiria's cheeks burned but she knew her father well enough to guess the kind of things he had been saying. If her reputation was ruined then no decent numbers would bid; some of the lows would pay good money to a man who could guarantee them a chance.

"I'm not a whore." she muttered, "No matter what he told you."

"I know that. I'm a good enough liar to sniff out one of my own." Seth said diffidently. "If those officials had half a brain they would have seen through your father in an instant."

"He bribed them." Tiria pointed out coldly. "Rats are corrupt, not stupid."

He shrugged. "If you act in a stupid way, people will see you as stupid. If the rats are willing to sell their wits so cheaply, I doubt they have very many to start with."

"You know nothing about us." The girl snapped, and flinched when he turned his dark eyes on her. For a moment there was a spark of outright hostility in his glare, and then he looked away. A smile played about his lips, and he shook his head. His voice had grown cruel and distant.

"I didn't need to know about you, did I? You didn't exactly quiz me on the customs that your bloodthirsty ancestors invented. As far as I can recall, you agreed to follow me before you had even seen me, and you asked my score before you asked my name. As much as you mock me for choosing that number it was more than enough for you to agree to me screwing you on a filthy chapel floor. I don't recall *knowledge* ever being a priority for you. Or did I miss a long, lingering conversation somewhere along the line?"

She reddened, and he sighed. His voice was still harsh, but the fury had gone. "I know a little, Tiria. I know that you're far more intelligent than you pretend to be. I also know that as soon as you found out what I am, you started being afraid of me."

She managed to choke out a few words. "I'm not."

"You, little wife, are a terrible liar." He leaned back in his chair and closed his eyes. "There's nothing wrong with it. I am not your friend, and I would far prefer that you keep up your own pretence. A stupid, frightened child is pathetic; a clever, fearless woman is a dangerous toy to keep, even for me."

"You're back to calling me a toy." Tiria gave a long-suffering sigh and folded her arms. "You still haven't told me why you brought me here."

He opened one eye. "You're here because I need you."

"I'm getting worked half to death by soft idiots because you 'need' me?" She had to bite down the urge to slap him, and instead managed to vow through gritted teeth: "If you really need me, then I swear I'll run away if you don't tell me the truth."

"You'll die in the wasteland or you'll die in the city? What an agonising choice." He shrugged, clearly indifferent. Tiria didn't understand, but she glared at him until he sighed. "If I tell you the truth, there are people in this city who will kill you for it."

Tiria's stubbornly set chin and folded arms clearly annoyed him, because he motioned for her to take him seriously and leaned forward, his voice low and intense. "I need you to be stupid. Remember that if you want to stay alive. The best way to be stupid is to know nothing. At least then, if they catch me, you can lie a little more convincingly."

"And if I tell the truth? Will you be in danger?" She drawled this in a way which made it clear that she didn't believe him. Seth bristled and his eyes grew dark and dangerous.

"If you try to speak against me, every word of it will come around to bite you."

"I'm not stupid enough to repeat back your lies, Seth. And you're not so proud you can't see that I've already worked out that something's going on. I might not be able to tell them what it is, but I'm sure that if the council get suspicious it'll stop whatever you're doing, won't it?"

He regarded her levelly for a moment, and then grinned and reached back for his wine glass. Despite the sudden joviality Tiria could see that he was furious; for the first time since she had crept into his rooms, she was genuinely afraid of what he might do next. Without thinking about it she reached inside her shirt, and when her fingertips met George's rough back she found that she could at least draw a breath. She pulled the little lizard free and let him nestle in her lap, willing herself to be as calm as the dragon was.

Seth's hand had been hovering over his knife. When he saw the lizard his eyes opened wide in genuine amazement, and he bit back a burst of laughter. "I thought you were pulling out a knife." He said.

"This is my secret." Tiria said, and then looked up from the lizard straight into her husband's eyes. "Now, tell me yours."

CHAPTER 7

"The most difficult thing that you have to grasp," Seth drew the words out slowly, "Is that none of this has anything to do with you. If you keep asking me why you're here, or why I chose you and not the next creature someone threw at me, then I'll stop telling you anything. I refuse to implicate myself simply to flatter your ego."

"As long as you don't lie to me, I won't interrupt." Tiria replied, and her voice was just as patronising as his own. Unlike Seth, the tone didn't come naturally to her, and so she sounded more sarcastic than he had. It was difficult for her to sit still now that she actually might find something out, and so she bit her tongue so hard that she tasted blood and nodded for him to speak. The man shot her an amused look, which she resented, and then began to speak.

"The people who live here are more frightened of me than they are of you, Tiria. When I was born they were afraid of my father, and when he was born it was my grandmother who made them tremble.

Think of all of the years of ballots which your people slavishly followed, and then imagine a single family keeping their own tradition for even longer than that. Perhaps the first people volunteered to become hunters, but by the time my father was born everyone knew that one day he would patrol the wastes.

My grandmother used to tell me that when our ancestors left, the world was still burning. You could see smoke pouring from the ruins, and when you walked in the rain it burned your skin like salt water in a cut. I expect you know more about that world than I do, since your family goes all the way back to the end times. But my family chose to venture into the wastes, and because they had seen those things, the people they left behind were afraid.

Some stories say that my ancestors lied about what they found, and used their lies to make themselves more powerful. Some say that they were rewarded for their courage, and that is how they rose. Either way, by the time that I was born, my family was one of the most influential in the city. The other children used to look at me in envy, for my fine clothes and my scavenged treasures. But the teachers used to pity me, and that was worse. They imagined me dying for those riches, and they were probably right. One day, my grandmother never came home. One day, my father did not make it to safety. And one day, I shall be swallowed by the sunlight too.

"I grew up knowing these things, but they were only stories to me until my turn finally came to leave. It was the day after my father disappeared. My first duty - and the first duty of every single one of my ancestors - was to find my father's body. It took me three weeks. By the time I found him, the ants had eaten his eyes. Every scrap of clothing had been stolen, and even his hair had been cut off to be woven into cloth. Every part of him had been used apart from his flesh, which was so withered and dry that I barely knew him. He had been stabbed in the belly - his hand was covering the wound.

"I thought I would feel horror - disgust - when I found him. I already knew what kind of world I was venturing in to, and I had seen death before. I was so prepared to be sickened by his murder that in truth I felt almost nothing. I stayed by his body that night, and tried to make myself cry, but there was nothing left in me to weep. Instead, I found myself marvelling at the way his body had been used. There was nothing about it that told me he had been disrespected.

"Aside from being stabbed, there were no wounds. No broken limbs, and his corpse had not been abused. His clothing had been taken away carefully - it must have been, because they had returned his hand to its resting place. Even his shorn head fascinated me, because it was so neatly done. Every part of him that could be used, had been taken. The part of him that was a living being had been left alone. I didn't think his murderer was the same person who had robbed him. I knew that night, and I have believed ever since, that the people who found his body were merely trying to survive."

Tiria nodded. She was too tactful to tell him about her own experiences with the dead, but she felt sure that he could see the truth on her face. When the winters were too harsh or the summers too bright, a single piece of cloth could save a person's life. She was also too clever to point out that a rat family might decide it was better to sacrifice a threatening stranger than their own children. Seth must know that, too.

He met her eyes for a moment, and then took larger mouthful of his wine and continued.

"I came back with his body and brought it to the council. I told them what I had found and, rather stupidly, I told them my thoughts about the scavengers. It was the first time I had faced the council alone, and I was foolish enough to think that they would value the truth. That night, a group of men came to my rooms and demanded my oath that I would stay silent. If I must speak, they told me, I must tell everyone that my father was defiled by the savages of the waste. Do you understand why they wanted this, Tiria?"

She thought slowly, and then remembered her own experiences with the council. Whenever she had spoken about her life and family outside of the sanctuary, they had scowled and shouted at her. Whenever she had opened her mouth, one of the servants had struck her into silence.

"They don't want people to know what it's really like out there." She worked out. Seth nodded, and then leaned forwards.

"It's more complicated than that. See yourself as a council member – a powerful man or woman whose family have ruled over hundreds of people for generations. Then look out into the wastes, and think about all of the thousands of people who don't even know you exist."

Tiria imagined Agni spluttering with rage and smiled. Her expression became more serious as the true implication set in. "I'd do anything to keep people in here."

"Exactly. And now imagine that you're a man who has spent his whole life patrolling the wastes. You know that the ground has stopped burning, and that the people aren't as dangerous as you think. What you don't know is that the council will do anything to keep you quiet."

"You think your father was murdered." The girl breathed, and then drew a shaking breath. "Who by?"

"I don't know." Seth shrugged and leaned back. "That's why you're here."

"Me?" She bit her lip, and then worked it out. She knew that the wastes were habitable. "If people started listening to my stories about the wastes, then whoever did this will want me to stop..."

The man smiled, a thin grimace. "I'd pretend to be very stupid, if I were you."

Tiria shook her head urgently. She was very tired, and the wine was buzzing through her mind as horribly as the dread which pooled in her stomach. Words refused to make sense, and she found herself babbling, "No, but..."

"You can defend yourself when you have to, and you're sharp enough to know when someone's trying to trick you." Seth pointed at her hip diffidently. "I know you're hiding at least one weapon on you, and I know you know how to use it. You also hate everyone who lives here, including me, which is a huge advantage. If I pretend I'm in love with you, I can trust you not to take it too seriously."

She planted her hands on her hips. "Not that nonsense again."

He looked at her as if she were stupid. "Why else would I bring a savage little rat into my home?"

Tiria reddened, and paled, and struggled for some way to tell him how ridiculous and mortifying he was being. She couldn't think of any other way than slapping him in the face, but she didn't think it would work out well for her. While she struggled, hand curling into a fist, Seth started talking again.

"My father had only one wound. That means he had not tried to fight his murderer off. Whoever did it was standing next to him. They could have been embracing him, or shaking his hand. He trusted people." The man's mouth thinned as he thought about that particular weakness, and then he scowled and looked up. "Do you understand?"

"I'm your bait." She looked up fiercely. "But you can't just throw me at them. If I die, I won't be able to tell you who did it."

"Then fight back." He shrugged. She gaped at him.

"How can you be so cold? I didn't ask to be mixed up in any of this! I don't care about you or your stupid father, or the idiots who live here."

As she spoke, her bleary mind realised that it wasn't true. She cared, because she'd been living here for long enough to recognise their faces. She had seen children looking up at their families with trusting eyes, and she had seen the fear on adults faces when they looked up at her. She represented everything that the council wanted them to fear, and she bore the brunt of their loathing for it. Their terror was palpable, and their anger was terrifying. If the people here were found by the rats, no-one would think to listen to what they had to say. It would be a mass slaughter, and Tiria already knew who would win. The council must be frightened of that, too... but they would have no idea they were making it worse.

Looking at Seth's face, the girl realised that he had planned this, too. He had left her here, alone, because he wanted her to know these people. He had made them afraid of her on purpose, and he made sure that she came to them as angry and bitter as he could make her. Tiria the rat, feral and vicious, had proven every one of the council's stories and crawled through their hallways like a grim warning.

Seth had manipulated her from the very beginning. She stood up shakily and spat at his feet, hating her anger but desperate to get the sick, burning fury out of her stomach. Seth looked bored, and waved an indifferent hand at her. "You're tired. Go to bed, little wife. We've already spoken for too long. You're not in any more danger than I am, and I'll sleep soundly tonight."

"You have a guard dog." She growled.

"Well, you have a lizard. I'm sure it has a terrifying hiss." The man drawled, and pushed her out of the room.

CHAPTER 8

The next morning, before dawn, Tiria was woken up by a strange tapping noise. She sat up blearily and then, in a moment of panic, picked up George from his side of the pillow and stuffed him inside her night shirt. The lizard hissed indignantly and scratched her neck as she shook her hair over the collar, hiding his bulbous eyes.

"Come in," She called out, and reached for her knife.

It was a girl who came in to her room, although that didn't make Tiria loosen her grip on the knife. She had been attacked by far younger children in the wastes, and she was sure she would never trust anybody again. The girl paused by the doorway to adjust her eyes to the darkness, and then bobbed down in an awkward curtsey.

"I'm sorry to bother you, miss. Master Seth has returned to the Sanctuary."

"I... oh?" Tiria corrected herself, remembering that she was not supposed to know that. The girl by the door risked a shaky smile.

"Yes, so missus... she says that there's no call for you to stay here anymore, and so she wants to... she asks if you'll move out as soon as possible. She wants to clean the room."

"Scrub it raw, you mean." The girl said, rubbing her forehead and yawning. The other girl blushed and nodded. "Well, where am I meant to go?"

"To... to master Seth's rooms?" The servant looked amazed by the question, and Tiria pretended her groan was a yawn.

"Does he know?"

"Yes!" If possible, the girl looked more amazed. "He asked for you."

Now it was Tiria's turn to look amazed. Rather than give herself away to this girl, who she was certain would be reporting back to Agni the second she left the room, Tiria made a great show of yawning and rubbing her eyes. "If my husband wants me, he can wait for me to have breakfast. He's kept me waiting long enough, after all. Bring me a bowl of porridge and a cup of tea."

The servant's mouth dropped open, and her voice became scornful. "Tiri..."

"Don't make me tell you twice!" Tiria scowled as fiercely as only a rat could, and threw herself back against the pillows. George lost his grip for a moment, and redoubled it with vengeful enthusiasm as soon as the world had righted itself. By the time his prickling spikes had softened, the servant had fled.

She had hardly dared expect it, but the cook actually sent up a tray of breakfast. The porridge was burned and sour, and the tea had probably been spat into, but Tiria enjoyed every mouthful. After so many weeks, the victory tasted so sweet that she could have been eating iced cake. She took her time packing her things, pulled on her scruffiest clothes, and left her cell of a room with a light step.

She had barely made it through three corridors when a hand shot out, and someone dragged her into a corner. Tiria stifled a shriek and fumbled for her knife, dropping her bag as she struggled. She felt her knee connect painfully with flesh. The assailant cursed and let her go. The girl reeled around, blade drawn, and gasped out a great shriek of air when she saw who it was.

"Walker! I nearly killed you!"

"If anyone else had said that, I'd have laughed." He wheezed, clutching his stomach. "An inch lower and you would have killed my grandchildren, Ti!"

She scowled and sheathed the blade. "I'm sorry."

"No you're not. You think I'm an idiot for grabbing you." He retorted, still curled around his stomach. He grinned wryly when she smirked at him, and made an effort to stand up straight. "Well, shall we call that a draw?"

"I won." She felt her lips twitching and made herself sound annoyed. "Why did you scare me, Walker?"

"I heard the news." He whispered loudly, and then looked up and down the empty hallway. "I had to talk to you before you left. I know that Seth's come back."

She shrugged and leaned back against the wall. "So what? I'll still come and visit. I'll tell you which of your rabbits would make the best stew."

He winced. "They're full of chemicals, Ti."

"Adds to the flavour." She replied, as she did every time. The man relaxed a little and slouched next to her.

"I wanted to tell you that I'll speak up for you, if you get accused of anything. I'll tell Seth that nothing happened."

She blinked at him, bewildered, and then blushed bright red as she recalled the only rumour Walker admitted he listened to. "Why do you want to do that? Nothing did happen! And Seth doesn't..." She clapped her hands over her mouth guiltily. Doesn't care. Her mind said, but she knew she could not say it. Seth's plan hinged on him being besotted with her, so she couldn't even whisper the truth.

"Seth doesn't know you." She managed. "There's no way he'd know if you were lying or not."

"Does he trust you?" Walker looked painfully earnest, but almost childish in his concern.

"He doesn't trust anyone." Tiria waved a hand grandly and then sighed. "Honestly, Walker, you have nothing to worry about. Nothing happened."

"But people are saying that I wanted it to." The man said, so softly that for a moment Tiria wondered if she had truly heard it. The mere suggestion of those words sent a chill up her spine. She didn't understand the feeling. It might have been fear, or surprise. Anything that made her life more complicated, she knew now, was putting her into even more danger. With his few words, Walker had also reminded her that he was in danger, too. Who knew what people were saying about their friendship?

Never mind that her heart thudded far too quickly for a sweet few seconds. There was no desire in it, only fear. She couldn't let anything happen to her only friend. The closer he was to her, the more he could be hurt. She had to push him away.

"I didn't want anything to happen." She said in a flat, dead little voice. It was true, but she hated herself for the cold, cruel words. Walker looked narrowly at her as she continued, "I'm glad we have nothing to lie about, and I'm more glad that nothing happened. I wouldn't lie with one of you soft, stupid city people for all the rabbit stew in the world."

He flinched, and then looked down at his feet. "As long as you're safe." He managed. "Let me know if... if you need me to speak for you, Ti."

"Tiria." She said coldly.

"Ma'am." He whispered, with a sick looking grin. Before she could reach out to him, he had turned on his heel and gone.

By the time she reached Seth's apartment, Tiria's mood had turned from fatalistic to deadly. She pounded on the door with the earnest hope that the wood would splinter, and when it refused she kicked it. Seth opened the door with a smile and waved her inside.

"I thought you didn't like acting like a savage." He quipped, ignoring her foul mood. Tiria threw herself into one of the chairs and, to her own horror, burst into tears.

"What's this!" Seth exclaimed, and the shock in his voice made her sob even harder. It wasn't right, that Walker knew her so completely and had been shoved away. It wasn't right that this man owned her life, and cared so little about it that he didn't even know she could cry. Tiria felt as if she was going to be sick, with both of them whirling dizzily in her head.

Oh god, his eyes... they had been so full of tears that they had shimmered, but he hadn't wanted her to see him cry. Even in his pain, he knew that a single tear would have been a risk. This place was a seething nest of venomous lice, and now that Tiria had felt them bite it was impossible to tell herself she didn't care.

She did care. She cared so desperately that she could feel her heart being torn into pieces.

A strange sensation caressed her cheek, and for an awful moment she thought that it was Seth. She pulled away in disgust, but the sensation stayed. Raising trembling fingers to her face, she felt the odd softness of spines and all of the fight drained out of her. George had made his clumsy way onto her shoulder, and his sticky tongue was carefully catching each tear as it ran down her face.

"I know." She told him. "I don't want people to cry, either."

The dragon looked at her quizzically, and then made a lunge for her face when she pulled him away. She planted him firmly on her knee, hearing Walker scolding her as if he were standing beside her. Too much salt!

I care. She thought again, and ran her hand over George's back. The frozen numbness of the last months bled away, and suddenly she saw the people she cared about in shining focus. There weren't many of them, and two of them glowed so brightly in her mind that she closed her eyes. Her mother, broken and desperate with the lows. Her brother, lost in the wilderness.

"I'll make a deal with you." She said out loud, knowing Seth was listening without needing to look. This time she knew that he would not dare to argue with her. The strength in her voice was her own, far beyond anything she had ever summoned before, and it scared her to feel it echoing in her body. Seth was silent, but he moved in front of her, and she raised her reddened eyes to meet his. "I'll help you, and in return, you will take me out of this place. You will do everything you can to help me find my family. If they're dead, we will bury them together. If they're alive, you will break our contract and let me leave with them."

He reached over, his hand open, and waited for her to grasp it. "Deal."

CHAPTER 9

As soon as the news spread that Seth had returned, the city turned into a flurry of activity. He was rarely in his rooms, always answering summons or going to show a specialist something he had scavenged from the wastes. The botanists were given seed pods, the scientists were handed ancient tubes of ointment and dull plastic tubs of pills. He even had books in his bag, although they were too heavy for him to have gathered more than three or four. Tiria resisted the temptation to leaf through the volumes. The man had a trick of appearing when she thought he was far away, and his sharp eyes didn't miss a trick. After two days she had grown used to sleeping curled up on the sofa, but she could not get used to being constantly watched.

She still had her chores. It was a relief to scrub floors since it gave her a few hours away from Seth. Even jobs she used to hate had their own charms; if she got absolutely filthy, she had a good excuse to visit the showers instead of going straight home. If she was sent to clean an extra room, then she made it last as long as possible. As the days dragged past she got used to coming home and seeing Seth standing up, moving past her to bolt the door shut as soon as she stepped off the mat. The dull clunk of the locks should have made her feel trapped, but it reminded her of the hatch clanging shut in her father's home. Strange, that his twisted memory should make her feel better, but it did. The sound cut her off from all of the petty viciousness behind it, and all that was left was herself and the stranger she pretended to understand.

One night she got home late, her hair still dripping from the showers. Seth looked up from the book he was reading, greeted her, and beckoned her over. Taking her elbow, he led her into the bedroom and then pointed at another door. Tiria blushed, pulling away. She had never even been into his room before; he had sternly forbidden her to bother him.

He pushed the door open and showed her a shower, as white and sterile as the decon rooms on the upper level. She laughed, mostly out of surprise, and looked up at the man enquiringly. He tried not to smile at her reaction and settled on his usual cold indifference.

"I'm tired of you keeping me up every night."

"Won't this make it worse?" She raised an eyebrow at him. "I'll have to come through your room."

"I'd rather that than keep the front door unlocked half the night." He folded his arms. "What part of *looking for murderers* makes you think staying out late is a good idea?"

She bit her tongue and then looked wickedly at him. "Just make sure you're not doing anything I shouldn't see." He reddened, and the girl relented. "Thank you, Seth."

Tiria thought that the new arrangement would make things worse, but after a few days she realised it was having the opposite effect. Now that she had seen his whole suite, Seth seemed much less mysterious. He ignored her when she was in his room. Tiria suspected that he had never been watchful; she had pinned suspicion onto the natural reluctance he had for sharing his rooms.

He had been alone for nearly a decade. His father had been killed when he was still a teenager, and although she heard whispers of women and affairs, even those had ended long ago. Most people could barely remember a time when Seth hadn't been alone, stalking the wastes like a ghost as the citizens trembled.

It was a ridiculous notion, but there was some truth to it; the man avoided the communal areas because whenever he was there, every eye would be on him. When he walked down a corridor people would fall into a hush, or whisper behind their hands. It was only in his rooms that he had any privacy, and so sharing them was a violation of his need for control.

Tiria sympathised, but she couldn't pity him. Over the years his loneliness had turned into cruelty, into the habit of looking down on the fearful and despising the curious. If he overheard gossip he would have a biting response, and if someone fell silent then he would goad them with his cold black eyes. When Tiria refused to be cowed by either of these, he had invented an uncertain, mocking side which sometimes made her want to slap him, but more often made her taunt him back.

They spent their time sniping at each other, but after a few weeks there was no malice in it. It turned into a kind of game, as they deliberately baited each other and wondered how the insult would turn around on them. Rarely - very rarely - one of them would surrender and hold their hands up in defeat. But usually their bickering lasted for days before they ran out of ammunition, and they were both far too proud to concede.

It was only when one of the barbs struck too close to home that the game would end. Then, they would spend hours or even days not talking to each other. The tense atmosphere made their close quarters unbearable.

The first time it happened, Seth had absentmindedly made a comment about Tiria's father which had made her whiten and recoil. If he had apologised then, then it might have healed the wound, but he only saw her pain when it was too late. For a few days she refused to meet his eyes, and returned to her old habit of staying out late and leaving early in the morning. The man struggled to find some way to apologise - an impossible task, when he had no chance to speak to the girl. Finally, he searched through his scavenged goods for a gift, or a bribe, or whatever the rats called pretty, useless things. Wrapping it carefully in thin paper, he wrote her name on the parcel and left it beside her sofa.

It took her a ridiculously long time to get home, and even longer to sound out the letters. He pretended to be asleep, but watched her through the doorway of his room. She opened the parcel and took out a silver bangle.

"This will catch the light. The savages would see me a mile away." She said, knowing he was watching her without looking up. He didn't make a sound, and she didn't look around. The girl got into her bed without another word, and her eyes closed. The next morning she stayed late to ate breakfast with him, and he saw the bracelet shining on her wrist.

"I thought you said you didn't like it."

"There are no savages down here." She said, idly taking another piece of toast. Biting into it, she shrugged. "Besides, I reckon its worth a few loafs of bread on the surface."

He coughed to hide a laugh and raised his coffee in a mocking toast. She smiled, and returned the gesture. Then he plonked the mug down and leaned forward, eyes black.

"Now, are you really stupid enough to let the rats know you've found solid silver?"

She grinned. The bickering was back.

There were a few things, though, that they never used against each other. Seth learned never to mention the girl's family, and in her turn she never asked about his. They also never teased each other about their plans. Whenever they spoke about Lawrence, or the committee, they were both so guarded that the most innocent question from the other could make them snap.

The last thing that they never argued about was their mockery of a marriage.

The vault seethed with gossip about it. When Seth had first brought Tiria to the city, he had disappeared so quickly that most people were convinced the whole thing was a joke. There was a rat, true, but there were other reasons that he could have had for bringing one home. Perhaps she knew too much, or she had information about one of the runaways. Perhaps he had traded her safety for someone's hiding spot. Either way, nobody really believed in the marriage story, however adamant the sentry was about what he had seen.

Once Tiria moved into Seth's apartments, everything changed. Suddenly, everyone believed they were together – if not married, then in some kind of arrangement. They lay the blame on the rat, of course. The usual gossip was that she was pregnant, and he was protecting his child – although, the rumour continued, who knew whose child it *really* was? Conception was difficult enough that they could understand the risk, although as the months passed and the girl's belly stayed flat that rumour died. In its place was a miscarriage, or worse, a lie that she had told to guarantee her safety. How Seth must hate her, the gossips said. She was a whore and a liar, which was bad enough, and a feral little rat, which was worse.

Walker told her all of the rumours, and more. He let her know who was inventing the most sordid stories. Tiria memorised their names and reported them back to Seth, but the man shook his head. No-one on the list had any reason to harm either of them. They were simply gossips, not people trying to raise trouble.

Seth heard the worst of the rumours, and then took steps to create a story of his own. Like all of his plans it was meticulously thought out, and he followed it with a precision which almost made it bearable for Tiria.

The hunter took his wife to meetings and gatherings, so that they would be seen together. Sometimes she simply had to sit with him in the front row and be seen. Other meetings were more embarrassing. The vault had a wealth of group counselling sessions, classes and even religious gatherings. Tiria had to mumble the words of ancient blessings and thank the priest for the benevolent peace the chapel gave her. Her cheeks ached with all of the fake smiles and she wanted to spit the sentimental drivel off of her tongue. She wasn't pleased to meet them. She wasn't happy to share her thoughts with the group. Peace was only with them because they were leaving people outside to rot.

Seth was a far better liar than she was, but she got the sense that he wasn't having to try so hard. He had already proven he had no qualms about touching her, while she still felt a searing wave of embarrassment every time she accidentally brushed against him in their rooms. He had opinions about every inch of her body, criticizing her if she hadn't brushed her hair or fastened her top shirt button. Tiria stubbornly ignored him, and found herself watching him just as keenly so that she might return the favour. The result was that she became painfully self-conscious. He finally agreed to an embarrassed truce after she caught him with his fly unbuttoned.

One morning they attended a meeting where the kitchens were asking for any new recipes. Tiria whispered to Seth that she ought to teach them how to make hundred-year-old baked beans edible, and he immediately volunteered her to go onto the stage.

"This isn't time for one of your jokes!" She hissed. He narrowed his eyes at her, his usual challenging look.

"You're here to talk about the wastes." Seth said under his breath. "Don't make this personal, you idiot."

Normally that would have made her back down, but she was in no mood for it. She stood on the stage and spoke nervously about food in the wastes, but the whole time she glared at Seth. Afterwards, the citizens giggled behind their hands and made comments about the loving couple.

That night, after they had locked the door, Seth didn't retreat into his room but beckoned Tiria to the fire. She thought he was going to yell at her and readied herself to shout back, but instead he met her eyes levelly.

"We can't keep arguing in public."

"Other people do it all the time."

"We're not other people." He sighed and shook his head. "We can't be emotional about anything we do, or they might use it against us. If I have to keep explaining to you why we're doing this, then sooner or later it'll get back to the committee."

"You and your stupid plans." She muttered, and then sighed and scratched her head. "Alright."

"Alright." He echoed and then held out his hand. She reached out to shake it, and squeaked when he abruptly pulled her upright. His eyes dancing, he let her go. "Now, we need to work on our marriage, little wife."

She folded her arms, trying not to look as defensive as she felt. He noticed the gesture - of course - and patted her shoulder. "Don't worry. I can't read you any better than you can read me, but we need to make it look like we can. It has to be believable."

They looked each other in the eye, and then broke down into helpless laughter. It was ridiculous. Tiria shook her head and wandered over to the bookshelf, running her fingers along the spines.

"People don't stand in front of each other and say *let's act married.*" She said archly. "They just live their lives with each other."

"You're right." He sat on the arm of the sofa and kicked his heels against the floor like a child. The woman pulled a face at him and gestured to the bookshelf.

"Let's pretend I'm in the library and I'm trying to choose a book, and you decide to do... the... husbanding thing."

"Ready, steady, go?" He murmured, grinning.

"Bite me."

"I don't think that's something wives ask in public." He stood up and dodged when she swiped at him.

"If you're going to be an ass I won't play your stupid game."

Seth ruffled the girl's hair and made a great show of looking at the shelves. "What kind of book are you looking for, my love?"

"I'm not sure, *dearest.* I just finished *Persuasion.*"

"Ah, I always knew you were a romantic." He declared, and made a great show of looking over the books. Out of the corner of his mouth, he muttered, "Ask me what books I like."

"Seth," She caught his arm and smiled sweetly up at him. "What was your favourite book when you were young?"

"I'm so ancient I've forgotten." He replied, "But when I was young-'er' I liked *Wuthering Heights.*"

"I'd like to read that, too. Then we can talk about it. I'd love to know what you daydream about." She kept her sweet smile and pecked him on the cheek. "Is it an absolutely romantic story?"

"It's charming. It starts with a brutal old man seeing the ghost of a woman he damned to hell."

She grinned and the act fell away. "That does actually sound pretty good. Do you have a copy?"

Seth reached up to the top shelf and took down a very battered book. At first, Tiria thought it was one that had been rescued from the wastes. Then she saw the laser-cut sharpness of the vault's printing press. It would have been written down from a recovered book and then re-printed. Seth had read it so many times the cover had nearly fallen off.

"Be careful with it." He said, handing it to her without hesitating. Tiria took it, but she didn't open the delicate pages.

"Are you sure?"

He looked at her and surprise crossed his face. He wasn't surprised by her, Tiria saw in a flash, but stunned by his own actions. His fingers twitched as if he wanted to take the book back, but then he nodded. She held the book a little closer, and reached up, and this time when she kissed his cheek she did it with genuine gratitude.

"Thank you." She said, and darted away before he changed his mind.

After that, Seth made their 'marriage' feel like a game where she simply had to play along. Tiria still struggled, but their newfound friendship made it much easier. She told herself not to blush when he touched her. Holding hands was no different from when he handed her food over their dining table, or passed her a book so that he could help her sound out a word. The grateful kiss had broken through her shyness, and that meant that she could do it again. It helped her to think of every kiss as the same simple gesture and not as a lie.

Tiria did notice something odd about their game. When she was alone with Seth she wasn't shy at all, but whenever they were playacting in public, she felt as clumsy as she had on the night when he'd found her. She knew that there was no point in feeling that way, but that face didn't do much to help. Every time she tried to do something she felt awkward, and when the man casually sat beside her or looped his arms around her shoulders she felt her cheeks heating. For once, her husband had the tact not to tease her about it, but Tiria found it so humiliating that she would duck into the bathroom and run her hands under the icy water until they were completely numb. She would have dunked her head in, too, but it would have looked peculiar.

Her blushes were convincing enough to send more rumours through the underground tunnels. Nobody doubted that she was in love when they saw her redden at Seth's lightest touch. The man himself was far more enigmatic, but the whisperers would have expected nothing less. While he remained aloof, they did notice him leaning close to whisper to the girl, and smiling when she stood up in meetings and spoke to the groups.

Seth seemed intent on encouraging the little rat to become a normal human being, even going so far as to escort her to the seamstresses and help her choose clothes which were pretty rather than functional. His determination was utterly eclipsed by Tiria's. She devoted herself to blending in. Her long hair grew darker as the sun-streaks faded, and her light brown skin softened and took on a healthy sheen. Her eyes were as piercing as ever, but there was a new gentleness in the way that she moved. Tiria could have told the gossips that she tiptoed because she was scared of tripping over in the heeled shoes that vault women wore, but it wasn't important.

Eight months after she arrived in the vault, people started greeting her with no idea of who she really was. When the girl was at work she was as insipid as always, but people began to stop her to ask after her health. The rat would have scurried away or snapped at them. The woman answered them in a friendly, if stilted, voice. She smiled at their questions, and told them about her life outside of the shining corridors.

People began to gather around her in the canteen. The rat's stories were fascinating. They giggled about them, and teased her for making up such fantasies. Tiria tolerated the shallow idiots for as long as she could, but it was rare for her to finish her meal without wanting to shake one of the jeering citizens. When she slammed her tray down and stormed out of the room they assumed she was running back to Seth, eager to spend the rest of her lunch break with the man she loved. Tiria heard the citizens guessing the sordid things that filled the time, and her blushes were always so obvious that the gossips said they must be true. Their laughter followed her down the corridors and straight into the blessed quiet of the science labs.

The girl spent every lunch time playing with the dogs and teaching George to paddle in the metal sinks. She spent every afternoon avoiding the citizens meaningful looks, and by the time Seth took her to one of the evening meetings she was always itching to shout obscenities across the crowded rooms. Then, Seth would whisper a joke into her ear, or pull his chair a little closer than it needed to be, and somehow that made everything feel more like a game again.

CHAPTER 10

What did Seth do during the days? Tiria would come home to find half of the room rearranged. Maps were drawn, covered in untidy black letters, and then recycled in a dizzying whirl. The dog either looked exhausted or bored, and the room was either spotless or filthy. Mechanical devices appeared and disappeared, and weapons gained bright, sharp edges before becoming mysteriously blunt.

Once, the girl opened the door and nearly tripped over a neat line of metal locks which were set out like a train track. A chipped stopwatch was clicking away on the table. Seth was hunkered over the line picking each lock in turn. When he finished he snapped off the clock, swore fluently, and then kicked the locks into the corner.

"Most of them are rusty." Tiria said helpfully. "You can just chip through them with a file."

"That takes too much time, and it's noisy." Seth snapped, and started lining the locks up again. Tiria nudged one a few inches to the left and earned a glare. Shrugging, she headed into the bedroom and dug her book out from the crowded shelf. Flinging herself down onto the bed, she started to lose herself in *Wuthering Heights.* Cathy was just sneaking off with Heathcliff onto the open moors when a shadow fell across the page.

"That's my bed." Seth said. Tiria made a great show of marking her page before she looked up.

"I would have read in my room, but it was full of your ego."

He sighed. "Stay there if you want to. I'm going out."

"Out?" She echoed absently, and then her eyes opened wide. "You mean *out,* out?"

The man nodded and gestured towards the other room. That was clearly enough of an explanation for him, and Tiria didn't actually care. She shoved herself upright and caught at his shirt. "You're taking me with you."

"I'm only going for a few hours, and you're hiding from the terrifying savages, remember?"

She bit her lip and sat back, deflated but not defeated. "Nobody will see me."

He ignored that. "I'm going to break some more locks out of the doors in the city. I only want to spend a few minutes out there. If I take you then you'll probably run off or go exploring, and I don't have time for that."

Seeing that his blasé words had hurt her, he smiled apologetically and reached out. Tiria flinched, but he only touched her cheek with his fingertips before drawing away. "I'm sorry, Ti. I know it's difficult for you to stay here. It will feel so much worse the next time you come back, believe me. Imagine going through decon again, but this time you know you're months away from seeing another sunset. I have to force myself to crawl through that hatch, and I don't love the wastes as much as you do. They were never my home."

She was silent for a long time, and then her eyes turned a little watery. "I didn't think you cared how I felt. You're only saying that so I don't try to run away."

"Whatever you say." He shook his head. "Forgive me for being candid."

"I don't know what 'candid' means. I just want to breathe real air."

"You will, just not today." The man stood up. Tiria chewed her lip, and then brushed a traitor tear away. Forcing herself to smile, she waved a mocking hand at him.

"If you die, I'm keeping all your junk. Stay away as long as you like." She threw herself back onto the bed and laughed at his annoyed expression.

"It's not junk. Get off my bed."

"Take me with you."

"Goodbye, Tiria." He turned on his heel and raised his chin arrogantly into the air before he left. Tiria heard him suppressing a laugh from the other room, and then the door clicked closed.

She lay still for a moment, barely feeling the soft fabric under her bare arms. The mischievous thrill of breaking the rules suddenly seemed so childish that she wanted to cry. There was nothing worth smiling about. The story she had been reading was about people who had never even lived, and yet they got to run in the wind and feel the sunlight on their skin. She was real – a solid, breathing person – but she wasn't allowed to feel anything, or go anywhere. She felt so insignificant that she raised her hand in front of her eyes and half expected it to fade before her eyes. It did – shimmering and blurring – but then the welling tears spilled down the girl's cheeks and she started to sob.

Her whole world was Seth's plan, and her role in his creation was to lie. She couldn't say or do anything which wasn't a part of that lie. With no truth to cling to, she was frightened that she was losing herself entirely.

Seth came back even sooner than he had promised. He smelled like chemical soap – an almost overpowering wave of sterile pointlessness.

He shook Tiria's shoulder impatiently, thinking that she had fallen asleep on his bed. When she raised her head he saw her tear-reddened eyes, and stepped back. He looked almost guilty, if such a thing were possible. Tiria couldn't make herself speak to him. His cleanness offended her. If he had smelled of dust or metal she could have at least shared in that.

The man watched her uncertainly. He found it hard to believe that she could be homesick for rotting ruins. The vault held heat, light, water and food. It educated and nurtured its citizens, who lived for decades longer than the rats. Surely, Tiria knew that the vault was a better place than the wastes. He felt as if she was insulting his home by detesting it so obviously, but he was too fond of her to be angry. Biting back his first, tetchy words, he sat down beside her.

"You would have run away." He couldn't help himself, the words were already spoken before he thought of them. She sniffed loudly and looked away from him. The man frowned, and then his voice grew quiet. "I honestly had no idea you were still so unhappy here."

"I'm not unhappy. I'm not anything." She croaked, and then buried her face back into the mattress with a sob. "I'm not doing anything except breathing and waiting for the air to run out."

"You're..." He struggled for the right word. "...bored?"

She groaned and punched the pillow. "You don't understand. I can't be bored. I can't be *anything*. There's nothing down here that lets me be myself."

The man looked puzzled, and then he made an odd noise and scrubbed at his face with his palms. "There's a gale blowing outside. The dust nearly burned my skin off. I didn't get far before I had to turn around." He held out his arm, and Tiria finally raised her head to peek at the burns on his hands.

"You should have worn gloves, or tucked your hands into your armpits." She cleared her throat and managed to sound scornful. "My mother would have flayed me twice over for being stupid enough to go out in a dust storm."

He smiled crookedly and scratched at the marks. "I am sorry, Ti." He said softly. "I didn't know you were homesick."

"What's that?" She asked, and when he explained she laughed shortly and shook her head. "I don't miss father's shelter. I miss having the freedom to... to do things the way I've always done them. Outside I know that whatever happens, I can survive it. I know what to say and what to do. I don't need anyone's help to survive out there, I can make my own choices and fight for them. What can I do down here?"

Tiria gestured around at the room, and then scowled and made the motion wider to draw in the whole vault. When Seth met her eyes she drew a shaking breath and then smoothed out an unfortunate crease on the cover of her abandoned book. "I like playing games, and tricking the council, but so would a hundred other rats. You could get any woman to be your puppet, and lots of them wouldn't make as many mistakes as I do. You said you chose me for this – and that you needed me – but nothing in the Tiria you created has anything to do with who I really am."

"That's why I lock the door." Seth said shortly, and then stood up. "We can't just keep running into the wastes whenever we get sick of lying."

"We?" She echoed. He blinked and met her eyes for a second, and then gave her a sick smile.

"I actually care what these people think of me."

"I care."

"Don't bother pretending around me. I've never lied to you about being a bitter, arrogant asshole. As soon as that door locks we don't even have to look at each other. Be whoever you want to be. But I can hardly smuggle you onto the surface every time Agni makes you angry."

"Oh, and going up to scavenge old locks..."

"Fair point, but I wasn't going to the surface to transform into a nicer man!" His words were still sharp, but his eyes sparkled with sudden laughter. Tiria felt herself smiling automatically, and had to bite her lip to keep from looking foolish. Months later, when she knew Seth better, she wondered how much of his nonsense he actually believed. At the time she was convinced that his first excuse – that he didn't want her to run away – was the only one he truly cared about. He seemed to pick up emotions like dust, and shake them off just as indifferently. It made him impossible to read. While Agni and Walker let their thoughts spill from every word and gesture they made, Seth absorbed the opinions of whoever he was speaking to and reflected them like a pool of still water. So Tiria believed that he understood, or at least that he sympathized, and resigned herself to more months trapped under the lifeless earth.

Her blushes became fewer, because Tiria found herself watching Seth in a different way. She admitted to herself that her body felt odd when he met her eyes. It became easier to separate that unbidden feeling with the lies they were play-acting. She could tell when Seth was lying to the citizens, and so she started trying to work out when he was lying to her. His eyes would lift at the corners as if he was trying not to smile, and his hands would open wide in a pantomime of innocence. When he pretended to be angry, he let his voice tremble with the laughter he couldn't betray. Everything seemed to amuse him, even Tiria's frustration at the endless lies she had to memorise.

When they locked the door to their room she always expected the laughter to fade from his face, but even when he was rude and withdrawn he still looked at her with bright eyes. It was because he was handsome, she told herself, or because he was mocking her. She blushed at the thought, because she hadn't even hesitated over the word *handsome.* What had made her mind fix onto something so ridiculous?

Tiria had thought Seth was thin and weather-worn. Perhaps the strip lighting suited him better, or his clean clothes. Her opinion of him, she told herself, had not changed. Still, she kept watching him, and eventually convinced herself that the reason he looked happy was because he genuinely enjoyed her company. He had despised her outside of the vault, and had deliberately avoided her for the first few months. Now that she had broken through his isolation Tiria thought that she had won some twisted gift. He was not her friend, because neither of them were capable of it, but at least they saw each other through open eyes.

The fact that Seth confided in her made Tiria feel warm inside. She remembered it sometimes, when he met her eyes after a particularly outrageous lie. She kissed him more tenderly on those days, and felt her body soften when he held her close.

For a few weeks they kept the act up even as they walked back to their rooms, enjoying the playfulness more than their lifelong sullen silences. During a meeting where they had been teasing each other and laughing like lovers, Tiria forgot that it was a lie. There was no deceit in it; she was laughing because she was happy, and she was happy because she was spending time with her friend. He never laughed or smiled with other people. After so many weeks of arguing with herself, she finally convinced herself that Seth must feel the same warmth that she did.

It took her days to summon the nerve to ask him. In the end she waited until he was sitting by the fire, and she curled up against him as she had a hundred times before in their game. He stiffened, and put his book down.

"What are you doing?"

"I..." She blushed, and then forced the words out. "I was wondering if you were... if we could..."

He stopped her, quite gently, placing his hand on her shoulder. "Don't get confused."

"I'm not confused. I..."

"You are confused. You know we're not here for that."

"But I *am*." She objected, and when his eyes hardened she knew she had said too much. She hadn't even been thinking about their contract until the words came out, but once they were spoken they couldn't be taken back. He stood up and pushed her away, and all the gentleness in him vanished.

"Don't you dare even *mention* that ballot," He growled, "God forbid you come to me for your *own* sake. I might have listened to that. Don't you understand anything about... about..."

"No." She interrupted him flatly. "You were supposed to teach me."

He stared at her in silence, and then a look of such disgust crossed his face that she had to look away. When she dared look up, he had stalked away into his room and slammed the door behind him.

For the next few days their act was mechanical and dull. Seth cancelled as many meetings as he could, preferring to disappear into the depths of the city than to even look at his wife. Tiria pretended that she didn't care, and spent her time working harder than ever.

She seethed under her calm mask. She wasn't *confused*. The warm, writhing feelings she felt around Seth were crystallised. She knew her friendship with him was a fact, and that he trusted her. She wanted him to acknowledge that certainty as much as she wanted him to understand her need for it. She wanted the facts to eclipse the lies until she couldn't tell which was which.

Seth was the one who was confused. He had shaped her lies for so long that he had no idea when she was telling the truth.

She wasn't hurt by Seth's rejection. She had been expecting it. After all, he had never shown her that he actually wanted her. Even as she thought that, a memory surfaced and made her stomach tighten. He had, once. When he had left her here, he had touched her. She remembered the hardness of his hands, so unlike the soft pretence of the past few months. She remembered that there had been heat, not laughter, in his dark eyes. And she remembered how her heart had raced before she had torn herself free.

If you came to me for your own sake, I might have listened. He had said, and his voice had been raw with anger. *Maybe I shouldn't go,* he had murmured a lifetime before, and she had shoved him away.

He had laughed when he left, and she hated him for it. Her loathing settled into the pit of her stomach, and she felt it burning through her veins like searing molten gold.

CHAPTER 11

For three days Tiria avoided her husband. She spent so much time in the science labs that even Walker noticed, and chased her away. Without his company she slowed down, taking twice as long to finish her work. She loitered in the communal showers after each shift, fighting against her confusion and turning up the temperature until the water had burned her skin. She had to force herself to leave the smothering steam. Walking back along the sterile corridors made her head ache. Opening the door made her heart pound. Every night it was like pushing open a scavenger's hatch, expecting to be looking into the wrong end of a gun.

She was almost right; on the fourth day Seth was pacing furiously across the carpet. "Where have you been?" He demanded, and dragged her in before she could think of an answer. "I've been waiting for you."

"Then you should have sent a message." She snapped at him, shaking her arm free. "Or come and found me yourself. I'm not a stray dog."

His mouth thinned, but he started bolting the door shut. The familiar action calmed him down a little. "We've been invited to a dinner."

"What's a one of them?" Tiria thought back to the sumptuous parties in *Jane Eyre* and her eyes shone. "Do you mean a banquet?"

He blinked, and then barked out a rough laugh. "Yes, if you insist. We have to dress up and... mingle." He muttered the last word with a darkness which made Tiria laugh. If anyone could make a banquet sound like a funeral it was Seth. She combed out her damp hair and buttoned her jacket back up.

"Well, shall we go?"

Seth shook his head. "It's tomorrow, Ti."

"Oh, then you didn't need to yell at me." She folded her arms and glowered. "Apologise."

He scowled at her and Tiria planted her hands on her hips, feeling like simply folding them didn't show that she was impatient enough. "Well, what is it?"

"Agni delivered the invitation. She was quite keen to tell me how much time you've been spending with another man."

"So? What do you care?" She waved her hand diffidently and turned away. He growled and grabbed her wrist.

"For the *hundredth time*, Tiria, our whole plan hinges on..."

"It hinges on you being in love with me, not the other way around." She pointed out icily. She suddenly felt sick, as if all of her anger had boiled in her stomach and sent white hot heat into her veins. "You're the one who brought me home. Most of your friends think I tricked you into it. Rats don't feel love, did you know that?"

"Don't spout their nonsense at me." He shook her. "It *has* to go both ways. If people think you tricked me, it makes me look weak. If people think you don't respect me, then they won't respect me."

"Apart from that, though, you don't care? Let's not get *confused* here."

He fell silent, and let her go. Tiria shook blood back into her hand and swallowed back the bitter taste in her mouth. She had secretly hoped that Seth might find out that she had been hiding with her old friend over the past few days. Somewhere deep down, she wanted to know if he'd be upset. Their argument had made her feel... odd. She hadn't been able to work out his thoughts or forgive him, but each morning she had woken up thinking of him, her body feeling far too warm under her soft blanket, and wondered what might have happened if she had said a few different words. Now, Seth had heard the rumours - and he was hurt - but for all the wrong reasons.

"I didn't do anything I shouldn't have." She said quietly, suddenly tired of the whole thing. "Walker is my friend. I stole George from him. While you were gone he taught me how to read. I didn't want to be here after... after you shouted at me, so he let me help out in his lab. He doesn't even know we fought; I told him you were working and didn't want to be bothered."

Seth narrowed his eyes at her, but now there was a shade of doubt in them. It wasn't until he sat down that Tiria felt confused. Surely he should still be angry? She tried another question. "It doesn't mean there aren't still rumours. What do you want to do about them?"

He looked at her and shook his head slowly. "I don't know."

She scoffed. "You always know."

"No!" He gave her a scathing look. "I don't know if I believe you, Ti. I don't give a rat's ass about the rumours; I just need to know that nothing happened."

"I guess it'll prove that I respect you, or something." She muttered sarcastically. He shook his head again and rubbed his temples as if they ached.

Tiria waited, not at all sure what he was thinking about, until he looked up and his eyes met her own like a burning coal. "What is it about you, Ti? I barely know you. How do you read me so well?"

"I don't know what you mean." She said. He laughed.

"I mean that you're right. I've dealt with worse nonsense with one eye closed, and it shouldn't have bothered me. But the second I heard it, I was livid. It makes no sense. Your friend has only seen you for a few measly hours this week, and I'm jealous of that. If he had touched you I feel like I would have strangled him."

"Don't do that. He's an awful fighter." Tiria replied, feeling as if her voice was drifting somewhere above her head. She chewed her lip for a second and then asked, "Did you get angry while Agni was there?"

"No." He shook his head scornfully. "I have more self-control than that."

"She wanted you to get angry." The girl replied. "She told me weeks ago that she was going to tell you about me and Walker. She knows it's nonsense, too. But she wanted you to get angry."

"I'm not angry." He stood up and ran his hand through his hair, fitfully messing it up. "I'm trying to figure out how to fix this."

"Stop what?" She asked again, frustrated. "I told you that nothing happened!"

"No that, you idiot!" He returned angrily. "Don't act like you don't know what I'm talking about! I can't risk your life if I'm in love with you!"

She gasped and pressed her hands to her face. It felt as if her heart was dropping into the ground, as if the almighty pressure in the earth was crushing her and holding her at the same time. "You're not." She said in a small voice. "You're pretending."

"I wish I was." He growled. Pacing to his desk, he searched through a stack of papers and then cursed and slammed the folder shut. "Ti, you need to make me hate you."

"No." She said, raising her chin stubbornly. He turned on her. There was a glimmer of something vicious in his eyes when he pressed her:

"Why? Because the ballot forbids it?"

"Forget the stupid ballot. You had your chance to hate me and you made me suffer for it. I won't help you now just so you can act all superior again."

Seth made a frustrated sound and started pacing again. Tiria resisted the urge to throw something at him. She took George out of her shirt, using the time to calm her racing heart and give herself a chance to think. Her heart refused to slow. She crouched down next to the fire and set the lizard in his nest beside the blaze, watching him cuddle into the warm fabric.

Her fingers were trembling, she noticed in a detached way. She had been willing this to happen, and now she was completely numb to it. Somewhere in her mind she was crying, or screaming, or laughing - some deep, intractable pain which was so raw that she couldn't even recognise it. Somewhere, she knew what to say.

The part of her that sat by the fire stared at the animal, who she loved. She knew that she loved George. She could hear it in words, in the part of her mind which was indifferent to the way that her skin burned. She could understand love when her heart fluttered with tenderness; it raced with Seth. She had no idea why her body spun towards the agonies of fear when her dreams held her in his arms. She had no words for that, and so she sat beside the fire and said nothing at all.

The books she had been reading had held something of the mystery, but they made it far richer and more puzzling than she had ever believed it could be. It was always held in words, embraced by the sharp pointed letters until all of its passion bled away. Rats had no words for it, and they never turned it into stories. She loved her brother, she loved her mother. They kept her alive. She was not supposed to love anyone else.

The ballot was cold and impersonal to prevent it; the pain and anger of losing a loved one was far beyond the control of any law, and love tied together couples whose tempers, weaknesses or infertility should have broken them apart years before. There was nothing practical about it. She agreed with Seth fervently over that, at least. So why had he used that word, when it meant nothing and spoiled everything?

"What does it feel like?" She asked, unable to look around. He stopped pacing and she heard him scratching his stubble irritably.

"What?"

"Love." She said the word as if it tasted foul in her mouth, and then shook her head when he made a scoffing sound. "I don't know what I should say to you."

He crouched down beside her, took her chin in his hand, and looked searchingly into her eyes for a long moment. She stayed quite still, wondering if he could feel her heart racing under his fingertips, until he let her go. Whatever he had been looking for had apparently satisfied him - she wasn't mocking him, or being crude. She was genuinely curious. He sat cross-legged on the other side of the hearth and leaned his head back against the sofa, tapping his fingers fitfully on the floor.

"You don't have to say anything to me, Ti. I shouldn't have said anything to you."

"Oh, because I'm not involved?" Her voice was sharp, and she had no interest in softening her words. "I was going to stay away, this time. I didn't want to come back. You hurt me. Don't argue, for god's sake. I don't think I'd trust a word you said. And I hate you too much to try."

He didn't flinch, but an icy coldness settled into his eyes. "Are you afraid of me?"

She laughed, and the brittle sound finally made him look away. "You want that, don't you? I won't pretend to be a coward just to soothe your wounded pride. No, I'm not frightened of you. I never was. I didn't care who you were or what you wanted until you left me here, and then I learned how to hate you. I wanted you to come home so I could scream at you, or else make you touch me again, anything so that all of the things we left unsaid could at least have an ending. God, I loathe you. You're as low and sly as a snake - worse, because you wanted to drag me into the dirt with you. But I wasn't afraid of you."

Seth looked away. His eyes were quite unreadable in the red light, and Tiria wrapped her arms defensively around her knees. "I feel like I know you better than any of the people here, because we're the only ones who have been outside. And I guess I don't know you at all, because I don't understand what you're trying to do now. I think there are two of you. I hate one of them. I hate him so much my stomach hurts. But the other one makes me feel..." She stopped, shrugged, and then picked restlessly at a splinter on the floor. "I don't know. That's when my words run out. So that's why I'm asking you."

"Are you asking the version of me that you hate?" He asked, smiling crookedly. She shrugged.

"Whichever bothers to answer first. If you're an ass about it I may hit you over the head with something."

"Go ahead. Do you really think I'll let you insult me without returning the favour?" He pulled a face at her, and Tiria was relieved to see that his leaden mask had softened back into the mocking smile she remembered. She raised her eyebrows and gestured for him to continue. Seth counted off his insults on his fingers.

"You're a brainwashed, bitter little rat who made it far too difficult to walk across the wastes. You fight like a demon and you are stubborn to a fault, but you love your family so much you surrendered everything you have just for a slim hope of finding them again. You have no self-esteem, because you think your value comes from finding them. Frankly, I find the whole thing sickening. I refuse to believe a woman as clever and fierce as you can be such an idiotic martyr."

"If you're going to insult me, at least use words I understand." She murmured. He blinked at her, and then waved a hand vaguely.

"I'm trying to explain what I hate about you."

"Oh, I'm already blushing. Carry on."

He scowled at her for using her falsely-affectionate voice, then scratched his chin and looked away. "I don't understand how you can be so driven to help another person, when you come from a world where even living into your teens is a miracle. I've never seen anybody fight so hard to act like they don't care, when inside they're overflowing with that kind of... of..."

"Love." She supplied. "I love my family."

"Then why ask me what it feels like?"

"I just don't know why you suddenly decided to do it. I loved my brother since the day I was born. I never had to choose to do it. When I think about you I can only see questions. I could argue with myself for years and still I wouldn't be sure if I loved you or..." she bit her tongue and looked away.

"That's exactly what it is." He said, and just like that he stood up. His voice grew bitter. "I can't stop arguing. It's burning me up. I've been working for years to get this far, and I refuse to throw it away just to protect a stubborn little rat."

"Wait!" She scrambled to her feet and followed him. He stopped and looked down at her, and she resisted the urge to stand on her toes so that they would at least be closer in height. He waited while she struggled for words, and then gave up.

"What is it, Ti? Some deal you want to make?"

"Shut up." She growled, and then reached up and kissed him. She had no idea where she had found the courage to do it, her hands shook when she touched him, and when she drew herself closer she expected him to push her away.

It was like she remembered, except far more frightening - far darker - far more real, because when his arms closed around her it was because he wanted to pull her against him, not because they were fighting. And then he was kissing her back, and all of her fear fled from her mind as her chest filled with warmth, and her heart raced. He did push her away, in the end. There was no fierceness left in his hands as they fell to her waist, but his eyes were full of white-hot anger.

"What is that going to cost me?"

"I'm not trying to trick you." She tried to pull him back, but he refused. Almost crying in frustration, she glared back into his eyes. "Can't you tell that this is real?"

"No." He stroked a strand of her hair behind her ear and then pulled it sharply, goading her to flinch away. When she refused, biting her lip, he kissed her forehead. His voice was rueful. "I'd let you try to convince me, but I suspect I'd be too willing to fall for it."

"Then why don't you convince me?" She demanded, ignoring the tear that was trailing down her cheek. "How do I know you're not trying to trick me? The last time you touched me you were just trying to make me angry."

His eyes narrowed, and he abruptly tangled his hand in her hair and pulled her to him, kissing her so fiercely that she caught her breath. When he let her go, he looked straight into her eyes. "I made you *angry*?"

"Furious." She shook her head. "I hated you for weeks."

"Weeks." He grinned and ran his fingers along her jaw line, stopping when she shivered. "I touched you once, and you were angry at me for weeks?"

"I still am." The girl pulled away and nearly shoved at him. "You never finished what you started."

He caught his breath and then pulled her back, holding her wrists quite loosely. "Think about this very carefully, Ti. If we do this, nothing else can change. I promise you, you'll get nothing else out of this. If you're doing this for a single other reason than because you truly want it, then we should stop right now."

"Should I ask you the same thing?"

"No." He looked a little mischievous. "I want you too much to play games with you."

She shivered and blushed. "I'm not trying to trick you. I want this."

"I don't believe you." He laughed, and drew her down with him to the carpet. Raising her shirt over her head, he trapped the girl's arms and moved down over her body, smiling when she caught her breath. His fingers moving heatedly over her skin, he pressed his lips to her throat and smiled at the sound of pleasure she couldn't quite bite back. "Convince me you want this, Ti."

She freed her arms, looping them around his shoulders, and arched up under him until she could crush herself against him. In the heat and the darkness of it she wondered how he could speak.

She wondered how he could breathe, or think, and then he moved into her and she couldn't wonder at all.

CHAPTER 12

The banquet was a stunning affair.

"Don't call it a banquet." Seth hissed for the fifteenth time. Tiria gave him an arch look and ignored him.

The largest room in the city was the canteen, but the pale concrete walls were barely recognisable in the soft lights which had been placed around the walls. They weren't candles, Tiria realised, but rather electrical lights designed to flicker and glow. It must have taken someone a long time to work out how to make them, she thought – and they gave off so little light that they weren't practical. Why not just use real candles?

"Try to set your dress on fire with a light bulb." Seth suggested when she asked. Seeing her scowl, he made a shooing motion. "Remember to drop and roll."

"I bet you don't even know the right answer. Who should I talk to?" Tiria asked. The man thought for a moment, and then nodded towards a woman in a green dress. Tiria memorised the woman's face and then made her way slowly through the room alone.

Her dress was difficult to walk in. She had found out that all of the clothes here were made from recycled fabrics, which had been pulped and boiled and washed so many times that they had gained that ethereal softness which she found so breath-taking. Unfortunately, the women of the city had retained their love of long, flowing evening dresses, and so the room was full of volumous skirts which tangled around their ankles rather than slipping smoothly down their milk-white legs.

God only knew where Seth had found her own dress. The one thing more amazing than the fact that it fit, was the speed with which her lover had stripped it from her body after she tried it on. It clung in the most awkward places and revealed parts of her body which had never even seen the sun. It was a soft, chalky red which made the rich colour of her skin even more obvious. Seth clearly approved - she felt his eyes on her more than once - but Tiria wished she could knot the silly thing up into something more practical.

"The savages will come through the ducts." She whispered, remembering what she told Walker and looking up with a smile. "And we'll have to set out skirts on fire to smoke them out."

Seth wanted her to be obvious, she thought with a resigned sigh. Making her way over to the woman in the green dress, Tiria fiddled with her hair and coughed until she turned around. The woman's kindly face froze when she looked at the girl.

"Oh." She said.

"I'm Tiria."

"I know."

The girl puffed out her cheeks and whistled softly. "Well, that's a relief. I thought I'd have to introduce myself to every idiot in this room. What's your name?"

"Mrs Parr." The woman made no move to shake her hand or smile. Tiria knew that using their second name was the way that the city people made themselves seem aloof. Many of them only used their first name with their friends. Her people changed their families enough that second names had no way to continue - if they followed their name with anything, it was usually their score. Tiria Fifty Five guessed her name was technically Mrs Kearney, since it was Seth's second name - but she couldn't make it fit.

"It's a nice party, isn't it? I haven't seen this many people all shoved in together since the ballot."

The woman raised her nose into the air. "Do you really think it's polite to talk about that here?"

"The ballot?" Tiria pretended to think about it. "I don't see why not. We go there every year, and we turn out okay."

"That's debatable." The woman said icily. Tiria grinned at her - the snide grin she had learned from Seth, and took a sip of the wine she had been handed as she walked in. It tasted metallic.

"We grow barley in the fields for beer." She said idly. "It tastes better than this stuff."

"Fields?" The woman looked a little incredulous. "Nothing grows in the wastes. You must be thinking of greenhouses or... or sewage works."

"No ma'am." She took another swig from her wine, enjoying this. "One you get outside the midlands, they say there's even green grass. You can sit in the fields and feel the wind in your face, and if you sit in the shade the sun doesn't feel as hot as it does in the ruins."

"You don't know what you're talking about." The woman said grandly, and then she glided away. Tiria watched her with her hands planted on her hips, thinking rapidly. It was true that she had never seen the fields herself, but everyone seemed so sure that they existed - and besides, there was always fresh bread in the market, if you had enough money to buy it. It cost the same as twenty turnips or five tins of food, so most people only had it as a rare treat – but it was there.

She ambled through the party, annoying the most pompous guests and telling them every detail of her life outside of the city. It was what she was supposed to do, but after an hour her throat was raw from prattling on. She pretended to be pleasant enough when she first met each person, slipping in comments as if she was making casual conversation, but as with the first woman she struggled. They were so determined to believe she was a liar, and when they were rude to her Tiria was happy to be rude in return. Some of them walked away when they saw her near them. Seth, the girl noticed irritably, was surrounded by men and women who were talking to him in eager voices.

Scavengers. She thought, loathing them. They want the things he brings back – toys, jewellery, books – anything apart from the truth. His family died waiting for the wastes to become safe, and all the worms care about are the spoils.

Seth saw her glowering at him, scowled back, and returned to talking to a chubby man who wore a forced smile on his clean-shaven face. It was one of the officials, Tiria knew, but she had no idea what he was in charge of. Food, by the look of him.

Someone cleared their throat beside her. "You're Seth's girl, aren't you?"

She turned and gave the man an appraising look. "Most of you lot call me the rat."

"I've never seen a rat look so pretty," He said with a slight smile. "Forgive an old man for hoping you weren't married."

Tiria had never been flirted with before, so she was nonplussed by this. "You've never seen a rat at all."

He shrugged and beckoned for her to walk around the room with him. "I admit I never got as close to one of you as my nephew has, but the clansmen I met in my younger days were forthright enough. They just didn't think looking attractive was a practical use of their time."

"It's not. Seth made me dress up." She said, and then her mind caught up. "You're Seth's uncle?"

"Didn't he mention me?" The man rolled his eyes. Tiria grinned.

"You know Seth. He doesn't like giving away secrets - even the secrets everyone else already knows."

"Did he tell you why he's like that?" The uncle's eyes sharpened when she nodded and looked quickly around the room before lowering her voice.

"I know about his father."

"What did he tell..." The man straightened up and his voice became loud and jovial. "Seth, my dear! We were just gossiping about you!"

Seth stopped beside Tiria and glared – not at his uncle, but at the girl. "If you think this is a good use of your time, you're even more stupid than I thought."

"Maybe I should go and give necklaces to old men, like you do." She retorted, stung. "I was only talking to..."

"You're not here to talk to him. Especially not about me." The man's voice sharpened. "If I haven't made that clear enough you're welcome to go back to scrubbing the floors."

"Charming." The uncle murmured into his wine glass. Seth shot him a dark look, but didn't answer. Tiria grit her teeth and remembered what he had told her about loyalty, and about showing people that she respected him, and about nothing else changing outside of the four walls of their room. None of those thoughts were particularly comforting, and she felt her hand closing into a fist ready to hit him.

"Go on, pretty girl." The uncle said, smiling at her as if the whole thing was a joke. "Get yourself another drink and find your scientist friend. Leave us grumpy old codgers to argue in peace."

She gave Seth one last glare and left. The men watched her go with the same expression on their different faces, and then both tried to hide it when they looked back at one another. Without another word they parted, drifting back into the crowd.

Tiria was having trouble finding out anything that might be useful. She already knew that people would not talk to her, but she had hoped they would ignore her and let her eavesdrop, as they had when she was scrubbing their floors. Dressed in her silly gown, she was as awkward and obvious as a cat in a birdcage. Giving up, she slumped back against a wall and sipped grumpily from her wine. Even the drink seemed to have been chosen to annoy her; after just a few glasses of the sweet, tart liquid her head was buzzing.

There was another room off the main hall – a kitchen, Tiria knew, although she had never been told to work there. The catering official used horrified words like contamination when anyone suggested the rat even sweeping the floors. As she watched, her bored eyes saw people peeling away from the crowd and slipping nonchalantly through the door. If they had all left together she would have thought nothing of it – but why were they trying to be secretive? Tiria looked around for some way she could sneak in, but unless she went through that door there was no way. She slipped closer to the kitchen and rested back against the concrete divider, listening intently. She couldn't hear what they were saying through it, either.

Grinding her teeth, she looked around for an answer. Then she remembered something, gasped, and made her way out of the room altogether. Running down the corridor, she yanked open another door and hurtled into one of the cleaning cupboards. It was a tiny, rank room filled with brooms and mouldy buckets, but when she had worked here she remembered smelling fried bacon. Where would the smell come from, if not the kitchen? She clattered around in the dark for a few minutes until she thought to look up. There, on the ceiling, was a grate into the air vents.

She couldn't waste a second. Hauling one of the metal shelf units around, she clambered up the steps and pulled at the grate. It refused to budge, and she nearly cursed in frustration when the shelves wobbled. They shuddered, and she braced herself against the ceiling hard to steady them with a strangled shriek. The steps wobbled again, even more, and she realised that the ceiling was moving. The grate didn't pull down, it pushed up! She gasped and gripped the edge of the vent, pulling herself up onto her elbows just as the shelves crashed down to the floor. A fog of washing powder billowed up, and Tiria coughed and shook her head, trying to see. The powder stung her eyes, and she could only feel her feet dangling in the air. Then, in pure desperation, she threw out one hand and found the hard knot of a rivet on the floor. She dragged herself forward, her shoulder screaming with the effort, until she finally dragged her torso through the grate and lay, gasping, inside the duct.

It made a small tunnel. It wasn't so thin that she couldn't turn around in it, but it wasn't large enough for her to move quickly. She crouched and half-ran along it, smothering her coughs and choosing her route by instinct, not by conscious thought. She heard the swell of voices from the banquet below her, and kept going. Then the pipe got darker, and she stopped running and crept along to the next grate.

The kitchen was almost in complete darkness, but she could see there were several people gathered around each other. They had clearly been arguing for some time, their hushed voices roughened by drink. Tiria couldn't recognise a single voice in the slurred syllables, nor recognise the tops of their heads. They talked about things that didn't interest her for a long time, and she started to wonder if they simply disliked the noise and brightness of the other room. Then one of them said Seth's name.

"What are we going to do about him?" They asked, when they had the group's attention. Tiria peered down at him, but the man was just another nondescript shadow. "He has to be up to something."

"He's always up to something." Another man said, his voice a weary drawl.

"Yes, but... what about the girl?"

"What about her? If Seth likes screwing trash from the wastes, then let him."

"He doesn't want to tie himself to any of the families." Someone else cut in, their voice urgent. "We should have matched him with someone when Mara died – anyone, if only to keep him tied down. He's too dangerous to be left alone. If he turns on us, who does he have left to protect?"

"The rat?" Someone asked, and there were a few sniggers. Tiria felt her hands curling into fists, and forced herself to pay attention. She memorised the voices, the words, but the people all spoke over each other and her head started to ache. The urgent man tried to speak again, and after a while the others calmed down to hear him out.

"If we could ensure his loyalty, then all of this will be over." He said. "We have to make him understand that life in the city is worth protecting. That he can't... can't just bring filth and whores in and out whenever he feels like it. It's like he's laughing at us."

"Let me get this straight." Someone drawled. "You want to dictate everything Seth recovers from the ruins?"

"You can't salvage a savage. If that's what he's bringing in now, then what will it be next? A mutation?"

"So your plan to protect us is to parade your daughters in front of Seth."

The urgent man bristled. "There are hundreds of other pretty girls in the city."

"I'm sure you know that for a fact." Someone else muttered, and their neighbour failed to muffle her burst of laughter. Tiria wondered if they knew how stupid they sounded. Did they think Seth was so shallow? Then she heard what else they were saying. The other women had wealth, or powerful connections. They had proven they could bear living children. They... they...

Would her husband want those things? She had no idea. He was already wealthy, and well respected – but he seemed to be constantly on guard, watching for the next trick or arguing with one of the officials. She chewed her lip and wondered if he would prefer to be safe than get his revenge.

"We'd have to deal with the girl, first." One of the women said, as if she agreed with the urgent man. "What plans have been put in place?"

"She's under Seth's protection." A man said. "We can't touch her."

"And she's a feral little bitch." Another cut in. "I wouldn't want to be the one to do it."

"No, no. Are you all rats yourselves, to be so bloodthirsty?" A calming voice washed over them like water. Tiria relaxed a little, and then her blood chilled again when the man continued, "She's known to have a temper. If she is provoked into fighting... accidents happen. If she is killed, what a shame! If she hurts somebody... that's a crime." He paused, and his gaunt silhouette moved its shoulders in a shrug. "We'd be bound by law to execute her."

"What if Seth just goes out and gets himself another one?" Someone muttered, but most of the people were nodding at each other. Tiria felt her cheeks burning in anger, and backed out of the duct as silently as she could. Whatever they said next, she had no stomach to listen in. As she crawled back along the tunnel she heard them heading back into the banquet, and heard their cold, drunken voices joining in the revelry. Biting back nausea, she made her way back to the cleaning cupboard and sat there for a long time, dangling her legs into the open air.

She had no desire to re-join the party, so she righted the cupboard as best she could and then traipsed back to Seth's rooms. It was only when she got there that she realised that the door would be locked. Sighing, she sat down in the corridor and saw that her elaborate dress was covered in washing powder, with grease and dirt from the duct. Grimacing, she tried to rub some of it off and gave up, growling a curse.

"Clearly you had a more enjoyable evening than I did." A man drawled. Tiria shrugged.

"You don't want to make jokes, Seth. I found something out."

"I wasn't joking." He waved a hand nonchalantly in the air. "After you left, everyone was talking about your terrible manners, running out like that. Then they started telling each other the things you had been whispering in their ears all evening." He grinned and unlocked the door. "People believe there are farms in the wastes! I think the council will sleep poorly tonight."

"They've already made their plan." Tiria said, waiting for him to lock the door behind them. She threw herself down onto a chair in a puff of washing powder, and repeated back what she had overheard. Seth listened in silence, his face darkening. When she repeated their plans to find him a wife he laughed and shook his head, but when she finished by telling him about the officials' plans for her, he stopped.

"You need to keep a close watch on your temper, Ti." He said earnestly. "Anyone could be in on it. Anyone could try to rile you. All they need is a threatening look and..." He mimed firing a gun, and then sighed and slouched back in his chair, staring at the ceiling. "Well, at least it gives us an advantage."

"An advantage!" She echoed, incredulous. He looked down and smiled crookedly.

"They think you're a mindless, angry little savage." He said slowly, and deliberately added. "Since you're not, you should have no trouble controlling your temper for a few days."

She threw a cushion at him pettily. "They're the ones trying to kill me. The way you're talking, it's my fault they're trying to find you a boring soft city lady to have babies with."

"Not to mention all that money and power." He reminded her with a smile. "It's tempting. Perhaps I should kill you myself."

"You're welcome to try." She shrugged. He looked her up and down, and pulled a face.

"I wouldn't want to kill anyone that filthy. Maybe you should just walk around in that dress for a few days, no-one would want to come near you."

She looked down at it, gave him a glowering look, and then stood up and stripped down to her underwear, tearing the offending garment off. Seth choked back a laugh and nodded at the fire, grinning when the dress went up in flames on the heated metal plate. The smoke was strangely perfumed, halfway between metallic and chemical, before it was sucked into the air vents.

"They'll tell me off for not recycling it." Tiria muttered. Seth stood up and joined her beside the fire.

"We don't want them to guess what you've heard. You're not in serious danger unless you fall into their trap. We just can't risk them finding out they've been spied on." He said, and then less seriously added: "Besides, it'd do them good to run out of a few supplies. If we could cripple the artificial sunlight generators in the agriculture levels, no-one would argue about leaving."

"People starve in the wastes." Tiria said quietly. "It's a terrible thing, to destroy food supplies."

He looked sidelong at her. "I was joking, Ti."

"You shouldn't joke about that." She replied, and then shook herself out of her mood and reached up to kiss his cheek. "Are we done being sinister for the day?"

"There's nothing else we could practically do tonight." He said absently, scratching his chin as he thought. Tiria grinned and kissed him, mischievously guiding his hands to rest on her naked skin.

"I can think of something."

"Does it involve you having a shower?"

"It might," She made herself sound aloof, "If you come with me."

He grinned and wrapped his arm around her shoulders, pulling her close against his side. She squeaked at being trapped, but quietened when he looked down into her eyes with a warm smile. "Well done, Ti." He said softly, "You did well tonight. I'm proud of you."

Tiria blushed and looked away, undone by the way his eyes caught her own. It was not passion - she knew that darkness and would have shivered if she had seen it - but this was not like that. She knew it was something different, perhaps something better, but when he held her closely and there was no artifice in his voice, he scared her most of all. Her heart warmed at the praise, but she choked on the words she might use to accept it or to reply. She could find no solid ground in this love he had so grudgingly given her, and so while her body ached for him her eyes frantically searched for the dust which would swallow them both in the end.

He understood, or at least saw her confusion, and rested his forehead against hers for a long time, eyes closed.

"Never mind." He murmured, and kissed her again.

CHAPTER 13

Tiria went about her work as usual for the next few days. It was difficult to do; she felt like someone was constantly behind her, and every shouted word made her flinch and reach for her knife. It was never anything more sinister than the maids yelling at each other, but after two days being on edge was exhausting. Seth frowned at the dark shadows under her eyes, and ran his thumbs gently along the smudges as if he thought he could wipe them away. He was typically aloof, though, pointing out that she was exhausting herself for no reason.

"The more tired you are, the more annoying you get." He repeated every time she yawned. If she swore and threw something at him he was equally implacable, shrugging as if she had just proved his point.

"You're not helping." She snapped, and pressed her cold hand to her aching forehead. "They're not threatening *you*."

"No," He said peacefully, "They wouldn't dare. They also wouldn't dare attack my wife in the middle of the day, unprovoked. They want you to provoke them, or they won't do it. So there's no point looking over your shoulders every two minutes, or losing sleep."

She groaned and buried her face in the pillow, her words muffled by the fabric but undeniably crude and very unflattering. Seth ignored her, but that night he locked the door, turned off all of the lights which mimicked sunlight in their false windows, and sent a note to Agni telling her that Tiria was unwell. The girl slept until almost midday, and woke up feeling as if ten pounds of iron had been lifted from her spine.

"They'll think I'm pregnant." She told Seth when she found her way into the main room. It stung her to admit that she had been sick with fear, and the words were bitter. He pointed at a tray of cold food, intent on studying a crumbling map.

"If the idea disgusts you so much, I suggest that you play-act the flu." He suggested flatly, and then fell back into silence. Tiria rubbed her eyes and propped George onto her knee, feeding him bits of tomato and cucumber as she drank her coffee. The dragon looked almost as bleary as she did. The girl realised that she had been so caught up in imagining assassins that she had forgotten to give the little lizard the attention he was used to. For the rest of the day, she sat in front of the fire with George delightedly climbing from her legs to her shoulders and back as she lost herself in a book.

She had almost finished the novel a few days later when she went back to work. Her muscles had started aching from sitting around for too long, and she knew that if people thought she was hiding then the officials might get suspicious. She returned to her chores with a vengeance, and finished so quickly that she had some free time before lunch. Instead of going to the canteen, she turned left and made her way to the science labs.

Walker whitened when he saw her, but caught his breath in a second and stepped towards her. "Ti! Tiria!" He corrected himself, as he had every time since their argument. "I heard you were ill."

The girl nodded, and went to give him a hug. He froze, and then patted her awkwardly on the back. She let him go. "I shouldn't have been so harsh. I just didn't... I didn't know if you'd be safe."

He blinked and then laughed uneasily. "Well, if you're here can I at least assume that I'm off the endangered list?"

"Whatever that means." She muttered, and put her book onto the table. "Seth leant me this. It's lovely, but I've nearly finished it. What should I read next?"

He hesitated, and then something sharpened in his eyes. "Tiria," he asked in a strange, stilted tone: "Can I look after George this afternoon?"

"George?" She asked, confused. "Why?"

"He's not very strong." The man said in a forced voice. "I'm worried that you'll make mistakes at work, since you've been ill. It might be dangerous for him."

"He's always..." Tiria started, and then saw the fear in Walker's eyes. Pressing his finger to his lips, the man pointed upwards at one of the lights. Tiria squinted, and saw a little black dot. What was it? Walker mimed someone cupping their ear with their hand, and she understood. People were listening.

"I'm using caustic cleaners this afternoon." She managed to invent slowly. "They can't be good for him to be around. Maybe if you kept him - just this once - and maybe you could check he's healthy and... and let Seth know if there's anything wrong."

Walker drew a deep breath and another forced smile appeared on his face. "I hope everything will be fine." He said, and then picked up the book. Leafing through the pages, he calmed down his clearly shaken nerves. "I wasn't expecting you to come and see me, Tiria! I'll look for another book for you."

"No." She said, taking George out and easing the protesting lizard into one of the incubator boxes. He pressed his paw against the plastic and puffed his beard at her, before she gave him some crickets and he scurried around the tank in delight. Was he in danger? Tiria watched the tiny creature and her heart sank. "I'll come back later. Thank you for... for everything."

He smiled shakily. Tiria slipped out. She couldn't bear to see another minute of such horrible fear. If she hadn't been to see him then he couldn't have warned her, but surely the people listening must have realised what he was doing? Since Seth had returned George had turned from a secret into a joke. Everyone knew the little rat never let go of her pet. She felt his missing weight as a living loss, and zipped her jacket up more tightly as she headed back for her cleaning supplies. Suddenly, she wasn't hungry.

Agni sent her to clean the chapel that afternoon. It was dark and lonely when the god-people weren't organising their meetings. Tiria had always preferred it that way. Out of everyone in the vault, the chapel workers pestered her the most. They were convinced that she had led a terrible life on the surface - but they didn't mean that she had been forced to eat stale food or drink sour water. Instead, they spoke to her about her soul. She had been bad, they told her, not even asking what she had done. She needed to ask for forgiveness.

Tiria wondered who she should ask. The people she had killed were dead; the people who she had fought had richly deserved it – and hadn't they fought back? She was hardly depraved in the other ways they winced over. Seth teased her about all of the men she had apparently seduced in the wastes. There were nameless crowds of them, if every gossip was to be believed.

"Go to confession and list them all alphabetically." He suggested, grinning. "I'd like to see what colour the priest goes after that."

"You want me to humiliate myself?" She asked, miming horror. The man toyed with her bracelet.

"It'd tell us whether the priests are feeding gossip to the citizens." He said thoughtfully, and hid a smile when she narrowed her eyes at him. "What, Ti? Don't you think that's worth knowing?"

"Absolutely!" She leaned closer and made her voice low. "I guess I could tell them all the things we like to do when we're alone. I wouldn't want to lie to a priest... and I think some of your ideas would make the gossip *very* scandalous."

"Please. A vicious serial killer brought a rat into his bed. If you don't think they're already saying..."

"I know they're saying it. They don't know it's true." She interrupted, and grinned wickedly. "I should..."

She never got to the end of her sentence, but by the time they had finished she would have had far more to confess than any priest would want to hear. For the next few weeks she had to bite back laughter every time Seth took her to the chapel, and when she was cleaning it she hid whenever she heard a footstep. It would be too much to listen to the pompous men trying to coax her into telling them her secrets.

Today, she listened for footsteps with more nervous energy than ever before. It was so quiet in the chapel that she could hear her heart thudding in her ears. After months of wishing the citizens would leave her alone, she felt their absence as a physical threat. In a rush of panic she remembered that it was the officials who were after her. They could easily change people's work schedules to keep them away. She thought that, and then the lights flickered, and every diamond of coloured light bled into darkness.

Don't fight back. She repeated to herself. She flattened her back against the wall. The darkness seemed to move, but it was too thick and soft for her to see anything. She felt as if she were truly deep under the ground, trapped in this darkness with no way to claw her way back to the sunlight. What if the lights never came back on? What if the power generators had broken, and they were all trapped in the smothering darkness?

Something touched her shoulder, and then a blunt force thudded into her knees and threw her off balance. The hand at her shoulder dug its fingers in and pulled her back, and when she was upright she felt the hard pressure of a human body behind her instead of the wall. The man wrapped his arms around her shoulders, and she heard his breath panting in her ear.

"Don't," She whispered, her breath hitching in her throat as he moved his hand over her body. Every part of her needed to move, to fight back, but she forced herself to stay still. Trembling with the effort, she clenched her hands into fists and suddenly realised what he was doing. He wasn't interested in her body; his hand was searching for the tiny lizard who was safely back in the lab. The attacker must know that if he hurt George, she would have fought him with all the strength she possessed.

When the man realised that the lizard wasn't there he grunted and shoved Tiria forwards. She collided with the wall and cried out in pain. She scurried into the corner, searching with her throbbing hands until her fingertips met the wall. Crouching down with her arms crossed over her face, she felt tears of frustration sliding down her cheeks. She bit back her frightened breathing, knowing even the smallest sound would give her away.

A foot crashed into her side, and she screamed in agony. He could see! How could he see in the dark? She clutched at her side and rolled up into a tighter ball, feeling the hilt of her knife pressing against the bruise. The man watched her - she could feel his eyes on her, and hear his breathing - but he said nothing. She waited in trembling anticipation, not able to see where the next blow would come from. Suddenly, the lights snapped back on and she covered her burning eyes with her hand.

The man had gone. It was as if he had never been there.

She wiped a trail of moisture away from her mouth and stared dully at a red smear that it left on her fingers. She must have bitten through her lip when she was trying to stay quiet.

She abandoned her cleaning rags and made her way home, pressing her hand against her side but lowering it proudly when she had to walk past anyone. They could see the blood; they stared at her struggling to walk - but none of them could meet her black eyes. Every part of her screamed at her to fight, even now when it was pointless. When she got home she punched a cushion but it wasn't enough to stop her hands from trembling in anger. Gritting her teeth, she snatched up one of the jars and hurled it against the wall. It shattered, and she followed it with another, and another, until the hearth was littered with shards of fire-blackened glass. Then she collapsed down onto the ground, clutched her hands to the burning pain in her side, and burst into tears.

She had no idea how long she had been there when Seth came home. She heard the locks snapping shut, but she couldn't force herself to look around. Then there were hands on her shoulder, and in a blinding moment she was back in the chapel. She shoved the hands off so hard that her side blazed in pain.

"Ti." Seth caught her head between his hands and rested his forehead against her own. She gulped and bit back tears, and then gripped his shirt in her hands and forced herself to calm down. It took a long time, and when she let go she saw that his own face was white with anger.

"I broke your jars." She whispered.

"Fuck the jars." He retorted. She bit her lip at the pain and let him raise her shirt. Her whole side was inflamed in red and purple bruises, and there was a deep, clotted gash where the hard edge of the stranger's boot had ripped into the skin. Seeing the damage made it feel worse, somehow. Tiria tore her eyes away and buried her face in the arm of the chair.

"I'm going to get a doctor." She heard Seth say. She nodded, but it had taken her dizzy mind too long to catch up, and the door had already closed by then. The darkness was slow and rich and red, not black, and then she felt arms closing around her and struggled against them as her side throbbed and twisted. A needle slipped into her arm, and then there was pain, and softness, and sleep.

She woke up in Seth's bed, looking up at a complete stranger. The woman saw that she was awake and put down a book before shining a light into the girl's eyes. Tiria cursed and squeezed them shut.

"You didn't hit your head." The woman confirmed, and clicked the torch off. Her voice lowered conspiratorially. "What happened?"

"I fell down the stairs." She muttered. The doctor smiled and tutted.

"What a nice boot-print the stairs left you." She drawled, and then picked up her bag. Tiria watched her in something close to wonder. It was so peculiar to see another person in these rooms. For months, she and Seth had been the only people here, and they had always locked the doors behind them. He must have been truly worried to have let this woman in. As Tiria was thinking that she saw her husband in the doorway, his dark eyes fixed on the doctor. He escorted the woman out, pressing something into her hand as payment, and locked the door.

Tiria pushed herself up onto her elbows, and then managed to get upright. The pain was less blinding than it had been, and her head felt thick and a little dizzy. It must have been the same drug they had fed her at the ballot, she thought in a haze. That one made her numb, too.

"Lie down, you idiot." Seth snapped the second he returned.

"I'm fine."

"Fine." He retorted as if it was a swear word, and then sat down heavily at the end of the bed. "Who was it?"

"I don't know." She searched through her shaky memories and told him what had happened. When she described the darkness and the way her attacker had still been able to see, the man froze.

"Are you sure he could see?" He asked. Tiria gestured to her side, where the bandage was starting to itch.

"It was pitch black when he did this."

"God." Seth stood up to pace across the room, and then shook his head. "I should have guessed they'd get him to do it. I hoped he'd have more self-respect than that."

"Who?" Tiria asked. Her husband looked over at her, and then spoke reluctantly.

"My uncle. He's the head of security. He answers to the committee... and he has access to the military stores. His men train with him in the caverns. His favourite trick is to put on a pair of night vision goggles and ambush them in the dark."

Tiria's hand dropped to her knife before she realised that it wasn't there. Seth saw the gesture and smiled thinly. "There's no point going after Hart now. He would have been following orders, and we still have to work out who gave them."

"Your own uncle." She said with disgust. "Why would he do something like this?"

Seth gestured around the room, to the books and ornaments and heavy furniture. "The hunters inherit all of this. He was left with nothing. My grandmother as good as disowned him. When I die, he'll get it back. He has every reason to want me disgraced. I just never thought he had the guts to go through with it. Now that he has his orders, he doesn't need to be subtle."

"Why did he hurt me?" Tiria asked, her mind racing. "Why not just scare me? He had already worked out I wouldn't fight back."

Seth thought for a moment, and then said very carefully: "If we had a child, Hart wouldn't inherit a single button."

"Forcing a still is a serious crime." The girl pointed out. "He wouldn't risk execution on the off-chance that I was pregnant."

"He probably thought you were. It's what the gossips were saying after you were sick. Besides, he thought you would give him an excuse to kill you. You didn't fight back, so he did this." Seth growled, and then he looked up. "Ti, I'm so sorry."

She looked down at her hands. Her silver bracelet was stained with blood. "We made everything so much more complicated than we planned, didn't we?"

"I'm going to summon the council." Seth burst out suddenly. Tiria wondered if he had even heard her. He met her eyes warningly when she tried to interrupt, and continued: "They'll be just as angry as us that this happened. Or they'll be angry that it failed. Maybe I'll be able to work out who gave Hart the order."

"If they weren't good at lying, you never would have needed to bring me here." The girl shook her head and looked down. "I don't think it'll work."

"I don't care what you think." Seth snapped, his hands clenching into fists. "They hurt you. They could have killed you."

Tiria caught his hand and then reached up to run her fingers through his hair. The man stilled, but his eyes were still full of anger. The girl rested her forehead against his, wordlessly comforting.

"Breathe." She murmured.

He shivered and then spoke, and his voice was so forlorn that it sounded as if it were coming from another person.

"It's starting again. I thought someone had a grudge against me, but if Hart did this then... then the whole council must be trying to hurt us. That means that they were the ones who killed my father." He swallowed, looked over at the door and his hands grew cold. "They made everyone so frightened of me that even the people I grew up with won't speak to me. I've been alone for so long I can barely remember how to trust anyone. They must see how much I love you. Now they're trying to steal you away. They're punishing me, and I don't even know what I've done!"

"They wanted to scare me, not kill me." She replied softly. He squeezed her hand.

"If you ran away now, I'd never be able to hunt you down. I think they've worked that out. You'll never be allowed to leave this place alive."

She tried to make it into a joke. "Just tell them I'd never betray the city."

He smiled wanly and closed her in his arms. "Every runaway I buried said exactly the same thing."

CHAPTER 14

It was the first time that Tiria had seen Seth in his official role. All of the rumours and hearsay hadn't prepared her for the way he changed. She had expected him to use his arrogant mask, but as soon as he was dressed in his smart council clothes, he became something else. He stood differently – his normal saunter changed into a stiff, formal posture which betrayed no weakness or strength, but was stoically neutral. He wore an icy expression she longed to kiss away. There was a man under it who could tease her, or grow fierce with anger, or be moved to gentleness in her arms. That was the man that she knew, and she wondered if the council members had ever met him. This polite, cold creature was barely human.

His eyes were his own, though. They still blazed with anger when he looked at her, even now that she had begun to heal. She beckoned him to the bed and smoothed his hair down, then nuzzled against his cheek.

"Don't show them you're angry." She said. "They want you to be angry, right? Go in there and smile, and see who tries to goad you. Don't shout at them, either. Smile politely and then we'll work out how to drag them outside for the savages."

He touched his forehead in a wry salute. "Lock the door behind me, Ti."

"I will, if you ever leave!"

She walked to the door with him, slowly and painfully, and leaned against the frame as he took the key out of his pocket to hand to her. He pressed it into her palm, and then very carefully rested his hand against her side. For a moment he obviously struggled to find the right words, and then he cursed under his breath and kissed her.

"I love you." He said. She couldn't help the smile that crossed her cheeks, but her voice was tart.

"Are you ever going to go?"

He straightened up, and just like that, he changed. Even the anger in his eyes disappeared, and when he glanced back at her he looked just as cruel and indifferent as he had the day that they had met. Tiria shivered, and as soon as he walked away she locked the door.

Seth heard it shut behind him, and felt the last scrap of concern fade into irrelevance. The girl was safe; he had no reason to return or to worry about her until the meeting was over. He deliberately pushed her out of his mind and turned his thoughts to the committee.

He had called the meeting in a blind rage, and only realised afterwards that he was playing into their hands. Usually, he could think three steps ahead, but this time he had done exactly what they wanted. Hart had been a little more enthusiastic than they had planned on, perhaps, but the committee were far too clever to let one man trip them up. The fact that Seth had been underfoot for years was bad enough.

The committee met once a week. Although Seth was usually outside they kept a seat for him, but after a few years his absence become a joke. He attended to give them reports, or to receive his orders before he left for the wastes. Neither of those things required much debate; he stood in front of the table and spoke in a level tone, and then he left before anyone could argue.

When he was twenty, Agni had interrupted his report with a scathing speech. He was too curt, she said. The council had no way of telling whether or not his claims were true. For all they knew, he had been sunbathing for three weeks before coming home with a few horrible lies to keep them quiet. Seth listened very politely, and after his next hunt he came home with a large bag. Looking straight into Agni's eyes, he opened the bag and tipped out three human hands. The council shrieked as the waxen meat thudded into the polished oak table. Seth pointed at the first one, ashen brown and soft.

"That was the runaway." He said, and then pointed to the second and third hands. "Those are from the man who caught him."

"Where's his other hand?" The head of rationing croaked. Seth looked at Agni, and smiled thinly.

"Meat is meat."

She turned green and ran to the rubbish bin, where she threw up loudly. Seth picked up the hands and shoved them back into the bag, pulling a ring off the runaway's finger before he did. This, he dropped onto the table.

"That's what I'd normally bring you. Do you want me to keep bringing you more?"

After that, the committee had avoided making eye contact with him. There was something unhinged about the hunter, they thought. Seth had a way of looking into a person's eyes and seeing everything they were trying to hide. He could look at a sky-struck citizen and know exactly how they would try to hide. Perhaps it was his training, or something he was born with, but either way the committee didn't want to stare into madness any longer than they had to.

Agni knew differently. She could tell when someone was laughing at her.

Seth definitely wasn't laughing after his wife was attacked. When he walked into the room the whole council could see how serious he was. He didn't shout, or accuse anyone, or make a speech. He simply looked around at the gathered men and women and said, "You all already know what happened. I'd like to find out why."

"We have more important matters than your wife to discuss." One of the women drawled. "We are trying to run a city, here."

"I appreciate that, Sorda." Seth looked at her with a pleasant smile. "This concerns you, too. From what I understand, the attack happened because of a power cut on the second level. While the lights were out a woman was brutally attacked. Are you telling me it's not your fault?"

"A power cut?" The woman frowned and looked at the notes in front of her. "No, there hasn't been a problem on that level in three weeks."

"Oh?" The man raised an eyebrow and looked around at another member, a small round man with narrow glasses. "Then there must be a problem with the security. All of the breakers have cameras, right?

It would have been impossible for someone to tamper with the lights without the guards knowing about it."

The round man sweated and pushed his glasses up his nose as they slipped. "We can't monitor every CCTV screen around the clock. I understand the... uh... 'power cut' only lasted for a few minutes. It would have been easy to miss. Lamentable, yes, but not a serious fault."

"It is a serious fault." Seth said, still sounding pleasant. "Are the cameras just for your own protection, since you're *lamenting* rather than investigating violent crimes? I imagine that if your wife had been assaulted, you would be more willing to find the man responsible. "

"Surely the man responsible is the assaulter himself?" Someone else drawled. Seth glanced around into the calm eyes of a man about the same age as himself. The head of filtration rarely bothered to speak to anyone, let alone the head of hunters. Arthur's whole life seemed to revolve around confiscating contraband cigarettes and mixing plant food in level four. When he saw Seth's curious expression, he smiled a little and waved his pen in the air. "You should all be more helpful. I would feel safer if this man was caught. You all seem a little too happy about a violent man sauntering through your corridors."

"Is Tiria well?" Agni asked suddenly. Seth scratched his head and took a sip of water, amused and annoyed by the sickly sweetness in the woman's voice. When his mind had cleared, he forced himself to speak formally.

"Whoever did it hit her hard enough to bruise her ribs. Doctor Acle examined her if you would like proof; I don't think she'll be able to scrub floors for a few days."

"That's not why I'm asking." The woman leaned a little closer, the fat on her arms seeming to ooze across the table as her cloying voice slipped into his ears. "You must be so upset."

"Not really." He shrugged and reached for the water again. "She said she's used to people acting like savages."

There was an uproar, and the man hid his smile in his glass. The vault dwellers prided themselves on their utopian lives, and looked down on the rats like children stamping on beetles. Being compared to the savages was like someone slandering their entire family. And to be insulted by the girl - the rat! They all snapped at Seth at the same time, and their voices rose into shouts before they began to calm down. Seth watched them, looking into their eyes and seeing who was really offended, and who was play acting. The actors had been lying all along, but it was only when everyone was fighting against their emotions that he could clearly see the artifice.

There were more liars than he had expected. His stomach churned, and he pressed his fingertips hard against the glass. Clear, solid glass. He made himself breathe, and then he looked around again. There were more than he expected, but not as many liars as he had feared. Some of these people could have really hurt him, if they were in on it, but they looked as mortified as each other. The older men and women were all sincere. Agni was a liar, of course, but Sorda and Arthur knew nothing about the plot. That surprised him. They were both young, and hungry to prove themselves. Ousting the last man in a long line of hunters would have secured their power for generations.

Seth thought quickly. With this many people plotting together, he had no way to force his way to the truth. He still had no idea whether they were part of the conspiracy against his father, or whether the rat had made them close ranks. If he knew what they had killed his father for then he would know what each one had to gain or lose, but while he didn't it was like shooting in the dark. While the lights were out, he and Tiria had found some very powerful enemies - and no way to prepare themselves for a second attack.

"Well, if none of you can provide me with any answers, I suppose I'll have to look for them myself." He said breezily, and pushed his chair back. As he had hoped, several of the liars moved to stop him. They glanced at each other, and then the head of civil order cleared his throat.

"We can look in the chapel, Seth. That's what I have a team for."

"I'm better at it. I wonder if your team will find anything." Seth returned. The man paled, and then looked at his accomplice for help. The woman chipped in.

"Your talents are needed elsewhere."

"A runaway?" He knew there wasn't one, but he wanted one of them to lie to his face. They were too clever for that; they shook their heads in unison until one piped up:

"We're worried about the ambushes outside of the city. You said the savages caught you and... her... when you were walking here. We need to know if they know we're here."

The savages? Seth nearly laughed out loud at the thought. They were so full of radiation sickness that their brains had dripped out of their eye sockets. Literally, in some cases. Still, it was a good an excuse to leave the vault, and he had been hoping for a chance to get away. If he had some room to think without worrying about another attack, then he could figure out his next move.

The irony of hiding in the wastes to get *away* from violence wasn't lost on him.

He listened carefully to their hastily made-up mission brief, nodding in all the right places, and then told them it would take him a week to prepare. He listed all of the things he needed to do - a gun that needed its sights re-tuned, a giger-meter that had become erratic, supplies that he needed to gather - all things which they shrugged at. They didn't need excuses, they just needed him to leave. As soon as he was gone, Seth thought, they would make plans of their own. If they had an ounce more courage they would simply refuse to open the hatch to let him back in again, but they were too clever for that. The only thing that scared them more than the hunter was their fear of the unknown. Until they found someone to replace him, there would be no-one able to hunt down the traitor runaways who could sell them to the wastes.

They had been training a replacement. He realised it in a rush. His long absence at the ballot had pushed them to it. He had thought Agni was just being pert. Soon, he would be disposable.

They agreed to him leaving in a week's time, and they didn't seem to care that his excuses for lingering were as idiotic as their reasons for sending him away. Seth breathed out a shallow sigh of relief. There wouldn't be another attack; he had bought a week of safety in exchange for their nonsense chore. A week would be more than long enough for Tiria to heal. He could take her out of here. They wouldn't expect it, Most of the citizens would recuperate for months over a broken toe. They probably expected Seth to leave her here, alone and vulnerable, ready for them to swoop down with their claws bared.

Seth smiled politely at the committee, and left.

CHAPTER 15

For the next few days they carried out a battle of silent wills. Tiria wanted to know what the council had said, but she knew from the closed-off way that Seth had made excuses that it wasn't worth asking. He, in his turn, didn't want Tiria to know how much danger they were in. For the few days they had left in the vault he became hyper-vigilant, refusing to leave the door unlocked even when he was home, and glaring at Tiria as if his frustration would make her heal any faster.

"I'm going to work today." She told him, when she had managed to get out of bed unaided and drag on some clothes. He scowled, and she sighed. "You're driving me insane, Seth."

"You're not well."

"I'm not going to stay here swooning just because you've decided you love me today."

"I don't care if I love you or not. You're too weak to defend yourself and - apparently - too dense to realise how dangerous it is out there."

"I looked out for myself for years before you came along." She raised her head stubbornly. "I'm not going to hide for another minute. They're only stupid vault people, and this time I'll have my knife."

He didn't answer, and the girl muttered a curse before she started looking around for the keys. Before she could find them, a hand seized her wrist and then Seth spun her around, covering her mouth with one hand and holding her trapped with the other.

"Fight me off." He said in a completely placid tone. She squeaked and tried to pull away, but he dragged her back and moved his hand from her mouth to her throat. Tiria stopped struggling, gasping, when he pressed his fingers down lightly on her windpipe.

"Seth!" She croaked, and he eased off.

"That's all it would take, Ti. Even if you drew your knife, all they'd have to do is..." He moved his hand down to her ribs and pressed gently against the bruise. Tiria froze and shook her head, already growing pale at the promise of pain. The man let her go easily, and then caught her when she reeled away. She caught her breath and shoved at him before gripping the top of the sofa to steady herself. Her cheeks flushed with shame.

355

"I hate you."

"I know that. I want you to stay alive so you can tell me that every day." He smiled when she pulled a face, and then helped her sit down. "It's pointless to put yourself in danger just because I'm 'driving you mad'."

"To be fair, you are really annoying." She muttered. He nodded, cheerfully admitting it, and then sat down beside her.

"Bear with me for another three days, Ti. I want you to heal, and I have things I need time to work on. After that you can go and scrub all the toilets you've been dreaming of."

"Three days." She repeated suspiciously. "Will I still have to fight you off if I want to escape?"

"I won't provoke you into stabbing me in my sleep, thank you." He said snottily, and then mimed falling over in agony when she poked him hard in the ribs.

"That's payback." She said, smiling slightly. "I might stab you anyway."

"In three days." He held his hand out seriously, and grinned when she shook it. "Deal."

By lunchtime Tiria was glad that she hadn't left the house. She was also determined not to let Seth see how much her side was aching, because he was insufferable enough when he didn't have a reason to crow over her. She made it through the day without betraying herself, but it was more difficult to hide her pain when she was half asleep. Her fidgeting finally woke up Seth, who sleepily opened his eyes.

"Don't say anything." She whispered, and curled around to rest her head on his chest. He laughed softly, and when she finally found a comfortable position he pulled the blanket up around her. She fell asleep feeling his fingers gently stroking her hair, and when she woke up the next morning he was still there. He was wide awake, staring thoughtfully up at the ceiling. Tiria blinked at him drowsily. He was usually gone by now, not just out of bed but working somewhere in the depths of the city.

She whispered, "You could have woken me up."

"Why?" He looked surprised, and then worked out why she was confused. "I know you slept badly. I didn't want to wake you up. Go back to sleep, love."

She didn't really want to close her eyes but every time she blinked sleep claimed her. It felt like a few minutes, but she must have drifted in and out of a doze for much longer than that. When the heaviness drew back a little she looped her arm around Seth's chest.

"It's so strange." She said.

"Hm?"

"We've never really done this. Just being sleepy and warm and safe together. It's nice."

"It won't last." He muttered absently, and then jumped when she poked him. "What was that for?"

"If you're going to be all sinister and keep secrets that's fine, but don't spoil my happy little moment with your stupid snide jokes!"

He laughed and relented. "Sorry, Ti. You're right, it is nice."

"I'm so glad you agree." She sniffed, and nestled a little closer to his chest. "Seth?"

"Yes, I'm still here."

"My side doesn't hurt as much today. Will you give me a hug? I've missed it."

His arm immediately curled around her back, and she sighed and smiled. "Thank you," She mumbled, and then fell back asleep.

By midday they were back to sniping at each other, but Tiria didn't try to pretend she wasn't in pain, and Seth explained a little of why they had to wait. He didn't say that they were leaving. If Tiria gave something away in her excitement, or want to tell Walker, then they would never be able to trick the guards into letting her leave. Seth's notion that she was a bad liar wasn't quite fair, but he was more prepared to risk her anger than her life. If Agni or a council member came to ask Tiria what she planned to do, the girl would be able to answer honestly.

Seth told Tiria that when she was better, they would go to the lower levels and train so they would be prepared for another attack. She had to be strong for that, she agreed, and so for the next two days she threw herself into healing with pointless enthusiasm, rubbing oil on the bruises and taking painkillers and vitamin pills when simple rest would have done the same thing. The fact that Seth had so much medicine in his home astounded her, and she read through every of the advice leaflets.

Whatever combination of medicine she ended up dosing herself with apparently worked, because on the third day she barely felt a thing. Seth still looked unconvinced when she swore she was well enough to start working again, so Tiria did the subtle thing and simply dragged him into their bed. Afterwards, he claimed, he was almost convinced but - laughing as he dodged a hurled pillow - he thought he could do with a *little* more convincing...

"Seth," Tiria asked afterwards, when he held her in his arms, "If you don't have the ballot here, then how did you have children?"

He made an odd noise, reached over her and drank from a cup of water. "Do you really want to talk about that now?" Seeing the stubborn set of her face, he smiled crookedly and kissed the end of her nose. "Are you jealous, little wife?"

She shook her head, laughing when he tried to kiss her again. "Stop trying to distract me!"

"I've missed you." He said, and although his hands were greedy on her body he touched her side with light, careful fingers. "You've been malingering."

"I don't know what that word means. Should I get up and fetch the dictionary?" She sat up and pulled on her nightshirt, laughing when he dragged her back down into the sheets and kissed her. When she caught her breath she kissed the end of his nose. "I'm fine. I've missed you, too. Now tell me about your wife, or I'll smother you with a pillow."

"It was a girl I grew up with." He said, finally relenting. "After I started going out into the wastes, she decided that she liked me. I needed someone to talk to, so I agreed. At first I thought we were well matched, but when I tried to tell her about the wastes she always stopped me. I think she liked her idea of the danger more than the truth. It got tedious, but after a month out in the wastes I was always more than ready to fall into her arms."

"You didn't love her?"

"I knew her too well to love her. After a while I realised that she was afraid of me, just like the others. I had thought she was above that... that pettiness. But she enjoyed being afraid." He ran his hand along Tiria's leg, at first gentle, and then he suddenly leant forward and pulled her to him, his fingers digging into her skin and tangling in her hair as he kissed her. The girl gasped and instinctively struggled, and then surrendered to the rush of heat in her body and kissed him back, just as violently, sinking her nails into his back before shoving him away. He grinned and shook his head.

"She never used to fight back."

"What happened to her?" Tiria asked, letting him coax her gently back down to lie in his arms. He tapped his fingers against her stomach, his face taking on the closed-off look he wore when he was about to lie, and then he looked down into Tiria's eyes and changed his mind with a sigh. The words came slowly, but she had no doubt that every one was true.

"She had the first still when I was outside. I never even knew about it. She told me about the second one... it lasted a month longer, but it never took. The third one was so twisted and broken that it suffocated before she could even hold it in her arms. She took it down to the morgue, watched it burn into ashes, and then she took a knife and followed it into death."

"I'm sorry." Tiria whispered. He didn't answer, so she stroked his hair and tightened her arms around him. "My mother only had stills after I was born. Every time one lost its grip, she would carry it out into the wastes. She left her weapons at home, and walked out for miles until she found somewhere for it to sleep. My brother used to follow her, keeping hidden, to make sure that nothing attacked her. Nothing ever did. He said that her love, her sorrow, must have kept them away."

"Did you ever ask her why she did it?"

"She did it because it was the right thing to do." Tiria said softly, remembering the odd strength in her mother's placid eyes whenever she unbolted the hatch. Seth raised his eyebrows.

"But why did she do it that way? Did her mother do it, too?"

The girl shrugged. "I wouldn't know. Mama didn't have a voice."

He sat up, amazed. "You mother was a mutation?"

Tiria shivered at the idea and shook her head. "Her sadness stole her words away."

The man didn't look convinced. "What happened to her?"

"She gave birth to a mutation with six toes. Instead of reporting it, she cut the extra toe off and pretended the baby was normal."

Seth whistled softly. "When was she found out?"

"At the next ballot. She kept sinking lower after that, because everyone knew what she had done. My father was one of the only people who bid for her, and he held her score over her head every day of her life. After my brother ran away, father told the officials that she was the one who had made him rebel. He said that mama had never learned to obey, and that her son had the same sickness. They even said that she was a mutation, that the radiation had rotted her brain rather than her body, and that she had passed it on to Lawrence."

Seth scoffed at that. Tiria bit her lip and then fiddled nervously with the end of one of her braids. "If you hadn't bid for me, then I would be caught in the same trap. People look at my family and they see us rotting into savages, not rising to become highs."

He gently took her braid out of her hands, pushed it behind her ear and cupped her head between his palms. "You make me happy, Ti." He said softly. "I couldn't bear to lose that. Please don't think of what we have as just... part of the ballot."

Tiria bit her lip and shook her head. "It's good now. But if I fell out of love with you I would still have to stay. If you stopped loving me, you could cast me out."

"I'm not going to stop loving you." He said, and then scowled and scratched his nose. "God knows I tried hard enough."

She didn't answer, and he struggled for words. "Would you believe me if I promised... that even if I started hating you, I'd never send you back to that life?"

Tiria shook her head. Seth sighed. "No, you're too clever to believe me."

"You said you wouldn't keep me." She pointed out. "I need to believe that."

He leaned a little closer. "I'll keep that promise, if you swear to me that if you ever change your mind, you'll free me from it."

"You'll keep that promise anyway." She retorted. "You said yourself that what we're doing here has nothing to do with anything else. If you start getting protective of me I'll take one of those pistols and shoot you in the foot."

He wrapped her braid around his fist, riled. "Don't you dare threaten me. I'll kill you first."

"You're too besotted to even shove me out of danger." She goaded him. "How are you going to kill me - bore me to death with your stupid promises?"

He smiled thinly, and then shoved her out of the bed. She gave a muffled shriek as she fell, and landed safely on the thick rug. Spinning around, she stood and regained her balance just quickly enough to avoid one hand, but not quite quickly enough to dodge the other. His fingers closed around her wrist and he grinned for a brief second, before she twisted around and dragged him down onto the floor with her. She was ready to enjoy her own triumphant grin when she realised he had knotted her braid around his hand, ready to drag her head back if she dared to move.

"I knew I should have cut my stupid hair off." She growled, and held her hands up in a gesture of surrender. Seth smiled lazily and pinned her against the carpet.

"I like it."

"Of course you do. If I didn't have braids, you would never have won!"

He archly ignored that. "Are you still bored, Ti?"

She gave an experimental wriggle and shrugged, ruefully accepting that she couldn't move an inch. She settled on a different tactic. "How about you go off and mutter about whatever evil scheme you're planning next?"

"Happily, my evil schemes are all ahead of schedule." He said. He kissed her softly before he murmured. "You'll like what we're doing tomorrow."

She stilled, suspecting a trick. "What?" She asked slowly, raising a wary eyebrow. He smirked and paused for effect, and then announced:

"The council are sending me back into the wastes. I'm taking you with me. We're going to look for your brother."

"What?" She gasped, and all of the strength seemed to leave her limbs in one go. "Are you serious?"

"Very." He freed one of her hands so he could touch her pale cheek. He looked exasperated. "What's this, Ti? You're not scared, are you?"

"Scared!" She pulled herself upright and flung her arms around his back, kissing him so passionately that the man was caught by surprise. He laughed when she pulled away and drew her back, coaxing her sudden delight into something slower, gentler, far richer. She moued and tangled her hands in his hair, her eyes heated, but he held her still and kissed the end of her nose playfully.

"Slowly," He said. "We won't have time to enjoy this for weeks."

"We have all night." She caught his lips and kissed him. When he pretended to dodge she laughed and nuzzled against his throat. "Don't pretend you don't want me."

"We'll be useless tomorrow if we stay up all night." He teased her. She pouted and shook her head.

"What happens outside this room has nothing to do with your plans." Tilting her head to one side, she opened her eyes wide in a mockery of innocence. "Or have we changed the rules? Last I remember, you were still treating me like a dog in front of your friends."

"They're not my friends."

"I'm not a dog."

"At the very worst, you may have been treated like a cat. People like dogs."

"You like me."

He made a scoffing sound, and she pressed a little closer and kissed the side of his neck. "You like me." She breathed, and he laughed.

"Alright, you win." He caught her arms and pulled her more firmly into his lap, making a great show of unbuttoning the top of her nightdress before he pulled it away. She laughed, her hands unconsciously moving to cover her naked breasts until he looked severely at her and dragged her wrists down behind her back. "Now, little wife, what evil schemes do you think I have planned for *you*?"

Afterwards, Seth realised he was never going to get to sleep. His mind was reeling with too many things to let him rest. He climbed out of bed, stalked over to his maps, and tried to concentrate on them for long enough for his mind to settle on one thought. It was hopeless; after a long while he admitted to himself that he couldn't remember a single river. He found himself staring away from his work, at the woman who was sleeping in his room. Giving in to whatever his mind was playing at, he crept into the bedroom and sat on the end of the bed, watching her.

Tiria had not changed since he hated her. That was not a problem; he had not changed, either. But it was baffling to the man that the things which he had detested a year before were suddenly things he admired. She looked so much softer sleeping, but older, too. The fire that blazed in her eyes was extinguished, and as she dreamed there was a serenity to her which made her seem more complete.

He reached down and touched her cheek with a tenderness that he wouldn't have risked when she was awake. He knew she would laugh. He knew he would hate her for it, even though she never meant the sound to mock him, and his anger would turn into heat, and passion. In the morning they would both be bruised by the words that he had imagined. They would tell themselves that the hatred burning languidly in their veins was love.

Tiria's skin was dark, rich, and soft under his fingertips. She hadn't changed since he had hated her; she was utterly beautiful. She sighed, and her eyes sleepily opened.

"What's wrong?"

He pulled his hand away as if he'd been burned. He tried to make it into a joke. "Does something need to be wrong?"

She groaned and buried her head back under the blankets. "Go to sleep, Seth."

PART 3: OUTCASTS

CHAPTER 1

The next morning Tiria felt as though the bright white lights were dimmer. For the first time in months she felt the heavy weight of the earth above her head, crushing and suffocating the buried worms beneath. By the time they had packed all of her hair was standing on end. She pulled on the sturdy clothes the tailors had given her and wondered if her skin was really tingling, or if it was just the thick synthetic fabric. It was designed for the workers in the lower levels. As well as being hardy and difficult to tear, it protected her from chemicals and some of the radiation. The murky yellow cloth was almost as ugly as the patch rags the rats scavenged in.

Seth was taking George to the labs. Despite her excitement, parting from the little lizard had made Tiria want to cry. She clutched him close to her chest and felt his spines prickle her skin for the last time, and then handed him over with her lip stubbornly set. Seth had been tactful for the first time in his life, and had slipped away without saying anything. Walker would take good care of George, she knew, and she wouldn't risk taking the dragon into the wastes. Still, she felt his absence as a real pain, and wiped away a few tears when Seth was gone. He came back and saw her reddened eyes, reached out and awkwardly tugged her jacket straight.

"It's a bit big for you." He said.

"Everyone here is too well fed." The words sounded croaky, but after she had made them the urge to cry passed. Seth smiled at her sharp retort, and unlocked one of the cabinets. Tiria peered over his shoulder curiously. In all the months she had lived here, she only ever seen Seth open the cupboard in his bedroom. The main room was filled with his junk, but once he had it, Seth didn't seem to care what happened to it. Many of the things he fiddled with had been scavenged by his father, Tiria knew, or even by his grandmother. Seth didn't care whether his ornaments were valuable or beautiful, but he did care about who had brought them home.

Tiria had brought the chalice home from the church. Seth kept it on a low shelf by the fire. Tiria felt odd whenever she saw it. How many more generations would let it gather dust?

The cupboard gleamed when it opened, and Seth reached inside to unlock a second door. This time the lock was made of dull metal, and it clunked heavily when he turned the key.

"Large weapons aren't really allowed in the vault." He explained, and pulled out a bowie knife. She strapped it wordlessly to her belt as he chose more and more weapons, handing some to her and stowing more of them inside his rucksack. When he saw the bowie knife he scowled. "Are you stupid? Hide it in your bag."

"Do they think you talk the savages to death?" She asked, exasperated. He shrugged.

"They gave the first hunters a gun, but they soon learned not to use it. Those things usually make more noise than they're worth." Having said that, he pulled two handguns out of the safe and stuffed them both into his bag. "I'll give you yours when you're outside."

"No thank you. I saw someone use one once. It exploded and blew their arm off."

Seth snorted. "I'm sure it did. I'll teach you how to clean one properly. I've seen rats who think you just point and pull the trigger. It's about as sensible as the way they play with explosives."

Tiria grinned at the gibe and picked up her bag. It felt much heavier now, and she hefted it experimentally. It felt strange to be leaving a shelter with a full pack. Scavengers usually relied on a sharp blade and their wits. With a light pack they could run fast, and that meant they lived longer.

They made their way to the entrance, ignoring all of the people who gaped at them on the way past. They made their way to decon and pounded on the inner door until the guard demanded the password. Seth swore at him until he cursed back and let them through.

"What's she doing here?" The man asked, his hand edging closer to his gun. Tiria wondered how quickly he could draw it. If she was fast, she could knock him down and make it out of the hatch before he even knew she had hit him. The temptation to run was so strong that she felt herself trembling. Fresh air was only a few feet away. The guard looked back at her levelly, and his feet shifted into what was clearly a fighting stance. His arms were thick with muscles. Tiria remembered that all of the security team trained for hours every day.

The soldiers answered to Hart. She swallowed and took half a pace back, lowering her eyes. The man's aggressive stance relaxed a little.

"Are you two done facing off?" Seth sounded bored. He wandered over to the hatch and folded his arms. "She's guiding me back to her ballot, John. The bloody rats hoard as many things as they can find, and I'll be damned if they find us because some scavenger spotted something shiny in the ruins."

"She'll run off." The man looked narrowly at the girl, and she tried to look innocent. He scowled. "She'd sell us out for half a day's rations, and you know it."

"The council approved."

"The council." He sniffed, and shook his head. "If she's not with you or dead when you come back, I'll have to leave you out there in the sun."

"You'd never do that to me." Seth smiled sweetly and then crooked his finger at Tiria. "Come on, girl, let's go. You can decide which of your hands I'll lop off if you die on the journey."

She made a rude gesture with both of them. The guard's eyes narrowed, and then he pointed at her left. "That one." He said curtly. "She has a freckle on her thumb. I'll remember that."

Tiria lowered her hands and fought the urge to hide them behind her back. She had never been able to tell when the citizens were joking, and she hadn't realised how serious the guard was being. Thinking about it, Seth's whole job was to stop people from escaping from the city. He had probably killed people who he had grown up with. Of course they would want proof that she was dead. She was silent as the hatch clanged open, and refused Seth's offered hand when she scrambled up onto the surface.

The sky was vast.

It was dawn, earlier than she had thought it would be. The lights in the vault must have been a little bit out of time, which made sense – how would anyone know when the seasons were changing? Their days never got longer or shorter, but out on the surface the sun was just beginning to rise. Everything was bathed in a soft blue light which was so rich, so different from the sterile shades beneath the ground, that Tiria felt like she was under water. The dust cracked and shifted beneath her feet, and she crouched down to run her fingers through it. It was soft, and rough, and cool against her fingertips. When she stood up and brushed it off her hands she realised how smooth they were. Her skin stung when it rubbed against the harsh grit.

"The next few days are going to be lousy." She muttered, hauling her rucksack on. "I've gone soft."

"You'll be fine." Seth was distracted by scanning the horizon and spoke rather vaguely.

"Uh huh." Tiria folded her arms and tilted her head at him, waiting for the hatch to slam closed before she cleared her throat. "Why didn't you tell me that I wasn't allowed to leave?"

"Because you're a bad liar." He smiled at her to mask the insult, and then explained. "The meeting last week made it necessary. They're trying to get rid of me. There's more to this than just a nervous official murdering my father. Dad must have found something out - something dangerous, that they don't want people to know. They can kill an old man, but they can't erase whatever secrets he told to his son."

"What secrets?" Tiria asked. Seth sighed and scrubbed his face with his hand.

"There aren't any. The old fool never told me anything."

"But the council thinks he did?"

"I imagine so. They need to get rid of me to make sure I don't tell anyone else. Oh, and they'll kill you too, of course, but we already knew that."

"It was your idea to mix me up in this." She pointed out. "Let's not blame the council for doing *exactly what you wanted.*"

He pulled a face at her and then looked out across the city. The vast, ancient buildings cast great pools of shadow across the crumbling roads. Anything could have been hidden in any one of the skyscrapers or basements. "Now we can stop worrying about the council and work out what to do next. If we can find out whatever dad stumbled across, then we can work out why the council are so scared. The problem is that I don't know where to start."

Tiria looked at her feet, and then cleared her throat awkwardly. "The outcasts see far more than the scavengers. You said they found your father after he died. Maybe they overheard something."

Seth was busy taking weapons out of his bag and sliding them into their holsters, but he paused to flash a grin at her. "Your brother is an outcast, right?"

"Am I that obvious?" She rolled her eyes and started strapping her bowie knife to her hip. "The outcasts will shoot us on sight. They get hunted down by their own families. Do you know how many points killing an outcast earns you? I'm not talking about the petty traders grubbing a living out of the dirt. I'm talking about the traitor runaways, the criminals and the rotting walkers, the ones with nothing to lose. The only reason any of them survive is because they are utterly ruthless. If you want to talk to them, you either need an insider or bulletproof skin."

"It's a wonderful coincidence for you, all the same."

"Don't be too clever. Without me, you won't get near to Lawrence." She retorted tartly, and shoved the blade into its sheath. "Do you have a better plan, or will you help me find him?"

Seth bowed his head in mock-surrender and looked around at the looming buildings. "Where do we start?"

"I have no idea." She scratched her nose awkwardly and then started walking. There was only one way they could walk, whatever they decided to do. After a few streets the looming buildings of the city had toppled over like drunkards, leaning on each other and groaning whenever the air got cold. Even the vault dwellers, who had never seen the city, knew about the skyscrapers. When chunks of them broke away they had felt the roof shake above their heads. They climbed up a steep hill first, determined to get as far away from the vault as possible before they began their hunt. Seth explained that he had to be careful, always starting his searches in a different direction in case someone was trying to track him. They climbed steadily. After five miles or so they stopped to rest and looked back down the hill. For the first time, Tiria saw the broken city which she had been hiding under for months.

The girl was amazed at how far away the gaping wound of the central city was from the vault. She had thought that the roads they had walked along, and the impassable crumbling buildings, were monumental enough. She had imagined the vault was tucked under the treasures of the long-dead, but Seth had told her the vault was right on the outskirts of the metropolis. The citizens had expected to be a target, he said. The vault was strong, but a direct hit would have blocked the entrances and suffocated everyone inside.

Looking down the valley into the city's heart, Tiria fought back a shudder. The crater was as barren as a desert, blackened by fire until the edges were as smooth and slippery as glass. Whatever buildings had been there were long gone. No birds flew over it, and the brown strands of grass stopped growing miles before its cracked edges. Great schisms shattered the earth around it where the earth itself had trembled. The lip of the crater crumbled, spitting rotting chunks of decaying buildings into the depths. A constant stream of dust drifted and pooled in base of the crater, choking anything that could have survived beneath. Every breath of wind sent the dust howling into the air.

How many people had died there? The crater was large enough to hold thousands - tens of thousands. How many more were killed when their skyscrapers had crumbled into the screaming earth? Had every person from the ancient city found shelter in the vault?

She remembered the savages who had ambushed them and shivered. No, someone had been left behind. For all she knew, the rats had come from this city, too.

The crater banished them from the east, and the groaning giants blocked the path to the north. They might have risked climbing over the shifting stones, but there was no point. After the leaning buildings there was a river where great chunks of ice seethed in the torrent, crashing into each other and the banks and carving away great chunks of earth. It was impassable, Seth had said. Before the war there had been a bridge. Perhaps the bombs had destroyed it; perhaps the early citizens had destroyed it to bottleneck their own defences. Either way, the only way they could leave the city was along the road to the south, and so that was the way they walked.

"Have you ever explored the city?" Tiria asked. Seth shrugged.

"There's nothing there. The fire took most of it, and the ash eaters looted the rest when the first winter came. Even when their homes had been flattened they refused to leave. If you were desperate you could dig through the bones, but no-one has the stomach for that."

"Where else could they have gone?" She asked. "To the vault?"

"It was too late for that. The door was locked days before the bombs fell." He looked a little uncomfortable, and then gestured for them to move on.

They made it past the outer wall before Tiria worked out how to explain her plan to Seth. He seemed quite happy to follow her, wherever she decided to go. It was dizzying to think that, on the surface, she was more capable than he was. Last time they had travelled together she had deliberately made the journey difficult. Now she fell back into her scavenging ways with easy skill, loving the feeling of dust under her feet and the sting of burning grit that roughened the breeze.

They walked past the wall, and when the sun grew painfully hot they sheltered under a concrete arch that had the word *Bus* painted on the side. It was a word that Tiria didn't know, but seeing the bold letters made her remember something. She turned to Seth with wide eyes, the words almost spilling out.

"I know where one of the outcasts might be! I found a book in the ruins. A proper book. When I tried to hide it..."

"Hide it?" He raised an eyebrow, and the girl stumbled over her excitement.

"Reading is a crime. The officials are the only ones who even know the alphabet. They get to know everything, and the rats keep running around the ruins bringing all the good stuff to them."

"My cynicism is rubbing off on you." He tweaked her nose with a snide smile and then waved the other hand vaguely. "Go on. What does this have to do with your brother?"

"Well, I tried to hide the book, and I met this girl. She acted like I was an animal in one of Walker's tanks, except I could talk. She asked me all these questions. She could read, and write, so..."

"So you think she must have come from a vault." He finished.

"You say that no-one's ever escaped from yours." She looked at him briefly and then twisted her hands together when he returned the look with cool disdain. "*If* that's true, then there must be another one."

"It's true." Seth said shortly.

"So what if Law found the vault?" Tiria wished the words didn't sound as foolish as they did. "He was never found. They never even took him to the ballot to be sentenced, he just disappeared. If the outcasts do have a vault, that would be the perfect place for them to hide. He could have joined them after he ran away."

"Would another vault let him in?"

"Why not? They let Owl out." Tiria spoke without thinking. "Maybe they're braver than your people."

"But he's a rat."

"Bringing a rat into the vault? How terrible!" She raised an eyebrow at the man and smirked when he looked aloof.

"Maybe they got desperate. People can be awfully brave when they're starving to death." He chewed his lip thoughtfully and then smiled, trying not to look too disturbed by the idea. "There are other vaults, Ti. We had radio contact with them, years ago, but it stopped soon after the fallout fell. The log books from that time say that they must have died. We thought we were the last ones alive."

"The rats thought that, too." Tiria said softly. "Everyone's so good at hiding from each other that we keep forgetting anyone else is around. The only people who seem to know are... are the outcasts. Because they come from all the clans – it doesn't matter if you're a rat or a trader or even a slaver; if you run away, your best chance is to find the outcasts. Some people say they even take in savages before they go bad. If Lawrence is alive then he has to be there – or, even if he didn't make it – they watch the runners, Seth. They have to have seen him."

The man stopped walking for a moment and chose his words carefully. The desperate note in Tiria's voice made him uneasy. "Your brother ran away years ago. Even if they did see him, they might have forgotten by now."

"He might be dead or caught by the slavers." Tiria added, her eyes narrowing. "But dead bones and evil men won't tell me how it happened. There's a chance the outcasts will know, and that's enough for me to want to find them."

Seth nodded slowly. "It's a good plan. Lead the way."

CHAPTER 2

It took days to walk back to the territory Tiria had been born in. The girl felt as if each step was making her smaller. The buildings were as familiar as the freckles on her arms, and yet they looked impossibly alien. This was no longer her land; she would be stealing if she took even one pebble from her childhood haunts. Now, it belonged to someone else: to her father, and his new wife, and whatever spawn the twisted old man could cough from his shrivelled loins.

Tiria felt deeply sorry for the new wife. She had witnessed her father's selfish brutality over Elizabeth for years, until she honestly believed that it was normal for a matched couple to loathe each other. Now that she knew better, she wondered if most of the rats enjoyed their breeding. If the ballot wasn't about dutiful marital rape but something better, then it would make the struggle for survival so much more bearable.

Her father's new wife might have known that kind of pleasure. She might have come into his bed shyly, not fearfully. Tiria felt sick at the thought. Somehow, she realised, she had to know what had happened to her. Her father's cruelty had never been reported, and so he had never been punished. Perhaps the new wife would have had the nerve to run from him. Perhaps he had browbeaten her as ruthlessly as he had Elizabeth. Tiria's own silence, her refusal to see the crimes he was committing, weighed on her.

"I have to go home." She told Seth. "I need to see my father."

The expression in his black eyes was clearly an argument. To his credit, he didn't say a word. Seth immediately followed the girl when she changed direction. They walked silently to the hatch.

It was covered in dust - inches of it. That was all that they needed to see, but Tiria grit her teeth and yanked the metal sharply upwards. They had been expecting it, but even so the stench made them both recoil.

"I need to see." Tiria whispered. The man squeezed her shoulder for a second. She took a great gulp of clean air, tied a rag over her nose and mouth, and then crawled down into the room she had been born in.

Even the savages would not have sheltered there. The body lay in its own filth, encrusted with dried vomit and faeces. There were dark streaks of blood on the spindly legs, and the rags wrapped around it were foul with mould. The man's body was contorted and gaunt. It was not shrivelled in the normal way of dead things, but dried out. It looked like something had drained him until there was nothing left to bleed or dribble out of his shell. He hadn't been dead for long enough for the rats to find him, but a grey film of soft fur mouldered in his gaping mouth.

"Cholera?" Seth asked, his sleeve pressed over his nose. Tiria shook her head, unable to tear her eyes away. Did she feel happy? She couldn't tell.

"His wife would have reported that. They always burn the infected."

She moved over to the rough cooking area and kicked at the scattered tins. All of the cupboards were empty, and every open packet crawled with maggots. She pushed them away, too curious to be squeamish, and picked up a bottle that she hadn't seen before. Her face was carefully blank when she showed it to Seth.

"It's strange," She said carefully. "His wife isn't dead, and she's not here. You'd think she would be."

Seth took the bottle of bleach away from the girl and put it back exactly where she had found it, hidden among the empty food tins. "Very strange."

"If she'd burned him, I suppose someone would have seen the smoke before she had a chance to get away. It looks like she's been gone for long enough to be safe. We're better at hiding than she is, aren't we?"

Seth nodded, and Tiria felt her mouth splitting into a grin. She couldn't help it; her body trembled with laughter, and tears, and shock. Rooting in her bag, she pulled out a small bottle of medical alcohol and tore a rag off her spare shirt. Seth was already climbing out of the shelter when she stuffed the rag into the mouth of the bottle. She crawled out of the hatch and held the bottle upside down, soaking the rag with the pure spirit. Her fingers were shaking too much to light a match. She struggled and fumbled them against the sandpaper, and then she smelled the unmistakable bitterness of sulphur.

Seth handed her the match carefully, keeping the flame protected from the wind. She smiled again, lit the rag, and then dropped the bottle into the hole. It exploded with a roar, and other smells joined the stench of the rotting corpse as its clothes caught fire, then the mouldy hair, and then the furniture and blankets until the whole shelter was ablaze.

Tiria slammed the hatch down and watched the metal glowing as it heated up. Smoke billowed from the badly fitted edges.

They were far away by the time anyone could have seen it.

When night fell they made their way to the library, and made a camp in the dark, dry basement. When thin strands of morning light spilled through the floorboards Seth started teaching Tiria how to follow trails. It was easy near the bookshelves, where the only footprints belonged to one of the two girls. Seth taught Tiria how to tell where they were moving and where they paused. When they were muddled together he asked her to point to individual prints and name them. It was frustrating, but when they got back outside it was impossible. There were a hundred prints for every one they wanted to follow – dog, rat, savage – and the wind had carved most of them into meaningless eddies.

"Now we have to think like our quarry." Seth said, unperturbed. He pointed in the direction of the steps. "If you were going this way, where would you shelter? Which buildings would you avoid?"

"Are you saying she'd think like me?" Tiria was confused. "How do you track the citizens? They don't know how to hide in the ruins."

"Their prints are always the ones going the wrong way." He murmured, and then gestured at the horizon again. The girl bit her lip, and then pointed at a distant hill.

"You can tell there's a little water there. The dust is darker and there's some green stuff. I'd go that way. Is that right?"

He smiled, and started walking in the direction she had chosen. Tiria bit back a curse and caught up. "You're not allowed to say 'I told you so' if we walk the wrong way for weeks. If you know I'm wrong, then..."

"There's no right or wrong." He interrupted her, and she had the peculiar feeling he was repeating back something from his own training. "We have a reason to choose this path, and that's enough for now."

"I get to say 'I told you so' when we're lost, then."

"I'd hardly expect you to hold your tongue. You don't know how." He muttered. She cuffed at him, and they kept walking.

After a few days they reached the green patch, which turned out to be a series of low-slung buildings with their roofs completely consumed by moss. Tiria circled them in amazement. She had never seen so much green in one place before, apart from the lower levels of the vault. It looked obscene next to the grey-red of the dust. Thousands of years of decay had branded everything the same dull shade, but here the moss erupted from the buildings like mould. One on side there had been a hill which had crumbled onto the building, making it look as though the roofs had grown from the earth. On the other side there were solid concrete walls with no apparent way in.

"Is it a vault?" Tiria asked, but neither of them knew the answer. It took them far too long to find an entrance, and when they finally did the rough hatch was sealed up by moss and rust. Tiria took one of her last explosive cartridges out of her bag and pressed it to the hinges, thanking whichever god was listening that the citizens hadn't stolen away her belongings. She set off the explosive, and covered her ears when the sound echoed and boomed in a vast, empty space. The place must have been enormous. She uncovered her ears and helped Seth to wrench up the damaged hatch. All they could see was thick, cold darkness.

Seth looked quizzically at Tiria, and when she nodded he reached into his bag and pulled out a flare. It burst into bright light, and he dropped it into the hole. It fell for a long time, and then the dull thud of its landing made the same ghastly echo as the explosion. They stared down, and both recoiled before steeling themselves for a second look.

It was a single, vast room. The buildings on the surface were ridges in the roof, solid triangles designed to be as structurally sound as possible. The room could not have been sealed against the fires, nor could it have nurtured any citizens: it was simply a huge, covered space they had run to when the bombs started to fall. The closest thing to a supply was a pool of water which lay in the middle of the room, surrounded by moss-covered tiles.

They must have sheltered there. Hundreds of men, women and children had hidden under the jagged roof, crammed together, surviving the worst of the blast and the fires but knowing, even before the dust started to fall, that they would die there. Their bodies lay entwined on the ground, wrapped around each other in embraces and rictus. Smiling faces beamed down at them from the walls as images of people in tight costumes played in the same pool of water.

The moss must have started in the steam from the raging fires outside, or perhaps the ash-eaters had grown desperate enough to drain the pool. Something had swept through them, after the exits were buried and they were left in the dark. A makeshift tower had grown from one corner, but it barely reached halfway to the hatch on the roof. The starving people must have looked up at the small outline of sunlight every day, and fought each other to reach it. The tower was made from metal, plastic, and finally human bones. The moss had been nurtured by the rotting bodies. It had grown hardy enough to survive, finally crawling up to the roof and sealing the hatch once and for all.

"Let's get away from here." Tiria said, and pushed herself away from the hatch so fast her head spun. She took a deep breath of the fresh air and shook her head, seeing the mouldering skeletons whenever she closed her eyes. "God, my family lived less than a week away from this. If my family... if my ancestors had chosen to... *god.*" She shivered and then started running, following the crumbling road out of the car park and into the dust. Seth caught up with her.

"I've seen worse." He said quietly, "But it doesn't get any easier."

"How could any of them choose?" She demanded, rounding on him. "They didn't know a single thing! They could find a vault and never see the sun again, or... or rot into savages, or stay outside and eat dust until it choked them... how could they have made that kind of decision?"

"I think most of them had it made for them." He replied, and looked back over his shoulder with a grim expression on his unusually pale face. "The vaults closed long before the bombs fell. Everyone who was left outside had... I don't know, a few days? Maybe an hour? If I told you the world would burst into flames by morning, what would you do?"

"Laugh at you." She said glumly. He nodded and tore his eyes away from the beautiful green building.

"I wonder how many of them laughed. I would have. I don't think I would have believed it until the sky caught fire."

CHAPTER 3

After the green buildings, Tiria and Seth walked for several days without any real purpose. Whenever they saw a landmark they made their way towards it, reasoning that anyone running from the officials or hiding from the rats would need to find shelter every night. If the outcasts truly took in the runaways, then they would watch the landmarks. If not, then they probably hadn't seen anything of either Seth's father, or Lawrence. While they waited for the outcasts to show themselves the two journeyers slept in windmills, train stations and even, on one peculiar night, the carcass of an ancient prison filled with animal bones.

"Walker would love it here." Tiria said, poking a massive bone in wonder. Seth tried to explain what a *zoo* was, and she shrugged. Like most of the burned world, it seemed far better not to know. The ancient, crumbling bones held a strange sort of dignity which had nothing to do with their years locked up in concrete enclosures. Now, they were equal to the other dust eaters.

If she had stayed in her own territory and been balloted off with another rat, then her whole world would have been comfortably contained within the few miles she could cover in a single day. The further she got from her territory, the smaller her childhood became. Her home had been mapped in single streets, where her scavenging rights ended and another person's began. The town where she was raised was large enough to hold scores of rats, and she recognised the colours and sounds of other clans even though she never saw their faces. The ballot was a familiar stink to all of them. Every other memory was ensconced in her mother's silent footsteps.

The world changed. Tiria saw other settlements: smaller towns, and villages which they skirted around as soon as they saw the fabric banners of a ballot building in the distance. There were other buildings which grew from the ground on their own, like mushrooms, with no windows or no walls, just a skeleton of support pillars and a heap of gritty bricks. They explored each of these with a little less hope each time. They still hadn't found a sign of the outcasts.

"We should keep going." Seth said after a few more days. Tiria was busy fashioning a snare for the feral cats she had heard yowling while they found their shelter, and so she didn't answer. The man lay back on their bedroll and yawned. "The world can't go on forever. Sooner or later, we'll find *someone.*"

"Don't you know where we're going?" She had thought he knew the wastes well, or at least his family did. Seth smiled crookedly at her.

"How would I? We're hundreds of miles away from home. None of my runaways even made it out of the city outskirts, let alone into your territory. This is far beyond anything I recognise."

"Oh." She bit her lip and finished off her snare with a neat knot. It didn't really matter.

They followed trails and uncovered ancient paths, and although Seth was teaching her to do it herself she was a slow learner. They had found water once thanks to her, but only after they were almost gasping from thirst. Apart from that it had been Seth who had found almost everything. She busied herself trapping and scavenging, trusting him to choose their path while she kept them fed. There were precious few supplies this far into the wastes, but since there were so few people the animals were easier to catch.

"You're skinning the next one." She said, changing the subject. "I'll show you how."

"I'll just hope we find the outcasts before our next meal, then." He replied with an exaggerated queasy look. She looked exasperated.

"Coming from someone who chops hands off human quarry..."

"I only did that once, and I didn't have to eat the damn things afterwards." He grinned suddenly. "It's not a bad idea, though. I should have forced them down Agni's throat."

"You're disgusting." She smiled at him, and left to put the snares out. She walked a good distance from the shelter before she did, knowing that the cats could take fright at the slightest sound or the smallest scent. The house they were sheltering in was by an ancient iron gate which was bolted shut, but the wall it was attached to was loose and easy to clamber over. She dropped down onto the far side of the gate and walked along the road. The trees whispered around her, but she couldn't hear anything moving through them. The moon lit the ground in bright patches where the trees hadn't spread their umber leaves, and she kept walking and searching for a clearing.

The shock stopped her in her tracks. She stood, frozen, not even daring to breathe. Her heart thudded in her chest, and then she raised a hand to her face and drew a shaking breath.

The house was wondrous. Endless empty windows looked out onto a dried up lake, with a stone staircase sweeping gracefully between the two. The building was larger than her ballot theatre, and the walls glowed in the moonlight. Swirls of ornate carved stone and endless rows of copper statues seemed to move when she looked at them. She could just imagine the place covered in flowers, standing serenely in the sunlight with ancient long-dead women sweeping in their grand dresses along the very path she was standing on. She looked down at her filthy boots and jeans, and suddenly felt very small.

There were huge bones on the driveway, shining in the blue light as she walked closer. Tiria didn't bother to keep to the shadows. She ran her fingers over the looming ribcages and her hand met leather. It crumbled in her hand, and a few metal links chimed as they fell onto the stone pavement.

The house cast no shadow, since the light was so dim, but every window was shrouded. There were wooden shutters drawn across most of them, and others were boarded up. Seeing the roughly nailed wooden boards proved that this place wasn't so different from the buildings in the cities, but Tiria was disappointed. It would have been perfect if this place was untouched. It looked as though the dust eaters had fallen asleep when everyone else had died.

There were carvings on the steps which had been eroded by years of sand storms. Tiria made out a face, a reaching hand, an extended leg. She frowned and drew her hand away. Touching the statues seemed more profane than scavenging from the dead. Someone had idolized these stone creatures. Dust eaters were crammed into their holes like insects.

She eased the door open and stepped into the house. The door was so vast that she barely had to open it to fit through. It barely creaked on its ancient hinges. Normally, the girl would have realized what that meant – but she was too fascinated to be wary.

The building was not silent, but it seemed to breathe more like a living being than a mass of stone. Shutters swayed and sighed, and endless corridors collected the low groaning and spilled it back into the mouth of the atrium. The emptiness of it felt different from the decaying yaws of the ruins, though. There was a living peace to the building which made it feel like it was supposed to be that way. The shutters did not bang against the walls or creak, they simply moved in the wind. The hot summer wind was cooler, and Tiria realized that there was no dust on the floors for it to blow about. That made her pause. She had been in the vault for so long that she hadn't even noticed, but to a rat it would have been so obvious –

She was running before they could grab her. Hands clutched at her pack. Tiria dropped everything she was carrying and wriggled free. A scavenger wouldn't have done that. Perhaps if they knew she hadn't come to steal from them they would let her go. They had surrounded her in the dim light, walking silently on the polished floors. The whole place was so clean they hadn't disturbed any dust. They would have been able to see Tiria reflected in the waxed floor even if she hadn't been so obvious.

Tiria ran down one of the hallways and slipped on the soft carpet. Her leg burned as she slid down onto the ground, and she pushed herself upright on aching palms. It was too late; the people who had been chasing her pressed down on her elbows and kept her flush to the ground.

"What are running from?" One of them demanded. The girl shrieked and tried to wriggle free, and he slammed her back down to the ground. "Tell me!"

"Are you joking?" She cried. "You chased me!"

"Not us, fool! Why are you here? Who are you running away from?"

Her racing heart skipped a beat, and she stopped struggling. "Are you the outcasts?"

The man didn't answer, but she felt his grip on her relax. Tiria sat up and rubbed some sensation back into her shoulders. "I've been looking for you."

"We know that. We've been watching you since you walked through Hillingdon." The man's face was shadowed. A beard softened his silhouette, but his eyes glinted. "We know that bastard official is using you as bait. How did you sneak away?"

The girl's mouth opened and then closed. "He's not an official. He's my high."

"Your high." The man scoffed, and helped her to stand. The other outcasts milled around them, muttering to each other. None of them took charge – they spoke to each other and came to a decision, before the bearded man turned back to the girl. "He isn't a rat. He isn't an outcast. You know as well as we do that there's only one other place that could spawn a man like that."

Tiria looked down at her feet. Another outcasts leaned forward, and spoke in a low voice. "You have to say the words, or we won't help you find your brother."

Tiria answered immediately: "He came from a vault."

CHAPTER 4

The outcasts collected Seth in the same dismissive manner they had captured Tiria. She was afraid that he would attack them before they had a chance to speak to him, but the outcasts knew how to trap violent men. A woman screamed by the gate, and when Seth ran after the voice he fell straight into a pit. A net had been strung at the bottom. While he struggled and swore, the men leaned their heads over the edge and explained what was going on.

"Why not just talk to me?" The man growled after they pulled him out. The outcasts looked pointedly at his weapons, and Seth bit his tongue. When he saw Tiria he pointed at her. "Why not just send *her?*"

"She told us you weren't an official, but that doesn't mean we believed her." The bearded man said smoothly. Seth was suddenly very guarded.

"Ti is my low. I'm from the Ruislip ballot."

"Is that the name of your vault?" The man said diffidently. Seth froze, and then he lunged at Tiria so quickly that she cried out and fell backwards. The outcasts caught Seth's arms and pulled him back.

"That was clever." Tiria said coolly, "If they didn't already believe me, they do now."

"I'm sure you could tell them far more!" He snarled. She shook her head.

"They already knew, idiot! I wouldn't have told them one word if they didn't. We walked past three shelters on the way here. They know we came from one of them; they don't care which one. They only want us to stop camping on their land. If a single official comes after us it could betray every person in this house."

Seth calmed down a little, but he still breathed heavily. "Killing us would have been an easier way to get rid of us."

"We try not to resort to that." The bearded man folded his arms and looked stern. "We're trying to live our own lives, not traumatize our children. Bloodshed draws the vultures near."

"I'm a vulture, am I?"

"Would you rather be a rat?" Tiria growled. He turned his glare back onto her, and she remembered that an hour before he had been gentle, teasing. Now he looked ready to throttle her.

It took Seth a full day to calm down. When he finally spoke to Tiria, his words were so calm that she thought that he was lying. He understood, he told her. Of course she had told them. They already knew, so surrendering the truth was nothing against what she had to gain.

"We'd better find your brother." He added. Tiria swallowed. There was something off about his serenity, as if he had burned off all of his fury and revealed something darker in the ashes. He groaned at her suspicious look, and twisted his hands into his hair.

"I'm not going to apologise to you." He growled. "I'm angry you talked. I'm just trying to say that I can see why you did it. You shouldn't apologise to me, either, but at least admit you know why I'm angry."

She met his eyes and nodded, but couldn't force herself to form words. Until she had betrayed the vault, she had no idea that finding Lawrence was more important to her than Seth's happiness. Still, she felt guilty: what would she have surrendered if she truly thought they could find her brother?

The outcasts sent her to the basement, where she found an old man surrounded by crumbling books. The room was a little cold, and Tiria knew that the paper only had a few decades left before it decayed. The reek of mould was strong, but the pages the old man brought out were almost new. He explained that they had reams of paper, which they had found wrapped in plastic. Every page was covered in tiny letters – names, places and dates. The outcasts recorded the details of every person they saw, and they were terrifyingly thorough.

"It's kept us safe." The old man said. "We know who we can trust, and we know what they want."

Tiria forced herself to smile. It would take weeks to look through all of the names, and she didn't even know if Lawrence was among them. After an hour, her head ached. After two days, she wanted to scream. In the end, she returned to Seth and tried to heal their cool divide just because his glares were less horrible than reading another cursive scrawl.

Seth admitted that making a truce with the outcasts was the best thing that could have happened. He busied himself asking the outcasts every question he could think of. Most of them refused to answer, but some of the older people were happy to talk. He didn't ask anything that would compromise their security. He was interested in how much they saw, and how they kept surveillance on the entire wasteland. The answers were staggering. The outcasts were seen by the rats as a ragtag band of desperate criminals, living in fear off scraps of contaminated food. In truth, the outcasts had begun with the survivors who had kept to themselves during the apocalypse. The manor house, for example, had protected fifty people who had kept to their own laws even while the world was descending into anarchy.

One of their descendants was happy to tell the story. Her hair was thin and patchy, but she held her head up with pride. "My great great many-greats grandpa was a miserly old sod who had a very big basement full of food, wine and a lot of firearms. When the warnings came, he locked himself, great grandma and the servants into the wine cellar. He stood over them with a shotgun and a glass of brandy until they stopped trying to escape. After the bombs fell they thanked him, or murdered him. One or the other." She shrugged and scratched her head. "You can never tell with family legends, can you?"

Seth told Tiria the story later that night. Her head was buzzing from going through the books, and she told him that she had found out some of the story from the records. Seth whistled appreciatively, and the next day he followed his wife into the library. While she hunted for names, he hunted for the past. He became fascinated by the outcasts, and told Tiria that he had learned more history in a week with them than he had in all of his lessons in the vault.

The man slowly warmed to the outcasts, but their casual rudeness made him struggle. The bearded man welcomed Seth and Tiria into the mansion by refilling their supplies. Then he immediately lost Seth's grudging respect by asking if he really thought his six chamber pistol was good for anything except annoying rabbits. The man's knowledge of weapons was terrifyingly thorough. The outcasts hadn't been lying about their ancestors' love of firearms, and had learned to read from ancient gun catalogues and hunting magazines. Every night they cleaned the pistols and sniper rifles which they carried, all the while making comments about the way Tiria and Seth poked away at their 'toy' guns.

Tiria thought that Seth would snap at the outcasts sooner or later, but in fact he began to enjoy their casual insults. By the end of the first week he returned them in good humour. The outcasts had as many stories as they did bullets, and while many of them were obviously false, there was enough truth in them that Seth listened carefully. Tiria noticed that he stopped watching for threats out of the corners of his eyes. Some of his suspicious watchfulness had ebbed away.

"I'm glad." Tiria whispered that night, cuddling up with him in their blanket. "It's about time you trusted somebody."

"I trust you," He kissed her forehead and then looked mischievously into her eyes. "Although you never said 'I told you so' when we got lost. I'm worried that you're saving up a great deal of crowing."

The next morning, Seth took a sheaf of papers out of the vault to read in his room. The librarian frowned, but didn't try to stop him. The man didn't emerge for hours, and when he did he was unusually quiet. Tiria wondered what he had found, but when she asked he made a feeble joke and handed the booklet back to the librarian. She saw the word *Vault* scrawled onto the cover.

"Is it bad? Do they know where it is?" She asked. Seth shook his head.

"No, it's more history. It's just an old story, but it was about the vaults, so..." He forced a smile onto his sunburned face. The librarian flicked through the pages, and his eyebrows rose.

"This man has the same last name as you!"

"Everyone in the vaults has the same last name." Tiria pointed out. "They're more inbred than the slavers."

Seth rolled his eyes, and no more was said about the book. That evening, Tiria sneaked out of the dining hall to find it. She recognized the blue cover, and stuffed the pamphlet inside her shirt while she wandered through the house looking for somewhere to read it. Finally, she had the bright idea of locking herself into one of the bathrooms. She sat in the luxuriant, cracked bathtub, dangled her legs over the edge, and started to read. It was written in an odd, stilted way that seemed to avoid using any real words, but just barked information at her.

1st November, 2344 (FF)
Events: Dog Vault Destroyed
Notes:
Official Unit 201/27V set ambush (Ref. Tactics outline 8B3)

3 Unidentified persons: 2M, 1F believed to be as follows:

1M: Unnamed ambassador from Dog Vault, previously sent to negotiate with wasteland groups (Declined: lack of security clearance, insufficient time to assess other options). 1M was witnessed collaborating with 1F for 5 months prior to event (Ref: Event Outline 2343/CC). Actual role in ambush cannot be determined.

1F: Unnamed Official. Assumed to have informed officials of location of Dog Vault. Arrested by officials following events. Outcasts are advised to avoid contact when possible, due to unclear allegiance risk.

2M: Unnamed. Possibly scout from a different vault. Wore no uniform and no tribe colours suggesting deliberate anonymity. 2M sought assistance from 1M after the event, and was denied. 2M was traced as far as Officials territory before disappearing. Wider search of the area denied, as it is Rat and Official territory.

Dog Vault is still burning. Estimated survivors: Nil. Officials captured no prisoners. Attack was clearly an extermination and not a tactical move.

No further action needed.

Tiria frowned and kicked her legs against the plastic bath. So there had been another vault, and the officials had destroyed it. Why was Seth so put out by it? He already knew that the officials would slaughter the citizens. It was why his family had been silencing their strays for generations. She sighed, and folded the paper back up. If he wanted to explain, then he would. She had better things to worry about.

Over the next few days her husband became so surly that she started to despise him. She goaded him, trying to break him out of his shell, and finally he snapped at her.

"You're never going to find your brother." He interrupted her voice and gestured at the vaulted ceiling. "We could never read all these books."

Before Tiria could draw a breath, the librarian hurried over to them. His face was flushed with worry, as he realized how close both of the strangers were to strangling each other. "Look," He said, "This isn't the best way to search. We trust you now, don't we? Ask Lloyd if he'll take you to the next commune. It's only a few miles away, and they're much more organized than we are."

"Another commune?" Seth asked, tearing his eyes away from the woman's. "I thought this was it!"

"No." The librarian smiled wanly and gestured at the papers. "There are more of us than there are of... of anyone else in the wastes. We keep to small groups so the officials don't find out. They might catch a cell and think it's everyone, but there are two hundred families for every one they know about. The network stretches all the way to the ocean."

"Ocean?" Tiria whispered. Seth had gone pale, but he nodded.

Two days later, Tiria was shown into a far smaller library filled with metal cabinets. The building they had reached had once been a government office, and the thick stone walls were peppered with bullet holes. She wondered if she was in the wrong place, and then a clerk greeted her. He drew a drawer out of one of the cabinets and showed her scores of neatly sorted names. While the girl was running a fascinated hand along the paper cards, he asked her who she was looking for.

"His name's Lawrence." She said, and leaned closer. Hope shone from her eyes. There were so many names in the room – surely, Lawrence must be one of them. "I think he left my district last year, when I was chosen in the ballot."

"When did he become outcast?"

"Eight years ago. Maybe more." Tiria chewed her lip, and the clerk looked confused.

"Why would he stay in a hostile district for so long?"

Tiria shrugged. She wanted it to be true, but against the man's amused words she felt foolish. "I was there. I always thought he was looking out for me."

The man ignored that. He looked through the filing drawers for an excruciatingly long time. "I do have a Lawrence. I have four, in fact, but I can cross off the old man and the idiot. This one could be your brother. A man passed through Harrow and got taken into the Tin Roof Shelter for a time. He lived in that commune for six years, it says here."

"That's not long enough."

"Allow him a few months of aimless wandering. Outcasts aren't adopted until they've spent a long time in the wastes. The officials' spies never hold out for more than a month." He searched for a certain page, and then smiled and turned it so Tiria could read it. "He left in August."

"August," She echoed, and then counted on her fingers. The season was just beginning to change. "That wasn't so long ago."

"You could be lucky." The man agreed, and then he frowned and turned the paper towards himself. A few notes were scribbled onto the bottom, just beside a large X. He cleared his throat. "We followed him for a while. We always do, in case anyone gets it into their heads to make a cheap fortune by selling us out. We saw him getting caught."

Tiria's blood froze in her veins. "Who caught him?"

"Who do you think? The officials!" The man looked amazed by her ignorance, and then realized that she had been desperately grasping at straws. He mollified his words. "I said captured, not killed. They knew who he was, but they didn't shoot him. I'd say there's a pretty good chance they took him to the farms."

"Or to the ballots." Tiria remembered the executions in the theatre and felt sick. The man patted her hand, and she saw the shadow of his head moving from side to side on the table.

"We watch the ballots. When one of our own is executed, we make sure we collect the body before the savages get to it. It's the right thing to do." He shrugged. "Your brother hasn't been seen since he was caught. He's either lying in a shallow grave, or he's in the farms."

Tiria felt a bubble of excitement rising in her stomach. She ran to find Seth, and babbled out the story so quickly that he couldn't make out half of the words. He smiled, and agreed that they should go to the farms, but something in his voice was off. Tiria planted her feet in the ground, bracing herself. She should have known Seth would see the worst in things. Sure enough, his only question made her want to slap him.

"If the officials caught your brother, then why didn't they kill him?"

"We don't slaughter people without a reason! The farms keep the runaways away from us until the council works out what they're running away from. If someone forced them into it then they can be pardoned, but if not... if they did it for a bad reason..."

"So you're saying they're guilty until proven guiltier?" He looked at the sky, murmuring the words with a slight smile. Tiria looked uncomfortable.

"People don't get to break the rules twice."

"Or even once." The man muttered. Tiria chewed on her lip.

"If you think they're lying, then why did you agree to go?

He shrugged, evading the question. "I was completely lost."

"Yes, but why *really?*"

"Every liar tells the truth once in a while. I'm not just here to find your brother. The outcasts are organised enough to have tracked us all this way, but so many of them get captured. I bet that the officials torture them to get at all their insights. Since the outcasts know about the vault, the officials might know, too. I can't ignore a risk like that."

"*Might.*" She whispered back scornfully. "You said I would never find Lawrence. How are you going to hunt down a *might?*"

"I'm chasing a story. You're looking for a criminal who the outcasts decided to enslave, even though they execute people for doing far less. You think you're going to find him alive. That's not a coincidence, it's a fairy tale."

Tiria's stomach dropped in anger. She sat up without a word, moved over to the other side of the room, and curled up under her jacket. When she woke up the next morning she felt the weight of the blanket on her back and shook it off angrily. It took her hours to speak to Seth again, and three days before she slept beside him. She wondered why she always made excuses for the man, when he was the one who didn't know the difference between honesty and cruelty.

He never apologised. He watched her run out her anger, and then he forgot the whole thing. Tiria felt her hatred settle in her stomach, seething with bitter bile, and knew that one day she wouldn't be able to forgive him.

CHAPTER 5

Now that she knew where Lawrence had been, Tiria couldn't wait to leave. The first few days of travel were excruciatingly slow, and she burned with so much nervous energy that her head ached. They travelled for a week through the lowlands, and then they climbed to the top of a hill and saw a flat desert stretching in front of them. After a few hours walking on it, the dust turned to burned heather and sand which had burned into odd shards of glasslike rock. Their feet slipped against it, and it took hours before they found a rhythm of walking across the crackling surface. It was ridiculously difficult. The crushing weariness was made worse by the fact that they could see the road which they had to avoid. The officials brought their prisoners here in hours, while they spent days avoiding the only solid ground for miles.

Tiria was too excited to care that her feet were bleeding. The next day she woke up and could barely walk. She had to waste a precious hour and some of their water cleaning the blisters and bruises, and by the time she had pulled her boots back on the sun was high in the sky. Autumn was almost over, and the thick stink of rotting leaves made the air thick in their lungs. It was a peculiar smell for such an arid plateau. They were confused until they crested to the top of the next valley and looked down.

The farms were a blanket of green. The ground was so thick with plants and trees that they couldn't make out the red shade of dust beneath them. The low hum of bees and birds was obscenely loud in the desert air, and great fields of cattle lowed in the distance. They looked down in utter disbelief, and then made out the shapes of buildings. The most impressive ones were in the centre of the verdant land – two great silos, and a shining structure with real glass windows. Around the outside of the fields there were smaller shelters, more like shanty huts than buildings. Tiria counted twenty six of them before she gave up. There was one every mile, she worked out. The valley was so enormous that there could well have been thousands of prisoners living in them.

The shacks were still on dead dust. There were odd, artificial borders between the green fields and the desert which ragged men and women were diligently treating with pails of chemicals. Tiria skirted the convicts carefully, and they started walking along the edge of the hill. Neither she nor Seth could take their eyes off the silos.

"If I wanted to rule thousands of people," Seth said in a dazed voice, "Controlling the food supply would work far better than waving a gun in everyone's faces."

Tiria felt sick every time she breathed in the good, clean air. "People are starving and they... they just...!"

"Ssh." He grabbed her arm and pulled her behind a rock. They both held their breath and listened to footsteps growing louder, and then further away. When they were sure that the person had gone, they slipped out of their hiding place. Neither of them looked back up at the silos. It would have been like pouring salt into the wound. Seth lowered his voice.

"The officials only get away with it because the rats don't know. As far as they know, the farms are contaminated hell holes. Whoever thought of filling the borders with criminals was a genius. Even the outcasts wouldn't think to look at them."

The woman shook her head numbly, and then started walking.

"Where are you going?" Seth asked. Tiria paused, because walking had been such an instinct that it hadn't occurred to her that it could be pointless.

"We need to find someone who's alone. It's dangerous to show ourselves to a crowd."

"It's dangerous either way."

"Since we live in a world filled with savage mutations and rabid dogs that's not a great argument, Seth."

He bowed his head mockingly and gestured for her to lead the way.

The first man they met stuttered so fiercely that they could barely understand him. "At least he won't be able to tell the officials about us," Seth muttered, and the man overheard him. Tiria listened to his angry words and interpreted them with a smile. "He says he wouldn't even tell the officials to hold their breath after he farted."

"Does everyone feel that way?" Seth asked, looking sheepish. The man nodded, and then pointed to the next building in the valley. His meaning was clear. If they were looking for someone, then they would be in one of the shelters. All the strangers had to do was search.

It took them three days to make it half way around the valley. Aside from the fact that it was vast, they had to wait for darkness or long shadows before they could cross the rattling rivers, and when they had to go into the farmland itself Seth was careful to make sure they didn't leave any footprints behind them.

They asked at so many shelters that Tiria lost count. After about ten, one of the men said that news of them had spread. Whoever they were looking for would probably know they were coming long before they got there.

"That's fine," Seth said guardedly, handing over the chocolate bar he had promised the man in exchange for information. "How can we find out about him, if it turns out he's not here anymore?"

"Dead, you mean? Or running?"

"Either." Seth tried not to look at Tiria, who had gone a little pale. "We need to find out what happened."

The man shrugged and picked at his teeth with a shard of wood. He pointed to the silos, which were glowing amber in the evening light. "See those? They keep all their records in there. When we arrived they marched us through and wrote down our age, hair colour, eye colour, birthmarks..." He trailed off and shook his head. "When people die, they go in through the same door. I figure they must start crossing off their numbers after that."

"Records!" Seth whispered the moment they were safely away from the complex. "Ti, there must be a whole records room in that place! I bet... if they're hiding the food here..."

"Maybe." She rubbed her eyes and yawned. "We need to set up camp. It's too late to walk to the next shelter now."

"Shelter?" Seth looked over at the silos, almost liked a kicked puppy. Tiria swatted at him irritably.

"How many soldiers do you think guard that place? Let's forget about the records, and just think about all the food there must be in those towers. Do you really think we could just walk in there and have a look?"

Seth opened his mouth to argue, and then shrugged. The fervour went out of his wild eyes, and he slept deeply that night. The next morning he stumbled a few times before he tore his gaze away from the building and started looking ahead.

They had to skirt the hills that day, as the farms bowed out into the desert to avoid a craggy river. The water covered their tracks as they waded upstream, but by the time they had climbed out of the ravine and back onto the other side most of the day had passed. It was nearly dusk when they saw the shell of another building in the distance.

They sped up a little, their feet aching too much to scout the building for traps. The shell turned out to be a roof with the walls buried in the sand. It looked like one of the tortoises Tiria had seen in Walker's lab, but when she blinked it transformed into the shell of the moss-covered swimming pool. She shivered and stood a little distance away as Seth made his way to the door. They heard the scraping sounds of chairs being pushed back as people stood up.

Warm light spilled out into the dust. Tiria kept her hand close to her knife, suspecting an ambush, but then she looked up and her hand fell away as if it had been scalded. She gasped, and reeled back, and heard Seth curse as he caught her and held her upright. The silhouette in the doorway froze, and for a second the man was absolutely still. Then, in a sudden movement, he ran down the steps and skidded to a halt. He stayed there, inches away, as if he was afraid that touching her would scare the girl away. Tiria looked up into his hard eyes, and felt her head spinning.

"Don't faint, sis." Lawrence laughed harshly and tapped the end of her nose with a trembling finger. "Only pretty women are allowed to swoon at my feet."

"Lawrence!" She cried, and he laughed and caught her up in his arms. She sobbed and clung to him like a child, feeling his arms closing tightly around her back and breathing in the wonderful, familiar scent of his skin. She had missed even that, she realised, and couldn't stop herself from bursting in to tears.

CHAPTER 6

"What is this place?" Seth asked, looking around the curving room with interest. Around them, the other people in the shelter busied themselves reading, or mending clothes, and pretended that they weren't eavesdropping.

"It's a housing branch." He said, as if that explained everything, and then relented when Tiria poked him hard in the ribs. Poking her back, he continued: "You already know that we're workers on the farms. They can't have us sleeping in the farm lands stealing their precious food, so every night we have to hike back here and share out our rations. If one branch doesn't report for work, the keepers punish our whole section."

"You must be very fond of each other." Seth muttered in his usual blunt way. Lawrence bristled.

"Would you let someone else suffer so you could run? They always catch us after a few days, anyway. You've seen the glass plains. There's nowhere to shelter or hide."

"Still – "

"Drop it, Seth." Tiria interrupted, glaring at him. "This isn't one of your puzzles, it's their lives."

The man shrugged and opened his rucksack, taking out several portions of rice, trail broth and cereal bars. "I didn't say I didn't understand, I was just curious. If you're on rations then we'll make dinner tonight."

Lawrence shot the man the first genuine smile he had given him. "Thank you."

As they cooked and ate their meal, Tiria had to keep touching her brother, laying a hand on his shoulder or sitting close beside him just to convince herself that he was really there. The years had made him stronger and leaner, and his eyes were far sharper and more shadowed than they had been before. He held his head higher, though, and he spoke far more confidently than he ever had around their father.

"He's dead." Tiria blurted out as she thought that, and then when Lawrence blinked at her she blushed and tried again. "Father's dead. We found his body."

Lawrence froze for a second, and then shook himself out of it. He didn't ask the question, but Tiria answered it in a fast babble – how they had found the shelter, and the body, and who must have done it. The man shrugged and Tiria knew that she could have been speaking about a stranger. The man who had ruled over their entire childhoods was less than dust to the boy he had disowned as a son. The girl stumbled to a halt, and her own question was asked before she could stop it.

"Law, did you ever find... mama?"

He finally looked at her, and the pity in his face made her feel sick. "Oh Ti, didn't anyone tell you?"

He spoke carefully, but in those few words she had already guessed the truth. Lawrence had spent his first few years as a free man, and he kept a close eye on both Tiria and Elizabeth until his hiding place was discovered and he had to leave the city. Elizabeth hadn't been at Tiria's ballot because she was laid up with her new partner's child. The man himself had been swaggering around boasting that he would be returning home to meet his new-born son, but so many people bragged about the same thing that Tiria hadn't paid it any attention. As confused and frightened as she had been, it didn't occur to her to ask each man for his absent wife's name.

The child tore into the world so quickly that Elizabeth's had no chance of surviving. Tiria wondered if her half-brother was sorry for his selfishness as he starved to death without her. From one woman's life had come two grotesque deaths, and her disgusted partner had thrown the bodies out for the birds. That was where Lawrence had found them.

"Here." He said, breaking through her numb silence to hand her something. Tiria took it clumsily, and looked down with eyes blinded by tears. It was soft and fragile in her fingers - a lock of hair. She pressed it to her cheek and then curled up and closed her eyes.

Seth sat next to the silent girl and looped his arm around her back. He told Lawrence softly, "She's been looking for you both since you disappeared."

"I know." The other man replied. "It wasn't safe for her to find me. She came close."

"You were hiding from her?"

"It was the best way to protect her."

Seth laughed humourlessly. "You were both trying to help each other by cutting off your own legs. I don't know which of you is the most stupid."

"She's not stupid." The man gestured to his sister, and swallowed back a lump in his throat. "Help her, please. I'll just make her remember... more."

Seth shot the man a scathing glare and then turned away. Picking the girl up, he carried her to a dark corner of the shelter and sat down holding her in his lap. After a long time, she started sobbing, and Lawrence pressed his hands over his ears. Finally, unable to bear it, he opened the shelter door and escaped into the night.

Seth watched him go, and his arms tightened around the girl. He had promised to leave her here, but it was impossible. Even if this wasn't a prison, even if this was a living paradise, he wouldn't leave her with this man. He couldn't. There was a vein of cowardice in Lawrence which made him dangerous. Oh, the man in him had covered it with bravado, and the people in this shelter seemed to believe in him, but the child of Lawrence had no stomach for the life he had grown into. A man who couldn't even comfort his grieving sister had no place in her life. A man who might have lead her into a trap had much to answer for.

Tiria eventually fell asleep, her face white and tearstained, and Seth left her in the dim candlelight. He made his way outside and found Lawrence pacing around the building, his face fixed.

"Has she stopped crying?" He asked. Seth nodded, and the boy visibly relaxed. "Oh, thank god."

"She'll cry again when she wakes up. I'll warn you, so you can run away again."

The other man coloured. "I didn't..."

Seth gave him a long look, and then shrugged and leaned back against the building. He was struggling to find a way to talk to this man. After so many weeks of hearing about him from the loving words of his sister, he had been expecting someone far different.

"You don't like me, do you?" Lawrence asked quietly. When Seth didn't react at all, he sighed and stuck his hands into his pockets. "Yeah, that's what I thought."

"I heard about a child who loved his mother and sister so much, he was prepared to break the law for them."

"Noble stuff." The man said with an amused look on his face. "It seems to me that you're old enough not to believe in fairy tales."

"Tiria seems to believe it."

"Yes, she was always fond of stories. She used to listen to the gossip in the ballot – far more than I did. She would come home and talk about nothing else for weeks. I don't know if she believed it, exactly, but she preferred talking about that nonsense than anything important. I was glad." He frowned and scratched his nose. "With everything else that was happening, she had a safe, imaginary world to hide in."

"So you're saying you hid things from her."

433

"Did I say that?" - diffidently - "She's nearly ten years younger than I am. I wouldn't have told her everything even if she had worked it out for herself."

"Are you going to tell her now?"

Lawrence glanced back towards the shelter and didn't answer, but Seth recognised the fixed look on the man's face as one that he used himself. For some reason the man's deceit was far more convincing than his affection for his sister. It was as if he was a different person away from her - stronger, more fixed in his own ideas. He spoke about his love for her with a touch of ruthlessness that Seth almost admired. Still, he had to push him - he had to know what Tiria had risked her life for.

"She wants to stay with you." He told the man, and saw him flinch with the dull satisfaction of knowing he had judged Lawrence correctly.

"She can't."

"We both know that. But if you want her to leave with me, you're going to have to be the one to convince her."

Lawrence's eyebrows rose. "Somehow I find that hard to believe. She seems to trust you."

"She made a deal with me." It was strange to talk about it out loud, but once he started Seth found it a relief to admit it to someone else. He explained the whole thing, even though it left a bitter taste in his mouth. "Even when she hated me, she was willing to do whatever it took to find you. That's how much you mean to her."

Lawrence gave the man a narrow look, which Seth scowled at. It wasn't so much the unspoken accusation as the fact that Lawrence was being superior over a sister he hadn't seen in nearly a decade. There was a depth of cunning in both siblings which they both tried to disguise. While Tiria hid it in her artless, forthright honesty, the man disguised his as bravado. The brother she adored was nothing but shadows and memories, and Seth wasn't going to be accused of anything by a liar. His defence came out in a flat, clinical list. "What happened between us was... we agreed that it had nothing to do with our deal. I didn't take advantage of her."

"No?" The man counted off on his fingers. "You got her to follow you, she worked like a slave in your city, she told you the scavengers' code and showed you our shelters... do you think you had to sleep with her to take advantage of her?"

"She agreed to all of that."

"I'm sure she agreed to anything you wanted." Lawrence said snidely, and planted his feet in the ground when he saw Seth's hand close into a fist. The man realized what he was doing just in time, and his words came out in a low hiss.

"I don't think you'd recognise the truth even if I shouted it at you. I don't know what else to tell you, Lawrence. Is it so hard for you to believe that Ti gave herself to me out of love? And god help me, but I took what she was offering. Yes, I wanted her, but I would never have touched her without her consent. And I can tell the difference between real consent and... and a trade."

Lawrence made his reply slow and deliberate, as if he was explaining something to an idiot. "As long as she's safe, I don't care if she has to whore herself out to every high in the wastes."

Seth lashed out at him which a cry of disgust, catching the other man square across the jaw. He knew in the blur of fury that this arrogant cretin had no idea how to defend himself, and yet he barrelled Lawrence into the dust and pressed his hands against the man's throat, bracing against his returning blows without flinching.

"Take that back." He growled. "She's your sister."

Lawrence croaked and swallowed, and as soon as Seth took his hands off his windpipe he coughed out a harsh laugh. He didn't say a word, but his raucous laughter made the other man's hair stand on end. Pushing himself away, he scrambled to his feet. In that moment he understood the man's character. Lawrence's whole mind was laid clear to him, and the revelation left him breathless.

"You never wanted her to find you."

Lawrence stood up painfully, brushed the dust off his clothes, and looked up. "I have my own life to live. I won't always be under the thumb of whoever beats me into submission."

"And you think about your baby sister like that, do you?" Seth sneered, trying to hide his anger under a mask of mockery. Lawrence laughed and shrugged, returning the mockery with outright, brazen honesty which he hurled at the man like bullets.

"That was my childhood, Seth. It would have been Tiria's, too. Whenever the old bastard followed her into the wastes I threw stones, broke glass - did anything to scare the coward into leaving her alone until he beat me, instead. That is the safety I bought her, and I paid for it. I deserve to look out for myself, and now she's old enough to do the same. I don't need your judgement. I'll find my version of freedom and she find hers. She can sell herself to you with my blessing, if it keeps her alive."

"What are you doing to find your freedom?" The other man asked, so softly that Lawrence blinked and stepped forward. When he didn't answer, Seth gestured to the land around them. His voice was sharp with anger. "You're locked up in a feeder plant with criminals. You're all just waiting to be executed. You can't even eat without signing into a register. I don't see how you can boast about abandoning your sister when all it's brought you is this misery."

Lawrence shook his head and then, without warning, punched Seth square in the jaw. The man fell back sprawling against the building, gasping in pain at the unexpected blow, and when he drew himself back upright the man's fist was lowered. He looked surprised, as if he hadn't expected his fist to cause any damage, but his face was red with anger.

"I won't let my sister be used against me again." He spat. "You take her away from this place, and you make her hate me. I won't let the only pure thing in my life sink her claws back into my spine."

CHAPTER 7

Tiria didn't cry when she woke up, she screamed. Most of the clan pressed their hands over their ears and ignored her, rushing to leave the shelter before they were late for work. Her cries stopped quickly, but she changed to such a low, wrenching moan that even the diffident workers shivered. One of the women dropped to her knees beside the girl and shook her.

"Shut up! Do you want the officials to hear you?" Catching sight of the girl's white skin, she hesitated and then lowered her voice. "What's wrong?"

The girl couldn't answer, but her hands crept to her stomach and she sobbed. The woman understood immediately, and hauled her upright. Walking her over to the fire, she set a pot of water to boil and looked up at the loitering workers.

"Tell the officials that Lawrence is sick. Find him and tell him to get back here *now*."

Soaking a rag in the hot water, she pushed the girl up against the metal wall and pressed the compress to her stomach. The blood had soaked through Tiria's clothes.

"How far along were you?" She asked. Tiria stared at her numbly, but the question stirred her from her shock.

"I don't... a few months? I don't..."

"Is it your first one?" The woman's brusque hands stopped working when Tiria nodded, and she sat back on her heels. Sympathy wrote itself across her face. "I am sorry."

"What did I do?" She asked, her voice colourless.

The woman shrugged and threw the dirty into the boiling water, fishing a clean one out with a stick. Another wave of pain made the girl shudder, and she forced her eyes open. "When will it stop?"

"I don't know. No-one here has ever miscarried."

Tiria looked up at her in shock. "Do you mean...?"

"No." The lady said softly. "That would be impossible. They don't miscarry, because they're not allowed to breed. They don't want more mutations running around, and the radiation on the farms is..." she swallowed and shook her head, then raised her arm and pointed to a small scar. "They inject us with these things, and after that we couldn't make babies even if we tried."

"You're missing out on a treat." Tiria managed through gritted teeth, and pressed her hands back onto her stomach. After a second she took them away, as if she couldn't bear to touch herself, and closed her eyes. "I didn't even know I was pregnant."

"Nobody ever takes on their first one. Just tell your high that and you'll be fine." The soothing words sounded sarcastic in the criminal's rough voice. Tiria opened one eye to give her a withering look, and then sighed.

"He won't be angry. He didn't want me for this."

"That's his problem. You know you have to keep trying."

Tiria shook her head, and this time her wan voice was stubborn. "No, this is the end of it. He promised he'd leave me here."

"Leave you!" The woman's eyes opened wide. "Because you were carrying?"

"No, I made him promise. I want to be with Lawrence."

"You can't stay here." She burst out, and then looked at the girl's waxen face and bit her tongue. She tried a different tactic. "Do you know why Lawrence was sent here?"

"He ran away." The girl replied. The woman pulled a face.

"They wouldn't condemn a man for that. You know as well as I do that they fine them points and

441

send them back to the ballot with their feet beaten raw."

"He didn't do anything else." Tiria tried to push herself a little more upright, and then her arms shook and she gave up. "I can't imagine him stealing, or raping, or..."

"The officials call it *depravity*. They stop us from breeding but they say he's a criminal for..." She stumbled over the words and looked away, until Tiria caught her arm. The woman looked down at the hand, the bloodstains in the whorls of the girl's knuckles, and drew a deep breath. "The first time he was caught, they gave him the chance to join a new clan. They took him to the ballot. The woman who chose him reported him less than a week later. He wouldn't breed with her, she said."

"But - Seth and I waited for months." Tiria whispered, lost. "It takes time to trust people."

The woman looked at her despairingly. "That's different." Seeing that the girl still didn't understand, she ground her teeth and forced the words out. "Lawrence can't make himself feel that way about women. Just men."

"Father found out." A voice carried across the room, and both women flinched and looked up. Lawrence had arrived just in time to overhear the last few words. He was holding the door open for

Seth, but his eyes were fixed on Tiria's. Both men understood what they were seeing in seconds, and a spectrum of emotions burned across each of their faces before they came to sit with the women.

Lawrence spoke quickly, as if the words had no choice except to come pouring out, a confession and a childish nightmare tangled together. "Father saw me meeting someone in the ruins. After that I was just counting down the days until he reported me. He would have made my life hell, and yours. I left before he had the chance."

"I thought you left because..." Tiria started, and then looked away. She was feeling dizzy, and she didn't know if it was because of the pain in her body or the ache in her heart. Seth was beside her, she knew. She could feel his arm around her back, his cool hand on her forehead, but all she could see was her brother's pale face. "Didn't you do it for us?"

"I'm sorry, Ti. I didn't have had the nerve to protect you - to confront him - until I was scared for myself." The man spoke bitterly, and she could tell he was telling the truth. Rather than ask him more questions, she nodded and rested her dizzy head against her hands.

"Ti." Lawrence took her hands, and her voice was worried. "Wake up, Ti."

"What can we do?" The fear in Seth's voice made her shiver, but she couldn't force herself to move. He started using his cold voice, the one which meant he was thinking more rapidly than he could act. She heard the woman speaking, but by then the words were a meaningless babble. Then there was darkness, and the words in it made sense to her, and she had always known the truth, hadn't she? She loved her brother, because she loved him without thought, and the voice in the darkness wept for the endless fear which had hounded him for something as simple as love.

It took Tiria two days to recover. She came out of her sickness red-eyed and silent, but once she was able to walk she stubbornly refused any help the others offered her. The other outcasts came and went. Lawrence went with them. Seth followed them to the fields on the first morning to map out the positions of the other worker shelters and the farming complex where the officials lived. He returned to Tiria at midday and began to tell her what he had seen, but his wife stopped him mid-sentence.

"Are you planning to break into the complex?" She asked, already knowing he would nod. As soon as he did, she shrugged and looked away. "Then I'll see everything when we get there, won't I?"

"I could go on my own." He had taken to touching her as if she were made of glass, and Tiria hated it. When he tucked a strand of her hair behind her ear she caught his hand and pressed her fingers hard into his palm.

"This isn't one of your soft runaways, Seth. We only get one shot at this."

He pulled his hand away easily, returning her baited tone. "Then you'd better get strong quickly. Right now you're no help at all."

"It's as much your fault I'm sick as it is mine." She snapped, and then flushed and looked away. To her surprise, the man wrapped his arms around her and pulled her close. He held her for a long time, silently nestling against her neck. He didn't say a word, because apologies or promises would have been empty, but when he let her go his eyes were as cool as always.

"I'm sorry, I shouldn't have said - " She started, and he pressed his hand to her lips and shook his head.

"I'll never be angry at you for talking about this. Never, Ti."

She remembered what his first wife had done, and how indifferent he had sounded when he had spoken about her death. Now that she knew him better, she could see through the act. That shard of the past had crept back into his life, and as always he used his coldness to hide his true feelings. Had his wife hidden her thoughts in the same way? Had they spent their days politely saying empty words, and never talking about the things that were hurting them?

Tiria swallowed at the idea and shook her head. It wasn't right to talk about the babies that slipped away. If you cried for them, you would never stop. It was better to think about them as *nothing*. But now she felt such an aching emptiness that it was impossible to pretend she hadn't lost *something*.

"I want to try again." She said. He searched her face as if he was searching for the words she hadn't said, and then gently wiped her tears away.

"Are you staying with me?" His voice was quiet, and he deliberately made the question flat, not pushing her towards one answer or another. Tiria shrugged - what else could she do, now that she knew she was putting Lawrence in danger? - but then she stopped herself and caught her husband's hand. He deserved more of an answer, and she knew she was ready to admit to herself that it was what she wanted, too. She couldn't find the words, and so she cuddled a little closer and felt him kiss the crown of her head.

"I've only ever made stills." He said softly. "If you want to try again, you don't have to stay with me. I understand that."

"It could be that I can only make stills, too." She replied, hurt by his quiet surrender. "That's a stupid reason for either of us to decide on."

"Do you have a better reason?"

"I'm tired." Her voice was thin and pale, and for a long time she was silent. Seth stroked her hair, and his uncharacteristic silence unnerved her into finally finding her words. She caught his sleeve. "Seth, I'm tired of keeping secrets and trying to guess who's lying to me. I'm not clever that way, and even before I got sick it was making my head hurt. Will you promise me something if I stay?"

"A trade?" He asked suspiciously. She bit back a rude reply and shook her head instead.

"I don't want to play games any more. You brought me here like you promised, and you were ready to let me go. I never really believed you would. But now things have turned out this way and... and we have the chance to start again. No secrets, no bargains and no ballot - just you and me, and whatever insane plan you think of next."

"You want me to make a bargain promising not to make any more bargains?" He muttered, but held up her hand when she tried to interrupt. She smiled

447

and cuddled up against him, letting him think it over. She suspected he was taken aback by the idea of living outside of his tricks and secrets. It was as if she had suggested he walk into a savage's den unarmed.

"Deal?" She prompted him, unable to stand the suspense. He looked down at her and kissed her forehead.

"Deal. I'm not even going to shake hands on this one." He kissed her again and then smiled. "I don't want you to think I'm already breaking my word, little wife."

As the days passed Seth and Tiria thought seriously about how to break in to the farming complex. To the outcasts, it must have looked as though the two strangers were indifferent to each other. Seth spent all of his time asking the workers endless questions, making notes and impatiently demanding more details than the man could recall. When he looked at his wife, it was only to ask her opinion on something.

He spoke with a coldness which the others immediately picked up on. Tiria could have told them that he was simply bad at showing affection, and that his coldness was his way of stopping himself from worrying, but nobody ever asked her. Most of the workers were outcast rats, and they knew it was a normal way for a ballot couple to act. The fact that Seth had spent any time caring for Tiria after her miscarriage made them uneasy. Time was more precious than kindness, and losing a still was about as common as a head cold.

Tiria reflected her husband's reserve like a lake of cool water, and after a few days the comments about the strangers ceased. The more normal they appeared, the less the farmers worried about them upsetting their ordered way of life. The less the farmers worried, the less likely they were to betray them to the officials.

Tiria spent every spare moment working, making two sets of workers clothes and setting aside supplies as well as repairing and sharpening their weapons. She enjoyed this last task the most. While she was wrapping strips of leather around the hilt of a knife, she could listen to her brother's stories or tell him her own, sharing their forgotten years with each other until it seemed as if they had lived each other's lives. After a few hours it occurred to her that Lawrence was probably lying and exaggerating his stories as much as she was. There were so many things neither of them wanted to share.

She didn't tell him about the vault. He had no way to escape from the farms. Even if he did, the citizens would shoot him before they let him step under the surface. It was easier - safer, she corrected herself - to lie to him.

After they made their agreement (she refused to even think the word *deal*) Tiria had felt bizarrely shy around the man. It was as if they were starting their whole relationship again, but this time they were utterly exposed. It was a ludicrous thing to worry about around a man who had seen her naked, the girl scolded herself, but still she was embarrassed by how quickly she blushed when he met her eyes, or how her heart raced when he found an excuse to spend a few moments with her. He scouted the land during the day and questioned every worker late into the night, scribbling endless notes until someone yelled at him to put the lights out. Tiria fought to keep her eyes open, but she was always fast asleep by the time he laid down next to her, and he was gone by the time she woke up.

It would have been frustrating enough, but living with the farmers made it worse. Seth may have been awkward about being affectionate around other people, but the workers had no such problem. They had lived together for so long that the idea of having a private life was alien to them. They laughed and cried and fought and kissed each other in endless groups which shifted and changed as often as the wind blew.

One night Tiria gave up. She slept with a stone under her pillow so that she would wake up early, and when she did she kissed her husband until he opened his eyes and reached for her. They made love rather clumsily under their blanket, but afterwards they held each other more tenderly than they had in weeks. Then, suddenly mortified by the realization that the others would have overheard them, Tiria sat up and started pulling her clothes on.

"Are you finished with me?" Seth asked in his snide way. She looked around and blinked, a blush burning her cheeks as the words hit home.

"I don't like being overheard."

"Can I tactfully remind you that having sex was your idea?"

"It was either that or start clawing at the walls." She muttered.

Seth's expression changed from amusement to a studied coldness. Then his cocksure grin came back - the one he only wore when he was mocking her. "You're probably right. No point in savouring the moment, is there? We both got what we needed."

She didn't answer, but while they were getting dressed she pulled on her clothes so roughly that one of the sleeves tore. She poked her finger through the tear with a curse and then buckled on her belt.

"I don't understand why you're making this so horrible." She hissed at Seth. He looked surprised, and then his smiled faded.

"Ti, Do you love me?"

Tiria looked away. She looked towards the light of the sunrise, and then back into the soft darkness.

"I know that what I just did wasn't love." She said flatly. "Are you angry because I didn't..."

"No!" He caught her hand when she scowled and moved away, and corrected himself more quietly. "No, Ti. I just had to ask, that's all."

Tiria shook him off and then met his eyes. "Your stories spend pages and pages talking soft nonsense like that. We don't have pages. We didn't even have an hour together. There isn't time for it."

"There will be." He kissed her forehead and then looped his arm around her waist. "Ti, one day you'll work out what the hell I'm asking you, and it won't be from your books or from asking other people, you'll just know."

"Jane Eyre left her husband to burn." Tiria replied. "I wouldn't do that to you."

"Why not?" He looked at her sidelong. When she laughed, he smiled, but there was no humour in it. He looked down at their linked hands, and resisted the urge to pull away.

CHAPTER 8

At the last moment, Lawrence decided that he was going with them. It was purely practical, he said. They needed to act like convicts until they were past the farms. He would show them how to do it.

"After that, I'll wait outside. If you need to hide I can take you to the best spots faster than they can chase you."

"It's dangerous." Tiria said. "I don't want you to be there."

"Which one of us is the terrifying criminal, little sis?" He retorted, tweaking her nose. The girl hid a smile, and caught his hand.

"You promise you'll stay outside? This isn't your fight, you know." She had already explained to her brother what they were planning on doing. The silo was too important to keep as a secret; they wanted to find proof that the officials used it, so that they could expose the whole thing to the rats and outcasts. If those two groups banded together, they might be strong enough to overtake the farms and actually use the farmland for some good. Lawrence was deeply cynical – not about the plan, but about the idea of the rats being sensible around so much food.

"They'll strip every leaf and leave the ground to fallow." He pointed out. "They'll stuff themselves this year, and still starve in the next."

"That's their choice." Seth replied. "They're already starving. They should know why."

Lawrence shrugged. "I guess if I'm going to be liberated by lots of hungry rats, I should probably help out."

"Still..."

"Shut up, Ti." The man glared at his sister and then folded his arms. "It's not as dangerous as you think. Most of the people here can't read. They could have built that building anywhere, but while it's surrounded by illiterate criminals it's safer than a locked vault. Why would they bother guarding it, when nobody knows it's there, and the people here don't know what it's worth?"

"There must be some guards." She retorted.

"Around the food, yes. You'd be stupid to go to the silos without a hundred men to back you up. That's why you're going to go in the back way."

"Back way?" Seth leaned forward, and Lawrence immediately leaned back. He looked supremely proud of himself.

"I'll take you there."

They set off in the middle of the night. The guards who patrolled the shelters changed shifts at midnight, and the first hour of the replacement's patrols were always slow and sleepy. They walked along the river bed until dawn, and then crouched under a bridge and waited for the workers to make their way into the fields. They moved more slowly after that, knowing that only one person would need to see them for them to be caught. They took turns scouting ahead, relying on hand signals and stepping so softly that even the river barely rippled. By the end of the first day their eyes were stinging from being on the lookout, but they couldn't stop and sleep. As soon as the workers returned to their shelters they began walking again. They climbed up from the riverbed into the fields and started making their way along one of the paths.

Tiria ran her hands through the plants in amazement. The farm levels in the vault had made her think that fresh food stank of chemicals, and made the air too thick to breathe. The leaves there had been unpleasant to touch, and had to be washed off so many times that the taste was almost completely removed. The plants they walked through had been warmed by the sun all day, and nurtured with flowing water from the river. A purifier had been installed upstream, and the sweet liquid made the soil smell sweet and fresh as the night started to cool.

The plants were tall and verdant, and every single one had such a rich scent that Tiria knew without looking what they were walking past. Tomatoes smelled bright, and corn smelled sweet. Lettuce smelled so fresh she could inhale it, and potatoes were dull and earthen. They picked crops to eat as they passed them. Tiria could hardly bear to hurt the towering stems, but the wondrous perfume was hard to resist. That night they feasted on autumn apples and blackberries, green beans and tomatoes.

"Why are you on rations?" She asked Lawrence. "Why not give you this?"

"If they catch us eating it, we're punished." He said, and shredded the leaves from a strawberry. "It's *their* food, you see. We only grow it."

They fell silent, and walked until they could hardly keep their eyes open. As the sun started to rise they found a hiding spot between two compost bins, and fell asleep in a tangled lump of limbs.

It took two days for them to travel to the outskirts of the complex. Lawrence pointed towards the closest side, where scores of people and storage crates were gathered in a gravel yard. Barbed wire ringed it, and every other person held a lethal looking gun. They had to move dangerously close to the loading bay to get around a field overflowing with blackberry brambles. As they walked, Lawrence pointed things out to them and whispered.

"The boxes get loaded onto carts, usually, but sometimes they bring trucks. There are fields full of grain which they process to feed into the engines. They make an awful noise, and when they drive past the air stinks."

"Where do they go?" Tiria asked. She was crawling on hands and knees to stay behind the cover of a rock. Lawrence climbed down behind her.

"I don't know. The road keeps going. For every ten loads that go back to the territories, a hundred go into the desert."

"There must be something on the other side."

"Obviously! If there was any cover out there at all then I'd be halfway across the desert looking for it! With their guns I reckon I could be a mile away and still get shot. The people who try it don't last for very long."

They moved around the complex in a wide circle, and eventually the crowds of guards began to thin out. The west side of the building was a forbidding concrete wall, with no windows or doors. Metal scaffolds spanned the sides of it, holding up chutes which wove in and out of the building proper. There was no way in, and so there were no guards at all. Tiria wondered how on earth they would break in when Lawrence turned away and started leading them through the fields. He did not explain where they were going, but by now the other two were so used to his ways that they followed without question. His unerring sense of direction had helped them avoid so many patrols that Seth grew suspicious and asked the man how he knew his way around.

"I was planning on stealing one of the trucks." Lawrence replied, as if it was nothing. "I left my shelter and spent a month out here. When they caught me they didn't punish me; they sent me back to the shelter and then cut off everybody's rations but mine. Every worker was assigned to ditch duty, so they had no chance to take food from the fields. I tried to share my ration with them, but there were so many of them..." He tailed off and rubbed his face with his hands. "I'm surprised they didn't lynch me. It's probably what the officials wanted."

"Why didn't they?"

"Because we're not inhuman, Seth. Because they knew it was the officials who were starving them, and that I hadn't been trying to hurt them."

They fell into an awkward silence, and pushed their way through canes until their hands felt bruised. Lawrence stopped so suddenly that Tiria bumped into him, and they both fell onto the metal hatch.

"Is it a vault?" Tiria asked, amazed. Her brother looked at her quizzically, and she remembered he didn't know about the vaults. Before he could ask, she started prying the hatch open. A rich, acrid stink bubbled up, and she fell back with a disgusted cry.

"Sewer." Lawrence said, and then looked at Seth with a slight smile. "We have to crawl through. It takes us right into the building."

The man looked at him levelly, and his jaw tightened stubbornly. "Thank you."

Tiria wished she could forget the half hour they spent in the dark. Every step was through ankle-deep water, but sometimes it felt so foul underfoot that she had to force herself to move on. The tunnel was flat, thank goodness, but it twisted around so that they had to keep their hands raised to feel for the walls. Sometimes the slimy bricks moved as insects scurried over their fingers. When they got to forks in the tunnel Lawrence told them which way to go. Tiria dreaded to think how long her brother had spent down here to know the labyrinth so well. They seemed to walk forever, but finally they felt the rungs of a ladder and started climbing up.

Lawrence pushed the hatch open an inch, peeking cautiously out. He smiled in the sudden light and climbed out. The others followed him.

They were in a room so vast that it might as well have been outside. The whole thing was lit by electronic strip lights. The hatch was concealed behind two vast cylinders, which Lawrence whispered were full of food. Sometimes the bay was used as a slaughterhouse, he said, and so the sewer opened here so that they could hose down the blood. When he had broken into the building before a herd of pigs was being killed. He crept in masked by the chaos, he said, but he still had nightmares about the sound.

"I'll wait here." He said. "You won't find your way back through the tunnels without me, but I don't want to find myself looking down the wrong end of a gun." He drew a deep breath, and then gripped Tiria's shoulder. His eyes fixed on Seth. "If you come back without my sister, then I'll lose you in the dark."

"I'm not going to do that." Seth replied icily. Tiria tried to smile at her brother, but she was scared and couldn't make her mouth obey.

"How long will you be?" Lawrence's fierce expression didn't change. "You're looking for documents, aren't you?"

"About Seth's home, and about this place." Tiria agreed. "We have to prove to the people in his commune that this is really going on. If they believe us, then they might stop bickering with each other and help." She didn't mention the council or their threats, but secretly relished the thought of showing every citizen the proof before their superiors knew what was happening. Food grew in the wastes. The rats would be inspired to rebel. The territories were ready to be overthrown. If the citizens were brave, they could live in the fresh air.

It was probably exactly what the council were trying to hide. Using it against them would be delicious.

Seth shook his head, unable to guess how long they would be. "We need to find a records room."

There was something else in his voice that Tiria recognized from the manor house. When he was talking about her plans, he spoke as if he was enjoying himself, or at least actively interested in whatever they were doing. When he had his own plans, he became so determined that it rang out in every word.

The building was vast. The silos formed on long, curving edge. The rest of the complex nestled into the crescent. Next to the vast towers the offices looked tiny, but there was nothing insignificant about them. The whole complex gave the impression of being dormant. There were guards, but they were not alert enough to notice two people blending into the shadows. There were officials, who were so caught up in giving orders or reading notes that they wouldn't have noticed a wasp if it stung them. There weren't any convicts, of course, but a huge number of people in jumpsuits worked on the control panels and conveyors which bled off the silos into the loading bays.

There were so many people that the deserted records wing was a shock. Hardly anyone was there, and the ones who were kept their heads lowered and could not be distracted. The filing cabinets were kept along a long corridor, not a closed off space, so that the officials could find their paperwork as they crossed between offices. Tiria's heart sank when she saw the scores of files, but Seth started to smile. Each of the segments was precisely labelled.

"I want to look for *Vault*." He said, predictably. "If they know about us, then they'll have a report on it. I've never seen so many papers! There's a whole section on *fruit flies*, for god's sake!"

"It's too bad there isn't a section labelled 'proof the officials are evil'." Tiria muttered. She didn't even know what to look for. Since Seth had an actual idea, she followed him, but as time dragged past she started feeling frustrated. Seth had helped her find Lawrence, and in exchange she had agreed to help him find his answers. The fact that she had no idea what the right papers were made the whole thing idiotic.

They might have taken a hundred pages, but Seth kept shaking his head and moving them on. He was looking for something very specific. Tiria guessed what he was thinking. If the officials did know about the vault, then their reports might mention Seth's father. It seemed like a slender chance, but Seth probably thought it was worth the risk.

Whenever they heard a guard approaching they ducked behind the cabinets and unsheathed their knives, ready to attack the second they were seen. They had seen the massive alarms on the walls, and knew that if they were caught by a single person they were as good as dead. One corridor had the cabinets fitted into the walls. When the footsteps started they tried to run, but their boots made too loud a sound. In desperation, they threw themselves down onto the ground and crushed themselves against the base of the cabinets, praying that the guard wouldn't think to look down.

He walked slowly, and they saw that it was an official. He wore a long coat which concealed most of his shape, and Tiria felt the old shiver of fear that all rats felt around officials. His face was masked, even here, and his hands were concealed by white latex gloves. The mask must have made it hard to see. He walked past them while they held their breath.

Seth sprang to his feet, and then noticed Tiria shivering. "What's wrong?" He whispered. She bit back a laugh.

"He nearly saw us! He..." She gestured to her own face, indicating the white mask the man had been wearing. Seth glanced back in the direction the man had gone.

"I thought they did that to frighten people. Why do you think he's still wearing it?"

"Maybe it's his real face." Tiria whispered, and had to smother a wild giggle.

They hunted through the curving corridor as it looped around, until they were almost back at the silos. They were arguing about whether to try to find another floor when a loud noise made them both jump. The lights started to flicker, and the harsh klaxon screamed through the room.

"Lawrence!" Tiria gasped, and instinctively ran towards the sound of charging feet. "They must have caught him!"

"Ti!" Seth chased after her and seized her arm. "Don't be an idiot! What could you possibly do to help?" She grimaced and tried to pull away, so he shook her and pulled her into his arms. "Ti, stop. Please. Think about this!"

She struggled, but slowly came to her senses. "We have to help him!"

"What can we do?" The man looked straight into her eyes, and even though she searched desperately for an answer Tiria knew that there wasn't one. There was half an army in between them and Lawrence, and even if he was still hiding they would close in on him long before help could arrive. What kind of help were they? Two rusty pistols against a hundred well-oiled rifles?

Still, she couldn't accept it. "Seth, we have to..."

He shook his head, and then pulled her against the cabinets. He pointed at the wall, forcing her to point too so that she would actually look. "It curves around. We can flank them, not run straight through them. Maybe then we'll be able to do something."

She nodded and started to run. Seth was a slower runner, so he fell a little behind. After a few minutes Tiria heard him swear, and she heard his footsteps stop. Seth stood frozen in the middle of the corridor.

"Seth!" She cried, and then ran back to make him snap out of it. "Come on, we don't have time for this!"

The man shook his head and pulled away from her, moving as if he was underwater. "Ti, this is... I never imagined they..." His eyes narrowed, and he ran along the stacks with sudden urgency. Tiria almost laughed with frantic relief but then he stopped again and tried open one of the drawers. It was locked; he swore loudly and slammed the heel of his hand against the metal. It boomed in the silence.

"What are you doing?" The girl grabbed his arm, aghast. "Seth, they'll hear us. We have to go!"

"Go, then!" He rounded on her, and his eyes were black as tar. Every atom in him that had been helping her was eclipsed, and all that remained was the cold, determined creature who had hunted his own people for years. Tiria fell back in horror at the transformation.

Seth drew his knife and turned back to the drawer, trying to pry it open with the point of the blade. Tiria felt her mouth drop open, but when she tried to see what was written on the cabinet she couldn't make it out. What could possibly be in there that was worth risking their lives for?

"Seth," She said softly, pleading with him: "They'll kill him."

"What am I supposed to do about that?" He growled. Tiria recoiled and shook her head.

"We have to try. We have to do something." She heard her voice growing desperate. "I don't want him to be alone."

"Go and join him, then." Seth had pried open a sliver of the drawer, and he slid his knife to the lock to cut through it. He yanked the front, and the draw slammed open. Folders tore and creased against the broken cabinet. Tiria snatched one of them up and opened it. She made out a name written along the top of each paper before Seth tried to take them back.

"These are about my mother." She held the papers behind her back and felt them crumpling up in her hand. "Why do you want these?"

The man held out his hand with barbed impatience. "Give them back."

"Did you know these folders were here?" Tiria saw the shadow in his eyes before he stubbornly returned her glare, and she felt a desperate laugh bubbling up from her stomach. "God, what's so important about a few bits of paper?"

He didn't answer, but his eyes moved to the folder she was holding. Tiria stuffed it into her bag, backing away down the corridor. "Why so you even *want* them? Law needs us!"

"There's no way to save him. You already know that." He moved towards her with dangerous, unhurried steps. The grim truth had made Tiria's blood run cold, and she only remembered how to breathe when Seth gripped her wrist and growled, "Give me my papers back."

"No." Before she could think about what she was doing, Tiria drew her knife and held it out in front of her, stopping him from coming any closer. "You're wrong. We can help him. I'm going to try. If you don't help me I'll... I'll tear these papers to shreds."

"Will you do that before or after you stab me?" He sneered. It was the callous voice of the hunter who had won her from the ballot a year before. Tiria shivered when she heard it and lost her grip on the knife. That was all it took – a single moment of weakness - before Seth lunged forward and twisted her hand behind her back.

He shook the dagger from her numb fingers and then pulled her wrist higher so that every movement made Tiria feel like her shoulder was about to wrench loose. Keeping her arm locked with one hand. Seth ripped open her bag and took the papers. Then he shoved her hard against the cabinets, She cried out and struggled, stopping with a wrenching gasp when his hand closed on her neck and he dragged her head back.

Tiria let out a cry when she saw the knife in his hand. How could he draw a knife on her? - but then, she realised, he hadn't. It was her knife. Then he moved and it was closer, too close, and the point of it was cold against her throat and his furious eyes were burning into her own, his voice a poisonous growl. "I told you if you threatened me, I would kill you."

"You said you loved me." She whispered, refusing to look away. He smiled thinly, and then drew the knife back and slammed it as hard as he could towards her. She shrieked as it flew just past her ear and stabbed into the cabinet hard enough to pierce through the thin metal.

Seth let her go and she reeled away. She spun around to face him again. He ignored her, pulled the knife free, and slid it into his own belt. "I'm done here. Come with me, or don't."

Tiria stared at him and slowly, deliberately, lowered her hands back to her belt. The knife was chipped and blunt, but she held it with strong fingers and when it was between her and Seth, her trembling stopped. He watched her with a level expression, and then shrugged.

"Goodbye then, Tiria." He murmured with a slight smile. She scowled and raised the knife a little higher, flinching when he grinned.

"You're pointing that toy the wrong way, little rat. The cats have your brother in the loading bay, remember?" He pointed, and the girl instinctively turned to look. When she looked back, he had gone.

The sound of running footsteps weren't his, the girl realised. There were too many of them, and they were running towards her, not away. Clutching her useless knife in one hand, she ducked into the shadows and sprinted towards the bay.

The corridors seemed endless. The sirens grew louder as she left the administration rooms, and she clapped her hands over her ears every time she passed a speaker. When she was far enough from one she could hear her panted breathing. Her lungs burned but she forced herself onwards, stumbling on exhausted legs, until the corridor opened up in front of her and she sped into the loading bay. She caught herself just in time and ducked behind a pile of crates instead of barrelling into the crowd.

Lawrence was surrounded. He stood proudly in the centre of the room, his gun still clutched strongly in his left hand. There must have been fifty men and women around him, but he didn't seem scared. Whenever any of them got too close he would raise the gun and point it directly between their eyes. Still, the whole circle was edging closer, and Tiria knew that soon any of them would be able to grab him.

She looked around desperately and then thought to look up. There were only boxes in the room, but at some point the bay must have transported something far different. Sharp metal hooks littered the ceiling on long, rusting chains. They were all fixed onto longer chains, which ran in a straight line back to a control belt. A metal balcony held a control panel and a large cog. It looked like it had made the long chains move backwards and forwards, but now it was so rusted that it would never move. Holding her breath, Tiria crept around the boxes and hauled herself up the ladder. The balcony shivered under her, and she gripped the metal floor as she crawled along it. If a single panel fell away then they would see her, and the whole thing felt as if it was crumbling under her hands.

She made her way to the cog and stood up, hoping the control panel would hide her from the officials. Her knife was blunt, but it could chip its way through rust. The small sounds she made as she sawed into the crumbling chain were masked by the shouting guards, but her heart still raced. The chain link was so thick that it seemed like it would never break, and every minute that she wasted was a minute Lawrence didn't have.

The chain shuddered, and a low groan echoed through the bay. Some of the guards looked up, but it was too late – squealing and rasping, the ancient chain burst out of the cog and sprang out into the loading bay. The hooks began to scream down: hundreds of them carried by their chains and swinging violently down to the ground. The guards cried out and covered their heads, and the sound of cracking bone rang through the air. Some threw themselves to the ground, but the dead weights of metal were snapping and falling like anvils onto the ground. Any one of them could have hit Lawrence, and Tiria cried out as she watched him ducking away. In the chaos he started running, and Tiria laughed with relief until he stumbled and fell. His footprints were thick with blood. One of the hooks had crushed his foot.

Tiria forced her frozen feet to move. She ran along the balcony towards the ladder, desperate to get to her brother. They could still escape. She could help him walk, and they could hide until he healed. They could...

A sheet of metal fell out from under her feet. Shrieking, she grabbed at the next panel and felt the sharp rust cutting into her hands. It was agony, but she pulled herself up and looped her foot over the edge before the floor tilted and buckled. It seemed like the world slowed down for a moment, as tarnished nails popped free and her hands slipped. Then she was falling, and the world went dark.

PART 4: RATS

CHAPTER 1

Tiria woke up. When she tried to move something dug painfully into her wrists. She wrenched her heavy eyes open and flinched at the light which glared at her from every surface. It wasn't sunlight, or even the artificial light of the city, but a piercing blue light which seared through her eyes and made a sharp pain dart through her head.

Silently, she closed her eyes again and felt with her hands. The surface she was lying on was hard, not cold but not warm enough to be comfortable, either. She could feel the edges of a metal ring if she stretched her fingertips right out, but if she tried to move any more than that the pressure in her wrists was unbearable. She tried to open her eyes again, and saw the throbbing outlines of her bruised hands crossing over in front of her face, her filthy nails, and the shining metal cuffs which were binding her to the ledge. She could feel other bands of metal against her elbows and ankles, keeping her pinned down. It was impossible to move enough to look any further; her breath fogged the metal surface, and she stared dully at her writhing fingers.

"I need to get up!" She called out, dragging her head upwards at a weird angle so her mouth wasn't pressed against metal. "Unless you want to scrub off your stupid bench, you'd better let me use the bathroom!"

A door slid open, and she heard footsteps. Solid boots ringing on a solid floor. The man said nothing, but he must have pressed a switch because the cuffs suddenly sprang open. Tiria sprang upwards in relief, and then winced and huddled back down when her arms screamed at the sudden blood flow.

The looming man waited for her to look up, and then pointed at a drain. Like everything else in the room, it was made of metal. The room seemed to be on a hill, and the floor sloped downwards towards it. Tiria guessed they must be in a building that had subsided in the ruins. She crouched over the grate, and then glared at the man until he looked away.

"Where are we?" The girl asked. "Where's Lawrence?"

The man sighed impatiently, but didn't say a word.

When Tiria was finished she rinsed her hands at the metal sink and wiped them on her clothes. It was only then that she realised her travelling clothes were gone; she was wearing a plain dress made from rough fabric which scratched her palms when she rubbed them dry.

The man stood by the cuffs, waiting for her. Tiria balked and shook her head. Still, he said nothing. When she hung back and clutched the edge of the sink he simply took her shoulder and pulled her away. He was unbelievably strong. However much as the girl struggled, she couldn't slow him down. His touch was indifferent as he snapped her wrist back into one of the links, and then he pressed the heel of his hand firmly into her spine until she cried out in pain and dropped down to the bench. She heard the other handcuffs snap closed, and then the man was gone.

She curled her hands into fists, and waited. She refused to curse or shout out after him. It was clear he wouldn't care.

The next time she needed to relieve herself, she used the chance to look around the room. The walls were made of solid concrete and the ceiling was smooth and low. There were no vents to try to climb inside, but she saw an odd lump on one corner of the wall which she guessed was a listening bug. She looped her fingers around the edge of the grate and pulled, but the metal was welded solidly to the floor.

After a few inches the pipe narrowed. The only way out was through the door.

She quickly adopted nervous habits, rolling her forehead over and over into the bench to try to warm the tepid metal, pretending the pressure on her skin could ease every itch in the rest of her body. She had no idea how long she was locked in the room for; all she knew was the endless blue light, and the only way she knew that time was passing was when the bland food they gave her made its way through her body. There was nothing to hear, however hard she strained her ears, and nothing to look at or to do. At first she retreated into her dreams, but soon she could not force herself to fall asleep for another second. The boredom was excruciating. After an endless time her monthly bleeding began. She wept her failure and shame out silently, pressing her eyes to the bench and hoping that their listening bug didn't have a way to see her.

The next day - or, at least, two meals later - the door clicked open without her having to shout. She twisted her head around to see, but all she could make out was a pair of dark green boots before her head started to ache. The normal guard was still and quiet, but the new man walked around her and his breath wheezed a little. When he stood behind her Tiria felt her hair standing on end.

"What are you looking at?" She demanded. She had been kept in silence for so long that she nearly jumped out of her skin when he answered.

"Tiria Fifty Five." She imagined him smiling while he drawled the words. He didn't sound the least bit angry, which made her uneasy. There was no reason for them to have chained her down unless they were punishing her for something, but the man sounded as if he wanted to be friends.

"I'm Tiria. You know that; you have my fingerprints." She replied in a low growl. "You probably know what my score is better than I do."

"Do you think it's higher, or lower?" The man's voice was pleasant. Tiria laughed, and felt a hand patting her shoulder. "Have a guess, Tiria. The last record we have of you states that you were chosen by a ninety two! Did you make the most of your time together?"

"You tell me." She tried to jerk her shoulder away from him, and then grit her teeth as she realised how pathetic she must look. The man tutted.

"When did you find out your high was an imposter?"

"An imposter?" Tiria echoed, and then snorted. "He seemed pretty real to me. Did I imagine him, then?"

"I'm sure you imagined a great many things." Suddenly, the good humour was gone from the man's voice. He leaned closer, and she could feel his hot breath on her ear. It was slightly too moist. "You should tell us every little daydream you've had, Tiria One. You've missed two ballots, and we'd like to know why. We'd like to know how and why your imaginary friend stole you from us, and we'd like to know where he took you."

"Why should I tell you anything?" She sniffed and moved her head, facing away from him. The hand on her shoulder grew heavy.

"I won't tell you why, Tiria One. I'll leave it up to your imagination." He straightened up, and she heard him talking to the guard in a different voice - officious and curt. "She's not with child, and we've already waited long enough. I'll let the others know we're starting while she thinks it over." They both walked to the door, and then Tiria heard the smile creep back into the man's voice. "She'll think more clearly in the dark."

The light snapped off, and the room was plunged into such thick darkness that it was like being smothered. With the solid metal pressing against her face, Tiria fought off the feeling that she had been buried alive. It took her a few moments to ease her frightened breathing, but once she was calm she dug her fingernails into her palms and forced herself to think. After so long in the blinding light the darkness soothed her racing mind, and her thoughts were clearer than they had been in days.

Everything the stranger had done had seemed utterly intentional - even down to speaking to the guard. She felt the blood trickling between her thighs and bit her lip. They had been keeping her here until she bled. Pregnant women were untouchable. The lives they carried were worth enough to double their rations and keep them from scavenging until the infants were weaned. Tiria swallowed and pressed her nose into her shoulder. She had been safe. She wasn't any more.

The man had left his threats up to her imagination, and suddenly she saw them in front of her slow-witted eyes. She was a prisoner, and she was nothing to them. Stripping her score away hadn't just taken away her rights. It had erased every good thing she had ever done. It wasn't just an empty threat - they would have already written it into her file, so it would follow her forever. It would be impossible to climb up again from such a pathetic number. So, without any past and without any hope for the future, they had given her one chance: to tell them everything she knew about Seth.

Was that so terrible? For all she knew, he could be locked away in the next cell. He could be back in his rooms sipping ancient brandy from a golden chalice. He could be dead.

Tiria cursed under her breath as the darkness sent black pain into her heart. Seth. What use had his love been to her, in the end? It hadn't been real, not a second of it. He used it the same way he used every smile and every threat: to shape the world into things he could control. She had willingly believed every word he had told her, and he had used it to bring her here. Even if he had been captured, he was doubtless already twisting his jailer around his fingers.

Betraying the vault would have been an easy choice, apart from one thing. As much as she hated Seth, she hated the officials far more. He was one man, and they were many. What had she done to deserve their hatred? Her score was supposed to be precious, a number which shaped her life and was shaped by her choices. They were meant to change it only if she had done something particularly good or bad. How could they just wipe her out? Her only crime had been to disappear - and that was hardly her fault. Seth had taken her away with their consent, and it was Seth who had locked her away from her own people for so long. She could have been breaking into the farms to find help, or to report him. What crime had she committed? What could they prove?

She shook her head and huffed out a sigh. It was pointless to think about it. They wanted to know about the vault. She was clever enough to know they didn't care about anything else.

Perhaps that was the answer. While they thought she knew anything, they would keep her alive. Sure, being tied to a metal slab for the rest of her life wasn't hugely appealing, but it was still life. The longer she kept her secrets, the longer she would be safe.

The next time the man appeared, he was as silent as her guard. It wasn't until he unsnapped the cuffs from her wrists that he made a sound, and Tiria was so preoccupied rubbing sensation back into her aching shoulders that she missed it.

"What?" She looked up, and froze.

The man grinned back at her. One side of his face lifted in a jovial smile, the other half sagged down to his collar like rotting bread dough. Yellowish lumps blossomed from his cheek and crawled up towards his eye, ringing the opaque white marble in flaking pustules. Tiria gasped and shoved herself backwards, her skin crawling.

"Mutation!" She croaked, and then remembered his hand had touched her shoulder. She scratched at it frantically. "You're a...!"

"Surprise." The man sneered, and then nodded at the guard. "Have you met Patrick? He doesn't have much to say for himself these days."

Patrick looked bored, but when the mutation glared at him he opened his mouth to show her. Tiria felt the blood draining from her face in horror. Where the man's tongue should have been there was a thick lump of flesh, more meat than organ, which squirmed around behind his purple lips. His teeth stood out at odd angles where the swollen tumour had shoved them away. She tore her eyes away and tried to stop herself from being sick.

"Don't touch me." She croaked, trying to make herself as small as possible. "Don't come near me!"

"What are you afraid of?" The first man moved closer, and she stared fixedly down so she wouldn't have to see his sour-curd face. She focused on his coat - dark, warm, a name badge, *Robert Sq... - ...* before a hand moved into her line of sight. She gasped as the man's fingers gripped her wrist. "Even you rats know that it's not contagious."

"You're rotting." She pulled away and stood up, backing into the corner. "You... savages..."

"Yes, it is a rather unpleasant side effect." The man scratched at his face and didn't seem to notice when a large flake fell away. "They're always so upset when we cast them out. You'd think we were killing them outright, not just taking their medicine away."

"Medicine?" Tiria whispered. It couldn't be true – there was no way to slow down the rotting sickness, everyone knew that. But then, the officials had more chemicals to play with than Walker had in his entire lab. It was a world away from the crude tablets and ointments the rats survived on. When she found the nerve to look up she saw that they were pulling masks out of their pockets. When they dragged the thin stocking material over their faces, they looked as normal and ambiguous as any other official.

"Shit." The girl burst out, and then buried her head in her hands. Why else would they all cover their faces? How could she have been so stupid? She wrapped her fingers around one of the cuffs. When they tried to take her away, she clung on and fought them off until Patrick physically hauled her away. He grunted as he lifted her over his shoulder, and the noise was more animal than human. She shuddered but couldn't will herself to claw at him.

The thought of his rotting flesh touching her skin made her retch.

"This won't work." Robert muttered. He unlocked a cabinet under the bench and pulled out a syringe. Tiria shrieked when she saw it and fought in earnest, but she was weak – too weak – the endless imprisonment had wasted her muscles into nothing. She felt the needle slip into her skin, and then her entire body felt as heavy as lead.

She drifted in and out of a haze, and when she woke up they were watching her. That's how it was, for days and for weeks. She would refuse to cooperate with them until finally she passed out from drugs or pain, and when she woke up the questions would begin again. The same routine, and the same questions, for weeks without end.

They wanted her to admit that there was a vault. Tiria knew that as soon as she had answered their questions they would kill her. She lied, and made sure Robert knew she was lying.

"He took me to a church." She repeated again and again until the words no longer made sense. "There was coloured glass on the floor. We stayed in the... he called it a vestry."

"You lived in a ruin for fourteen months." Robert shook his head. "And what did you do there?"

"He wanted what you want. He asked me all these questions about the ballots until my ears were ringing. It took him months to make me say a single word, so I don't hold out much hope for you two."

"We're very persuasive." The man replied smoothly, not batting an eyelid. "Where was the church?"

"I dunno. The savages got to us a few times and turned us about. I've never had a good sense of direction. Maybe you should tell your mum not to chase the rats next time." She laughed at him obnoxiously. "This is boring. Either do something or leave me alone. I'm not going to tell you anything."

He squeezed her foot. "You're wrong about that."

For the next few days they never left her alone. Every breath she took, every move she made and word she spoke, was watched and recorded. She longed to throw herself down and scream, but her world was exposed and floodlit and she couldn't even cry.

Robert was very careful. He refused to raise his voice or insult her. There was nothing threatening about the things that he said to Tiria, but every pleasant word made her stomach crawl. She could never work out how much he already knew. He confused her so much that she began to stutter, not trusting her own tongue to tell the lies she had so carefully invented. Robert knew that they were lies, but he never said so to her face. He humoured every story with the same slight smile, and then he left her in Patrick's hands.

Patrick tried not to hit her. He was too strong to risk hurting her so badly, and on the rare occasions when he swiped at her he quickly pulled her up from the floor and checked her head for bruises. He never looked guilty when it happened, but slightly irritated, as if his own strength was keeping him from his work. It was terrifying to think that a few words were the only thing keeping Patrick at bay, but Tiria was more indebted to those words than any other protection in her life.

The torturer was easily irritated. Tiria supposed it was because of his twisted tongue, which kept him from saying anything apart from doglike yowls. He must have been able to speak once, because his fishy lips shaped the syllables, but the tumour had grown as he had aged and finally rendered him mute. She wondered if it was still growing, if one day it would push back into his throat and choke him to death. She closed her eyes and daydreamed about it while the man was sliding pins under her nails or pressing a soldering iron to her skin. When Robert asked her his pleasant questions she told him her theory, and laughed when Patrick growled and shoved her into the wall.

"Now then, Patrick." His companion chastised in a mild voice. "That was rude."

The giant kicked angrily at the chest beneath the bench, and the tools inside it rattled against each other. Robert shrugged. "Yes, but that's necessary. If she answers our questions she'll be a free woman. You don't want to spend the rest of your life looking over your shoulder for a rat with a grudge."

"I don't believe you." Tiria pulled herself upright and brushed off her dress. There was an odd lightness in being utterly defenceless, and she smiled sweetly at the interrogator. "I know too much to be set free."

"What do you know?"

"I know the officials torture innocent people if they find out about the farms."

"The rats don't care about anything, so long as they have something to chew. They eat *each other,* for God's sake! We give them rations. After that, they wouldn't care even if they did find out the truth. They're happy to let the criminals slave away. They get their rations, and it means they don't have to venture further into the wastes."

She swallowed and tried not to think about people filling their bellies with the rotting weeds that the officials didn't want. "I'd still tell them that you tortured me."

"Do you think they'd care, Tiria One? If I took you to the ballot they'd be baying for your blood."

She coloured and looked down, and Patrick caught hold of her hair and pulled her head back. She yelped and clutched at her neck as it arched, while Robert asked her in his soft voice: "What else do you know?"

"Nothing." She croaked. "Not a damn thing."

Robert shrugged and his eyes met Patrick's. "I'll be back in two days. Break her. Be as rude as you like. If our little guest is clever enough to work out how this ends, then she should be clever enough to want to avoid it. Make her talk."

CHAPTER 2

After two days even Patrick looked tired. He had worked through the night, keeping her awake until her head pounded and using every trick he knew. The man was creative, but he didn't like to repeat an idea. Besides, even before Robert had disappeared, the torturer knew his work was pointless. The girl absorbed pain as if it was her due, and whatever he did to her seemed to be half-forgotten by the time anyone asked her any questions. She would laugh whenever he grew frustrated, and remind him that he wasn't allowed to kill her.

The problem was that the officials had never lived in the wastes. They had no idea of the gauntlet the rats had to pass through to survive. Most of them would accept this level of pain just to find a good stash of food. The techniques the officials used on their own traitors were nothing compared to the way rats turned on each other.

"It has to happen." Tiria said softly, once he started looking guilty. "If it wasn't us, it would be someone else. Robert doesn't understand that. He wasn't raised to be disposable."

Patrick put the tool away. He untied the girl and brought a bowl of warm water and soap, cleaning the blood from her skin before Robert got back.

"He doesn't like the sight of blood?" Tiria guessed, remembering the odd pallor to the man's skin whenever he had interrupted Patrick's work. The man shrugged and nodded, and they shared a rueful smile.

"Do you write?" She asked Patrick. The man looked at her narrowly, and the girl shrugged. "I know how to read. I don't write so well, but I could read your words."

He dropped the food tray down on the edge of the bench and left the room, bolting the door shut behind him. Tiria sighed, wondering what he was going to try next, when the locks clanged a second time. Patrick stomped through with his usual ponderous speed and handed her a notebook.

Where did you learn how to read? The first page read. Tiria frowned, thinking of an answer, and jumped when Robert emerged from behind her guard's back. He snatched the notebook from her hand. He smiled at the question and handed the book to Patrick with a shrug.

"It's obvious that Elizabeth taught her. Is this what you've been spending your time on?"

The man shrugged and scrawled a note, handing it to his partner with a bored expression. Robert scoffed at it. "Whatever helps you sleep at night, petal."

"How do you know my mother?" Tiria asked, interrupting them for the first time ever. When they both looked up at her, she pressed, "How did you know she could read?"

The man looked surprised at her even asking. "Don't you know why you're here?"

"I'm here because I disappeared." She replied automatically, but the words withered on her tongue when both of the men shook their heads. "Is it because I broke into the farms?"

Patrick made an impatient gesture, pointing to Tiria, Robert shrugged. "If she doesn't know, you might as well tell her. Answer her questions, but only a page at a time. If she really wants to know, she'll have to earn it."

"Write in small letters." Tiria whispered as the other man left. "We can fit a lot on one page."

Large letters. You will give me three answers per page. What do you want to know?

The girl hesitated, and then blurted out the one thing she already knew the answer to. "Mama was a mutation, wasn't she? Her voice..."

Patrick didn't bother writing an answer. He simply looked at her. Tiria bit her lip and looked down at her bare feet, which dangled over the stained floor.

"I'm not mutated." She muttered. "All mutations give birth to ... to even worse children. Savages who tear out their mother's wombs from the inside."

The man snorted and stood up to leave. Tiria caught at his sleeve and earned a swipe for her troubles. She dodged the worst of it and then wiped her stinging eyes with the back of her hand and sat up stubbornly. "Alright, I'm sorry. I guess I'm just a... a mutated mutation. One that came out right. It must happen."

Patrick pointed down. When she looked at him blankly he sighed and picked her up. The man balanced her on the sink, and pointed in the tiny tin mirror above it. While she wobbled on the slick metal, he supported her whole weight on his shoulder and caught her foot. He held it up to the mirror and tapped his finger against the outside of it.

There. There, where she had never thought to look, was the guilty mark. Tiria caught her breath and gripped her foot with her hand. Her abrupt movement made the man lose his balance, but he caught himself on the wall and lowered the girl to the floor. She caught herself against the sink and dragged her foot round in a graceless loop.

The scar ran along the outside of her foot, just below her smallest toe. There was no way she should have missed it, She had never looked at the outside of her feet when she washed because... who did? She had spent a lifetime letting her eyes skip over her own skin, and she had missed the one detail that Elizabeth had hidden from the entire world.

Elizabeth's daughter was born with eleven toes.

When she pushed the blade down through flesh and bone into the dust, the child had screamed. She burned the useless meat and held her baby tightly, knowing that the man she lived with would only see a bawling brat. He could have worked out the truth, if he had half of a mind to, but Elizabeth hid in her silence and her bitterness until he only cared for the shell of her body and her hard work. When the baby was brought to the ballot, she had looked up at the officials and dared them with fierce grey eyes to see the scar and condemn the child forever.

We can protect her. The doctor had whispered. *You know that, Elizabeth.*

The woman's arms had closed protectively around her child, refusing to give her away, and finally the official had waved them away. The first words on Tiria's file were a lie.

"I know this story." Tiria managed to whisper, reading Patrick's curt summary. "It's not about me. The mutated baby was her first, not her last, and the officials stole it away."

Patrick shrugged and picked up the pen. *She left us in disgrace. A twenty. By the time your rumour started I guess everyone had mixed it up why she was so low in the first place, since no-one knew the truth.*

"Then why isn't my brother mutated?"

His father wasn't, and Elizabeth barely was. He is a mutated mutant, like you wanted to be.

Tiria winced. "Who was Law's father? Was he the reason mama left this place?"

Your turn to answer questions now.

"But...!"

Patrick scowled and threw the book against the wall. Pages exploded outwards, fluttering through the air like birds' wings. Tiria refused to flinch back from it, but she folded her arms in mock-impatience at his attempted threat.

"I'll tell you three things, then. One: the man who took me away was called Seth. Two: he stole papers from other ballots to make a fake identity.

My home territory is filled with pointless little dregs and lows that most of you officials don't care about one bit. So three: he got away with it because your smug friends saw that he acted all superior, and lows just aren't like that. He told me they never even questioned him."

"Well done." A syrupy voice murmured in her ear. She flinched – how was such a heavy, monstrous creature always so quiet? – and turned to look at Robert. The official was frowning thoughtfully, and then he picked up a page from the floor and made some notes on the back. "Find out which ballots he stole from. I doubt any man would travel hundreds of miles to find an A12B147 form. We should be able to work out his route."

Tiria nearly planted her fist in her mouth. How had her idiotic few words given away so much? She bit her lip and tried not to look to mortified, but of course Robert noticed. He smiled and patted her knee.

"This is just the start, my dear."

CHAPTER 3

They drugged her again, and carried her out of the room. This time they shoved her into a strange box which rattled and swayed as she fought to keep her eyes open. When the doors opened and Patrick picked her up again, the long metal corridors were gone. She tasted dust and hot metal, and knew they were outside. He set her onto her feet, and took her hand like a child.

"Wak." He chewed the word, a bovine lowing. She pulled her heavy feet up and forwards, clinging to him to stop herself from falling into the dust. For now, she told herself blearily, they needed her to stay alive.

The building swallowed them up, and while her eyes adjusted to the darkness Tiria's legs nearly gave way underneath her. She recognised this place. Not the room or the building, but the smell and sound of scores of milling people, and the drunken laughter of the rats. The masked officials' faces turned towards her, but when they saw Patrick's huge hand on her shoulder they looked away. Men and women stared at her from the examination tables until their officials asked them questions, and then they simply forgot about her.

It was a ballot. Tiria nearly laughed out loud. Was this the best threat they could think of? They were going to send her back to the ballot? No matter if she was a low; if someone bid for her, then she had a chance to break free. She was almost feeling cheerful before the door opened behind her, and someone else was carried through.

Lawrence's head lolled back against his guard's shoulder, and a bright blossom of blood bloomed from his forehead. Tiria gulped and reached for him, but by the time her heavy hand could move he had already been taken through to the next room. Patrick knocked her hand down gently.

"Be grateful there's something in your pretty head worth protecting." Robert's voice was muffled by the mask, but he patted her shoulder in a friendly way. "We're not allowed to do that to you."

"Law..." She mumbled, and then her head was too heavy to lift. For a long time they stayed there, watching the rats come and go as they were examined. Tiria listened to the questions that they were asked. *How many days did you spend outside of your shelter? How often did you have enough goods to trade? Have you been angry with your family? Has any member of your family been acting strangely? Have you had a rash, or a stiff joint?* They were all questions designed to see if they had mutated, but now that she knew some of the truth she heard the unspoken questions they were truly asking. *Have you been hiding goods from us? Has your family obeyed the rules? Has anyone asked too many questions?*

She turned and leaned her head against the wall. It's cool surface reminded her of the bench, which was oddly comforting, because at least there she had known what to expect. Patrick sat down beside her and drew her down to rest against his shoulder. She didn't know whether to recoil or sleep. The confusion kept her awake.

"Pa..." she managed heavily. "If they muta... do they join... you?"

The man shook his head slightly. His stockinged face looked up a little towards Robert, and he sighed. The sound gurgled in his throat.

"I don't know what you're complaining about." Robert replied. "You know these things drag on."

Patrick shrugged and stretched his legs out, for all the world as if he was going to sleep. The other man kicked at his boots until the guard groaned wetly and sat up straight.

The last of the rats trickled through, and were either sent back to their families or escorted through the same doorway that Lawrence had been carried through. Tiria squinted through the door whenever it opened, but she couldn't make out anything in the shifting shadows beyond it. She knew what they were doing. She couldn't bear to admit it, but she knew. Seeing her captors' faces had given her a small glimmer of hope that maybe the mutations had a choice, but now she felt dread rising in her like the rotting sickness.

Robert kicked at Patrick again, and the man made an obscene sounding mutter before he hauled Tiria to her feet. She swayed dizzily, but this time it was easier to walk. The drug they had given her had even worn off enough to let her drag her feet as they bore her towards the door. It was like spitting in a river; Patrick barely seemed to notice.

The room was empty. A tight corridor lead off it, twisting and turning through mazes of ancient wires and scaffolding, until they were suddenly at the edge of a great open space. A stage yawned in front of them but they didn't step onto the boards. Instead, Robert stopped in the wings and planted himself in a good place to watch. Patrick held Tiria's elbow and gestured for her to look out at the stage.

The backdrop was painted with a fading moonlit lake, with long-necked birds swooping across it. It was so unlike the shabby theatre of her own ballot that for a second Tiria was awed. Then she looked across at the other wing, and saw the crowd of mutations. They were marched onto the stage naked, their hands crossed over their private parts as they wept and stumbled over the boards. At her ballot there had only ever been two or three of them, and usually old men and women who had been eating from contaminated tins all their lives. There were at least ten people in this crowd, and two of them were barely in their teens.

Just like in her own ballot, the mutations were brought forward one by one while the officials pointed out their flaws to the roaring crowd. Afterwards, they were humane and quick - as soon as the officials slipped the poison into their veins the mutations collapsed. Tiria could see the nearest mutation shivering, his eyes bulging in fear, and as his turn came nearer a thin trickle of urine ran down his leg.

When it was over, the officials held out their hands for silence. The crowd hushed immediately. When Lawrence was brought onto the stage, the rats heard every footstep.

"No." Tiria whispered, and spun around dizzily to stare at her captors. "Please..."

"Something to tell me, Tiria One?" Robert asked smoothly. She stuttered and stumbled over the words which rushed to her lips, and as she struggled she heard the shouts of the officials listing out Lawrence's crimes. *Runaway. Outcast. Non-breeder.* The crowd muttered to each other and then their cries began to drown out the official, who was still reciting the endless list. Every cold word inflamed them more, until they were shoving at each other to get nearer to the stage. The mob of people clawed at the criminal, spitting on his bare feet and screaming at the officials who held them back.

Tiria sank to the floor and clutched at Robert's feet. "Please... please stop them! I'll tell you everything."

"You'll do that anyway, my dear." The man kicked her away. "I didn't bring you here to listen to you beg."

"Then why...?" She sobbed, and then looked around at her brother. His face was white as a sheet, the gaping wound in his head still oozing thin, greasy blood. He didn't seem to see the people in front of him, or hear the official who was now howling over the baying crowd. His eyes were unfocused, and it took him long, slow moments to turn his head whenever someone made him flinch.

"I'll show you." Tiria burst out, and grabbed at him desperately. "Please don't hurt him. I'll take you to the vault, I swear it. Don't kill him."

"He's dead already." Robert said, sounding bored. "Those idiots in C Shift don't know how to pull their punches. The poor sod's bleeding into his brain."

Patrick picked Tiria up from the floor and set her back on her feet. While Robert was walking away across the stage the other man's hands closed around her shoulders. His grip moved to the base of her neck, forcing her to look forwards and nowhere else. Each hand was like a vice, and no matter how much she struggled she couldn't look away.

Tiria longed to close her eyes, but how could she? If Lawrence looked around he would see her. He could look into her eyes and see that she loved him. She could smile. She could make the whole thing less awful than it truly was, as if the bloodthirsty crowd and the cold, ruthless officials could be softened by one pathetic smile. But he didn't look around; his eyes were soft and dying, and when they raised the needle his gaze couldn't even focus on it. He lifted a trembling hand to the stage lights, trying to catch the glittering stars, and as the needle slipped into his spine a smile lit up his face.

The whole world froze into a single heartbeat.

Lawrence stumbled forwards. Robert planted his hand into the man's back. Lawrence gasped out a rattling cry and fell into the crowd unblinking. The rats reached up and clutched and tore until their hands were slick with blood, and Tiria screamed and tried to reach him, reaching out and sobbing until Patrick's hands locked around her arms. She struggled and bit and clawed and Patrick looked up, and she saw that Robert was laughing. She felt his faceless cruelty searing into her soul.

CHAPTER 4

"We fed your brother to the savages." Robert said it so diffidently that she thought she had imagined it, until she felt the words rushing towards her like rolling flame. Pulling herself away, she drew her knees up to her chest and stared at him. The man's pleasant smile never faded as he rested his hand on her bare foot. "There wasn't enough left of him to bury, and someone recognized their aunt amongst the starving bastards. Meat is meat."

"He was already dead." Tiria managed to croak out the words Robert had jeered at her, and then raised her chin and spat at him. "You can't touch him anymore."

"Me? They didn't give him to me. C Shift got the pathetic traitor, and I was given little Tiria One." Robert smiled at her. "If they'd given him to me, he would have been fed to the savages while he was still *alive*."

She sighed and looked down at the floor numbly. It was shining and clean; they knew they didn't need to hurt her any more. Every time she closed her eyes she saw the gleaming needle and the soft, childish happiness on her brother's face. She saw the crowd baying for his blood, and their nails sinking into his skin. Nothing could be worse than that.

"Do you want to go to the vault or not?" She asked, and it felt as though her voice was being dragged from her stomach. "Take me there and shoot me, if you want, but stop talking about Law."

Robert opened his mouth, but a huge hand fell on his shoulder and stopped him. He glared up, and Patrick shook his head slightly. Piqued, the man stood up. "Watch her." He ordered, and stalked out.

Robert waited for the man to leave, and then let his breath out in one rattling huff. He pulled a notepad out of his pocket and scrawled a few words on it before pressing it into Tiria's hand. She couldn't make out the letters through her swimming eyes until the door closed, and she realised for the first time in weeks that she had been left alone. She looked down at the note.

Cameras are off. Cry for him. I'm sorry.

She stared blankly into space. She couldn't cry. She closed her eyes and inhaled. She felt air moving in and out of her body, and felt her heart thud when she fought against drawing the next breath. She gave up, in the end. That was what she had always done, wasn't it? She couldn't even convince her own flesh to listen to her. Where had it brought her?

The next morning they unlocked her cell when she was still half asleep, and escorted her out into the corridor. Tiria's numbness had faded, but she was halfway between not knowing and not caring. She followed them obediently.

They walked through several corridors before the girl realised that she already knew where she was going. The walls were made of polished steel, and the floor was cold and sterile, but the place felt so much like the city that it was almost like coming home. She must be in a vault, she realised, but it was utterly unlike the one she had lived in before. Where that one was clearly made to shelter its citizens, this one looked like it was trying to arm them. Everything about it ran smoothly, from the electronic locks on the doors to the cameras in every cell. Nobody looked like they gossiped in the corridors or smoked contraband cigarettes in the ventilation chambers. Most of the people they passed saluted when they saw Robert and Patrick. All of them had some kind of deformity.

What had happened here? The officials had all come from this vault, that much was clear. They seemed to have more technology and resources than anyone else. Tiria guessed that the most important people from the ancient war had sheltered here, ready to keep fighting. It made sense that generations later, their descendants would think the same power was owed to them.

She was not far from the truth. Where the council simply wanted to run their city, the officials wanted to rule the country. It had been easy to frighten and bribe the dust-eaters into obeying them, when the whole world was wrecked by famine. Nurturing and controlling the farms had been the deciding blow in their war against the rats.

After that, the ballot system had been created to control, not to protect. The rats and savages were merely collateral damage. Still, the officials had paid for some of their duplicity; they had needed to open their vault before their waning power was forgotten, and the radiation had still been strong enough to warp their bodies. The rats had adapted, had grown stronger to survive and had already begun sacrificing their offspring if they were too weak to survive. The officials learned that trick too late; by the time they started their own culls, the mutated genes were so widespread that it was just a matter of how the corruption appeared.

Their medical knowledge and technology helped them to find a treatment, but it was hardly a cure. It stopped the rot from seeping into the nervous system and the brainstem, but one missed dose could let a deadly cell through. They cast out the savages before they were insane, and turned away from their pitiful pleas. The pain of casting out their brethren made them cruel, and they hoarded all of their precious medicine far away from the rats. If one of them began to mutate, they simply exterminated them.

The early swarms of rats could have overpowered the officials in days. Now, their numbers culled and their dissenters banished, they crawled through the ruins as a dying breed. The only thing that really threatened the officials were other vaults, and so when one of the rats disappeared for weeks with someone who could read enough to forge ballot papers, they leapt at the chance to wipe one out.

Tiria knew none of this, although she guessed a little by peering into every doorway they passed. She was clever enough to connect what she knew about the city and the farms with her own childhood in the ballot, but she had no idea how desperate the officials were to hold on to their lands. The concept of owning land was meaningless to her; territory rights only meant that you could keep the things you scavenged: other people weren't allowed to steal supplies from your shelter. Every scrap of land she had grown up on would be passed on to the next person chosen by the ballot, just as she could claim anyone else's shelter if she took that person as her low. One rat hole was like any other, and they weren't sentimental.

The idea of owning land or the people who lived on it was laughable, even though it was what the officials had always done. The rats couldn't conceive of them as their owners; they saw them as people who helped enforce the rules the dust-eaters had lived by. That was how the officials kept the dissenters down; the rats were more offended by rule-breakers than they were.

Patrick and Robert escorted Tiria up a flight of stairs and then waited outside of a medical bay. The girl read the letters on the sign without interest, using them to distract herself rather than to amuse herself. Perhaps they were going to inject her with their poison too, now that she had admitted there was a vault. It didn't look like a painful way to go. She didn't like the idea of being dead, but Lawrence had smiled when he had fallen. Perhaps it wasn't so bad.

The man in the medical bay insisted that she be cuffed to the table before he went near her. His squeamishness reminded the girl of the doctor in the city, a lifetime ago. She lay on her front when they told her to, and stayed so still that they didn't really need to lock the cuffs around her wrists and elbows. The doctor walked around her for a while umming and erring, and then she felt rubbery fingers squeaking against the base of her neck.

"She's very thin." The man said. Tiria heard Robert hiss through his teeth.

"Just do it."

"It's far too potent." The man objected, but then he fell back into silence. Tiria guessed that the other men had glared at him, or that they were too high in score for the doctor to argue with. Did the officials have scores? She was wondering that when she heard the snip of a pair of shears. Her head suddenly felt very light, and she struggled to move to see what they had done. She moved too easily, and she realised: her hair had been cropped short.

"It's so it doesn't catch in the stitches." The doctor explained. Robert tapped his foot impatiently on the floor, and the doctor muttered a foul word under his breath. "Hold still, girl."

The gloved fingertips were back on her neck, pressing into the soft divot of skin at the back of her skull, and then she felt the sharp heat of a blade cutting through her skin. She shrieked and struggled, but almost as soon as the pain had begun it faded away. She caught her breath and felt something hard and cold under her skin, pressing against the first knot of her spine.

"What is it?" She asked. The doctor didn't answer, but Robert walked up and rested his hand on her shoulder. Perhaps it was meant to be comforting, but when the doctor started stitching the incision closed it was just another restraint.

"It's a tracking device, Tiria One. Just in case you were thinking of abandoning us in the middle of the wastes."

She *had* been thinking about that, but she was hardly going to admit it. She settled for a bored grunt and felt the doctor smear a tingling gel over the scar.

"Don't scratch it."

"Scratch?" She wiggled her hands mockingly through the handcuffs and heard the doctor snort back a laugh. Robert patted her shoulder and then his breath was hot in her ear.

"You think we're stupid, don't you?" He breathed, watching her to see even the smallest twitch. "If you even think about running away, I'll track you down."

"Will you take this thing out when we get to the vault?" She asked. He laughed and shook his head.

"Poor little Tiria. It's twisting its wires into your spine even as we speak, my dear. Long after I shoot you in the head it'll keep sending out its signals. We'll be watching you until you've withered in your grave."

She winced and closed her eyes. The uncanny iciness of the disc suddenly felt much worse. "It's sweet that you'll give me a proper burial."

He grunted and unlocked her restraints, hauling her to her feet. "Time to go. Start walking."

They began at her old ballot. The interrogators blindfolded her until the rattling box reached her territory, so that she couldn't find her way back to the officials' vault. It took hours, and her legs shook under her when she climbed out of the vehicle. This time, since she wasn't drugged, Tiria could see that the box was a van much like the rusting shells in the towns, but with rubber tires and a growling engine. She stared at it in wonder as it rumbled away. The men pulled bags onto their backs, and Patrick fastened a long chain from his belt to her wrist.

They made their way north, towards the city. Tiria wondered what lay to the south. She had never been there. She was half tempted to lead the officials there and let them guard her as she explored unknown lands. Robert was too clever to be fooled, though: he could tell when she knew her path, and when she was unsure. The girl fixed her destination in her mind and started walking.

Her feet blistered and bled on the first day, but by the third she had started to grow strong again. Every day they covered more miles, and every night Patrick unpacked a medical bag from his supplies and silently treated her blisters. He never seemed to feel the hard travel, but Robert moaned constantly about the hot sun and the cold wind, as well as the grit in his boots and the sand in his eyes. They stopped ten or twenty times a day to let the man rest, and when they started walking again he yelled at them both as if it were their fault the journey was taking so long.

Tiria hoped that his rages would bring the savages down on them, but they never did. They walked for a week, and nobody dared to attack them. They saw the writhing creatures in the distance, but they stayed away. Even the savages would be intimidated by the sheer size of Patrick. When he treated Tiria's bleeding ankles her whole foot could be enclosed in one of his hands. She wondered if it was a part of his mutation, or if his whole family were that large.

Robert snored loudly and startled himself awake. Rolling over in his blankets, he blinked blearily at the sight of the huge man dabbing antiseptic onto the girl's feet. "You've left her unchained." He mumbled, and then pushed himself a little more upright. Patrick lifted up the chain that linked Tiria to his belt and shook it, but the other man scowled. "You know the rules. As soon as we camp, you chain her up. What do you think the girl will do if you fall asleep, sing you a lullabye?"

"I don't know any songs." She replied flatly. "If you two want to croon to each other, be my guest."

Robert ignored her and rooted in his bag, digging out the metal spike which they hammered her chain into the ground with each night. Patrick made a disgruntled sound and pushed the girl's bare feet off his lap so he could reach over and grab it. Tiria was about to make another sarcastic comment when something knocked against her hand. She folded her hand around the smooth surface, not looking down while her captor rammed the picot into the hard-packed earth and looped a rung of her chain around it.

Tiria kept her prize hidden until both of the men had fallen asleep, and then slid it around in her palm. It was a plastic bottle with a white lid. Something was written on a label, but it was too dark to make out the letters. She knew what it was, though. Robert had scores of bottles stuffed into his bag, and he doled out a share of them to Patrick every morning before necking his own. Tiria remembered what they had said about the savages needing medicine, and her hands closed around the plastic. The bottle would be missed. The pills must be more valuable than diamonds. Moving slowly, barely daring to breathe, she unscrewed the lid and poured a handful of the white lozenges into her hand. They felt waxen and fragile. She tore a strip off the bottom of her shirt and tied up the pills in a little bundle, which she shoved into the waistband of her jeans. Then she carefully rolled the bottle back towards Robert, biting her lip as it tumbled over the uneven ground. It came to rest a few inches from his bag. He would think it had spilled out on its own.

She hadn't thought of any real plan while she was walking, but now that she had the pills an awful idea came to her. That day she led them slightly to the right of their path, ambling across the valley rather than changing direction. That would have made them suspicious, whilst the meandering route merely seemed like the absentminded trail a rat would naturally travel along.

This wasn't the way that she and Seth had walked away from the city. It was the slower route they had taken to get there. She suspected that Seth had chosen it to try to get her lost. It was a stupid plan on his part; rats prided themselves on memorising every scrap of pavement they crossed in their territories. Tiria led the officials along the crumbling tarmac and felt the reassuring lump of fabric pressing into her hip.

She wasn't going to do the *right* thing, exactly. Her plan didn't really have an ending, she just wanted to see what would happen. She was probably going to die, but that was going to happen anyway. It would be nice to see Robert sobbing and begging for his life before he sent her to hell.

"We'll get to the vault tomorrow." That night, Tiria spoke softly while Patrick was frowning over her healing feet. "You'll kill me when we get there, won't you?"

Patrick shrugged one shoulder towards the snoring Robert. The girl understood: if he was ordered to, then he would. She doubted Robert would hesitate. She edged a little closer to the man.

"I'd like to know about my mother." She whispered. "Please. No-one will ever know. I'll forgive you for killing me if you tell me."

The man's eyes flickered, and for a moment such savagery crossed them that she flinched away. Then, in a whiplash change of mood, he pulled the notebook out of his pocket and scrawled:

It's your own fault you're here. You can't forgive me for doing the right thing.

"I suppose not." Her voice was soft. "What else can I offer you?"

He looked at her coldly, and then wrote something else. He tore the page off with a violence that made her flinch, and scowled when she took it.

I lost my voice and everyone forgot that I still want to be listened to. I'd like to see Robert hold his tongue for a day. You've listened to me. I will miss that. What do you want to know?

Tiria bit her lip and then looked up at the man. She forced her eyes to linger on his ravaged face, to see the odd colours the rotting flesh had stained the living skin and not look away. He returned her gaze with a hostile light in his eyes, and she shook her head.

"Does... does it hurt?"

He nodded and then, strangely, smiled. It was a twisted expression but it lit up his whole face and he suddenly looked much younger. Looking down at the notebook, he picked up the pen and flashed her another smile. He wrote quickly, his writing growing more spiderlike as his hand grew tired. He tore the leaves off to hand to her as soon as they were full.

Tiria read.

I never knew Elizabeth, but everyone knows the story. She was born in the Officials Vault. No ballot for us. Hard to breed for some, too ugly to try with others, but E was normal and people wanted her. She hated it. Cut off her extra fingers and toes and asked to join the rats, but official leaders said no. Her family was too high. She knew too much. She went to ballots without a mask on and disappeared for weeks into wastes but always came back.

One day she comes back and tells her father she met someone. Not a rat, not an official, but a man from another vault. It was the first time we knew any other vaults had survived – ours has been open since the first fallout cleared. He was told to find out where the other vault was. She follows her man and finds out everything, tells us how to find the vault and how well defended they are.

Next thing her reports stop. Stupid woman was besotted. She wouldn't spy on him. She told the man everything about us: the radiation farms, the ballot, the culls and savages – everything. She told him we were taking over the wastes, and that we would destroy every vault to hold on to them.

Her man leaves her here and goes to look for other vaults, to warn them. While he was gone we attacked. Everyone was dead when he got back home.

Elizabeth had seen the attack too, and she understood what she had done. She fell down crying. Her man found her in the ruins and knew she had betrayed him.

But what did he have to lose? He picked her up and told her everything.

He had searched for miles and found a hunter from another vault. He told him everything. The hunter swore he would help look for other vaults. He said that his vault would dismiss any rumour as soon as they heard it. The hunter said that to convince anyone they had to find all of the vaults, not just one or two, and get them to talk to each other. Between them, they must have enough proof to sway the council.

E's man told her to tell the officials everything. He knew she was our spy. He said that we should know the vaults were coming to destroy us. She told us every word, and she never spoke after that.

Of course we tried to find him after that, but both men had disappeared. We finally found E's man's body about the time her son was born. The hunter probably went back to hiding in his hole. He was banished, and over the years only a few of us kept searching for the vaults. Found some, dead or suffocated or burned.

Your vault is still alive. If we don't kill it, they will kill us.

Tiria let her breath out in a rush and crumpled up the last page. "But they don't know anything! The council killed the hunter when he tried to warn them."

Patrick's eyes narrowed. Seeing the clear disbelief in his face, the girl tried frantically to explain.

"He was Seth's father. As soon as the council heard there was anything outside the vault they turned on him. The people in that vault... you don't understand." She waved her hands futilely in the air. "They don't want to attack you, they just want to sit underground and squabble over shiny things."

Liar. Patrick wrote, and walked away from her before she could stumble over a reply. *Why would your high steal documents about this if he didn't care?*

"He wanted to know why his father died."

He knew enough to bid for you.

"Well then, he..." Tiria stumbled to a halt, and remembered the hunter's grin of triumph when he had found Elizabeth's folder. He had known exactly where to look. He had even warned her, hadn't he? *Don't you think this is too much of a coincidence?*

Robert watched her struggle, and then patted her shoulder with his meaty hand. He wrote slowly, and the words were beautifully shaped. *Did you believe everything he told you?*

"I told myself I didn't. I guess it's not the same thing." She risked a watery smile and shook her head, clearing it of its insistent thoughts. "I wanted to believe him. It was so much more... more colourful. I would have followed a high and carried his children and dug in the dust for the rest of my life. Seth made living seem so much better than just surviving. It didn't matter that I was breaking the rules, because he always had a story that made it okay." Tiria caught Patrick's eye and hesitated. "Do you... do you have a family?"

No. Too mutated. The man gestured to his body without embarrassment, and Tiria looked away. When she read the notebook again he had added: *Robert is married. Our parents rotted. No-one else.*

"Wait - he's your brother?" Tiria looked from one man to the other in frank disbelief. Patrick pulled a face, or at least his dribbling maw twisted a little more comically than usual, and then he tapped the paper with his pen.

Why do you think I let him talk to me like that? Anyone else, I'd smash their face in.

"I talk to you like that."

You're a rat. Prisoner. Your words don't matter.

"I'm Elizabeth's daughter." She reminded him archly. The man smiled.

Tomorrow I will kill Elizabeth's daughter and all of her words and questions go away. That's what I mean: words don't matter. Robert will be swearing at me long after you're gone.

Tiria shivered and pushed the paper away. "I want to go to sleep." She said in a small voice. The man patted her shoulder again. It was like being comforted by a brick wall. He tore off a last piece of paper and handed it to her. When she read it the words blurred in front of her eyes.

I will wake you early so you can see the sun rise. I won't let Robert hurt you more than is necessary. It will be quick and it won't hurt much. Those are all the answers you will need.

CHAPTER 5

The sun was fierce the next day, and even before they broke camp they could feel their skin reddening and stinging. Tiria tugged fretfully against the metal chain, trying to shade the links so that they wouldn't burn her. The wind was surprisingly cool, and whenever the slight breeze drifted over the party they all slowed down and opened their arms, embracing the first fitful signs of winter. Soon, the nights would become as deadly as the noonday sun, and they would have to tie rags over their faces to stop their skin from cracking in the extreme cold. Robert pulled his collar a little higher with a muttered oath.

"How much further is it, girl?" He demanded like a petulant child: "My feet hurt."

"Not far." Tiria could see the jagged outlines of the brick buildings. After an hour they were close enough to make out the wind spilling clouds of fine dust from the rooftops. She dragged her feet as they walked closer, and by the time they were in the village square Robert was almost seething with impatience. Patrick tugged her on with a glare, and then growled as the hot metal links seared his skin.

"We're here." The girl said sulkily, pressing her back against the edge of a ruined wall. The dust and bricks had buried the bodies, but she could still make out the shapes of the savages under the dirt. The men hadn't seen them yet. She dug the bundle of pills out of her belt and clutched them in her sweating palm.

The sun was far too bright. The savages had ambushed them here before, but they were starving and bold. So few scavengers passed through their village that they had attacked despite the heat. Tiria breathed steadily, and watched the shadows.

"Where is the entrance?" Robert was looking around avidly. He kicked the cornerstones of the buildings and stamped on the ground, listening for the boom of a hidden hatch. The girl didn't answer, but she curled her hands behind her back and sank her fingertips into the crumbling bricks. The shadows were seething, like a liquid, with the sun glinting off the ripples of fingers, and arms, and faces... faces...

"Here! Your medicine! They have your...!" She screamed, and threw the bundle as hard as she could. It burst open, scattering white pills into the dust, and the shadows came alive. The dark liquid creatures exploded into men and women whose eyes bulged and hands constricted as they fought and tore at each other for the pills. They shovelled handfuls of dirt into their mouths, frantically trying to find the precious medicine. The ground seethed and was splattered with dark blood and clotted strips of flesh before the savages stopped fighting each other and dragged their hollow eyes around to the intruders.

They were frozen into place. The only human who moved was the girl, who grunted and writhed against the man who had his hand clamped around her mouth. The smaller man stared at the savages in horror.

Tiria sank her teeth into Patrick's hand. He let out a bellow and dropped her. "They have your pills!" She shrieked at the savages. "In their bags! Thousands of..."

Her words were cut off sharply as Robert turned and struck her hard across the face. The girl reeled away with a cry and stumbled. She fell so hard that her head cracked against a brick. The sickening noise rang around the courtyard, and then the savages screamed and exploded forwards, arms outstretched towards the men, faces twisted with fury.

Tiria shoved back against the darkness but she came to far too slowly, blinking her eyes open and then squeezing them shut with a cry of agony. The sun was too bright, and she rolled onto her side to press her face into the dirt. The ground was warm and sticky, and she smelled the unmistakable stench of blood. Gagging, she shoved herself away and retched when the world spun. She fell back against the ground and pressed her hands over her ears, trying to block out the screams and the slow, wet popping sound of tearing flesh.

Something fell heavily onto her back, and she whimpered and try to shove it off. A hand pressed against her mouth, and then she heard a low, garbled sound. It was impossible to understand under the pitiful cries of the mutilated men, but the savage leaned closer and tried again. Its breath stank, and the fingers which dug into Tiria's cheeks were shrivelled and hard.

"Lie still." The savage grunted, and then dragged itself over the girl's body. Tiria froze, her spinning head unable to understand the fact that a savage was talking. She struggled under the savage's dead weight, and the creature grunted and dug its nails into her skin. Shuddering, the girl lay still.

"Listen if you want to live." The savage's breath was warm and moist in her ear. "My name is Maggie."

"Sava..." The girl mumbled giddily. The creature huffed a laugh.

"Say my name or I'll rip you open."

"Maggie."

The savage sighed, and her whole body relaxed. For a moment her stomach-churning gargle became feminine, and childishly vulnerable. "Thank you."

"Are you going to kill me?" Tiria tried to free her hand, and groaned as even that small movement sent pain shooting through her body.

"Probably not. It's hard to tell." The savage pressed her withered hand onto the girl's forehead. "You hit your head. Your friends left you to die. Tell me why."

"They're not my friends." She closed her eyes and tried not to breathe in too deeply. The stench was unbearable, and she dreaded to think what Maggie looked like. Something was moist about her; a clammy moisture soaked through Tiria's shirt and tickled her spine. "They want me dead."

"So you wanted us to kill them." The savage looked up – the pressure on Tiria's shoulder disappeared for a moment – and then the woman's lips moved against her ear. "Lucky you. Do you want to see?"

"I'm going to be sick." Tiria moaned, and then choked and turned her head to vomit into the dust. The savage grunted indifferently and let her sit up. The girl stared at the ground, watching it spin, and wiped her mouth. Maggie wrapped her arms around her back and held her upright until the spinning stopped. "Thank you."

"I used to be a nurse." The savage creaked out another laugh, and flecks of greasy spittle flew across Tiria's vision. "I used to dish out those pills you threw at us. Now I can't even open a bottle." She reached over and rattled one of the pill bottles in front of the girl's face. She flinched at the harsh sound, and pushed it away with a trembling hand. The savage's claw was twisted, the fingers knotted and broken, and it was encrusted with black, crumbling sores which had cracked and filled with sticky, blood-stained dust.

"I can't look at you." Tiria whispered. Maggie put the bottle down carefully into the girl's lap.

"Open it."

Tiria did, pushing the lid down before she twisted it. She expected the savage to snatch the bottle and swallow every single pill, but the creature merely tipped the white lozenges onto the ground. Her breath rasped in her throat, and the emaciated paw crept towards them. Then, shaking, she stopped.

"Would you take them, if you were me?" She croaked. Tiria didn't answer, and the savage sighed. "Put them back in the bottle."

It took the girl a long time to do it, as every pill had turned into two and her clumsy fingers didn't know which one was real. Maggie waited patiently, as if the girl was a child playing with a puzzling toy. Every time another savage crawled near to them the creature would rear up and snarl, digging her claws into the girl's shoulders until she cried out in pain. The other savages kept their distance, glaring balefully at the pair of them.

"They send people to us who can still think." Maggie explained in a low hiss. "They can find food, build shelters until they start twisting up. If they don't help us we take a finger, or an ear. They know they'll be the same as us soon enough. We keep our distance until their minds rot." Again, she made the low laugh. "You've made me into a queen."

"Won't the medicine wear off?"

"Yes, thank god!" The savage exclaimed so loudly that some of the other creatures scurried back. "Do you think I like seeing what I've become? Remembering the things I've done? I've licked bird shit off rooftops. And them! Them!" She gestured to the others, her hand flying past Tiria's ear. "Do you think we start liking the sight of rotting flesh just because it's all around us?" She shuddered so fiercely that Tiria felt her hands trembling, and her voice dropped to a feral growl. "I wish I'd never swallowed your medicine, bitch. All I felt was the need, the want, and then it all faded away and I... I want to go and sink my hands into that man's fat head and swallow the meat."

Tiria took a deep breath and dived away from the grasping arms. The world spun sickly, and she stumbled and collapsed back to the ground. A hand closed around the back of her neck, and then she was pulled upright so quickly that she gagged.

"I'm dying anyway." She croaked, and felt tears sliding down her face. "I watched my brother bleed into his brain. The same thing's happening to me. You might as well..."

"Dying?" The creature laughed and shook her. "You're in shock, but you'll outlive me. If you weren't moving so much you'd be fine. Didn't I tell you to lie still?"

Feeling scolded, Tiria hung her head. She had been so used to the idea of dying today that she felt almost cheated. Not looking up, she held up the bottle of medicine. The savage grunted and shoved it away.

"Give me ten. My territory is five days from here. I can see my children again, and then get away before I can hurt them."

Tiria counted out the pale disks and handed them over. "They work for a whole day?"

"More or less." The creature clicked the pills between her fingers. "You'll be able to live for a year on the rest. Take two if you want to keep the anger at bay."

"Me?" Tiria laughed shortly, and pressed her fingers to her aching temples. They were so grimy with blood and dirt that they looked almost as grotesque as Maggie's. "I don't need them."

The creature drew a breath to say something, and then let it out in a sigh and patted the girl's shoulder. "I'll take the pack to the south. Don't look around until we're gone. I'm a slender, beautiful woman and if you remember me any other way I'll rip your eyes out."

Tiria nodded mutely, and listened to the rustling, cracking sound of scores of savages crawling away. Some of them were chewing, their mouths wide open as they crunched and drooled, and she leaned forward to be sick again. She would have to look eventually, if only to give her nightmares something to cling to. She lay back onto the damp filth and closed her eyes.

She woke up gasping when someone groaned. It wasn't a savage – in the red evening light she could see they were all gone. Struggling upright, she looked around but it was too dark to see anything except a few crumpled shapes. Some were savages, their skulls crushed as if they had been smashed together. Others... she couldn't bear to look at the others, not yet. She crawled away from the wall and heard a grinding sound as the end of her chain dragged across the bricks. She stared at it numbly, not understanding what she was seeing. There was a swath of denim caught on the last link, and when she moved a thin red smear followed it across the courtyard.

She struggled over to one of the travelling packs and pulled out a bottle of water, pouring most of it over her aching head before draining the rest. It was lukewarm and bitter, but her stomach finally settled. She shoved all of the scattered supplies into one bag and hauled it over her back.

The groan rang out a second time, and she saw something move. Biting her tongue, she crept forward on her hands and knees and recognized the broken shell of Robert lying in a pool of blood. Great chunks of flesh had been torn away, yet they hadn't killed him. Perhaps it was Queen Maggie's snide way of refusing to help the girl, but Tiria doubted it.

An empty pistol lay beside the man. She guessed that he had threatened the savages until they had given up – but too late. Instead of the quick, savage death that they had given to Patrick, the man had been slowly bleeding out for hours.

"You're dying." She croaked, and smiled for the first time in weeks. "Good."

The man looked up at her and coughed up a mouthful of blood. It was dark and full of black clots, and dribbled down his cheek into the dust. She had a horrible feeling he was laughing.

"So are you." His voice was the merest whisper, yet there was a grain of honesty in it that made her believe him. She leaned closer and shook her head.

"Do you want your last words to be a lie?"

He smiled, and a fatalistic strength shuddered through his body. His eyes opened wide, and she could see the blood-stained whites all around the dizzy pupils as he spat, "That tracker's not the only thing we shoved into your body, bitch. You... *mutated mutant.* Heh!" He laughed and gagged on a mouthful of blood before his wild eyes met her own. "It's about time you started rotting like the rest of us."

She stared at him for a moment, and then understanding washed over her. She gasped and scrabbled at the disc that was lodged into her spine. She tore at it with her fingernails until her neck was slippery with blood, but there was no way to get deep enough to drag the disc out.

"What did you do?" She whispered, and then shook the man until his teeth cracked hard together and shrieked at him, "What did you do?"

He couldn't answer, he was dead. His eyes stared up into her own, dead and laughing, one glaring and one milky and blind with splitting pustules. She shoved him away in horror. Rotting, he had said, like the rest of them. She scratched at her neck again and then cried out in a low, wretched wail.

She was free. What good was it to her, now?

PART 5: ICE

CHAPTER 1

Tiria spent three days in a daze. She wandered through the wastes without seeing them, grazing her knees on walls she didn't see and falling down slopes which loomed out of nowhere. The heavy bag of supplies bruised her spine but she never thought to put it down or to eat any of the food. When she slept, she simply lay back on the lumpy canvas and let the darkness creep over her. She didn't care that the stars were above her, and not the shelter of bricks or stone. She slept like the dead, long after the sun had risen. Every time she woke up her eyelids were burned from the sunlight, and her lips had split and cracked with thirst.

She found the river on the fourth day and sat beside it, listening to the rushing water. She knew it must be filthy, but she still stripped off her clothes and sank into the depths. Tiria couldn't swim, but when the ground dropped away from beneath her feet she kicked and kicked until the surface broke above her. When she was tired she crawled ashore and sat in the hot sun until it grew unbearable, and then she dove back into the water.

She had no idea why she was doing it, only that some part of her needed to be clean. The lukewarm shallow water felt sticky and smelled putrid, but the deep water was cold and clear. The current terrified her, and it took her three tries before she dared to struggle out into the middle of the flow. Her clumsy kicks grew stronger, and she learned how to swim down into the depths.

There was nothing there. The cold gave her a kind of peace, but there was nothing but darkness and blurry sand no matter how far she swam. Tiria made her way back to shore.

She pulled her clothes on, and forced herself to eat. The tough jerky made her jaw ache, but her head began to clear for the first time in days.

What could she do now? She could hardly return to the rats, and the officials would kill her on sight. The outcasts would never take her back after seeing her guiding the officials. The thought of returning to the vault made her feel sick, and she didn't want to be swept away to rot in the farms. She could trade, she supposed. She could hunt in the ruins for supplies or valuables, if she was quick enough to steal from other people's territory without getting caught.

Then, in the winter, she could have to copy the other traders and find an isolated family to shelter with while the snows fell. A woman had done that once in her own territory, begging them to let her shelter before she froze to death outside. Tiria remembered the desperate woman's face, so old despite her youth, and the grunts of her father as he rutted with her. It was a 'fair trade', he told her. She had nothing else left to sell.

Tiria shuddered and looked down into the shining water. It was autumn. What would she have left to sell, by winter? She had plenty of supplies to survive on for a few months, but when she started trading they would disappear quickly. The colder it got, the more expensive food became.

She could hunt people, she thought. She could kill savages, or track down runaway slaves. Surely somebody would shelter her in exchange for that? She could run a long way along a trail before she got tired, and Seth had taught her...

The thought of the man made her wince, and she violently bit off another piece of jerky. No. She would never resort to that. She would rather be a beggar and a whore than trust a single thing the man had taught her.

Besides, who knew how long she had left? A year? Some people only had a few months before the tumours burst through their skin. She rooted through her bag, and found the plastic tablet bottles the officials had brought with them. Altogether there were just over a hundred tablets. They had thrust the sickness into her spine a week ago, but she hadn't felt ill. Perhaps if she only took one pill and then waited for three or four days, she would earn an extra year. She could do a lot in a year. The madness might still creep in if she took so few pills, but what use were a hundred measly days of certainty?

She looked through the rest of the supplies. There were more than she had guessed, and as she lined them up in front of her Tiria started to smile. There was a lot of food – cereal bars, dried fruit and nuts, fifty dry cubes which could be boiled up to make soup, and two whole bars of chocolate. There was a penknife, whetstone, flint and matches. She dug into the bottom of the bag and her fingers found the edges of a small metal box. When she opened it she discovered a medical kit, with bandages, sewing tools, ointments and two tiny syringes tucked into cunning sections. She peered at the syringes curiously. They were both stocked with glass vials of clear fluid, and the word *Amoxicillin* was printed on the side in red letters. Tiria frowned at the word, her lips moving as she sounded it out. She wondered if it was the same thing as the pills, but she doubted it. She packed the bag up again and left the riverbank.

For the next week she walked steadily. She decided to get as far away from the officials' territory as she could. Once she was far away, she would be able to decide what to do. The road curved steadily uphill, out of the low valley and into the highlands around it. For several hours she walked through empty fields with hulking metal insects rising out of them. Thick metal wires littered the ground, and she stumbled over one of them before she thought to scavenge them. It took a long time to roll up the strand, but with twenty meters of wire in her backpack she felt safer than she had in days. That night she slept in a copse of dead trees and wrapped the wire around them until she was enclosed like a bug in a cocoon.

She untied the wire the next morning and asked herself why she had done it. Who had she been afraid of? The savages were too feral to risk baking in the sun, and there was nothing for the dogs to hunt here. It was a desert; if she stayed in the highlands she would starve to death and her body would shrivel up in the hot wind long before she went savage. Who would risk their lives to finish the job? The question made her laugh out loud, and she pressed her fingertips to her lips. She couldn't think of an answer. All of the clans were all as dangerous as each other, and they all had their own reasons for wanting her dead.

She thought: *They'd tear each other to shreds to get a chance at me.*

The thought made her pause, her fingers curving around the cold wire. She couldn't defend herself from any of them on her own, but they all had enough power to cripple each other. If she was clever - and very, very lucky - she might be able to pit them off against each other.

She stuffed the wire into her bag and started running again, looping back around the highlands and coasting down the ridge of the hill into the next valley. The great scar of the city seared the horizon, and beyond it she could see the thick, brownish smog that hung over the river. Nobody ever went there. Nobody wanted the city. It belonged to the dead.

Tiria shook off her superstition and forced herself to plan a route downhill. There were places to shelter in the city, and food clutched in the hands of the dead, and the radiation wouldn't hurt her too badly. She was already mutating, so she had nothing to be afraid of if she was careful to avoid the crater. That was where she would hide. She scratched her neck, and felt the odd disc of the tracking device clicking against her spine. That was where they would find her.

The time she had slept in the hills was bad enough; the nights in the foothills were the most frightening of her life. She was too close to the territories to be safe from the officials, and every time her tracker caught against her hair she flinched, thinking their soldiers had found her. There weren't just imaginary dangers, either. The closer she got to the city, the more she was scared of an ambush by the savages. Tiria wrapped the wire between old fire escapes and strung her blanket across into a hammock, but even then she flinched awake at the slightest noise.

She hiked back into the village on the outskirts and made her way to the courtyard the savages had claimed. The stench hit her before she saw the bodies. The savages' corpses were gone, dragged away into the shadows as if they never existed. A few weeks ago she would have imagined the creatures ripping at the rotting flesh and shoving it into their gaping craws, but now she wasn't so sure. There had to be more to the savages than just their brutal reputation. This was the third time she had crossed the hatch-marked tiles, and the second time she had watched people die lying in the red brick dust. Only the buried bodies were still there; the savages had taken their comrades back into their haunts, but not to eat them. The bodies of Patrick and Robert still stared blankly up at the blinding sun – perfectly good meat left to moulder until the stink made Tiria's eyes water. Black flies covered Patrick's abdomen where the savages had torn him open, and as the girl watched a mouse crawled out of Robert's swollen purple lips. The animal's hide was bald and boiled with tumours. The girl watched it without the slightest danger of queasiness.

"You took their bodies away to bury them." She said aloud, gesturing to the empty ruins around her. A strange hissing sound made the hairs rise on the back of her neck, and she scratched the implant fitfully. "I know you're there. I want to talk to Maggie."

"She's dead." The croaking sound was more like a growl than a voice. Tiria squeezed her eyes shut and planted her feet in the ground.

"What happened?"

"Her family planted an axe in her head." A new waft of pungent air puffed over the courtyard as the creature crawled closer. "They didn't even recognize her. They just screamed."

"Were you expecting anything else?" Tiria stubbornly refused to open her eyes. "Maybe that's how she wanted to go."

"Maybe." The savage laughed, and then his icy hand slapped into the girl's ankle. She shrieked and then bit her lip so sharply she tasted blood. The hand slid slowly up to her knee, and then pulled her down to the ground. "Don't scream again, girl. It makes the voices want to come out and play."

"What's your name?" She asked, pressing her hands over her eyes. The creature moved so close to her that she could feel its breath moistening her cheek, but it didn't touch her again. She used its confusion to press it again, "What did you look like?"

"Darren." The voice was almost human. "I was twenty six when I turned. I used to have blue eyes."

"What colour..." Tiria almost peeked, and then remembered that the savages had milky, translucent orbs that oozed with greasy tears in the piercing sun. "Never mind."

"Never mind." He echoed roughly. "Maggie said you'd be back. Did you bring more medicine?"

"Do you want some?"

He laughed. "Of course I do. We all do. But think carefully before you start using them as leverage. Tearing you to shreds will be just as satisfying as being able to think clearly for a few measly days." His gloating voice changed a little, and Tiria felt a calloused fingertip prodding at her ear. "The voices get awfully angry sometimes, but we're still alive underneath them. Why won't you look at me?"

"I'm afraid of savages. I'm not afraid of a voice, even one that says nasty things."

"Clever." He snorted a laugh, and moisture slapped against her raised hands. She squeaked in disgust and twisted further away. "It won't work, you know."

"I don't know what..."

"You won't be able to argue with voices when you start to rot. We all tried." He sighed and patted her knee. "I took Maggie's pills so I could try again. I'm so tired, little rat. Tomorrow I will let them win."

Tiria shivered and winced as her nails bit into her forehead. She hadn't consciously moved her hands into fists, but the fingers had constricted and gouged dimples into her skin. She couldn't even trust her own body – even though nothing had changed since she had found out the truth, and even though she felt perfectly healthy, she second-guessed every twitch and aching muscle until she wanted to scream.

"I'm not here to give you medicine." She muttered. "I'm here to ask for your help."

He scoffed, "Why would we help you?"

"Because I'm asking." Her voice was so soft that she heard it tremble, but when the creature didn't answer she pressed on more strongly: "I've seen who you are. I want to listen to your names and hear what the officials have done to you, so that when I start killing them I can scream it into their faces. I still have the strength to fight them and I'll give you all of my medicine so you can help me. After that I'll be just like you. It's my last chance, do you see that? I want to use it to really hurt them."

"You haven't seen anything." The creature pointed out stiffly. "You won't open your eyes."

"I'll be afraid of you." The girl admitted. "I can't help it. Maggie told me not to look."

"I'm Darren." His voice was stubborn. "Look at me."

She opened her eyes, and the light was so bright that for a moment everything blurred and shimmered. The light slowly ebbed away, and the man's face swam into focus. It was a man, she could see that – although a few months ago she wouldn't have even thought he was human. His eyes were an opaque blue which looked blind, but he looked back at her levelly. His mouth was puckered as if he was dying of thirst, but his ears and jaw and cheeks all looked normal. His nose was the part of him that was grotesque, a rotten scar that razed across his face and between his eyes, reaching up into his hair line as if it would split his head in two.

"Is that your mutation?" Tiria croaked, pointing. He smiled and nodded.

"Who am I, then? What would you tell the officials about me?"

"Nothing." She shook her head. "I can't tell anything about you from what you look like."

He laughed, and a weird snorting whistle came out of the wound. "Oh, come on now! Think like the little scavenger you are. Look at my face and I'm sure the words will come back to you. What am I – violent? Bloodthirsty? Diseased?"

She gulped and nodded, but didn't look away. Darren closed his eyes, covered his nose with one hand, and just like that he looked human. When he spoke, his soft voice reminded her of Walker's. "You can say anything you like to the officials, but as soon as they see us all those words will fly out of their heads. After we're banished they burn our photographs so that nobody remembers us from before. Most of us forget our own names within a year." He sighed and took his hand away, keeping his eyes shut. "We don't need your sympathy, little rat."

"Revenge, then." She pressed her hands to his cheeks, watching his eyes fly open in shock. "I know it's happening to me. I won't go without a fight."

"Careful." He croaked, "That could just be the voices shouting in your head."

"If it is, then I'm glad." Tiria smiled wolfishly. "The officials made me go mad. If it helps me to kill them then it serves them right."

The savage studied her for a moment, and then raised his hand to her own and gently pushed it away. Closing his fingers around her own, he studied her calloused palm for a moment and then sighed. "I should probably be telling you to go home. You have time left. You can still run and laugh and kiss your family good-night. Don't sacrifice those moments; you'll be savage sooner than you think."

"It will be too late by then." She whispered. "I can still outsmart them. It's the only way I'll win."

He looked at her narrowly, and then smiled. "Like I said, I should be telling you to go home, but I won't. If you give me the medicine I'll gather up the ones who can help you. You'll need them to be sane, I guess, if you're trying to outthink the officials." He held his hand out, and Tiria hesitated. The pills were a year of life. If she gave them away and this man betrayed her then she would have lost everything.

Was revenge worth so much?

"I'm rotting anyway." She muttered, and clicked the bottle open. "Let's make them pay."

When the sun started to set the savages sent her away, warning her that the voices were deafening in the darkness. On that night and for the next two days Tiria hiked along the city wall, looking for other entrances into the ruins. There were a few, but the wall had buckled over some of the great iron gates, and buildings had collapsed and blocked the others. It would have been difficult to get into the city through them, but not impossible. She tore a page from Patrick's notebook and drew a semicircle half way down, mimicking the way the wall closed off the valley. Every time she found an entrance she made a mark, finding out that if she drew lines between them it echoed the odd patterns of roads she could see between gaps in the crumbling stones. She marked any tall buildings which stood out to her but couldn't work out how far from the wall they were; the buildings were far taller than any she had ever seen.

When she was satisfied that her rough map was finished she memorized it and headed back to the only clear gateway. As she walked she scrawled a note on one of the blood-stained pages in the book and made her way to the vault. Her boots left prints. She walked backwards and trudged through puddles, making the trail as obvious as possible.

The hatch was still hard to find, but she stamped on every suspicious bit of ground near the wall until her boots found steel. She slapped the note down onto the ground and pounded on the hatch as loudly as she could. It only took her a few moments to sprint away and duck behind a fence. The hatch creaked open, and the soldier inside it looked out suspiciously before catching sight of the note. He frowned and picked it up, and Tiria watched with dark satisfaction as his face turned white.

I will tell them everything.
Come and get me.
Rat.

CHAPTER 2

Tiria sprinted into the ruins as fast as she could, her rucksack thudding painfully into her back with every passing mile. Every time she came to a junction she headed north, barrelling into the heart of the dead city with her heart in her mouth and her breath rasping in her ears. There was no way the citizens could be chasing her already, unless their soldiers were stupider than she had thought. When her legs started screaming she slowed down but kept moving, wanting to put as much distance as possible between herself and the vault. The further she went, the more she could double back on herself. She wanted to plant endless mazes of tracks. She could find hiding spots, and places to set up traps. She needed time, and luck, but most of all she needed to be quick.

The road dimmed as she ran, and it took her a few minutes to work out that it wasn't just because the sun was setting. The red bricks were gradually becoming darker, as if they had been dipped in ink. Tiria slowed down and climbed the ancient, rusting metal staircase to the top of one of the taller buildings. She caught her breath on the last flight and looked around.

The crater in the middle of the city was still a good distance away, but she could see it more clearly now. The bowl-like edges were seared in black glass. Tiria knew that if she got too close to it the radiation might kill her before anyone had a chance to catch up. It was tempting to head that way anyway. She had nothing left to lose and no-one would believe she was stupid enough to do it, but her stomach churned at the memory of the savages. Radiation exposure made mutations worse, and she was determined to cling to her sanity for as long as she could.

She crouched down in the corner of the staircase and pulled open her bag, stuffing a handful of dried fruit into her mouth. There was probably another hour until the sun set. The city had a solemn silence to it that made her head hurt; nobody ever came here. Even the savages stayed away. The radiation and the dangerous listing ruins made it unsafe, and the buildings were crammed with the burned long-dead that nobody wanted to steal from. Tiria looked at the blank, burned eyes of the building opposite her and shuddered.

You wanted to stay alive, too. She thought to any ghosts who might be listening. *You have no reason to hate me.*

The ghosts didn't answer, but Tiria imagined that the eyes became simple windows once more. Tucking the food back into her bag, she climbed further up the staircase and ran along the roof until, three buildings along, she found another fire escape. This one creaked and groaned when she stepped onto it, and she flinched at the harsh noise in the silence. She held her breath and then ran down it at top speed, feeling every wrenching note shuddering in her bones as if the entire building was tumbling down on top of her. The staircase shuddered but held.

When she reached solid ground Tiria burst out laughing, relief dancing in her veins. Then she looped her wire around the rusty support posts, and hauled on it with all her might. The fire escape screamed as the metal bar snapped away, and then it began to warp and pop away from the wall. Tiria fled, dodging the chunks of brick that every support tore away from the building.

When it landed, she made her way through the dust and untied her rope. Her hands stung, and she rubbed the shards of rust away from them impatiently.

Now that there was a gap in her trail, she moved more slowly. The officials wouldn't need to follow her footprints. They only had to look at their tracking machine to know where she was, and she would be dead before she knew she was surrounded. Tiria hoped that they would be as cowed by the city as the vault dwellers; there couldn't be anything valuable in the endless streets, or they would have been searched decades ago. The officials had marked the city out of limits, and none of the Rats had argued.

There was a coldness to the city which had nothing to do with the weather. The screaming of the dust eaters still rang through the hollow doorways, and the violence of their deaths marred every stone. There were shadows on the walls which were so clear that Tiria could make out every splayed out finger. Their faces were unnaturally long. It took her a long time to realize that the dust eaters hadn't been shaped differently; their chins had dropped down as they screamed, and they had been branded that way forever.

She gritted her teeth and kept walking. The officials would be cautious. She was better at scaling ruins than people who had never had to choose between safety and survival. If she was careful then they wouldn't be able to follow her. The tracking device was powerful enough to speak across the wastes, but she doubted it could pinpoint the exact vent she was hiding in.

Discounting the officials, she walked through a narrow alley way and stomped heavily into a drift of gritty mould. If they followed her from the vault then the citizens would be here first, and they would be angry enough to ignore the ghosts. Their soldiers would sprint after her footprints, too blinded to realize they were already lost. By the time they realized she was hidden they would be frightened, and easy for the officials to surround in the dark.

That only left Seth. If anyone found her, it would be him.

Tiria looked back at the trail of footprints and bit her lip. The next time she passed a building she hauled herself up it, clinging to the bricks and panting with effort as her shoulders ached. The bricks cracked under her calloused fingertips and chunks of them fell away from her scrabbling feet. When she reached the roof and looked back there was a clear path from the ground to her hiding spot.

"Stupid." She muttered, and started moving again. The tiled rooftops bled into one another, and by the time her legs grew tired the wind had swept her footprints away. Tiria smiled, and started heading back towards the vault, memorizing every junction and testing rusting ladders and loose tiles. By the time she reached the outer wall she wasn't afraid anymore. They had weapons and machines, but this was her territory.

The first of her hunters entered the city through the main archway. Tiria crept along the rooftops and watched the distant shadows wavering in the heat haze. One of them was Seth - she would recognise his loping, casually complacent stride anywhere. Her heart leapt into her throat, and for a moment she could hardly breathe. The mixture of fear and confusion was stunning. He was alive – and clearly the officials hadn't caught him. He sauntered towards the tipsy city with a confidence which made her feel sick. Only his eyes were wary – two piercing black orbs which caught the slanting afternoon light and made him look demonic. Tiria tore her eyes away, and forced herself to breathe.

She didn't know who the other figure was. A burst of jealousy coursed through her before she realised that the slim, effeminate silhouette was a man - short, yet solid, with weapons shining at his hips. The ridiculous fool hadn't even thought to hide the gleam of his weapons from spying eyes. She could see the sun shining off them from a long way away. Even the moonlight would outline them at night. How could Seth have let him walk out into the wastes like that?

Tiria stalked them silently for a few streets, trusting in her sure knowledge of the safe and trembling ladders to mask her sound. When she knew they would creak she leapt down steps or shimmied down walls, but she was careful not to stay on the same level as the men for long. They stayed in the middle of the road, brazen and obvious. She wondered if they wanted her to see them.

Seth barely looked around. Tiria was certain that he knew she was there. He didn't need to look for her; he knew she would have been following them since the second they ventured into the ruins. His companion moved nervously, looking into every corner, but even when she was in his line of sight he never saw her. He was looking for movement, or the soft sheen of eyes and skin. She ducked down or froze whenever he looked, and his untrained eyes never knew the difference between grimy fabric and wind-seared stone.

"She's hiding." He told Seth, in a voice which carried. The man didn't answer, but Tiria could imagine the scathing expression in his eyes. The other man's voice rose. "Why are we walking? We just have to wait until she lights a fire or runs out of food."

"Do you think she's stupid?" Seth demanded. Tiria ducked back behind a wall at the clear tenor of his voice. He knew she was watching. He knew she was listening. If he decided to find her, she'd better be ready to run. When she risked another peek the other man was arguing.

"She's a rat. Just a rotten scavenger, like all the rest. I know how to find her. What do you think I've been training for?"

"Ah yes, I forgot." Seth looked the other man up and down, shining weapons and all. "Hart taught you everything he knows. You have a lot of faith, Justin. He's never been out here."

"Of course he has. He couldn't have trained me without it." Justin laughed and missed the look on the other man's face. Tiria watched as Seth's surprise turned into understanding and then, slowly, dawning fury. Of course Hart had been outside. Who else would the council have sent to murder a hunter, if not his own brother? Seth's hands closed into fists, and then he took a deep breath.

The stranger hadn't even noticed. He was so inattentive that Tiria expected him to stumble over every brick in his path.

She followed them for another block, and then they reached a courtyard. There must have been a fountain there, once. She had seen drawings of them in the books she had read, with shining water blossoming out of them and falling into deep, limpid pools. This fountain was full of dust, and the wind blew grains of it from the high pedestal and whipped them around the empty plaza. The bowl that had once held water was dry. The ancient bones of a dust-eater were curled up in the bottom, huddled around like a child. Tiria had seen so many of them that she had thought they could no longer shock her, but she could read the woman's last moments like a story. The fires had come, roaring through the streets, and she had hidden in the water until the basin cracked.

Tiria crouched in her broken window frame and looked back into the attic room. There was nobody there, but she was suddenly aware of the colour of the singed walls, and the remnants of toys and games that littered the floor, undisturbed after all these years. She swallowed and looked back down at the two men.

"We'll need to split up if we're going to find her." Justin sat on the edge of the fountain and took a huge bite of a chocolate bar. Seth didn't answer, and after a few minutes the other man grew bored of trying to chatter and simply wandered off. Seth waited for a few minutes, and then he unzipped his bag and drew something out. He placed it into the fountain bowl, and Tiria's heart leapt into her mouth when she saw it move.

"This is not a trap." The man said clearly, not looking up. "I'll be gone by the time you climb down. This cancels any debt between us, my love. Tomorrow I'll hunt you down like the traitor bitch you are."

Tiria held her breath, and watched the tiny lizard licking curiously at the warm marble. She longed to leap down and snatch him up. She was frightened that it was one of the man's cruel tricks, and that he was testing her to see if she was truly watching.

Her best chance was to fire at them. Even if she accidentally killed George, she would show Seth how little she cared about anything from the vault. It would prove she was ready to kill whoever it took to survive. She told herself that, but as she looked down she couldn't even make her hand fall to her holster. The little animal climbed up the bones like a ladder, and then slid back down into the dust. She gave an involuntary gasp when he fell, and then clapped her hands over her mouth.

Seth looked straight up at her. Their eyes met, and she drew back into the shadows. His eyes were as black as obsidian, and they were completely empty. She held her breath, ready to run if his hand so much as twitched towards his gun.

He grinned like a wolf. Tiria didn't move, but her fingers constricted around the splintered window sill. She watched the man as he gently lifted George back onto his feet. When the annoyed animal was settled, the man walked away. He sauntered. It was terrifying. He was so convinced of his place in her world that he even had his hands in his pockets.

Tiria sprinted down the corridor and made her way down the ladder. She scanned the plaza for footsteps, but he hadn't returned in the few seconds where she hadn't been watching. The empty windows looked down into the square balefully, and she knew that she shouldn't risk it. He could be in any of those windows with a gun trained on her head – and, unlike her, he always hit what he aimed for.

Tiria knew all of these things, but her feet were already moving. She tore across the smooth slabs with her breath rasping in her throat, her legs wildly akimbo as she launched herself forward. She reached out with both hands and grabbed the lizard as she ran past, not caring that he sank his claws into her palms, and stuffed him into her jacket as she ran. A soft popping sound made her flinch, and she threw herself down against the stones just as the bullet tore a solid chunk out of the pedestal. She dragged herself upright and ran, kept running until her lungs felt like they were bursting, and then she found a ladder and started to climb.

The rooftop was safe. She could look down, and nobody could see her unless they were up there with her. She sobbed out her gasping breaths and opened her coat, seeing that the lizard was puffed up and black with feral anger. Weeping, she kissed his furious head and held him until he stopped trying to claw at her. Finally, he gave her a tentative lick on the nose.

"It was a warning shot." She whispered to him. George tilted his head to one side, and she rooted in her bag for some dried fruit. He ate it with grudging pleasure, and she stroked his head to calm herself down. "He almost got me. He wasn't even trying."

She couldn't take a chance like that again. She knew why he had done it. If the council's hunter died out here, then he would be blamed. If George was killed, then she would never forgive herself. They both had a weakness, and they were both clever enough to use it against each other.

"Tomorrow's going to be fun." She muttered, and stood up. "We'd better get ready."

CHAPTER 3

Killing Justin would have been easy, but Tiria knew better than to hunt him down. It was the obvious thing for her to do, and so Seth would be waiting for her to strike. It was far too dangerous to do anything he might be expecting; he only needed to guess her movements once to be able to kill her. He had effortlessly found her at the fountain – of course he had, hadn't he trained his whole life to track people down? He knew how she would act, and so he had known that she would be watching them. Tiria walked through the city chewing on her fingernails. What could she do that he wouldn't expect?

The traps she had set around the city might have given her an edge, but they were hastily made and clumsily concealed. Perhaps Seth would be distracted enough to miss one, but she doubted it. It was more likely that the new hunter would stumble over one.

Seth would be watching the other man, then. He would have worked out that the traps were there. He was so disdainful of the vault dwellers that he would expect the newcomer to trip over his own feet. While he was watching Justin, he wasn't hunting Tiria. The best thing the girl could do, she realized, was keep the idiot alive.

A gust of wind blew dust into her eyes, and she covered them with her hand. The breeze was icily cold, and she forced open her watering eyes to look up at the sky. A great black storm front was rolling across the horizon. It was still far away, but even the sight of it made her shiver. If she was at home she would be running back to the shelter already. The autumn storms were short, but viciously sharp. People got trapped in the howling winds and blinded by the heavy rain, or they froze to death in the artic night, or the savages dragged them out of their hastily made shelters and skinned them to steal the warmth in their flesh. Tiria zipped up her coat to her neck, making sure that George could breathe. She was already shivering in the icy air as she looked around for somewhere to wait out the storm.

The idiot hunter pulled his collar up to his ears, but didn't bother moving to the sheltered side of the road. His eyes were on the road, not on the sky. He seemed to be following footprints, which was baffling, as Tiria had not set one foot onto the dusty road. The divots in the dust might have been made by a crawling savage, or a dog, but the man didn't seem to know the difference. The girl crawled along the rooftop and watched him in amazement. If the traps didn't kill him, then he would surely walk right into a feral den and have his hands bitten off by dogs.

Something crashed down beside her head, and she shrieked and rolled away. It took her a second to leap to her feet, but as soon as she was upright she realized she had made a mistake. It hadn't been a weapon; a large chunk of ice had landed close to where she was lying. Justin had heard her scream, and could see her clearly now that she was standing upright. He cried out, and fired six rounds at her before another hailstone crashed down and splattered him with shards of ice. He yelped and ran towards the building.

Tiria realized that as stupid as he was, if she faced off with him on a rooftop his gun would give him the advantage. There was a wall on one side of the roof, about two feet high, a last barrier before the sheer drop. She sheltered from the worst of the hailstones behind it and looked over the edge of the roof. She saw the man hacking wildly at a doorframe. Lumps of rotten wood fell away, and the door creaked open a little. He gave a triumphant cry and started barrelling into it.

The hailstones had grown smaller now, but there were far more of them, and every so often one of the deadly chunks still fell. Tiria looked around for some way to escape. The fire escapes would be icy death-traps, and Justin would soon be inside the building. As she was looking another crash came from downstairs, and she peered over the wall to see the door swinging open a little more.

The wall wobbled under her hand, and she froze. It was designed to stop people from falling off the edge, and so it hugged the lip of the roof. A long crack ran straight through it. Without stopping to think, she pushed herself out into the open and sat facing the wall. She sank her fingers into the crumbling tarmac and then pushed both of her feet out against the wall. Hailstones bruised her upturned face, and she shut her eyes and shoved blindly. Her body slid in the ice, and she lost her grip. When the wall finally came loose she nearly fell with it, and had to scrabble to keep herself safe.

Then she looked down, and saw the crumbled body lying beneath the icy stone. There was no time to savour the moment; she fled into the building and sprinted through the empty rooms. If Seth truly was watching Justin, then he would be seconds away from killing her. She bit back a curse. She had not wanted Justin's death. It had been an instinct to kill him, and now her only defence was to run.

She fled through the streets, slipping on the ice and holding her hands above her head. The hail stones hurt, but she was sure that Seth would bide his time rather than venture out into the storm. The wind whipped the shards into her face, and her nose felt so numb it might as well have fallen off. She desperately needed to find shelter, but as the buildings grew shorter and stockier the exposure only got worse. Finally, she saw a solid concrete building with thick bars across some of the windows. Gasping, she tried to open the door and almost wept when the door swung open. It was a thick, metal door, and when she slammed it shut behind her she felt safe for the first time in hours.

It took her eyes a while to adjust to the dark. When they did, she saw a harrowing sight. Scores of twisted shapes littered the long hallway. The dust had been undisturbed since the bombs fell, and now her presence made it billow up into the fine, soft powder that spoke more of ashes than of dirt. There must have been scores of dust-eaters crowded into this place when the bombs fell. She crept through the unrecognizable husks and made her way around the corridor. After a few hundred feet the twisted shapes disappeared. They had all been clustered into the lobby. It must have been chaos. Were they trying to get in, or out? Did they think the people here could help them?

The next doorway led her to a room filled with more of the metal bars. There were ten separate cages lined up along two walls, with an office at the facing end. More twisting shapes were in this room, but only one or two in each cage. That was worse than the crowd, in a way. If the people outside were trying to escape, then they had willingly left these people to die. Tiria shook melt water from her cropped hair and tore her eyes away.

The nearest cell to the doorway was outlined with concrete, not metal, but there were still thick bars on the door where a window looked out. Tiria tried the door, found that it was open, and ducked into the concrete cage.

The cell bolted from the inside. There were long racks on the wall which had been raided for their weapons long ago, and a few decaying riot vests scattered on the floor. Tiria bolted the door and saw that the concrete around the solid iron was pockmarked with deep holes. Whoever had taken the guns had fought to keep them. She dropped the keys to the ground and leaned against the wall, letting exhaustion wash over her whole body.

She fell asleep before she could eat, and the sound of her rucksack spilling its contents across the floor only made her eyelids flicker. The wind and rain howled outside, and she curled up tighter against the cold. Patrick hadn't given her any winter clothes. She would have to find something in the morning, or the cold would kill her far faster than Seth could.

Her dreams writhed with cold, grasping fingers.

CHAPTER 4

"Hello, Ti."

The girl sat bolt upright, scanning the room for Seth as her hand fell to her gun. The room was clearly empty, and the metal door was still bolted firmly on her side. His voice had rung around the entire cell; had she imagined it? She raised herself cautiously to her knees and looked up at the ceiling, but it was bare concrete. Then she looked at the ground. There was nothing except a metal grate, far too small for a man to crawl through, like the one that she had crouched over as a prisoner. She held her breath, deciding that if she didn't hear anything else by the time she counted to a hundred then it had just been a vivid nightmare.

A dull clanging sound made her flinch. It was definitely coming from the grate. How could he be in there? She crawled over to it, cautiously teasing her fingers over the edges of the grille. It was welded in place, and she let out a sigh of relief before guiltily clapping her hands over her mouth. It was too late; the clanging noise stopped, and she heard the soft sounds of someone sitting down. The grate must run between the cells. He was on the other side of the concrete wall, a few feet away from her, unable to see her or attack her but still so close that her skin crawled.

"Are you going to shoot me through concrete?" She rasped, finding her voice. "I'd love to see the recoil on that."

He sighed and she heard him unzipping his bag. "You're an idiot. Your door locks from the outside, didn't you notice? I could leave you to starve to death in there, but it doesn't seem fair. I'll wait for thirty minutes after I hear you leave, and then we'll start again. If you want to keep running all night I'll kill you in the dark, but to be honest I'd rather get some sleep."

"This isn't a game." She muttered, and heard him laugh.

"As long as you end up dead, lovely, it doesn't matter how long it takes."

"Is that why you didn't kill me in the farms?" Silence followed that question, and she clicked her tongue against her teeth. "How did you know I was here? I know you weren't following me. It's like someone told you where to find me."

There was a pause, and then the voice came back. "I'm sure the officials didn't let you go without a tracking device. They must be following you too."

"Yes. They'll be here soon. They think I'm hiding in the vault." Tiria leaned back against the concrete and then opened one eye. "How can you use their tracking bug?"

"I can't." The man sounded for all the world like he was prompting her for the right answer. Tiria's tired mind buzzed, and she looked down at herself. The official's bug pressed against her spine and grated on the rough concrete, but she knew there was nothing else on or under her skin. Her clothes were the grimy jeans and shirt that the officials had dressed her in, and after they had cut off her hair she didn't even have any hair ties from the vault. Her eye caught the glint of metal, and she nearly groaned aloud. She had completely forgotten about the bracelet he had given her. Snapping it off, she threw it into the corner of the room and heard Seth laugh at the tinkling sound.

"You knew it'd be stupid to wear it into the wastes."

"How much of this did you plan?" She spat, shaking with emotion. "Why would you make me think... if all the time you were just using me to... to..."

"I didn't do anything." He actually had the gall to sound surprised. "You chose to make things between us real. I wouldn't have touched you if you hadn't been begging me for it. But I warned you nothing would change, and I meant it. Once we had broken into the complex I didn't need to keep you anymore. I *wanted* to." His voice turned sour. "I gave you that choice, too."

"I wasn't begging for anything." She said, flaring beetroot red. "I never had to. Anyone could tell that a pathetic sadist like you would be gasping for it."

"This is an argument I would be more than willing to let you win if we weren't both armed." He returned with a sudden flash of maniacal humour. Tiria rolled her eyes, but beneath the stupid expression her mind was racing. Seth was trying to be distant, but the argument clearly put him on edge. She could use that. Or, it could be that he was putting on an act, like he had so many times before. They sat in silence for a long time, listening to the wind howling outside the building, and tried to size each other up.

"I could have told the officials weeks ago. Do you know why I came back? Why I wanted you to follow me?" Tiria asked finally.

"Me?" Seth sounded tired. The girl could just imagine the crooked smile on the man's face. "It doesn't matter. *I* don't matter. If you kill me then the next hunter will take my place. It's done now. I gave you the chance to walk away. You won't get another chance. If you thought singling me out would change anything then you were wrong."

"I killed your next hunter."

The man's voice echoed in the grate. "There will always be another one."

Tiria closed her eyes and found herself imagining Seth's face, looking for the mask which she had seen him wear so many times before. She used to tell herself that she could see past the cracks to see what he was really thinking. As the seconds crawled past the icy realisation made her shudder: there was nothing beyond his simple words. He was telling her the truth, as bluntly as it had been told to him by his own father. Whatever hopes and dreams he once held had been buried for so long that now he genuinely felt nothing at all. He had been raised to be a puppet, and the council had sent him to the wastes to hide their secrets. If he questioned his duty, then he would no longer be fit for it. A hunter lasted only as long as he kept his thoughts to himself.

"You must feel something." She whispered, feeling as if her revenge was being stolen away by his utter indifference. She wanted him to feel –

what? Trapped? Helpless? She wanted him to feel as lost and betrayed as she did, was that it? Her fingers clenched into fists, and she saw that they were trembling.

Seth listened quietly, and finally his voice emerged. It was soft and so close to being soothing that it was obscene.

"Do you want to know why I chose you, Ti? It was the first thing you asked me. I promised that I would tell you when it was time."

She didn't answer.

"They told me to find the boy and make sure he died. I couldn't reach him, but I found his sister. I hid you in the vault and waited for him to come looking, but the selfish moron abandoned you. I took you out to look for him. You did very well, Tiria – I couldn't have found him on my own. But I had no idea the outcasts were so organised, or that they saw so much. I couldn't simply kill him. It had to look like an accident. Alerting the officials was the easiest way to do it."

Tiria stared at the grate, mutely shaking her head as she listened. It wasn't a conscious movement; the utter refusal to believe what he was saying stopped her from thinking beyond the next word.

Seth stopped trying to explain and grew blunt. "Your brother was a threat. I hunted him, and I killed him. It's what I do."

"'Lawrence wasn't anybody." She forced the whisper out, and hated him for being able to hear it.

"No. *You* weren't anybody. He was everything. His father was a hunter from another vault. The man abandoned his duties to chase a woman, and every man, woman and child he was supposed to protect was slaughtered. We had to make an example of him. My father slit his traitor throat, but he lost track of your brother. He made a mistake." Seth grew quieter. "I corrected it."

Tiria pushed herself away from the grate. She remembered the way Seth had stopped in the farms, pouring over the papers. He hadn't needed all the files, just Elizabeth's. Seth had abandoned his wife the second that he knew that Elizabeth was dead, and that Lawrence was trapped. His work was finished, and he would be untouchable in the vault until the day he died.

Come with me, or don't.

She suddenly saw her life through Seth's eyes. His voice had echoed and warped in the grate, and now it seemed like the only voice that fit.

Every word he had ever said had been a lie. Every tender moment they had shared was suffused with bitterness. Even the gift he had given her was tarnished, a pretty lie he had clamped onto her wrist to keep her under control. But she hadn't needed it, had she? She had agreed to everything he wanted, and because he never had to ask her, it never occurred to her that she could have said no.

He had made her think that finding Lawrence was her own idea, and so she had happily agreed to do whatever he wanted in exchange. He had promised to free her from the ballot, but even that was a trick. Once she led Seth to Lawrence then her husband had no more use for her.

The only thing that made Tiria doubt herself was the moments of stillness they had shared, when there was no reason to be affectionate at all. Even if Seth had been manipulating her he wouldn't have cared if she was unhappy. In their first weeks together he had bullied and tested her until he was satisfied that she would obey her contract unerringly. Nor had he used her loneliness and hunger for gentleness to coerce her into having sex. There was nothing he could gain by gentleness that she wouldn't have willingly given him as part of their contract – apart from love.

I can't risk your life if I'm in love with you! His fury rang in her ears, and she remembered the anger in his voice. He hadn't been pretending, he had been accusing her of destroying his intricate lie. She had done everything he wanted, and she had broken so far beyond the man's control that her obedience mocked him. *You need to make me hate you.*

She wanted to believe it was a trick. She needed to believe it was a lie. As the seconds crawled past, she rested the flat of her hand on the icy concrete wall and wished she could see his face one last time. All she needed was a few seconds. It would be enough to tell her whether he loved her.

Seth's father had been murdered. That was what he cared about. Nobody in the vault really cared about each other's conspiracies. A hunter was killed because he had lost a screaming child and a mute woman in the dust. Seth hadn't been threatened because the council thought he knew too much, but because he did not know enough. Until he unearthed his father's mistake he would be ostracized, and the longer he took, the worse his position became.

Tiria had been a tool, then an ally. Maybe Seth hadn't wanted to make her into a sacrifice. Maybe he hadn't cared. Either way, Tiria couldn't forgive him for it.

She curled up against the wall and pulled her canvas bag into her lap. The fabric was heavy, but at least it was warmer than nothing. She thought she would sleep badly, but she was so exhausted that as soon as her racing mind slowed, she passed out. Her dreams were torrid and vicious, and when she woke up her head was pounding. She nestled it into her hands, and gasped when sharp pain stabbed into her skin. When she looked at her hands she saw that both wrists were riddled with deep scratches. Her fingernails were dark with dried blood. Whatever she had dreamed about had made her tear at her own skin.

Tiria held herself still for a moment, trying to make sense of such insanity, but as soon as she closed her eyes the dream returned. It roared so violently in her ears that she gasped and threw herself forwards, gulping in breath after breath as she tried to force the grotesque anger away.

Her racing heartbeat slowed, and she finally found the courage to look up. This time she was more awake, and her mind belonged to herself again. When she scrabbled in her bag for her water flask the scratches started to bleed, and the feeling of the warm moisture on her skin made her feel calmer. She drank thirstily, and then ate two of the cereal bars the men had stashed in the supplies. There was no point rationing her food, Tiria decided. There was no way that a nightmare that bad would stay away for long enough to let her starve.

Swallowing back bile, she moved over to the grate and slammed the butt of her gun against it. The noise was the same as the dull clanging Seth had produced the night before, and she felt her heart harden. The soft noise of the man stepping closer to the wall made her want to scream. The sun had risen. The whole stupid game had to begin again, and he had been right. Until one of them died, they couldn't stop.

"I didn't force you to choose me." She spat. "By all rights you should hunt yourself, not just me. If we had made children, you would have to kill them too."

"What do you want me to say?" His voice took on a mocking note. "'I let the way I felt change what had to happen'?"

"I know that's a lie. If you felt anything at all, then none of this would have happened."

"Sure." His sardonic tone was back, a feeble echo of the brash tones he used to use. "I'll betray everything my family stood for because a rat has pretty eyes."

"Your family didn't stand for anything." She hissed. "Slaughtering children like animals because their parents fell in love... oh, how noble."

"I told everyone you were dead." He interrupted her with sudden anger, slamming his hand onto the grate so hard it boomed. "I lied for you."

"The council knows you're a liar?" She smiled. Seth's anger had made her feel inexplicably happy, as if he had given her a gift. She leaned her head back against the concrete and twisted around a little. "They wouldn't bother to send two hunters after me. They sent Justin after *you*."

Seth fell silent.

Tiria stood up, hauled her pack onto her shoulders and made her way to the heavy iron door. She scooped up the bracelet on the way past, hiding it in her jeans pocket. It took a lot of courage to slide the thick locks back against the wall, and she moved as quietly as possible. At the very last moment, a clot of rust squeaked against the frame. She shivered and rested her forehead against the metal, clinging to her last fragment of protection. He was probably standing right outside. She swung the door open slowly, bracing herself to slam it back closed, and peeked out into the corridor. It was empty; there were no shadows which could hide him, and apart from a row of footprints leading to the next cell the concrete dust was undisturbed.

The next cell was designed for prisoners, a small room edged with thick iron bars. She could see the shadow of a man spilling across the floor, but he was sitting quite still beside the concrete divider. Her heart raced: Seth's cell locked from the outside. If she could bolt it closed then he would be trapped. She bit her lip and looked at the lock, feeling her heart race. It was on the other side of the open bars. He would have a chance to shoot at her as she ran across, or grab her through the bars as she struggled with the rusted lock. Was it worth the risk?

"You've got thirty minutes, Ti." Seth said softly. She flinched and knew he had heard her involuntary step backwards, because he laughed and the shadow shook its head. "If you don't believe I'll wait then you should be running faster, not creeping through the shadows."

"I'm not afraid of you."

"Twenty-five."

She turned, took one last longing look at the lock, and then slipped away.

CHAPTER 5

The officials had finally made their way into the city. Tiria heard them as she sprinted through the streets. There was no point climbing over the roofs. Seth knew she was running. She just had to get as much distance between them as possible, and she knew for a fact that she could move faster than he could. Someone who spent their entire life buried alive didn't know how to run on the crumbling streets. The ruins were full of pot holes and hidden bricks and concrete posts. There were soft stretches of dust which dragged her down, and hard glassy swathes which made shockwaves ripple into her knees as she slammed her feet onto it. Tiria sprinted until black spots danced in front of her eyes, and then she started walking. She longed to sit down and get her breath back, but her legs would have seized up. She kept them loose by moving, and when she could breathe she started running again.

She found Justin's body by noon. It was stiff, and her hands slipped against the ice on his skin. She struggled to unzip his jacket and haul it off him, but as soon as the warm fabric was wrapped around her body her shivering stopped. She pulled the corpse's shirt off as well, planning to slip on the extra layer when she was safely hidden. As an afterthought she tugged his shoes off, stole the laces, and then pulled his socks onto her hands. The clothes were filthy and blood-stained, but for the first time in hours she felt warm.

She dug her hands into the corpse's belt and grunted as she hauled him over. There was a wet sucking sound as his face sunk into the mud, and a viscous bubble burst onto the surface. For a horrible moment Tiria thought he was still alive, but his naked skin was icy to the touch. Shards of ice clung to his jeans and slid into his flesh, drawing out a thin watery fluid. The girl winced and tugged at the waistband. The thick fabric was too muddy to tear, so she crammed her hand under it and searched for the hidden holster in the small of his back. Her fingers found leather, and then thin straps, and her heart sank. It was empty. In the few hours since the man had died, someone had stolen his gun.

She drew out the holster and stared at it. A sliver of paper was poked into the lining, and she pulled it out. Seth's neat writing mocked her.

Too late.

Tiria screwed up the note and bit back a wild urge to laugh. Seth was already armed, and so was she. An extra gun wouldn't make any difference, and the man was arrogant enough to ignore it. So why take it?

Once she had found out about the tracker it was easy to imagine him strolling through the ruins and shadowing her every step. She had been careful, but when she was focused on Justin he could have closed in on her. He had promised to leave her alone until the second day, but he had learned her movements and watched her kill, learning how to use her strengths against her. Stealing the gun was his way of challenging her.

He had promised her half an hour of safety on the first morning. Was he using the same trick now? Tiria looked around, and the hair rose on the back of her neck. Tiria scratched at it irritably and cursed when her nails caught against the scar. The disk was ice cold. Her fingertips seemed too clumsy, and she drew them away. Whenever she thought about the implant she remembered what it was doing to her. What if she was already going mad? She had laughed when this poor man had died, hadn't she?

Tiria dragged her mind away and let go of Justin's belt. His body slid further down into the mud. She had more important things to do than wallow in self-pity. Rooting in her bag, she pulled out the tracker bracelet and snapped it around Justin's wrist. The skin was mottled and bloated, and the polished metal shone from it like a star. Before her thoughts wandered again, the girl flipped Seth's note over and scrawled a new message. She shoved it between the corpse's fingers.

Watch them dance.

She ran towards the prison. The sun reached its peak, and the coldness turned into a sweating humidity that made it hard to draw breath. It was the perfect time of day to move quickly without worrying about finding cover. Nobody else was used to the heat; even Seth preferred to shelter at noon. The icy wind sometimes tricked peopled into venturing outside, but even in winter the hot sun was still vicious enough to make blisters burst from their skin. Tiria dragged her sleeves over her hands and covered her head with Justin's shirt, preferring to sweat inside the layers than to let the bright white light spill onto her skin.

She kept to the shadows when she could, and when the vast city wall loomed in front of her she grit her teeth and climbed back onto the rooftops. The wind whipped up the stinging dust and the radiation from the metal ladders was almost unbearable, but she hunkered down beside a chimney stack and forced herself to be still.

The officials crept into the city in small groups, their hands and faces covered in the stocking material which made their outlines grotesque. The dull brown shade of their clothes helped them to blend into the dust, but the wind whipped the fabric up around their legs until they were painfully obvious. Each group chose a different direction, and they all walked at the same measured pace. Tiria watched them with sharp interest. Their tracker wasn't as strong as she had feared; the officials knew where she was, but they had to search for her specific location. As long as she hid, they wouldn't be able to find her. There were far more interesting discoveries waiting for them in the ruins.

The savages were coming into the city through the sewers. She hadn't seen any signs of them, which was a relief. She knew they were there, and had been searching for them. Seth would be oblivious. When Darren had told her about the underground network she had been thrilled, until he had pointed out that the water was so irradiated it would make her hair fall out in chunks. Never mind the mutation, he sneered, radiation exposure would make her die long before the pills ran out.

The savages were used to crawling through narrow tunnels, crushing their soft bodies through impossible angles to reach safe, cool havens. It was how they survived, burrowing into the ground like tapeworms into a gut. Tiria had been tempted to risk the radiation anyway, but when Darren had shown her the entrance to the sewers she had almost been sick. It was a slit, not a cave, barely five inches tall and getting narrower. If the tightness wasn't bad enough, there were hanks of hair and flesh clinging to the sharp concrete edges where hordes of savages had caught their nerveless limbs on the edges.

"Changed your mind?" Darren asked her snidely. Tiria shook her head.

"How can you go down there?"

"There are fat, juicy rats." He said in a dreamy voice. "Have you ever been hungry enough to eat a rat?"

"Yes," She admitted, "But..."

"What was his name?" The savage grinned, and even though the expression was horrific Tiria knew him well enough by then to recognize that he was mocking her. She huffed out an exasperated laugh and swatted at his shoulder.

The savages' sense of humour was so dark that it came close to macabre, but once she had a chance to get used to it Tiria warmed to it. The savages who were dosing themselves on the pills enjoyed using their minds while they were still quick and unclouded, and the intelligence some of them showed was frightening. They had laid plans that made the girl's head spin, and they had the entire sewer system mapped out in their heads.

Tiria had thought that they would simply charge at the soldiers and tear them to shreds, but their plan was far darker and more vengeful than a simple slaughter. There was a terrifying brutality to the savages, which had sharpened their minds to a fine point. If their bodies hadn't been betraying them, then the savages would have been formidable. When she thought about what would happen to them once the pills ran out, Tiria hated the officials even more.

One of the savages was a sweet old woman who had turned after she was a grandmother. She spoke about her children with obvious love, and in the same breath listed all of the painful things she was going to do to their partners, who had cast her out into the wastes when her mind started to crumble. It was dementia, the other savages thought, but the radiation had soon overtaken it. The vault dwellers had no resistance to it at all.

Tiria asked Darren what the old woman was doing to help their plan. He looked embarrassed and confessed that he was giving her the pills because he felt sorry for her. He knew that she was going to be left behind, but he wanted her to remember her family one last time before the winter fell. She was too feeble to last another season.

The girl listened in silence, and then shook another handful of pills out of the bottle. She carried them to the woman herself, and listened to her stories until the sun started to set.

She only spent one day with the savages. Alongside making plans and telling her their stories the men and women had come to her with other advice. They knew that she was contaminated, and they knew what was going to happen to her next. Some of them tried to comfort her, but most of them shrugged off the pain and insanity as a normal part of life. Those ones offered her the only practical advice she could use: the voices would grow louder. There was no point in ignoring them, but while she was still sane enough to know what she was doing the anger could be useful. The savages looked at her hands and her weapons, and they listened to her plan for revenge. Yes, they told her. Let the voices tell you what to do.

Tiria looked around the city on the second morning and bit back her frustration. The voices were in the back of her mind all the time, getting louder with each waking nightmare, but she could not use them. She had to wait for people to come to her. The savages would be in position under the city, but they were useless until the officials arrived. Seth would catch up soon, and all she could do was wait and wonder how many precious seconds of sanity were slipping through her fingers.

Something scrabbled by her foot, and she flinched and looked down. It looked like a huge spider – but then it rapped against her boot again, and she recognized it as a filthy hand. Kneeling down, she peeked through a storm drain and saw one of the savages grinning up at her. His teeth were almost red in the dawn light.

"We've found iss." His voice was mushy, and a line of spittle poured continuously from one side of his mouth. It took him a little time to form the words, and he gaped a little in between sentences. "Darren says... are you sure?"

"Yes." She said softly, and raised her hand to stroke the lizard in her jacket. His sleeping weight was comforting, but not nearly enough for the awful thing she was about to do. "Please... please make sure they make it out alive. I don't want them to die down there."

"Not our faulss if they do." The creature shrugged and then winked at her. His mouth flapped open like a trap door as he turned away.

Tiria took a deep breath, shuddered at the lingering reek of the sewer, and then started heading back along one of the main roads. She was so brazen that she made it past three groups of officials before anyone saw her. A shot rang out, and she raised her hands above her head.

"Don't shoot!" She cried, and lowered them so slowly that the soldiers could see her trembling. "Patrick sent me! They need help! I'll take you to them. Robert is hurt!"

The officials sped closer. They still had masks over their faces, and in the cold wind their exposed skin was mottled and stark. One of the leaders edged closer to her and pointed a plastic tool in her direction. It beeped, and he switched it off.

"Tiria One." His voice was high-pitched and a little too rapid. "Where are your guards?"

"There's a hunter from the vault. He shot at them." The girl invented, making her eyes wide and her voice frantic. "Please, I don't want him to kill me too!"

As she had hoped, the circle of guards turned about and aimed their gun sights around at every possible sniping spot. If Seth was watching, he was doubtless diving into an uncomfortable hiding spot. The girl turned back to the leader. "Patrick got shot.

Robert set me free to fetch... anyone, really. He said you'd be able to follow my tracking device."

"I thought you said Patrick sent you?" The man challenged. Tiria blanched and shook her head.

"No – no – oh, I'm confused! It all happened so quickly! You have to come right now. He might be coming back!"

One of the rifles suddenly went off, and the crackling boom of the shot made the girl cry out and duck down to the ground. The sound seemed to echo for a long time, and then she heard the soldier cursing under his breath. "Winged the bastard."

"Keep your eyes peeled." The leader said shortly, and hauled Tiria to her feet. "This one wouldn't have turned herself in if she wasn't scared. Lousy cowards, these rats. Take us to the vault, girl."

"The vault?" She rubbed her eyes. The dirt on her hands made them itch, but maybe the red marks looked like frightened tears. "But... Patrick..."

"I haven't got the manpower to haul that freak back to the truck." The leader said impatiently. "We're not here for him. We're here to find the vault. Take us there, or we'll leave you out in the ruins and let that hunter skin you alive."

She mimed a shudder and looked up at the roofs. Darren had said that the officials would be predictable, but this was ridiculous. The only thing which the savages hadn't foreseen was how Seth would react. He wouldn't be stupid enough to risk being shot at again, but he would do anything to protect the vault. He was close enough to see her nodding. Tiria made the gesture as small as she could, and then cringed away from a sniper shot that never came. The leader took her wrist, and gestured for her to start walking as the guards kept a wary perimeter.

By the time they got to the edge of the city, smoke was trickling out of vents hidden all along the roads. The pungent smell of fertilizer chemicals made the air rancid, and the sound of people screaming was unbearable. As if on cue, the hatch in the ground sprang open, and hordes of people started pouring out into the sunlight. They clutched at each other and clawed at their eyes as the bright sunlight stung their delicate bodies, and then collapsed to the ground and coughed up lungfuls of smoke.

Tiria breathed in slowly. She had been afraid that the soldiers wouldn't let them leave. The fire had started in the vents, and the savages had carefully controlled it so that even the people in the deepest tunnels would have time to escape. Even so, there was only one way out. All it would have taken was one stubborn guard to bottleneck the whole thing, and then hundreds of people would have been crushed together in the tunnels. She drew back, easily pulling herself from the official's dazed clutches, and slipped back into the ruins.

Her wrists started to burn from the cold, and she drew herself into an alley way to wrap some of Justin's ragged fabric around them. As she was knotting it around the scratches she froze, and unpicked the last loop. One of the scratches had deepened, but instead of the usual red swelling that infection brought to the flesh, the skin around it had puckered a sickly white. The scratch gaped open, and when she tentatively pulled the scar outwards she saw that the broken flesh was black and rancid.

She tore her eyes away and choked as vomit surged up from her stomach. She retched and spat until her stomach was an aching hole, and then rubbed some of the gritty snow onto her forehead. It was too soon. She knew that the voices were growing stronger, and that her anger was far too heated to be sane. She had known that for days – but some part of her still hoped that she had time.

There was no medicine left for her to take, since she had given it all to the savages. They had looked at her dolefully as she left, and she had thought that they were jealous of her. Now she saw their true pity. They knew this would happen. The bile rose into her throat again, and even though she had nothing left to throw up her body shuddered and heaved. She blindly knotted the fabric around the ulcer and forced herself to stand.

If her body was already rotting, then it meant she had no time to feel sorry for herself. She had already wasted time being sick – and for what? To waste her food supplies? Tiria scoffed at her stupidity and started moving – not away, but back towards the vault. The screaming was getting louder.

CHAPTER 6

Walker fought to catch his breath. He had spent as long as he dared in the science lab, pushing animal tanks into panicking citizens' hands as they fled to the surface. The smoke held a sharp, chemical acidity which made every breath burn his throat, and by the time he freed the last few animals he couldn't even speak. The cats and dogs streamed ahead of him, running between the panicking humans' legs. He had been worried that they would run back into the depths of the burning vault, but their keen noses led them straight towards the fresh air.

The vault door stood wide open, and people were shoving at each other in their haste to get out of the hatch. They carried huge bundles of belongings, blocking each other's paths as they clung to their useless possessions. They had enough time to see the smoke and plan their escape, but most of the citizens had waited until the last minute before they abandoned their homes. Now they clawed at each other. Their selfishness was chilling.

Walker remembered the way that Tiria had spoken about the wastes. She had told him that the vault dwellers were just the same as her clan, but the scientist had laughed it off. He could not put the educated, cultured citizens side by side with the rats. Tiria was clever – but Walker instinctively believed that she was an anomaly. The rats could not be refined, and the citizens would not degrade themselves. Now, seeing them screeching and pulling each other back into the fray, Walker saw his people as just another clan.

The vault groaned behind them, and the floor began to shake. The crowd fell completely silent, and then the push began again. The pause had made them focus, and now they didn't care to fight each other for their treasures. They simply turned, and pushed their way out of the hatch. The ground tilted, becoming more and more uneven as the lower levels buckled. The fire alone would not have been enough to do it, but the blaze had started in the farming level. The noxious fertilizers belched poisonous gas into the pipes, filling them up until they were under so much pressure that a single flame...

The floor shook again, and Walker fell to the ground with a cry. It took him a second to pick himself up. Glass shards stuck into his hands, and he looked down to see the snake he had been carrying slithering out of the remains of its tank. Normally he would have been shouting a warning, telling people not to be bitten. Now, he stared at it until it vanished, and knew that it wouldn't make a difference.

He coughed and fell back to his knees, and someone hauled him to his feet and shoved him forwards. He had no idea who the stranger was. The crowd carried him without his feet touching the floor, until it exploded out into the sunlight and spilled away. Walker crawled forward from the hatch and dug his hands blindly into the dirt, coughing and spitting in the icy air. There was a white powder on the ground. He spat black, sticky phlegm into it and pressed his icy hands to his pounding temples.

The dogs found him. They had been kept in cages in the labs, and he had always thought that they hated him. Now they wrapped their warm bodies around him, and their tails waved a little in the cold air. The sunlight made their fur look beautiful. He ran his hand through it in wonder. The retriever turned and licked his nose.

"You like to be stroked?" Walker croaked, and dug his hands a little deeper into the fur. The dog yawned and lay its head down on the man's lap. The peculiar cluster of animals grew over the next hour, as cats and even rabbits started finding their way back to the familiar pack. Walker didn't see the snake again, for which he was grateful, but several of the citizens handed him back the tanks he had shoved into their arms. He looked around with a wry laugh bubbling up in his throat. What could he possibly do with the animals, now? If he released them they would turn on each other before they even made it to a safe burrow. The thought sobered him, and he ruffled his fingers through the dog's fur. He might as well say the same thing about the humans.

A commotion made him look up, and he saw that most of the guards were clustering around a stone wall. Walker's eyes followed the wall up, and when he couldn't see a ceiling above it his head spun. He squeezed his eyes shut giddily. How could there be nothing above them? The guards didn't seemed bothered by vertigo, but most of the citizens were groaning and pressing their faces into the snow.

The noise was coming from behind the wall. The guards had caught something, and it was struggling as they dragged it back towards the vault. Smoke was pouring out of the hatch now, and when they dragged the captive closer he caught a lungful of it and started coughing. One of the guards struck him, and he bit back the hacking sound and faced the man down. The citizens' weeping grew quieter – they all recognized Seth. This was his world, and when they were in it they were his prey. People pushed themselves back from the circle of guards, and watched with wide eyes.

"I know you did this!" Someone roared, and one of the guards struck Seth hard in the gut. The hunter doubled over, gasping, but when he caught his breath his voice was cold.

"Why would I do this? I'm still looking for the girl, you idiot! If she..."

"The girl!" The other man raised his hands to the heavens and then looked down. His eyes were a little giddy despite himself. Walker recognized him as Hart, the head of security. The man gestured for the guards to take Seth's arms, but although he lowered his head his voice was strident. "Your father was soft for the savages, too! I should have known you'd go the same way. Did you tell her to burn the vault?"

"Of course not!" Seth growled at him, but the man wasn't listening. His voice grew clearer, and he met the guards' eyes as he spoke.

"We should have killed this traitor from the start. He wasn't taking a lover, he was twisting that girl around his fingers and waiting for her to snap. You didn't have the courage to do it yourself, did you Seth? You couldn't light the match... oh, but the girl could! She was born for it, the savage little bitch. I expect we're all supposed to blame her for this, but who gave her the idea? Who showed her where the vents were? It wasn't me, Seth! It wasn't anyone here!" He finally lowered his voice again, his face beet-red, and only Seth could hear the last few words. "You just couldn't let me win, could you? Was it worth razing our home to the ground?"

The man replied, just as quietly. "It's a shame you didn't burn. I would have forgiven her for everything if she had managed that."

Hart's eyes narrowed. He swung his arm back, and as he brought it around Walker saw the glint of metal between the man's fingers. The knuckle duster made a dull cracking sound as it connected with Seth's ribs. The man grunted in pain, but struggled back to his feet. The guards still held his arms, but they flinched away from him when he lunged to either side. If it wasn't for Hart standing in front of him, the hunter might have managed to break free in a few moments. But Hart was cunning. His body was weighed down with weapons, and his words had made more people cluster around them. Seth might fight off his two guards, but another ten were waiting.

Walker's fingers constricted into the dog's fur, and it gave him a reproving little whine. He looked away to sooth the creature, and when he looked up again Hart's hand was shining in the winter sunlight. The snowflakes slid smoothly off the knife, polishing the steel to a lethal sheen. Hart smiled as he beckoned to Seth.

"Shake my hand, little nephew." His voice was magnanimous. "It's a clean death. You don't deserve it, but I'll be generous. I'll even kill the bitch for you after you're dead."

Seth eyed the knife, and then raised his eyes. The brows were drawn down so fiercely that the rictus looked more animal than human. The guards held him so tightly his skin was white around their gloved hands, and when he made an unconscious move towards his uncle the men behind him drew their knives. The sound of singing steel echoed around the silent crowd, and Seth looked down at his hands as they clenched and relaxed. There was nothing else he could do. Slowly, he nodded.

The guard on his right freed his hand. Seth moved as quickly as a snake. Hart had been expecting it; he grinned and stepped sideways, tripping up his nephew and sending the other guard flying across the ice. Seth regained his balance easily and stood up straight. He knew there were other men behind him; he didn't seem to care. His eyes were fixed on Hart, and on the knife.

Hart swiped at him, and Walker was just wondering how the guard could make such a clumsy feint when the man lashed out with his foot. Seth countered it. He moved so easily that it seemed like he was slow, but his eyes were quick and alert. He had no weapon, but he never took his gaze away from the exposed knife. He and Hart circled each other for a moment, and then they crashed together. Both of them grunted and swore and finally shoved each other away, unable to find a flaw in each other's defences. Then Hart's eyes flickered sideways. Seth missed it: he was too intent on the fight, and on its oddly unspoken rules. The men standing behind him moved forwards, and twisted his arms up into locks before he even realized they were there. Seth swore loudly and struggled, but it was obvious to everyone that this time he wouldn't escape.

Hart stepped forward, and smiled. He picked up the knife from where it had fallen to the ground, and raised its point to touch the end of Seth's nose. His grin widened, and he murmured something that only Seth could hear. The hunter's face darkened with anger, and the guard started laughing.

A shot ran through the clearing. The citizens screamed and threw themselves away as Hart fell backwards, blood blossoming from a hole above his eye. The eye rolled up, staring up at the wound as the other orb dilated and closed. The guards recoiled in horror. Seth pulled away from his captors with and whirled around, looking wildly into the ruins. One of the guards grabbed at him. Without thinking, Seth snatched up the other man's knife and slit his throat. The second guard cried out and moved forwards, grappling with the hunter until he fell back. Seth used the momentum to throw the man away, and then he threw himself beside Hart and tore the man's weapons from his belt. The guard dragged himself to his feet and threw himself onto Seth, but this time the man was ready. There was a cry, and the guard went limp. When Seth shoved him away a knife caught the sun, blood-stained and wedged under the guard's arm.

The whole thing took less than a minute. Walker pushed himself back against the dogs, his heart racing. He had never seen anyone move so fast. Seth had been distracted the whole time, fighting as an afterthought while his black eyes searched the ruins. The doctor wondered how lethal the man could be when he was truly fixed on his opponent. Seth had clearly wanted Hart to live; if he hadn't, then the man would have died as soon as he stepped in front of his nephew. It was only when he had offered to shake Seth's hand that the man had become truly deadly.

Seth pulled the knife free from the body with a grimace and then stood up, waiting for the rest of Hart's people to attack him. These men were more wary. They had learned more than just hateful lies from Hart – they had learned how to fight. One of them wove back and forth in front of Seth, sizing him up for weaknesses. The man smiled thinly and waited, letting the guard take his time. Walker saw another guard creeping around the outside of the group, making his way into Seth's blind spot and then approaching with his gun raised, aiming at the back of the hunter's skull.

Something barrelled into the gunman with a cry, and the man's gun flew away as the air was pounded out of his lungs. The thing that had hit him rolled, and then leapt to its feet. Tiria dragged herself back beside the man and pressed his own gun to his head. She looked into his eyes as she pulled the trigger, and then she kicked his twitching body away. Her eyes were just as indifferent as Seth's as she caught another guard, hooking her leg around his thigh as he grabbed her and throwing herself backwards into the dirt. It didn't matter to her why these men were fighting, only that they stop. It was blindingly obvious that she didn't care whether that meant maiming them or killing them.

It was a clumsy style of fighting which seemed to hurt the girl as much as her targets, but she was far faster than any of them. The men could not aim a gun or a blade at her, but she could tackle them and take them down. The guards weren't prepared for another enemy, and so Tiria clawed her way through the circling pack like a she-wolf. Many of the guards saw what was happening to their friends and fled, preferring the dangers of the ruins to the brutality of its people. Soon, the only one of Hart's men who wasn't groaning or dead was struggling to free himself from Seth. The man pressed his elbow into the man's throat, crushed him against the wall, and then let his limp body drop to the ground. Breathing heavily, he turned around and his eyes met Tiria's.

She watched him like an animal, her hands hanging beside her, panting as she lowered her head. They glared at each other for a moment, and their eyes were so impassioned that Walker shivered. Tiria abruptly smiled and cocked her pistol. The snap was loud and bright in the icy silence. She raised the weapon to aim it at Seth's chest, and then pulled the trigger. The empty chamber clicked, and the girl laughed. Then she turned on her heel and ran into the ruins. Seth cursed, picked up his knife, and sprinted after her. She was far faster. The watching citizens could see her drawing further away, but they had also seen the hatred in Seth's eyes. She wouldn't escape.

The girl had burned the vault. They knew that, now. They watched their hunter following her, and some of them rooted in their own supplies for kitchen knives, or picked up stones. The rat had destroyed their home. She was going to die.

Walker stopped himself from following the baying crowd. He coughed up another lungful of smoke. He couldn't help replaying the strange scene in his mind. Tiria would have killed Seth if her gun had been loaded. She had aimed well, and he hadn't dodged away when she pulled the trigger. Why not? Seth had stood still and watched while a girl aimed a gun at his chest. Walker would have been running for the hills! Had he known that the gun was empty?

Something was going on. It couldn't be as simple as a savage girl madly destroying the vault. He couldn't think that of Tiria, and now he knew that Seth didn't see it that way, either. Why had he let Hart capture him?

Walker looked down at the animals, and then he groaned and raised himself to his feet. Every breath felt as if he was inhaling icy metal shards, but he forced himself to move. He didn't take a weapon, but the dogs streamed past his feet. They had been fed and teased by Tiria for months before she left the vault. They knew her. They had found fresh air in the chaos of the fire. They could find a living girl hiding in dead stone.

CHAPTER 7

Seth closed in on her before she had made it half a mile. He had learned the city far quicker than she had, and somehow he always seemed to get closer when she needed to choose a direction to run in. Tiria wondered if he had deliberately funnelled her as she found herself in a vast shopping centre. The shops inside the centre must have been made of glass, but the bomb had shaken the building and they had all shattered. After a few years the wooden floors had collapsed, and so piles of glass and ancient brittle plastic ringed the impassable concrete crescent.

The only way out was through the same entrance that she had just sprinted through. She spun on her heel and started to run back, when a bullet whistled past her ear. She shrieked and threw herself onto the ground before the second one rang out. When the third one was replaced by a docile *click* she smothered her hysterical laughter against the icy tiles.

"Out of ammo?" She called out, biting back a hysterical laugh. Seth cursed and flung the useless gun to the ground. It sank into the ice, the hot barrel melting the soft powder around it until the weapon had left an ugly brown smear. Tiria wished she could stop laughing, but the words spilled out before she could stop them. "Maybe you're not a good hunter, just a good shot! What kind of idiot uses up all their bullets?"

"Oh, and you have some left?" He retorted. Tiria waved her gun at him mockingly, and then fired shots into the air until it was empty. The percussion made them both flinch a little as the roar echoed around the buildings. The man's face fixed – surprised, yes, but furious. "You fired an empty gun at me back at the vault."

She considered him levelly. "You let that man sneak up on you on purpose. By the time I worked out that you were trying to lure me out, I was already fighting."

"You still should have shot me."

"Well, you should have locked me into that cell." She shrugged. "Seems we're even again."

He looked nonplussed for a moment, and then his hand whipped down to his back and he pulled out a second gun. Tiria smiled when he aimed it at her heart, and when he fired she laughed over the useless clicking sound. "Justin missed me with all six of those bullets. He didn't save his ammo, either. Didn't you check?"

"I didn't think it would take more than six bullets to kill you." He hurled the gun straight at her. Tiria yelped and ducked, but the edge of the heavy pistol caught her across the shoulder. She felt the bruise rippling down through the joint, numbing her whole arm and making the scar on her ribs ache. She fought back the urge to clutch at the throbbing joint, and used her instinctive recoil to draw her knife and throw it back at him.

He moved; the blade whistled past his ear and clattered down into the dust. They both watched it breathlessly, and then Tiria flew towards it and threw herself down to retrieve it. The stones had dented and blunted the blade, but it was the only weapon she had, and as Seth closed in on her she raised it ready to defend herself. He stopped short, his boots scrabbling in the gravel, and his hands closed into fists as he watched her.

"Do something!" Tiria hissed, still holding the knife. He smiled wanly and shrugged. The girl glowered and dragged herself to her feet. Her shoulder was shivering now, and she switched the knife to her right hand. It was her weaker side, but at least she wouldn't drop it.

"We're going to run out of weapons at this rate." Seth said, eyeing the blunt edge. The girl narrowed her eyes.

"I'll throw stones before I let you win."

"I'm not trying to win. I'm trying to kill you."

"You don't get to do that." She returned flatly. She knew what she meant, but Seth obviously thought she was goading him. He laughed and drew his own knife, not rushing, just letting her know that they were evenly matched. He hefted the blade experimentally. Tiria saw his eyes narrow as he watched her for the slightest move. She only knew how to defend herself, not how to attack. All he had to do was work out how to get through her defences.

Well, he would have to work for it. Tiria grinned, turned on her heel, and sprinted back through the entrance and into the ruins. She didn't bother looking back. He wouldn't throw the knife, it was the only weapon he had left. She could hear a stream of torrid swearing and the pounding of running feet.

Seth must be getting tired of her running away, she thought dreamily. Still, she wouldn't be able to do it for much longer. She was getting tired now, and although none of her wounds had truly hurt her, the combined pain was slowing her down. If she wanted to escape, she'd have to find a way to slow Seth down. If she wanted to kill him, she'd have to work out what else to do. Running was the only thing where she was sure she had the advantage.

This time she chose her own path, not letting herself be intimidated by Seth's pounding footsteps. Her breath rasped in her throat, but she pushed herself onwards to one of the fire escapes which rattled when she climbed it. She hoped that it would be too weak for Seth to climb, but when she peeked back the man was supporting himself against the brick wall so the rusted metal didn't have to bear his weight. He seemed utterly fearless. The girl edged along a piece of scaffolding and then scaled down a chain on the other side. The links creaked as she climbed, and when she got to the bottom she swung herself hard around the side of the scaffold. The tower shuddered, and then twisted in the same direction. By the time Seth reached the top, the scaffolding was lying in a sighing heap at the base of the wall.

"Why don't you stay up there?" Tiria yelled, panting. "This is stupid!"

He didn't answer. She saw him turn his head like a bird, scanning the rooftop for clues, and then he disappeared from view. The girl held her breath. Every instinct she had screamed at her to run away. She forced herself to stay calm, because she had to *know.* There was only a slender chance that her plan wouldn't work, but she hoped that Seth was too set on catching her to think straight. He knew her too well to be careful; he expected her to keep running until her legs gave out.

There was a harsh rasping sound as sheets of metal ground against tile, and then there was a cry. Tiria waited for footsteps, but there were none. She breathed out in a rush, and then ran back to the base of the building. The interior staircase had an emergency exit at the base. It was the quickest way to the ground, and like most of the tall buildings it was the only one that led directly from the roof. Tiria hadn't scaled this building because it was like the others.

She made her way through the rubble and walked slowly towards the door. She couldn't see Seth, but she could hear him. She had been afraid of looking through the doorway at his corpse, but from the amount of swearing he seemed quite well.

The pit had caught her too, when she had first found this place. She had been nervous of using the ancient scaffolding, and had made her way down through the building itself. When she saw the fire exit the bright sunlight burned her eyes, and she hadn't seen the pit looming at her feet. She caught at the edge as she fell, and dropped down into the cellar without hurting herself. Apparently Seth had managed to do the same, although he must have been bruised from all of the sheets of corrugated metal falling onto his head. Tiria had dragged them precariously over the gap to make it appear safe, but they were too fragile to support a grown man.

The other important difference was that Tiria had found a doorway that took her out of the cellar. She had only been trapped for about three minutes. Seth didn't have that luxury; she had barricaded the door with so many bricks that even Patrick could not have broken through. He was trapped.

She didn't look over the edge to see if Seth was hurt. She didn't even let him know that she was there. She turned, and crept away.

CHAPTER 8

Walker soon learned that the ground was uneven, and that he had to lift his feet up to avoid stones. The dogs raced along with their tails happy blurs, but for the first mile he struggled to stay upright. The cool, flat floors in the vault seemed like an unspeakable luxury.

The dogs seemed to have different opinions about how to find Tiria. The collies were so intent that they snapped at the basset hound whenever it tried to take charge, while the Labrador and the pug only seemed interested in bowling each other into the muddiest patches of melt water. Walker wondered how dangerous the water was. The snow was falling steadily, and when he felt it melting into his jacket he shivered at the idea of irradiated water seeping into his skin.

It was dark by the time they closed in on Tiria. The girl didn't even try to disguise herself; she didn't seem to notice that anyone was nearby. The dogs hung back from her as if there was something deeply disquieting about her scent. She climbed into a concrete building, and the canine pack followed her. Walker held them back, and stepped into the building alone.

There was a savage cry, and the man found himself lying on his back with a sharp, grimy blade pressed against his throat. For a second he honestly thought that Tiria would kill him, and then the manic light in her eyes faded and she laughed. It was a soft hiss of sound that made his skin crawl, but at least she lowered her knife to do it.

"Walker." She whispered, and tucked the knife into her belt. "Are you taking the dogs for a walk?"

"I was looking for you." He said awkwardly. The girl gave him an odd, unreadable look, and then her legs shook under her and she sighed. She sank down to the ground, and when she pillowed her head on her knees Walker couldn't help reaching out to her. She looked so small, and so fragile. When he touched her hands she snarled and dragged herself away, then looked up with querulous guilt lining her face. Her eyes didn't seem to be able to focus.

"Ti," Walker murmured, "You're not well."

"It doesn't matter." She smiled. Her lips were cracked with sunburn and cold, but they were strangely crimson. For a surreal moment Walker thought she was wearing lipstick. He pushed her lip down with his thumb and looked at her teeth. The gums were bleeding. Her whole mouth was stained with blood.

"Don't." She pulled herself a little further away and then sighed. "Don't fuss. I'm too tired for you to mother me."

"It's too late for anyone to mother you." He said bluntly, sitting back on his heels. Tiria's eyes flew open. She was about to snap a retort when something made her bite her lip. She reached her hand inside her jacket, and drew out George. The tiny lizard was sleepy and slow with the cold, but he licked her thumb as she stroked him.

"He's too lazy to look after himself. You'll have to do it." Tiria said, her voice tart as she poked the lizard's stumpy nose with one finger. Walker held out his hands. The girl hesitated before she gave him the lizard, and her breath hitched, but when she finally let go of her pet she breathed out. "I don't have many worries left. It's good to let go of another one."

"You only have to worry about hiding from Seth." The man pointed out. The girl smiled crookedly and shrugged one shoulder.

"If he's clever, he'll leave me alone. I'm dying fast enough without his sweet help. He can leave me be, and not risk getting hurt in the fighting, and he won't have to look me in the eye when I go." She raised her eyebrows, and a wound on her face started to bleed. "Will you tell him that?"

"I'm not going anywhere near him!" Walker was horrified by her easy question. "Did you think he sent me?"

She nodded, her eyes widening with realization, and then she laughed. "How stupid of me! Of course he didn't. It never would have occurred to him! He never saw you as anything except a name. He never knew I was a real person except when I was with him. I ate his food and slept in his arms, and then he went to work and I didn't exist until supper time. We're both about as real to him as one of the stories in his books."

"But he loved you." Walker asked. Tiria nodded, smiled a little, and then wiped her hand across her mouth. She frowned at the smear of blood and then shrugged to herself.

"He still loves me. He wouldn't send you to me. He needs to do it himself."

"Then why did you think I was..."

"Because there's no other reason why you'd be here." She replied flatly. "I'm tired, and I don't understand. If Seth didn't send you then maybe the council did, or the officials thought you would be a good lure. Maybe you'll be shot down dead the second I send you away. Maybe they said they'd spare you. They won't. You'd do better to crawl through the sewers than trust a single person out here."

"Nobody sent me. The dogs led me to you. That's it."

She scoffed and rooted in her bag for something. She offered a foil-wrapped rectangle to Walker, who sniffed at the chalky bar inside suspiciously. The girl snorted a laugh and pressed it back into his hands. "They taste better than most of the food you'll find. Get used to it, and don't let anyone see how much you have!"

He peered into the bag she pushed over to him. There were about ten of the food bars in it, and two packets of dried fruit. In the vault they would have lasted him for two days. The dogs looked hopefully at the protein bar, and he carefully wrapped it back up in the foil. "How is everyone supposed to survive out here, Ti?"

"I don't know." She leaned her head back against the wall, looking uncomfortable. "Some of them won't. The sooner they learn how to use their hands and feet, the better off they'll be. They've got more weapons than any other clan, and they can pick more supplies off the officials when they send another squad out here. Maybe they can trace the tire tracks back to the other vault and live there –

it's not so different to the old one. Or maybe they can dig back into this city and make it good again. They have to be ready to fight, though. The officials won't stop until they think every citizen is dead."

Tiria told the wide-eyed man what she knew about the vaults, and the tangled history which had bound her family and Seth's father together. It felt odd to talk about it, as if every word was a little less true once it had been spoken aloud. Her own part in it seemed trivial. A slew of traitors, brave men, spies and rebels had conspired to undermine the greatest power in the wastes, and all that remained was a blood-stained woman telling fairy tales in a city filled with ghosts.

"Why is Seth still trying to kill you?" Walker asked. "He doesn't need to. The fire meant we were ready for the officials, you know. I'm sure that if we weren't already outside they would have trapped us in the tunnels, and we'd all be dead."

Tiria said flatly. "How would I have known that? I didn't do it to help anyone. I told the savages how to get in through the vents. They started the fires. They wanted to drive you out into the wastes because they *hate* you. The officials only came here because of me. They stuck a tracking device into my neck. I knew they were following me, and I still came here."

"But..." Walker was obviously trying to find some way to make Tiria innocent, and he struggled. The girl patted his arm awkwardly and then sat back. The man shook his head after a while, and his voice took on an odd, intrigued note. "Did you say you have a tracking device?"

Tiria nodded, and turned so that he could see the raised bump on the back of her neck. The man's fingers touched it deftly, and then he drew away.

"Ti, if you took that out of the city, would the officials stop coming? I mean, for long enough to give us time to defend ourselves?"

"Maybe." She chewed her lip for a moment, and admitted, "I don't know if I'd make it that far."

He studied the knot of scar. "We had some chips that the dust eaters put into their animals, before the bombs fell. I studied them when I was a child. I think if this is the same thing, that I could disable it or even reverse it."

"Reverse!" She turned to stare at him. "You mean, follow it back to where it came from?"

He nodded seriously. "We could find the other vault. If we're quick enough, we can attack them before they know we're coming and take it over. You said it yourself; we have better weapons. We're not mutated at all, and we're strong and well-fed. If we're quick..." Then his face fell, and he pushed himself back a little. "But you're not strong enough."

"And the only people who hate me more than the officials are the citizens." She offered helpfully.

She felt sorry for Walker. He clung to her advice like a starving man clutching food. He was terrified of the wastes, and he had no idea how to survive outside of the vault. Tiria had tried to teach him in the vault, but it was like she had told Seth. Words didn't teach anyone; he would have to struggle and work things out for himself before he truly knew what he was doing.

Having a rat with him would have made it easier, even one that he couldn't trust. Tiria was lucky the other citizens hadn't realized the same thing. Babysitting hundreds of spoiled adults would have driven her insane long before the mutation took hold. She shrugged and pulled her shirt off. "Well then, is your knife sharp enough, or do you want to use mine?"

He blanched and held out his hands. "No, no! I can't..."

"Look, if you don't do it now, then in two days you'll have to fight Seth to dig it out of my grave. At least pretend I chose to do the right thing."

She pulled out the medical box from her bag, and showed him the sharp penknife and the sewing kit.

Walker nodded as he tested the edge of the blade, and then his eyes widened and he picked up one of the syringes. "Where did you get this?"

"The officials had it. What is it?"

"An antibiotic." Seeing that she didn't understand, the man waved his hand in excitement. "They stop wounds getting infected. It takes us weeks to make them in the labs. Or it... it did. This must be more precious than gold out here."

"Gold isn't precious to us." She smiled and took the vial gently from his hands. "You might be able to trade with it."

Walker shook his head and packed it back into the case. "Take them with you, Ti. If there's the slightest chance you can get stronger, it's in here."

She took the box, frowning a little, and managed to thank him. Walker smiled and then his face grew more serious.

He gestured for her to lie down on her stomach. When he cut into her neck she cried out in pain, and his hands shook so badly the knife clattered to the ground. His fingers were still trembling when he raised it again, and Tiria grit her teeth as the quivering point scored tiny grazes along the cut. She wondered if he would keep sliding the knife down, pushing it deeper until it killed her. It was bewildering that he didn't seem to hate her.

She felt her blood spilling out from the wound. It felt oddly thin. Walker pried the chip out, cursing as the filigree strands clung to her spine, and finally pressed her wadded up shirt down onto the bleeding incision. Tiria sat up, reeled giddily, and then fell back onto her stomach. The watery blood seemed to burn her, and she slowly started to feel the pain. It was so far away it was like feeling it happening to another person, but the slow throbbing grew into sharp stabs and she rocked her forehead into the ground.

"Ti." Walker's hand gripped her shoulder, and then she felt his fingers other expertly dressing the wound from Robert's medical kit. She shook her head, and rolled onto her side. The man was frowning at the blood-stained shirt. "I accidentally cut through something else. There was a... like a capsule..."

"I know what it was." Tiria said, taking the shirt back and clumsily pulling it on. "Don't worry."

"It was dosing you – putting something into your blood." He insisted. "When I cut through the membrane it was full of yellow fluid. It all ran out."

She giggled and looked down at the stain. He was right; the red blood was mixed with buttercup yellow. It was quite pretty, in a disgusting way. "I didn't know that was possible! I should have slit my throat weeks ago."

"What was it?"

"I don't know. I didn't ask. They put it in me to make me mutate. There are pills which slow it down, but I reckon it's done its job."

He looked horrified and wiped his hands off on his shirt. "Why would they do that?"

"Because I wouldn't tell them how to find the vault." She scratched at the dressing for a moment and then lowered her hand. Her voice grew plaintive, almost childishly lost. "I did try to be good. It just didn't work out that way."

Walker moved, and the next thing Tiria knew she was being crushed in his arms. An attack – she thought – and then he sobbed and she realized that he was crying. She had never seen a man cry before – not even Lawrence. Seth only ever grew angry. Walker's shoulders moved, and his sobs were abrasive. He choked air into his lungs and his hands sank into the back of her shirt until the tacky fabric twisted. Tiria sat numbly and waited for him to finish. He had lost his home, and his safety, and any love he had once had for her. She would probably cry too, if she had been betrayed. It never occurred to her that she was the one he was weeping for. If someone insisted on wailing over her, then it wouldn't be a near-stranger she had befriended in a sterile pit.

He wasn't crying for her, was he? Her throat closed up. The more she thought about it, the more it twisted her up inside.

"You're hurting me." She shoved him away. "You have your tracker, don't you? Leave me alone."

"Come with me." He replied just as quickly. "I'll look after you."

"No." She pushed him again, but couldn't summon enough strength to be fierce. "Let me finish things here the way I planned. If you interfere you won't live through the week. Either Seth will kill you, or I'll go savage and tear your throat out. Go and take that tracker to the committee. I'm sure they need it."

Walker shook his head, but he looked nervously out of the window. The sun was rising now, and he knew that the darkness was the only thing that would keep him safe. The dogs shifted sleepily, sensing his nervousness, and Tiria patted his arm.

"Don't fret. The savages left the city as soon as the fire took hold." She hesitated, and then said, "You won't survive in a pack. When you get a chance to slip away, head for the mountains. Keep following the road North, past the green roofs. A few weeks after them there's a big mansion, all painted white.

The people there will help you. Stay with them. You can learn from them." She reached for George and stroked the tiny creature's back. He turned his head and glared at her, and then burrowed himself deep into Walker's coat. The man stood up with an effort, and lowered his hand to help Tiria stand. She took it, and smiled.

Walker thought forcing himself not to look back would be hard, but it wasn't. Tiria had acted as if she were already dead. The way she had spoken was so peaceful and factual that Walker hadn't even thought to argue with her. The signs of radiation sickness were so pronounced that he would have to use strong drugs to even slow it down, and he had no idea where to find anything that potent in the wastes.

George nestled against his chest, and sank his claws into Walker's skin. The dogs sniffed at the ground, and they started to walk out of the ruins.

CHAPTER 9

Tiria slept. There was nothing else she could do. She had no food, no supplies, and no real desire to move from her shelter. She listened to Walker's footsteps fading away, and then closed her eyes and let the madness into her dreaming mind. Her wounds grew infected and sickly, and her body burned with fever. Tiria slept peacefully for the first time in weeks.

The nightmares didn't scare her any more. They had teeth, and claws, but their eyes were soft and she sank into their warm bellies and felt safe. They prowled through the ruins, stalking between empty windows as if the streets had been made for them. When the buildings blocked their way they lowered their heads and butted their way through. Bricks and burned glass showered down from their spines like dust, and their beards turned black in the cold. Then they shrank, and cuddled into Tiria's hands, and the girl was afraid. They kept growing smaller, and she couldn't protect them. They had vanished into her hands, and she must not let anyone touch her, because any part of her skin could be sheltering the tiny dragons from the horrors of the world.

She stumbled out of the shelter and walked blindly through the streets. She did not know if she was dreaming or awake, but the sun burned her flesh and her feet froze in the snow. Her body moved around her, but she felt detached from it. Arms and legs were far away, and her heart was beating far from the part of her that seethed and felt and loved and hated. She stumbled over a rockery and clung to a fence, crying out when the frozen metal sheared away and sent her falling to the ground. The world kept spinning long after she had stopped moving, and she lay still. The clouds of smoke still billowed from the city, and they swirled above her. She ran her hand drunkenly through the snow. White above and below, and she was caught between the two. Tiria turned her head to one side and watched the city. From the ground, it looked like it was falling into the sky.

How many days did she spend dreaming? The nightmares became so physical that she found herself scrabbling at the dirt, breaking her nails against walls as they grew faces and mocked her. Seth had laughed at her so many times that she no longer believed he was real. The demon with his face haunted her, and she forgot to guard herself from his attacks. She trudged through the city without thought, and her hands hung limply beside her knife. It would have taken her a hundred years to draw it.

The girl's mind drifted, and she felt the eyes of the ghosts following her through the streets. She was so vulnerable that the real Seth was no threat. He needed her to fight back, she remembered blearily. He had to love her to wrap his hands around her throat, or his body around her own, and she had to make him hate her or there was no meaning to any of it.

Her mind cleared a little, and she felt the snow start again. Ice trickled down her neck. She shivered, and raised her bovine head, and Seth was beside her. Was she imagining him, too? His face had been stained black by the smoke, and grey flecks of ash clung to his hair. A rag was knotted around one arm where the soldier had shot him, and the wound had swollen so badly that he couldn't bend his elbow. A bruise on his head was livid, and his face was waxen from weariness and blood loss. His hand was on his knife. He didn't say anything. Tiria longed for the nightmare to come back.

There was no fire left between them. Exhaustion infected them both. They returned to each other because it was all either of them had left. One of them had to die, or the whole thing would have been meaningless. To have that meaning – a final, blissful moment of clarity – would have erased all of the pathetic nonsense which they had thought was so important when they started. The people whose war they were fighting had died long before, and if their shadows weren't worth dying for then their children could not see past them. Seth could not forgive the rats' crimes any more than Tiria could absolve the citizen's callousness.

But they had a fragile peace. They walked together in silence. The one who lived would be too weak to survive the wastes, and anyone they might have turned to had already denounced them. All they had was each other, and for those few minutes they shared the last moment of loneliness the world would allow them.

Tiria stopped, and drew her knife. Meeting Seth's eyes, she dropped it into the dirt. Then she sat down and drew the last of her rations out of her pocket. He disarmed himself and sat beside her, adding his own food to the pile. It was a pathetic meal, but they ate it slowly and made it last. When they were finished Tiria took the medical pack out of her other pocket and opened it, letting the man see what was inside. He looked impressed despite himself.

"You're hurt." The girl said, and gestured to his arm. "You've made a pig's ear of binding that up."

His eyes narrowed, and she sighed. "Look, Seth, we can fight each other until the sun explodes but I'm not letting you die of a stupid wound-fever. Especially since I wasn't the one who shot you."

He looked at her levelly for a moment, and then a grin crossed his face unbidden and he snorted a laugh. "This is ridiculous."

"It is." She said, smiling, and then shook her head. "But if you're going to die, then I want to be the one who did it. I know you're thinking the same thing."

"You turned me into a traitor." He said with a spark of his old anger, and then he shrugged. "On the other hand, I love you. So when I kill you, I'll make sure it's clean."

"How generous of you. If you hadn't betrayed my brother and sent me to the officials we could almost be friends." She beckoned him closer, and started unpicking the knots of his bandage. She could have cut through them, but picking up the knife would have been the last thing she ever did. His skin was warm and dusty under her fingertips. She undid the last knot and gasped a little when the bandage fell away. "What the hell did you do to this?"

He craned his neck around to look and then shrugged. Tiria pulled his arm so that the light fell onto the wound. She had thought that the bullet had only grazed him, but he must have been turning as it hit. The long gouge ended in a deep pit which was clotted with blood. There were sharp lines around the wound which told her that he had already pried the bullet out with his knife. The whole mess was swollen, and the centre of the hole was a disquieting colour – the early warning sign of infection.

"You might die before me after all." The girl muttered, and ignored his stifled laugh. She poured alcohol into the wound and cleaned it, while Seth bit into the back of his hand and stubbornly kept watching her. His suspicion was almost admirable; it would have been far easier for him to look away from the sight of his own suppurating flesh, but he kept his eyes locked on the girl's hands throughout. Tiria bit through the end of the sewing thread rather than reaching for her knife, but when she took out one of the syringes he stopped her.

"How stupid do you think I am?" His jaw set, and he pulled his arm away. Tiria planted her hands on her hips, almost jabbing herself with the needle.

"Walker said it's an anti... anti... something that stops you getting an infection."

"Walker! When did he get a chance to tell you that?"

She fell silent, biting her tongue rather than risk an answer. She had no idea how much time had passed, but she didn't want to give Seth an excuse to catch up with the only true friend she had left. Instead, she took the second needle out of the case and held them both out.

"You choose one, and I'll take the other." She said. "I scavenged them off the officials. I don't know what they are, either. If they're good I don't want you to get an advantage over me."

"Maybe you've already taken the antidote."

"That's right, I found a whole poisoner's workshop out here." She scoffed. He regarded her for a moment, and then pointed at one of the syringes.

"You take that one. We'll wait for an hour, and if you're still breathing I'll take the other."

She rolled her eyes and let him jab the needle into her arm. The tiny amount of liquor slid into her body. She wondered what on earth it could fix. There were so many things wrong with her that it would struggle to choose! She yawned, and realized her pain was ebbing away. The antibiotic must have been laced with some kind of sleeping drug. "Wake me up when the hour's over." She mumbled. "I want to stab you with that other needle."

"I might smother you in your sleep." He said flatly. She smiled sleepily.

"If it's really healing stuff you need to keep me alive to know for sure. It might be the only thing that saves your life. I can't see you giving up that chance."

He didn't answer, but she knew she was right. Her head felt as heavy as lead, and she felt the sky spin as she fell back into the dust.

Her dreams were empty. There were no demons, and the nightmares stayed away. Perhaps the drug had scared them off, but either way she enjoyed the thick darkness and fought to keep her eyes shut for as long as possible. When she finally dragged herself back to the surface she thought she was still asleep; she was warm, and comfortable, for the first time in weeks. She opened her eyes blearily and saw that Seth had made a fire, and that he had covered her with his spare clothes and laid his coat under her as a mattress. When he saw her moving he left the fire alone, sat beside her, and handed her the second syringe. She took it, injected him with the medicine, and then wrapped her arms around him and felt sleep reaching for them both.

The sun was rising when they woke up. They didn't move for a long time.

"Will you be able to go home?" Tiria asked softly. Seth shook his head a little, and then sighed.

"If I said you were dead they'd call me a liar. I'd have to take them your body, and I won't do that. I don't have to prove myself to them."

"They might need your help."

He scoffed a little. "They were going to torture you, Ti. They told me to bring you back alive. They sent Justin with me because he was supposed to keep me in check. I think Hart set it up. He knew I would rather kill you myself than throw you into their spiteful hands."

"No," She corrected him gently, "Hart knew that Justin would die. That idiot was so weak that the wastes killed him before I even had a chance to aim. He was arrogant enough to agree to follow you, that's all. Once he died there was no way you could go back. If you killed me – so what? You're the one who let Justin die. You're still a traitor."

He mulled this over. "It doesn't matter. I don't want to go back to them."

"The outcasts won't help you, either." She said flatly. "The officials will kill you on sight, and the rats never help outsiders once the snows start to fall."

"There's the slavers, or the merchants."

"Or the bounty hunters?" The girl winced when he nodded, and then looked pointedly at his shoulder. "You couldn't strangle a kitten with that hand."

"And what about you?" He asked, "What are you going to do after you've killed me?"

"I haven't really thought about it." She admitted. "I suppose I'd want to keep walking. I'd like to know what happens after the desert ends."

"That's hardly practical." The man muttered. "What will you eat? Where will you shelter?"

Her voice turned arch. "I don't need to be practical. I'm just making up happy lies." Then a raw note crept in, and she looked away. "What will I really do, Seth? Is that what you're asking? Look at me. You can see that I'm sick, can't you? Even if I made it out of the ruins there's a hundred people waiting to kill me, and I'm not strong enough to run away any more. So, *practically,* I'm going to starve to death in one of those black-eyed towers and be forgotten like all the other dust-eaters."

Seth stroked her hair, and she shut her eyes and felt traitor tears warming her cheeks. "We can go together," He said.

Tiria shook her head. She couldn't open her eyes. The man drew away, and she knew that the sliver of a chance was over. Even if she had wanted to confide in him, the moment had passed. And she didn't want to – she still hated everything he stood for, even though her fractured mind wanted to cling to the torturous hours of loneliness he had kept at bay.

"The vault is still burning." Seth said. "Those tremors were the tunnels collapsing."

Tiria hadn't felt the earth shivering in her sleep. She remembered that the buildings had crumbled in her dreams. "I gave them the same chance they gave me." She had only whispered when she had spoken before; her speaking voice was coarse and ugly. Hearing it made her angry. She suddenly wanted to claw out the rasping creature that was clinging to her throat. "The soldiers didn't kill the ones who ran. All of the innocents... they have a chance."

"Not much of a chance." He returned. His voice was suddenly smooth, like liquid poison. Tiria was too tired to be cowed. It wasn't a game anymore. They weren't friends, or enemies. He was just a man, another scavenger hiding in the ruins of the dead. In her eyes he looked smaller, weaker. He was just as tired and sick as she was, but he was too stubborn to see that everything was already over.

"I made sure you weren't with them." She smiled a little and ran her fingers through her hair, crumbling up the fat ashes between her palms.

"Didn't you work it out? That's why I lured you out of the vault."

"You let mutations into the vault." He spoke as if he was repeating a mantra. The words must have spun around in his head for hours. He couldn't believe she had done something so terrible, even when she was the one admitting it.

"I didn't let the mutations in. You did." Tiria unwrapped her bandaged arm and showed him the suppurating wounds. He looked at them in horror, and then shook his head. He stared at the dust unseeing, and the girl could see the pain in his face as something inside him finally shattered.

In that moment she longed for him to draw his knife, to slide the point into her flesh and stop the madness from tearing into her soul. She longed for that, but she knew he was far beyond it. There was nothing left in him with the will to fight her. Killing her would just spill blood, not save lives. Besides, she was already dying. The only reason to hasten it was to be merciful, or to have the satisfaction of seeing the end. Seth had never killed anyone for his own reasons. He had no notion of mercy or revenge. Without the vault, he was hollow.

His silence made white-hot heat spill into her stomach, and she grit her teeth as the madness roared. "Mutations and rats and officials, and we're all as bad as each other, aren't we? Your father tried to help us, and they killed him for it. If your useless friends had helped him, it might have actually made a difference!"

Seth looked away. Tiria gripped his chin, forcing him to meet her blazing eyes. He flinched away from her – from her mutated flesh, she thought bitterly. Her voice lowered to a damning hiss. "You're finished. You've protected those bastards all your life from people who have to tear each other to shreds for a taste of what your citizens throw away. Your friends shouldn't be afraid of a withered hand or an extra toe, they should be afraid of hundreds of people finding out their children died from sicknesses your doctors can cure with one little jab. Or maybe they should think about how desperate starving people have to be, to eat irradiated food and drink filthy water. And they *knew*."

She drew a harsh breath as the truth came pouring out, one bitter word after another. "Your council knew they were leaving people to die and they didn't care. Your pathetic citizens believe every word they're told by those cowards. They'd never listen to a mutated little rat like me, or a spineless pawn like you. So I sent them the savages." She grinned, showing teeth. "I wanted them to join in the fun."

"Innocent people will die." He managed to rouse some of his old fire, but she shook her head mockingly and let him go.

"Whole families are slaughtered every day. Do you think they deserve it more because they live in the dust?" She turned away and spat, "It's their turn."

"Savage." He hissed it at her. The broken, lost note in his voice had finally turned to outrage, and she knew that she had finally convinced him to hate her. The girl looked around, and she picked up her knife. She held it out between them, ready to throw it if he moved, and then she abruptly sprang forward and buried it into his thigh. He cried out and his hands constricted. Before he could ride out the pain the girl seized his weapons and backed away. She watched Seth staunch the flowing blood with a shaking hand. Then he dragged himself closer to her and stopped, reeling dizzily as his leg buckled and another wave of pain washed through him. Tiria caught him, and gripped his shoulders for a moment until she knew he would not collapse.

"I'm not a savage. I chose to do that." Tiria whispered. Her face slowly became a perfect, smiling mask. "Goodbye, Seth."

"Tiria." The word was so full of malice that despite herself, the girl felt a glimmer of fear. The man's eyes were black with anger. "I won't stop. I swear it. I'll kill you if it's the last thing I do."

"The only way you'll find me is if I let you." She managed to make the words sound arch, hiding the yawning, empty pain in her stomach. "I saved your life. If you really want to kill me, I'll be waiting." Her voice changed a little, becoming almost wondering. "Why do you think I'd be scared of you, now? After you so sweetly begged me to love you?"

"Run, Tiria." He pushed himself upright, oblivious to his leg, and she saw the stone he had gripped in his other fist. She backed away, and when he raised it she ducked away.

He didn't even throw the stone. When she looked back, he had dropped it into the dirt. He didn't stumble, or weep, or shout after her. He simply watched. Tiria felt her heart twist, and for a moment her feet froze into place. She could have gone back to him. She could have explained, but it was impossible. There was nothing left to save.

EPILOGUE

The girl woke up under a thin blanket of snow, and realized that she could no longer feel the cold. She was aware of it, and she knew that her skin was burning wherever the blanket had slipped, but her skin seemed to have become soft leather, wrapping around her organs without offering any sensation. It took her a moment to remember how to walk, and she had to force her limbs to move. She could not feel the pressure of the ground beneath her feet, and when she managed to make her icy hands work the only thing she could feel was the heartbeat beneath her palms. She left the blanket lying in the snow, and walked out into the city. The snow made it feel soft, and quiet, but the sound of distant cries and wailing was a constant burr under the screaming voices in her head.

Tiria walked without purpose, and without thought. The snow was untouched in some places, and in others it was thick with prints. She always chose the clean snow. There was something precious in its untouched drifts. It was the first time she had walked through the snow. Some part of her knew that it was dangerous, and that anyone who walked in the snow was likely to catch the infection which made blood spill out of every wracking breath. The small voice told her that, but the louder voices gleefully ran her fingertips through the white feathers, and made her spin around and laugh when the wind blew.

Something caught her, and held her still. She snarled and grappled with it, until it drew back and slapped her hard. Hissing, she recoiled and huddled down into the snow, watching the other creature with wary eyes. It looked familiar – a foul, faceless lump of arms and legs. It reached across to her, and she snapped at the fingers. They stank, and she gagged, but then one of them forced a white stone into her mouth and held her nose until she swallowed.

The creature sat beside her for a long time, until the ice faded from her eyes. Tiria shivered, and finally recognized Darren. Her head ached as if she had drunk too much wine, but she knew her sickness would only get worse. Ashamed, she hung her head and muttered a nonsense apology.

"It took hold faster than I thought." The other savage said. "I'm sorry."

She swallowed. Her thoughts came slowly. She remembered. She spoke.

"I swam in a river. The water sang with radiation, but I didn't care. I went in again and again, and drank it, and it glittered in the sunlight." Tiria ran her hand over the sores on her arm, and her voice grew almost inaudible. "I was almost happy, then."

"Be happy now." Darren stroked her hair back from her face, and then reached around her. He must have picked up the blanket, and carried it as he followed her through the ruins. The fabric was heavy with water, but a little warm from his body heat. The girl huddled into it.

"I did everything I wanted. That's more than most people get, isn't it?"

He was silent, and after a long time the girl started to cry. Great, heaving sobs shook her entire frame, and she felt the water freezing on her cheeks. The savage patted her back, and drew her closer, and she didn't mind the reek of him. It was the only thing making the crowing voices quieter.

Darren never spoke to her again. His tenderness was more animal than human, and after a long time his eyes took on a cast which swayed dizzily between sanity and emptiness. Tiria watched him, knowing that in a few hours she would be the same.

She ran her hands over his face, and then her own, and felt the sores beginning to form on her cheeks. The savage made a soft sound at her touch, and the murkiness in his eyes faded for a moment. He reached clumsily into his ragged pocket, and pulled something out. He pressed them into her hands, and she saw that the cloth package held hundreds of tiny white stones.

The savage forced her hand closed over the package, and as her fingers sprained and locked the girl forgot that she held the pills at all. She watched him stagger away from her, and looked up at the groaning skyscrapers. They were too tall, and they made her dizzy. She looked back at the white snow, and stood up. Now it was smaller, and she was stronger than it. She picked an untouched path, and walked along it. The movement roused her, and her senses came back, and Tiria sluggishly remembered to walk away from the seared glass streets. No snow settled there. The crater would burn her in a second. The animal in her wanted to survive.

She walked to the river, and watched it with the last scrap of awareness she possessed.

The water had frozen completely. The bergs of ice groaned at their tethers as the thinner ice pushed them back. The surface was rough, pitted with raging torrents that fought against the solid barrier above. Chunks of ice smashed down from the solid masses and broke through the slippery plate surface, causing jets of water to burst out like blood from a punctured artery. It was dangerous, violently so, but the ice stretched from the city and kept going, all the way to the opposite bank. The ice continued even there, easing itself up the soil and sinking long, hard fingers into the ruins beyond. The channels of water had frozen in the streets, and the city on the bank was criss-crossed with ruler-straight veins of sheer ice.

Tiria stared numbly at the city until the sun set. When the darkness came, the last of her mind went with it. She stared into the black sky for hours, trying to cling to her memory of the horizon. There was something beyond the river. There was something on the other side of the bank. There was hope, if only she could will herself to seize it. When the sun rose she would cross the ice, and be safe.

The city burned behind her. She stared, and the dawn started to break, and she could not remember why she was cold and still.

There was nothing on the other side of the bank. The darkness seemed to reach up to the sky, and as the sun started to rise the crimson light glowed back from the ice banks and flared back into the clouds. It was a heartrending, terrifying expanse. The girl clutched her arms around herself and willed fear not to rise up in her seething mind. There was very little left in her heart except confusion and anger. Her name came and went, and her thoughts fleeted about as swiftly as snowflakes. She looked at the crimson land, saw that it was becoming amber and finally yellow, and knew that somewhere in the colours there was beauty.

She remembered beauty. She loved it, far more than she had loved anything else. There were people, perhaps, or things that she had enjoyed... but her life had become smaller, and softer, and the part of her that remained knew that beauty was light. Beauty spilled over the ground in pools of pure colour.

Tears spilled down her cheeks and froze on her throat. There was beauty, then. The world still held that. She could cling to it.

The girl looked back. The city blossomed with smoke. She could still hear the cries, and she knew they were coming closer. The voices would find her. She would lose the beauty forever. Without it, there would only be anger. Her fingers closed up and constricted. The thought of turning away from the light made her want to tear, and maim, until the colours bloomed back from their flesh into her heart.

There was beauty, then. She turned to it, and raised her hand to her lips. The white stones trickled into her mouth, hundreds of them choking her and turning to dust on her tongue. She forced the whole mess down her throat, and stood unblinking as it scoured down to her stomach. It had been important to take the pills. She had known that, once. She followed the compulsion without understanding it.

Then she turned, smiled, and stepped onto the ice.

*

Other books by Vivien Leanne Saunders

Hunting
Let the Which Out
The *Riverbed* Series:
Mire
Tributary
Cascade

FIND MORE BOOKS, SNEAK PEEKS AND SHORT
STORIES ONLINE AT
https://sivvusleanne.wixsite.com/authorvls

If you enjoyed this book, please review it on
Amazon!

Printed in Poland
by Amazon Fulfillment
Poland Sp. z o.o., Wrocław

53414596R00388